"If you stru
said
"you
Now, again!"

☆ ———————— ☆

He lifted Alexa until she was able to clutch rocky handholds and look over the rocks into the gorge that the Aescir called Nenasytets, or "insatiable." A thundering falls poured down, split into two cataracts by a promontory like a spear. At the bottom of the falls, spray leapt upward above whirlpools that seemed to spiral down and down, choking on enormous jagged rocks, crying out in torment.

It would be so simple to leap into that pool. No one would ever find her. They might even mourn. What was her alternative? To seduce these people into accepting her, and then, finally to betray them? She was good for nothing else. Something in her agreed with that judgment. Already her fingers were releasing their white-knuckled clutch on the rocks. The spume was very white, very greedy, and it drew her. They would never know.

I promised Audun I would fight! She bit her lip, and the pain helped her repel the invisible sorcerer's attack.

"No," she gasped, "No!"

THE WOMAN OF FLOWERS

Also by Susan Shwartz

Byzantium's Crown

**Published by
POPULAR LIBRARY**

THE WOMAN OF FLOWERS

SUSAN SHWARTZ

POPULAR LIBRARY

An Imprint of Warner Books, Inc.

A Warner Communications Company

POPULAR LIBRARY EDITION

Copyright © 1987 by Susan Shwartz
All rights reserved.

Popular Library®, the fanciful P design, and Questar® are registered
trademarks of Warner Books, Inc.

Cover illustration by Rowena Morrill

Popular Library books are published by
Warner Books, Inc.
666 Fifth Avenue
New York, N.Y. 10103

 A Warner Communications Company

Printed in the United States of America

First Printing: November, 1987

10 9 8 7 6 5 4 3 2 1

Dedication

To Dr. Benzion Rapoport,
adept in rebirths

Acknowledgments

Special thanks to all my friends (writers, editors, and civilians)—and most especially to Evangeline Morphos—for putting up with "I'm blocked!" and "Do you know what those characters of mine are up to *now*?" throughout the progress of this book. My admiration to Nat Sobel for a stellar display of class. My obligations to Eileen Campbell Gordon, the extraordinary proprietor of Rivendell Bookstore, for providing research material and sage advice.

PART I

*   *   *   *   *   *   *

The
PRINCESS

Chapter 1

☆

The *Hvitbjarn* beached by Dnieper-mouth with a jolt that sent Alexa sprawling. A quick twist, one hand flung out for balance, and she caught herself from falling. It hadn't hurt, she realized. Her knife wounds had healed during the journey across the Black Sea from Byzantium. Pain? No princess of Byzantium, heir to the power of Isis and Osiris that was the first best gift of Divine Cleopatra to her consort, expected to feel physical pain. Except, perhaps, in childbirth. But Alexa would never have children now. Her brother, who should have been Emperor, was dead. She deserved to be dead too.

She would have traded her physical well-being for worse gashes than she had suffered in the disastrous fight at Byzantium's harbor from which Audun Bearmaster and his Aescir kin had rescued her. Any pain was better than the guilt she felt for drawing on forbidden sorcery.

All around her, the Aescir unloaded *Hvitbjarn* and her sister ships of the wine, silk, gold, jewels, and fruit they had gained in Byzantium. Shouting, they began to hammer extra timbers to the keels of their clinker-built ships so they could withstand the Dnieper's rapids. They did not trouble her. Probably, they thought she was still too injured to work. In the unwelcome leisure, her thoughts turned on treason, murder, and the foulest of battle magics.

"Still idle?" Audun Bearmaster padded up behind her, stealthy and almost as strong as the white bears that were his clan's sigil and constant companions. In his arms was a coffer that only an Aescir would have tried to carry. He dropped it at

3

her feet, then flung it to reveal rolls of papyrus and parchment sheets.

"Even if you are newly restored to health, Princess, you are lettered. Perhaps you might keep these records of our cargoes? Einar and Ragnar, here, will tell you what to watch for." The request was politely enough phrased that even if Alexa had not owed Audun her life, she could not have refused. *He seeks to occupy my mind*, she thought. The night before, he had encountered her on the shore, attributed her "wandering" to sleeplessness, and brought her back to the quarters she shared with two redoubtable Aescir women who watched her as they might watch a too-wily Syrian merchant when they bargained for spices.

Alexa looked up from her new task. The shore teemed with people and goods; it looked remarkably like the sack of some city. Guards prowled at the camp's perimeter; the threat of attack by Petcheneg barbarians was very real. It had intensified since the Emperor's death. Alexa studied the guards. So much for that scheme, then. She had no chance to escape, and nowhere to escape to. Einar came up and pointed at a cluster of chests.

Shortly after, Ragnar led her to count bales of carefully wrapped silks. Each of the big, ruddy Aescir assigned to guard her—though Audun called them her assistants—had a wave or grin for her. *They cannot know the poison I have made of myself.* They knew her only as the little princess whom Audun had watched grow up and to whom, along with her brother, he had given a white bear cub. But the cub had died, poisoned by Irene, their father's second wife, who dared to call herslf Empress and Isis on Earth. So Alexa had secretly engaged Audun and the Aescir to carry her and her brother Marric away from their City to a place where he could raise troops and gold to gain their throne.

That had been her plan. Blameless, it was, and it should have succeeded were it not for the rottenness Alexa had let seep into mind and soul. She had feared Irene, and been revolted by her son, Alexa's half brother—yet she had felt a salt fascination for them too. Isis on Earth, Irene claimed to be. Sorceress was more like it, mistress of magics that had more to do with Set than with the holy linkage that bound the

Empire and its rulers into one truth, and yoked the infinite and the mundane with an inviolable tie. Though Irene was barred from that union, her necromancy had given her the strength to grasp at the throne.

In power had lain Alexa's temptation, and there she had fallen. If magic had given Irene such power, what might it do for the Emperor's daughter, the rightful heir to the moon crown that her mother had worn so well? Half-Greek, half-Egyptian as the imperial family was, magic quivered in their blood, to be drawn on as sacrament and weapon. Barred from the one, she had seized desperately on the other. With a stepmother taunting her, her half brother lingering in her courtyard, avid to talk or touch, she had studied feverishly. Her studies had drawn her stepmother's predatory interest. Terrified by that, she delved further into her ancient scrolls, a lethal spiral that warped her judgment even as it stained her soul.

With her contamination came her hubris. Now she had dreamed of overcoming Irene herself, simultaneously avenging her father Alexander and presenting her brother Marric with the throne that they would then occupy jointly.

Her poor brother. At her call, he ventured from his army, which loved him, and came to her. She must have been drunk, or mad, when she and her brother had fought off their half brother's guards. His inept attempt at rape had maddened her further, but Marric had praised her courage. He could not see what she had become. The madness fed on itself like plague; not content with taking their half brother hostage, she had cut his bonds and hurled him beneath the hooves of their pursuers.

Alexa dropped the scroll she held and clasped hands to her temples. Though Ctesiphon had been wrapped in a carpet when he fell, she had heard his screams as the horses trampled him. She could hear them now, drowned out by hoofbeats, the hiss of Marric's sword drawn in her defense, and his furious reproaches.

"*My* Isis, not a murderer!" Marric had snarled at her, his hands bruising on her shoulders.

How dare he accuse her! That was when she had turned on him, too, red fire blazing from her fingertips, *words* spewing from her lips . . . at the remembered taste of those *words*, she knew she was going to be ill, and she leapt up and ran for any privacy she could find.

After an eternity of heaving and shuddering, she knelt upright and dashed her hand across her mouth. Her guards were nowhere in sight. But Audun Bearmaster stood over her, watching with a mixture of patience and compassion.

"Drink this," Audun said from behind her, and held out a carved horn.

"It will make me sicker," she whispered. She sounded petulant, even to her own ears.

"From water? A few herbs?" He continued to hold out the horn to her. If she did not take it and drink, he would make her drink it the way she had seen him stroke potions down the throat of a sick beast. The drink was astringent, oddly refreshing, unlike the mandragora she had swallowed in the evil nights of their journey across the Black Sea. That had kept the nightmares at bay while her body healed itself; this left her keener of mind, more vulnerable to those wounds of spirit for which she saw could be no healing.

"You are much too kind," said Alexa, little as she cared for kindness that restored her memories of her treason.

"Walk with me, Princess," said the Bearmaster. He led the way past the ordered frenzy on shore, the scattered embers of fires and hastily thrown-up dwellings, toward the dark quiet of the forests. Here, Audun's white bears wandered, hunting or waiting for scraps from the Aescir's fires. Two bears, one but a cub, raised their narrow heads as they passed. The elder rose to her hind legs, towering to almost twice Alexa's height.

Audun reached up to scratch beneath the bear's pointed muzzle. Jaws that could gnash through his arm opened and delicately bit on his massive fist. "So, sister, make your manners to the princess."

The white bear wove toward her. Alexa steeled herself to touch it, but the beast veered abruptly and moaned, then dropped to all fours. The cub, drawn by Audun's deep, furry voice, scuttled toward Alexa. Its black eyes and nose made Alexa laugh, remembering how the cub Audun had once given her and her brother had wrestled with them. Until the day it bit Irene, and she had it poisoned, it had never harmed a soul. She reached out to ruffle this cub's thick fur, but its mother slapped at her hand with a huge paw, then whacked the cub so that it tumbled onto its back and rolled into a heap of pine needles before it recovered its footing and ran off. The female lingered long enough to growl at Alexa. Then she turned her back and left.

That was no retreat, Alexa thought. The bear had withdrawn herself and her cub from contamination.

"So," Audun nodded to himself. "So."

Alexa drew herself up. "The bears shun me," she said. Surely Audun must have noticed it when they disembarked. Not a one of the great white bears would willingly come near her. How not? she thought. If the Aescir were men and women of all tribes—Rus, Finn, brightly clad Lapps, and strangers from Biarmaland by the White Sea—who pledged faith to one another, then, just as surely, the white bears who traveled with them, and whom, as a mark of great esteem, they would bestow only upon chiefs or emperors, were part of the *var*, or pledge of honor and loyalty each made the others.

"I know," Audun said. "I had meant to take you into Finnmark with me. But if the bears—"

"Doesn't that tell you what I am?" Alexa burst out.

"You are the daughter of Alexander, risen to his Horizon with Osiris in Glory," the Bearmaster told her. "That makes you his heir, along with your brother. As well you know."

"You saw," she raged, heading deeper into the tall trees, "you saw my brother Marric fall on the dock." A clear stream blocked her path, and she kicked a rock into it.

Audun's hands grasped her shoulders and turned her around as she might have lifted a feather. She was forced to look up into his face. He towered a good foot taller than she, with long braids and beard the color of one of his bears. He wore a heavy blue tunic and breeches, and shone with ornaments that would have been ludicrous on anyone but a Northerner: a belt buckle the size of her hand, wrought of garnets and braided gold, a chain that might have been hammered into pectorals for two priests on a feast day, immensely heavy bracelets and rings. But all else faded as she gazed up into his eyes. They were gray, but that was all there was of coldness about them. Though a beast's innocence and its potential for innocent vio-

lence shone in them, so did the compassion and wisdom of a
wise king or a priest.

It was painful to meet Audun's eyes, but how could she
look away? For the first time, Alexa wondered how it might
be if she confessed what she had become. She deserved to be
slain and cast unburied into the waste; but she remembered
that Audun had always been kind.

"I saw Prince Marric, all right," said Audun. "Guards cut
him off from you, and he fought like ten demons to reach
your side until they brought him down."

"You saw my brother die," she said flatly.

To her amazement, Audun shook his head. "I only saw him
fall. Princess, when we rescued you, you were gravely hurt,
and your wounds turned feverish. Yet if your brother had
died, you would have sensed it. Heaven and earth would have
revealed it, for he is Horus Incarnate, lacking only the rituals
to rule as Emperor. One land," he said, as Alexa had heard
him say since she was a child, "one lord—and he is that lord.
As you are rightful Empress."

He thought her to be as innocent as he! "I am not fit to rule
now," she said, and prayed for courage to force out the rest of
the story.

"What else should I have seen?" he asked suspiciously.

Alexa twisted her hands and half turned from Audun. "Answer me!" he ordered. She was ashamed that she could not
submit to the judgment that she had laid on herself: confess
what she had done and take whatever punishment she had
earned. Something at the corner of her eye drew her attention,
and she turned toward the trees. She could scarcely see them
now, and the day had been bright, too bright for such a mist to
spring up. Suddenly, she was dizzy, and the hair at the back of
her neck prickled, the way it did whenever Irene had drawn
too close to her and she had felt her magics. When Audun
demanded that she answer him, she hushed him almost ab-
sently, listening until she stood trembling.

"Something . . . hidden . . ."

"Is it a raid?" Audun asked. He shouted something into the
forest, and the mist faded.

Now that the mist was gone, they saw the war-party of
Petchenegs who had used it for cover come boiling out. The

three in the lead, briefly dismayed at seeing people who might spoil the stealth of their attack on the camp, grinned, then advanced at a run.

"Get behind me!" One massive arm swept her behind Audun and sent her sprawling on the ground. The Bearmaster drew his weapon—a heavy sword, rather than the ax most Aescir carried—and, bellowing a challenge, struck through first the guard, then the sword arm, of the first barbarian.

Alexa drew the dagger no one had thought to take from her. As she had been taught, she kept it sharp with whetstone and oil. When Audun sent another man sprawling, she pounced on him fiercely, the wickedly sharp blade slashing at his throat. Blood fountained out over her hands . . .

. . . *and in its redness, she remembered* words *that would free them from this trap,* words *that would save Audun to rule his clan and tend his bears* . . .

If he were spared, what difference did it make if she spoke those words once again? She was already accursed. Audun swung his blade with two hands in deadly arcs that the Petchenegs backed away from. Barbarians they might be, but they were fierce warriors who had killed many Aescir and many of the Empire. In an instant more, they would encircle him. She held her bloody hand before her face and drew breath to curse them.

Then angry grunts and roars echoed. Alexa glanced behind her, where three male bears reared up fully eight or nine feet high, then advanced on the Petchenegs. Immensely fast, one bear seized a man in deadly embrace. His bones snapped the way her half brother's had. War cries howled out as Einar and Ragnar followed the bears, and flung themselves into the battle.

She could not permit them to die for her. She focused on the blood that dripped from her fingers, summoning up the controlled lusts for power and violence that underlay Irene's powers. Scarlet light began to build around her fingertips.

"No!" shouted Audun. "Princess, guard yourself!"

The bloodlight began to crackle from hand to hand, building up power for an attack. Audun's order made Alexa whirl around, ready to hurl the fire at whatever wretch thought to flesh his knife in her. But no one rushed her with blade or ax.

"No!" Audun shouted again, as the power in her ached for the victims it craved. *It* craved, Alexa thought. She did not. After causing one brother's death and—for all Audun's comforting words—the capture and worse than death of another, Alexa would never crave victims again—would she?

Would she?

Not ten feet ahead of her, Einar screamed and fell, blood bursting from his mouth and nose. "Einar!" she cried. He had been good to her, had taught her Aescir songs and found her a heavy cloak. A bolt of red lightning lashed from her left hand to turn the man who had slain Einar into a shrieking torch.

"Stop it!" Audun shouted, as the lightning built up again, began to encompass her in a red nimbus like that she had seen encircle Irene after the cub bit her. With each spell, with each bolt of crimson fire, she would become more and more like Irene until the day would come when her soul would be weighed on the Scales against a feather, and she would be hurled into darkness for the crocodiles to devour.

I will die first! she swore to herself and sought to quench the fires she had summoned. They leapt and whined about her, the nimbus of flame fading, then surging up again. It was a temptation to cast the power roundabout—already she could smell pine and scorched flesh from the one man she had killed. Once she launched the flame, the trees would burn like so much tinder, destroying Aescir and Petcheneg alike. And now that she had summoned it, the fire must be launched, or it would recoil threefold upon the user. Marric had dared to come to her aid. Audun had the heart to fight a troop, Einar to die at his side. Could she equal their courage?

The bears grunted and howled. One, its ruff bloodied, weaved on its hind legs and strode toward her, seeking the enemy behind Audun and his surviving two men. *It senses the magic!* she thought. In horror, she watched as her hands came up, ready to burn the beast and save her miserable life for yet other murders.

"No," Alexa whispered. "I will not." In seconds, the bear would be upon her, would rip her head from her shoulders if she did not fight. Yet, if she did, what hope was there for her among the Aescir?

She forced her hands down, stammered out half-learned

words, and the fire that blazed about her flickered wildly, shredded, then leapt high over her head. The flame weakened, though one tongue lashed out and licked her face. She screamed and smelled her hair scorching as the bear reached her. A tremendous slap sent her rolling on needles and dirt.

The air was blessedly cool as she came up hard against the rough trunk of an immense pine. A blaze of light exploded in her skull as her head struck the tree. As the light faded into a chaotic red pulsing and then darkness, over the shouts of men and the howls of Audun's fighting bears, she heard hungry, vicious laughter.

"We can launch *Hvitbjarn* when you're ready, Bearmaster."

A man's voice brought Alexa out of comforting nothingness back into the world. It would be no easy world for her henceforth, she feared. She lay—so it seemed—in the rain. When she opened her eyes, she saw only blackness, with a few fugitive specks of fire that reminded her of the flames she had called up, then absorbed into herself. They would vanish, she assumed, and she would live out her life in blackness.

"Let's give her the chance to wake on dry land," came Audun's furry voice.

"Are we really taking her to Staraja Ladoga with us?" Disgust and fear trembled in the other man's voice.

"How fare our kinsmen the bears?" asked Audun.

"Well enough. Redcheek took no lasting harm from that one's magics. You saw what she did." The voice was chill with a condemnation she welcomed.

"Aye, that I did. All of it. The Princess sensed the raiders even before I did. And when I shouted, she turned her fires on herself rather than harm the bear, though it might have killed her."

"While you men sit nattering, this cloth is almost dry," said a woman's voice, so close to Alexa's face that she felt warm breath fan it. A hand tugged a cloth away from her eyes.

Violent light exploded before Alexa, and she moaned, almost sick with relief. "Not blind . . ." she muttered.

"No," said the woman, "but your eyes are badly inflamed." The dampened cloth slapped down again, blessed relief against her hot eyes, but not before Alexa glimpsed her surroundings: a ring of Aescir, circling a tiny hearth fire—not the blaze that she originally thought she saw. Audun's face was concerned, her nurse's patient and watchful, Ragnar's blotched from mourning Einar. The man who had spoken against keeping her with them had a face cold with horror. She had caused that horror. That knowledge hurt almost as much as the fire that had lashed her.

But she was not blind. Tears ran down her cheeks until she was cautioned about weeping. "Thank the Goddess," she whispered. A low rumble of thunder made her wonder if she dared invoke Isis's name.

"Shouldn't she eat something?" asked Audun.

"Not for hours."

"Then out, the lot of you," he said. "I must settle things with the princess."

Alexa heard them leave, heard Audun settle down close by the pallet on which she lay, then felt him remove the cloth from her eyes and brow. The Bearmaster's huge body blocked out most of the firelight; she blinked, testing her ability to endure what light was left. Then she gazed up at him.

"Now you know," she whispered.

"Now I know what?" he echoed her. "That you were desperate, and turned to sorcery? I could smell it on your messengers when you asked my aid." He snorted with indignation, much like one of his bears. "Offer me gold, would you? as if I were some mercenary—not that I condemn my kinsmen who sell their swords—you would pay to free you. As if I would not do so for your own sake."

Alexa rolled over on her side. "You knew all along?"

"I wanted to see if you would tell me. Child," the furry voice was deep and warm, "I needed to know how deep it had gone. Deep enough: you sense the things of darkness too fast for me to think you wholly untouched—and when you panic, you turn to black arts. But Alexa, you stopped. When I shouted, you took the brunt of your own evils. And," Audun laughed, "you were the one who alerted me to the attack. Infant sorceress or not, we probably owe you our lives."

"They will hate me in your home."

"My home? Staraja is just one of them. I had meant to take you into Finnmark with me, perhaps beyond—"

"Where the bears are born? You can't do that now."

"No," said Audun. "Not until you are cleansed."

"How can I ever be clean again?" Alexa cried softly. Tears rolled down her face, and when Audun patted her shoulder as if she were indeed the infant he had called her, she seized his hand and wept into it. No peace, no rest, and no curing—not anywhere.

For a long time, Audun let her weep. Then he reached down, grasped both her shoulders, and set her firmly upright. The jolt shocked the tears out of her.

"Listen to me," he ordered. Alexa gulped and was silent.

"I cannot take you to the Ice now. But I promise you, there is healing . . . if not among the Aescir, then elsewhere. I swear that I will take you all the way to the Druids of Penllyn in the Isles of Mist, if I must."

Hope sparked, then began to flicker in her heart. She pictured it as a joyous flame, all yellow and white, not the murky red of the—

"In return, Princess, you must do one thing for me."

As she started to blurt out that she would do anything, the Bearmaster held up a hand. "Among the Aescir, we have a saying that a man—or woman—should be sparing of speech, not hotheaded, not overly quick in boasting of great deeds lest the time come when he regrets his hasty words. You must think before you promise. For what I require of you, child, is your oath that you will fight for yourself."

Alexa stared silently at him. "But, to be clean again . . ."

"Yes, to be clean. To be cleansed, you say you would do anything. Would you confront Irene? As long as she can think of you as a paltry thing, feeble enough to die of a few wounds and your guilt, she may be content to let you waste away. And she has other concerns: her son and what to do with your brother Marric . . . yes, I know you refuse to believe that he still lives.

"But you fought. First you summoned and then cast aside those magics of which she is mistress. And this, child, this will force you on her notice once again. You are resolved, you say, to do 'anything' to be purified. What if she seeks to turn you back toward the burning, or, failing that, to destroy you?" Alexa bent her head. Her black hair fell forward over her shoulders. It smelled of smoke, and was scorched all along its ragged length. She looked for the dagger that she kept by her, and failed to see it.

"May I have my knife?" she asked. "I will not seek to use it on myself—or keep it." Wordlessly, Audun handed it to her, and she began to trim away the burned hair.

"You will look like you have been ill—or like an outlaw," Audun told her.

"Are not both true?" she asked, and relinquished the dagger. "Bearmaster, I swear to you that I will fight as best I can." Einar, who had died that afternoon, had taught her a poem, something about "spirits being braver, hearts more keen, courage sterner as strength dwindles." "In turn," she went on, "I ask a pledge from you."

Audun nodded, half-smiling.

"I will fight. But if I fail, I beg you, grant me a clean death."

Waiting for his answer, Alexa drew the burned strands of her hair through her fingers. Finally Audun took them from her and tossed them on the fire.

"Hair has power," he reminded her. "As we go upriver, we may meet more enemies such as the Petchenegs we fought today. I have heard that the men of Jomsborg travel through Gardariki, daring, even, to treat with the Red Empress. Do not leave anything that they could turn against you as a weapon."

"Jomsborg . . . I have heard of them," Alexa said. They had a fortress in a northern river-mouth that barred only two things from its formidable gates: women and fear. Their sigil was the black bear. Rumor hissed that they could shape-change. She shuddered. They were too much like the Aescir for comfort. "Irene . . . she sent an embassy to Grettir, jarl and reiver."

Audun shook his head. "Of that I was not aware," he said.

"It appears, Princess, that as we go upriver, you must be my adviser, as I am yours. For if we fail, the Black Bear and the Red Empress will mate in Byzantium, and there will be no law, no peace for us anywhere."

Chapter 2

☆

"The island!" came the shout from on deck. Alexa leapt to her feet, regardless of the twinges it cost her. Her bruises had faded in the four days it took to sail from Dnieper-mouth to Khortitsa, the island that lay like a monstrous ship at anchor in mid-river. Here the banks rose into towering cliffs, perfect vantage points for the Petchenegs whose arrows rattled against the *Hvitbjarn* and her sister ships. Beyond the island, the rock faces soared even higher, creating the deadly flume of rapids they must soon master.

Some of the arrows had not been Petcheneg. Instead they bore the marking—a black bear ramping in anger—of Jomsborg. On the evening when the first such arrow had been shown him, Audun had growled. His beard seemed to bristle and catch sparks from the single torch that illuminated the heavy carved gameboard on which they had been playing Senit. Audun's massive hand tightened on the stalk of the fox-headed playing piece until it snapped. Blood dripped from his hand onto the shaft. For an instant, Alexa imagined another shape—taller than Audun, clad in white fur—superimposed over the Aescir chieftain. He bowed wordlessly, and she blinked against the illusion of a white-muzzled head nodding high above her. Then he left. The shadow that lumbered behind him was that of a man.

She caught up the torch as if to follow, and then, wearily, put it down again. This was Aescir magic, and no matter for her to dabble in. All that night, she could hear the dark-voiced clamor of chants, the tapping of spirit drums, and the whine of horns. All that night, she had shivered. As often as she sprang up from her pallet, she forced herself to lie still, disciplining herself not to respond to the lure of drums and rattles, praying to Isis that she could forget the surge of hunger she had felt when Audun's blood stained the game piece red.

Today, though, had dawned bright and peaceful. The jutting cliffs no longer looked like terrible jaws. Audun's grin was unforced, unshadowed by illusion. Like the crew themselves, Alexa spent hours scanning the cliffs for enemies. Pelicans nested among the rocks and fished along the shore, her companions (she tried not to think of them as guards) said. Ragnar swore he had shot one on the trip downriver, and then swore worse when his fellows reminded him that the bird had sunk before he could retrieve it and confirm his boast.

Tonight, they would sleep ashore, if they slept at all. For, although the Aescir welcomed a landing on Khortitsa, it was no place to stay and feast. It was the last staging point before the battle upriver that would strain body, mind, and nerve for the next six weeks. The rapids could be ventured only in early summer, and the season was passing fast.

Every day was precious now, and Alexa's illness had cost them days already. She felt herself under constant scrutiny now: would today be the day she would crack, or tomorrow? Or could she heal herself altogether, without proving a further drain on the Aescir? She had promised Audun that she would fight for herself. She would make a beginning—now. Waving aside Ragnar's offer of help, she seized a bundle and jumped down from the ship onto the rock of Khortitsa, so strangely motionless after days on board *Hvitbjarn*. Ahead of her men and women of the Aescir splashed laughing onto the shore, yelling out greetings to the newcomers. Even the white bears bellowed happily. One tossed his head, a fish he had just caught dangling from formidable jaws.

Audun would have no time tonight for chess or Senit, Alexa thought, or for the rambling talks that were his strategy for acquainting her with the lands of her exile. Up ahead he

emerged from an exuberant embrace of two old friends at
once. He turned, plainly looking for someone. One of his
companions, a woman, pointed at her. Alexa ducked her
head, and hurried away. Her shorn hair brushed hot cheeks.
She did not want to be noticed. Her retreat took her outside
the throng into a grove where the cool shadows made her slow
her footsteps. She rubbed her eyes, feeling as if she had come
to the end of a bout of weeping, sighed, and glanced around.

Ahead of her, lances of white light pierced through the leafy
shadows; beyond them, the light seemed to form a curtain such
as the one leading to the sanctuary in the Temple of Isis at home.
Though logic told her that a clearing in the forest might shine so
brightly, she felt power prickling along her spine. What lay
beyond that light? Would she be permitted to find out? Cautiously, she advanced, hands raised to protect her eyes. Three
steps more, and she would walk through the light. Though she
might be blasted, she decided that she would rather be consumed walking toward the light than fleeing it.

Then she stood in the midst of the clearing, with sunlight
stroking down her back and sides, more soothing than a
skilled bath-slave. Alexa glanced eagerly about. The clearing
was ringed by a circle of arrows at regular intervals. The
center of that ring appeared to be an ancient oak tree so wide
that five women Alexa's size, their hands joined, might not
span its immense trunk. She walked toward it, and the scents
of blood and mead prickled in her nostrils. Clearly, this was a
place of sacrifice, yet she felt no unease in entering it. As she
neared the tree, she saw that in several places, bark had been
stripped away, and the living wood carved into the runes she
could not read, as well as into other shapes—a bear, a hawk,
even a lunar disk from the Isis rituals.

Alexa sighed deeply. For the first time in many days, she
was hungry. Reluctant to return to the shore and all those avid
eyes, she approached the tree, knelt, and held out her hands,
as if entreating it. The Aescir were generous to their guests.
She hoped any spirits to whom this shrine might belong would
be equally hospitable. Under the tree she found freshly baked
bread, a hard cheese, dried meat, and mead in a jar. Ignoring
the meat, she crumbled cheese into some of the bread, and
washed it down with the thick, potent mead. It tasted of herbs

and honey, reminding her of the honeycakes she and her brother had always pilfered from servants.

She yawned. How long had it taken her and Marric to realize that their honeycake thefts had been abetted by the very people they robbed? She remembered making off with a platter, and hearing a nurse laugh. Though her brother had laughed too, she had been furious. Her brother . . . for the first time, memory of Marric did not ache like a rotten tooth.

Audun was right, she realized. If he had died, she would have known it. All their lives, she and her brother had been close-tied, the knowledge that they were destined to rule together as Isis and Osiris on Earth drawing them ever closer. The night he returned to Byzantium, she had sensed it. Fear, grief at their father's death, and unadmitted guilt had made her summon him, had turned her days into a walking nightmare, her nights into traps in which her stepmother stalked her dreams, laying snares until the evening of his actual return. Even the sullenness of the summer heat had lifted; and she had felt a surge of joy and courage unaccountable to her until the moment she saw him standing in her courtyard, ready to guard her.

No, Marric couldn't be dead. But, their stepmother's power and character being what they were, death might be the best he could—no, that could not be true either. Marric had always been champion, protector; she had never known him to surrender. Let him survive. He had to survive to forgive her.

Warmth crept over her, and she yawned and stretched. That had to be the mead. Tears rolled down her face, and she started to blame the mead again until she realized that it was the power of this place, not the mead, that made her so certain that if Marric lived, he had forgiven her already.

But then, he always had been more generous than she.

How will you forgive yourself, Alexa? The question seemed to rustle from the leaves high overhead.

She had no answer for it. Though she had promised to try to live, she took no joy in the fact. Her memories of a sunlit childhood, a brother who loved her, even Audun's telling her that he trusted her seemed to belong to someone else.

Drawing her dark cloak over her head, a princess of Byzantium sobbed herself to sleep in a barbarian shrine.

Alexa woke to the music of chant, horn, and drum. Sunset was but ashes on the horizon. Even this far north, the goddess Nut spread her cloak over the world, bringing darkness and happy dreams. But this was no night for healing sleep. The circle of arrows about the mammoth oak resonated to the tromp of hundreds of feet and the vehemence of Aescir prayer. Now torches marked where each arrow had been placed. In the light they cast, white bears weaved back and forth, their muzzles lifted to sniff the air.

She drew herself up into a ball, her knees protecting breasts and belly, then leaned forward. There was power in the air, both within the circle and ramping hungrily outside it. Around the other side of the tree, Audun drew lots from a bowl, then displayed them to the Aescir ringing him. They shouted. Some even clashed their swords together as several of the younger men brought forward birds for sacrifice. Alexa watched, fearful of her own reaction, as the cock's necks were wrung. The blood! Whatever lurked outside the circle seemed to press in, hostile and avid.

The press of bodies, the reek of blood and smoke, the ragged brilliance of the torches pried at Alexa's awareness. She tried to concentrate on the here and now. Man faded into bear, changed into a creature half-human, half-beast, that lolled on all fours or danced upright. Light exploded as oil was hurled on the fire. Her mind reeled free of time and place, and she saw men and bears dancing on snow beneath a white sky crowned with trembling rainbows. Beyond them lay only ice and silence that threatened to engulf her. Think, she commanded herself, of playing chess with Audun, of how he grins at a clever move. Think of where you stand, of the people circling you . . .

. . . *yes, and what they will do to you when they find you spying* . . . the bears' giant shadows loomed up before her, swept over her, and she cowered back. As the crowd shifted, she saw that it was made up not only of Aescir but also of men and women in the brightly trimmed dress of Finnmark. The light gleamed off the brass and gold trappings they wore.

*What would they do to an outsider . . . blasphemer, already
accursed, spy upon their rituals . . . you must hide . . .* Audun
wrung the neck of yet another bird and cast the feathered body
down while the thing in Alexa's thoughts quivered with
hunger.

It was Irene, she thought, Irene following her in thought,
drawn to the sacrifice, anxious to steal power as she had already stolen a diadem. *Get out of my mind*, she thought. *Get
out.* She struggled to cast out the hateful presence but found it
too strong. As if realizing that Alexa could not banish her,
Irene's thoughts crept further into her mind, sending out tendrils that sought to lodge within her spirit and mesh together
in a web that would possess her, mind and soul.

*Make me . . . little daughter. Or join me. Oppose me, and I
will break your mind and feast upon your soul. Join me and
. . .* Irene's promises were the throaty, seductive purr that
Alexa had heard her use on Marric a time or two (before their
father had prudently sent him away) when she thought herself
unobserved.

Alexa set her chin, unwilling to respond. If she could not
expel Irene, at least she could forbid her to invade further. A
sudden slash of hostility abruptly thrust her consciousness
outside the here and now as a realm she had visited once or
twice in furtive glimpses into Irene's ancient books of spells.
It could resemble prison, palace, or vision of hell. Now it
seemed to resemble a beach at night, shrouded by fog that
roiled and spun with red glints. Ahead of her came the drowsy
lapping of waves.

Such a place—the priests of Osiris taught that before the
spirit reached the Horizon, it must cross a shore. Was this it?
The air hummed, sending veils of mist swirling in a heavy
wind, scented with carrion and poppy. The last time she
smelled that, she had attacked her own brother. She felt its
madness boring into her brain through her eyes. No, this was
no shore she wished to cross. Even the silence and the ice that
would strip her soul bare would be better.

Did she have the strength to escape?

Will you promise me to fight? She remembered Audun's
words. The red light . . . it was what there was; it was all there
was. If she renounced it, then she embraced only nothingness

. . . the numbing lullaby made her sluggish, mind and body. She forced herself to slam one hand against the tree trunk. Impact and splinters drew a gasp of pain from her and made her eyes fly open. The torchlight was red too . . . yes, but a man waved his torch and it flared out, a comet's trail of gold and white as brilliant as the sunlight that had bathed the glade that day.

There is white, Alexa thought. *There is health. There was even love once. I remember.*

"I remember!" she cried out, rising to her feet, walking out from behind the tree. "I remember your promises, too. Lies, Empress and thief, all lies!" She dashed out into the firelit circle where men and bears danced, her hand pointing in accusation as she shouted at the spirit that spied and waited beyond.

Audun strode to her side, and shouted words that the Finns echoed. The sense of hostile presence clenched itself, as if drawing in upon itself to attack, then faded.

Alexa knew better than to call that a victory. Irene had tested her victim's mettle, had gained from her reluctant mind knowledge of her location and allies. She would be back, and with more strength. Alexa put her torn fist to her mouth. The taste of her own blood made her spit and choke. She reeled, was briefly glad when Audun caught her, then pulled away.

"I can walk," she told him. Her guards trailing her, she left the circle of arrows. The sense of presence that had hallowed it and, for a brief moment that afternoon, healed her, was gone now, replaced by satisfaction and anticipation, mingled. Outside the circle, she staggered. Men and women emerged from various shelters to point at her and cry out about the interruption to the night's magic, but Alexa was beyond humiliation. A woman, older and larger than many, took charge of her and led her to an empty shelter. She felt herself covered warmly, heard a murmur of comfort and consolation, and then was asleep.

At dawn they left Khortitsa; the next day, they passed Kichkas Ford, and pressed on upriver. Now the cliffs gnashed over *Hvitbjarn* as the oarsmen forced the boat toward the rapids. Here the Dnieper was as wide as the great Hippodrome itself; hard to think that it would narrow into the howling sluice that even the Aescir, with their tremendous strength, feared.

As the hours passed, Alexa became aware of a rumbling that gradually grew louder and louder. When Ragnar lumbered over to sit beside Alexa, he found her gazing anxiously upriver.

"Is it Petchenegs," he asked, "or more magic of your own?"

"I have told you; I dare have no magic. That sound . . . do you hear it?" she asked.

"Hear what?"

"A terrible groaning noise. Is that the rapids?"

Ragnar nodded. "It will all get worse," he told her cheerfully. "As we go upriver, at one point, the cliffs meet overhead. You have to light torches if you want to see where you are. It is like rowing in a cave."

Alexa shuddered. "Truly?"

"No. But the river narrows, and the trees on either bank do brush one another at times. Do not be afraid, little princess. The bears have no fear, and after you chased away—"

"I?"

"On Khortitsa, you rose from behind the great oak and put to flight whatever evil spirit waited for us. You are our luck!"

"I beg you, don't call me that!" Alexa cried. The noise of the rapids intensified. Now it sounded like the moans of a man in mortal anguish. She suppressed a desire to clap her hands over her ears. If worst came to worst, *when* worst came to worst, she supposed she could heat wax and block her ears as Odysseus had done for his men. Thinking of the old story, she chuckled.

"Why do you laugh?" asked Ragnar, shouting to be heard. He looked at her with what she realized was admiration. The Aescir respected the ability to laugh in the face of danger. Alexa's higher voice carried over the roar of the water as she told the old story, and the man beside her laughed.

"Had I been Odysseus," he declared, mangling the name, "I should have jumped overboard, swum to the Isle of Sirens and returned with one of those beauties slung over my back." He looked at her sidelong, to find out if he had been properly appreciated. Alexa bit back a snort of laughter at the big man whose raveling braids caught the spray of the river and whose blue eyes held an innocent vanity. Before Audun yelled at him to grab a line, he asked for another tale, which she feared to give him, lest her words, like the Sirens, drag him down to share her own fate.

All that day, the rapids pounded in their ears. The current grew more swift; the oarsmen labored for shorter periods before they flung themselves down, gasping and complaining for brief intervals of rest. *Hvitbjarn* bobbed from side to side, twisting past huge jagged rocks. All on board tensed, ready to throw out a hand to grab something solid in case they were flung off their feet.

Cautious on the treacherous deck, Alexa busied herself carrying food to the straining rowers or providing salves when even their callused palms blistered, cracked, and bled. Twice, she had to shout at men before they consented to toss furs over bodies streaming with sweat from their labor at the oars.

"Not even Gerda, my wife, could tend them better," Audun approved.

People ate, tended the bears, or labored with only half their attention on the immediate task. *Hvitbjarn* lurched in the flume now. Ahead of them the river groaned, drowning out the cry of birds, the grunted complaints of the bears, and all but the loudest shouts. The oarsmen tensed, waiting for their first bout with the rapids.

"Secure yourselves!" With a lurch that snatched the scream from Alexa's lips, the boat nosed down first one falls, then a second, and into rapidly rushing water that frothed up white against the boat's sides. This was Strukun, named after the falls and the current. Alexa crouched down, daring to move only when she saw others venture forth. Spray dashed over her. Strukun seemed endless, invincible, and yet it was but the first—and least—of seven rapids in a series.

They would have no silence for the next ten days, she knew—unless it was the silence of the drowned. No sooner than they had weathered Strukun than Audun rose to prowl the ship, seeking to repair damage to the ship's hull, ordering men to lash toppled cargo more firmly in place. Alexa's hands and back ached from bailing, but she found the pain—shared by everyone on board if she could tell by the complaints and curses—reassuring: she was human; she shared human pains.

Gradually *Hvitbjarn* steadied in the water. After several hours, Alexa began to believe it might continue that way. All too quickly then, after a bend in the river, the roaring up ahead intensified, and the river turned white, as if brought to a seething boil. Leanti, with its roiling white water, was upon them. They shot from Leanti like an arrow from a bow.

If it got much worse, Alexa decided, she would lash herself to the nearest heavy object like Odysseus and stay there, unless, of course, she was washed overboard with it. The sky grew dark as, on either side of them, the cliffs rose to blot out the light. She ceased even to try to wring out her garments. From time to time, she crept out of what small safety she had found to bring food or drink to the oarsmen who sweated to keep the ship upright in the water.

Now the rapids ran in surges like immense waves on Oceanos' shore. They were in Baruforos now, named from the wavelike pattern that the water created or from the cliffs themselves.

The men were tiring now. Dark circles showed beneath their eyes, despite the weathering of their skin. Audun's white hair and beard hung in lank, dripping strands and he looked —how old was he? Alexa wondered. When he passed by her to shout a word of reassurance at her before moving back to the oarsmen, she could barely understand him, so hoarse was his voice. He gestured, and the oarsmen nodded, evidently gathering themselves for one last effort.

Up ahead thundered such a cataract that Alexa believed it must surely dwarf the legendary falls from which the Nile itself had its birth. Isis guard them all! she prayed. The ship veered toward the left, where the sheer rock of the cliff was so high that none of their ropes might suffice to let men use them to draw the ship along. The river arced out into a wide curve, like a grinning jaw studded with sharp, wet teeth toward which, inexorably, the water and the straining oarsmen were driving them.

Alexa jammed one fist into her mouth to keep from screaming. If they continued on this course, they would be dashed upon the rocks, the boat would be torn asunder, and they would all be pitched into the spray, to be battered to death or drowned. The river's curve widened yet further. Audun shouted hoarsely, and the men cheered. Ahead of them, between the rocks, was the gap toward which he steered them.

Another hoarse shout, which Alexa interpreted as orders to brace herself, and *Hvitbjarn's* keel scraped against mud and stone and jolted to a stop. The prow jutted upright, slanted defiantly. The man sagged at their oars, panting, too weary even to cheer.

Moments later, all hands began to unload cargo. Alexa struggled with a bale of furs as large as she and finally succeeded in toppling it from the deck onto the flat, wet shore, then went back for another, and another.

At some point she became conscious of someone leading her away from the boat toward a fire built in the shelter of a pile of rocks. Abruptly, she started to shiver, aware now of the cold, of the way her dank garments clung to her. She gulped at the first hot food she had had in days. The fire shimmered, and the dampness beading her lashes cast rainbows in front of her eyes. She remembered the ice and the silence, and shuddered. Ragnar patted her shoulder, and his friends grinned at her. She caught Audun's eye, and was pleased to see him nod gravely.

He heaved himself upright and came over to sit by her. "When my father, Ingvar, was Bearmaster in my place, I remember the first time I saw this spot." He paused, seeing that an appreciative crowd had gathered. "I would wager that you thought I planned to break the boat on the rocks, eh, Princess?"

Alexa ducked her head, her cheeks flaming.

"Aye, that was what I thought when m'father headed us for this spot. We unloaded, and never will I forget just how cold I was. But we had little chance to rest. No sooner did he get his own breath than he was bellowing for us to unload, and get out digging tools."

There were appreciative murmurs. Alexa glanced around at the listening Aescir, who must have heard this story a hundred times, yet had settled happily down to hear it again.

"And, Princess, do you know what Ingvar said next? That

since the river offered us no channel, we would make one!"
Audun paused long enough for his audience to groan. "And
so—we did. Took us a month. By the time we finished, I
don't think that even a skald or a Druid bard might have invented more curses than we came up with."

He rose, mead horn in hand, and passed from the circle of
firelight into the night. Alexa dared to follow. Her feet scuffed
in a puddle, and he heard her. "Mind your footing," he
warned. Here, between the rocks, the roar of the cataracts was
oddly subdued. She blinked, trying to locate him. Then her
eyes became accustomed to the moonlight, and she saw his
burly figure standing next to a slab of rock. She went over to
join him.

"Give me your hand," he said, and enveloped it in his own,
guiding it to the coarse-grained stone. "Those are the runes for
Aifor, the rapids we just crossed."

"There are other runes—is that the word?—here too,"
Alexa traced the angular signs that looked as if they had been
etched into the rock with an ax blade. If Marric were here, he
would know about runes; he had always a taste for barbarian
stories.

"Aye," said Audun, and emptied the horn of mead he carried at the stone's base. "The gods—yours or mine—have
smiled upon us so far. We set up this stone for a man named
Rafn, one of five brothers . . . Just at the bend in the river, he
went overboard. We never found the body. I mind well when I
sailed with Vifil. He had us set the stone up. Since then, each
time we lose a man, we carve in his name here."

Einar, thought Alexa.

"I'll hold the torch while you carve his name there," she
offered.

"No," Audun shook his head, and the torchlight cast the
illusion of ruddy youth on his hair and beard. "I want you to
carve it."

She knew no runes. Very likely, she could not even lift that
ax, much less wield it with the delicacy such carving would
demand. She shut her lips firmly on a protest.

"I will trace the runes for you and steady your hand,"
Audun told her.

He knelt to etch in the angular symbols, and Alexa tried to

think of how many strokes each would take. The ax was too heavy for her to lift, and Audun reluctantly handed her, not the blade she had surrendered ten days before, but a knife with a bone handle carved in the form of a bear.

The stone would blunt it. From his earliest days of training, Marric had taught her always to keep her knives sharp. She bent, etching the runes in deeply. As she carved the last angle on the last rune, though, the shriek of a hawk, stooping on its prey, made her hand slip. She hissed in aggravation, then finished the stroke. Blood from the cut dripped onto knife and stone alike. She straightened, wiped her hand on her skirt, and handed the knife back to Audun.

He closed his hand around hers on the hilt. "This is yours now," he said.

Alexa shivered, and Audun laid an arm about her shoulders. "You should come back to the fire, little lady. Have you not wished for land now, these many days? Starting tomorrow, you shall have it, though you may not be glad of it for long. We walk."

That night her sleep was deep and dreamless.

Chapter 3

☆

The portage began the next day. Alexa joined the line of bears and their handlers, all heavily laden, who were to walk the six miles beyond the rapids. Accompanying them were several men who bore only their weapons. Even the sun came out. Despite the wind, it beat warmly down upon her shoulders. She found herself cheerful, and strode out willingly. She had not felt so strong in what seemed like years. The bears sniffed as she passed, then gave absurdly human shrugs as if her tiny self were of far less importance than the rocks and trees and enthralling scents about them.

Not all the Aescir were huge and ruddy, she thought. Some of the people of Finnmark were dark, though not as small as she. One woman stopped and demanded that Alexa show her the cut on her hand. Finding it bandaged to her satisfaction, she walked on at Alexa's side until they were joined by others. Apparently, in carving those runes, she had passed some sort of test. *They might accept me*, she told herself. *They might*.

She found herself drawn into one of the interminable Aescir stories. The accent of the storyteller was strange, and the roar of the rapids distracted her. But as near as she could understand, the tale was of Penllyn, the kingdom in the Isles of Mists to which Audun promised to take her should all other attempts to heal her fail. Though Penllyn's ties with the Aescir went back centuries, they were not originally kin "until," said the storyteller, "we had more men than fields, and the land groaned beneath our bears' paws. Some sailed over the swan's road to the Isles of Mist looking for land. Oh, not as our sole home; Penllyn is far too from the Great Ice, which brings forth the bears—but as two families may dwell together on the same farm as friends and neighbors. Thus it began, but all under heaven withers and wanes. And the Reiver Jarl of Jomsburg had other dreams; the lawless man longed for conquests.

"Then as now, Penllyn's Queen kept the land hale. She is always young and fair. How not? when her life is allied to her lands. She lives only so long as she, like the fields, is able to bear. Though she herself may ride to battle, she usually summons a man to her side, a war leader as consort and lord. The Reiver tempted this man with a witch—his own daughter—as bribe and prize. For as men of Jomsborg run mad under the moon, shift their skins in the battle-lust, and are subject to the skin-change and the madness, witchery heats their women's blood. When the warleader saw her, lust cost him his honor; he lost his soul.

"And almost, our lords, and both of our land rights. For many years, Aescir and Penllyn warriors bled to bring back what they'd owned before. Time and again the crafty warrior, who knew too well the ways he'd betrayed, beat them back. Then came the Bear.

"Some say he was the son of a princess of Penllyn and an Aescir lord; others say that the bears found him wandering by the White Lake, a child in the cold, and carried him to the Bearmaster. In ten great battles, he beat Jomsborg back, thrust them out from the Misty Isles. Then he, the Queen, and the Bearmaster sat down and created a great accord, a peace that has lasted even until this day—though," the storyteller added, voice dropping out of its impassioned singsong, "not because Jomsborg has not tried to break it, time after time."

The story continued, but Alexa, her eyes on the uneven rocks of their path, walked on, wrapped in her own thoughts. The Isles of Mist: like the lands of Gaul past the reach of the Empire, she and her brother had always wondered about such places. Though her brother possessed several impeccably Greek and Imperial names, he had always—stubbornly—insisted on being called Marric, after a distant (and perhaps mythical) ancestor who came from the West.

But the idea wasn't totally without basis. At one point, she knew, Divine Cleopatra's first spouse had sent armies into the Isles of the Mist, as he had done in Gaul. But when he was murdered before he could wear the diadem of Empire, Cleopatra had looked elsewhere . . . to Antony Cosmokrator and his dream of combining the Empire with the Egypt they both loved. Empire moved to the Middle Sea. After Octavian's defeat at Actium, it had moved south and east as well, the Eagles of old Rome and the Falcon of infinitely older Heliopolis merging into a realm where the Emperor was both king and Pharaoh, and the Empress—his closest female kin—ruled as Isis on Earth.

"What happened to the Queen?" she asked abruptly.

The sudden, awkward gap in the story told her that the question had been an unfortunate one.

"The time came," one woman said, "as she grew older and her time of bearing drew short, that she knew she must pass within the Druids' grove and return her life to the goddess. But she had spent so many years fighting that she felt she could not leave this life before she had fully savored it. So . . . she fled, Princess Alexa. She fled with a trusted warrior,

the Bear's friend, into your Empire." Her tone was hot, un-
forgiving, even after these many centuries. Women never
could forgive one another, Alexa thought. If she herself
thought it would avail, she would have cursed Irene, even if
her own damnation followed. As it might in any case.

Another voice spoke up quickly, as if trying to cover over
the awkwardness. "Some say she bled to death, trying to give
birth when she was so old. The Bear himself never recovered
from this double loss. His Queen left an heir, but she was very
young. In the years while she grew up, he ruled alone, and
fought Jomsborg again and again."

"Some say," cut in the first speaker, "that he died in one of
those battles. Others—I among them—that he disappeared,
and will return should he be needed. But this much is true: as
long as he is remembered, the love of Aescir and Isles will
persist."

The Bear, Alexa thought. In Greek, that would be Arktos.
He might have been Imperial. Like her father and brother, he
had been betrayed by the woman in whom he had the best
right to trust. Walking blindly away from the women, Alexa
stumbled into the Aescir who kept watch against ambush.
They seized up weapons as she approached, then relaxed as
they recognized her. Ragnar and Ottar came up.

"Any sign of enemies?" she hated the way her voice shook,
and kept her head down.

Ragnar glanced closely at her. "Have you heard something,
lady, to distress you? I saw you walking with . . ." his voice
trailed off into unflattering references.

"They told me about the Bear, nothing more," Alexa said.
But it had been more than enough. A treacherous woman, an
empire that harbored her, a broken harmony: it hurt to think of
them.

Ragnar shrugged. "Would you see the rapids?" he asked.

"Is that wise?" asked Ottar.

But Ragnar had her by the hand and pulled her along the
path until they were half-bent over high rocks. The sudden
pressure of huge, hard hands at her waist, lifting her to a
better vantage point, made her twist. He pulled her back and
set her on her feet.

"Be easy, now," said her companion. "If you want to see,

you have to trust that I can hold you. If you struggle and fall, you are lost. Now, again!"

He lifted her until she was able to clutch rocky handholds and look over the rocks into the gorge that the Aescir called Nenasytets, or "insatiable." A thundering falls poured down, split into two cataracts by a promontory like a spear. At the bottom of the falls, spray leapt upward above whirlpools that seemed to spiral down and down, choking on enormous jagged rocks, crying out in torment. On the rough bank beside it, the strongest of the Aescir struggled to lift their ships from rollers onto their sweating backs.

How could they stand it? How could anyone? It would be so simple to leap into that pool. No one would ever find her. They might even mourn. What was her alternative? To seduce these people into accepting her, and then, finally, to betray them? She was good for nothing else. Something in her agreed with that judgment. Already her fingers were releasing their white-knuckled clutch on the rocks. The spume was very white, very greedy, and it drew her. They would never know.

I promised Audun I would fight! She bit her lip, and the pain helped her repel Irene's attack.

"No," she gasped. "No!"

The hands at her waist tightened, began to force her back over the drop. She writhed against them, until she had twisted half onto her back. She gasped as she saw the feral gleam in Ragnar's eyes. Having failed with her, Irene now sought prey less capable of defending itself.

"Put me down," she hissed, and felt the hands contort as if Ragnar tried, yet could not obey her. Instead, she felt herself forced inexorably back over the rock. Even through her garments, it scraped against her back and side. This was worse than her succumbing to Irene's blandishments about suicide; she would fall, Irene would withdraw—and Ragnar, if they did not execute him, would be outlawed, to wander, lifelong, convicted of having killed the woman it was his charge to protect.

Spittle appeared at the corners of his mouth, and he whined faintly.

"Fight it," she whispered. "Please, Ragnar. I don't want to die." To her astonishment, the words were true.

The Aescir's face twisted, and he shook with strain. Alexa twisted again, her hand darting to Audun's knife. She would not kill, no—not even if she could. But a small wound, the pain of which could break the concentration that made him Irene's thrall . . . she had the knife out when Ragnar's punishing grasp loosened somewhat. Thank Isis, he was fighting!

Now horror showed in his face as he realized that he fought to control his own body as much to avoid murdering her. His lips drew back in a snarl—was that the rage of a man or the frenzy of a trapped beast? Bearded jaws seemed to elongate, turn into a furred muzzle. In a moment it would rend her throat . . . or would it? Alexa raised her hands to push against his face, to scratch and claw . . . where were the others? Did they think that this was flirtation? If this resembled Aescir dalliance, their women were even hardier than their bears.

"The Bearmaster told *me* to fight," she told him. "Fight this!"

For what felt like hours, she lay suspended between rock and rapids, struggling to free herself without overbalancing. She had the knife . . . and she had the magic. One *word*, and she would be safe. She could even lift the memory of this from the man who held her.

The temptation swept over her like the torrent below, and she fought it. "Help me, Ragnar! Audun ordered you to protect me." Again, his grip loosened, and again and again, she reminded him of his oaths, until, gradually, his grip relaxed, and she was able to slide down the rocks to crouch on the path.

It hurt to breathe, hurt worse as she tried to rise. And she postponed the moment when she would have to meet his eyes for as long as she could.

Finally, she looked up. Ragnar's blue eyes lost focus. He blinked, then reeled. Then, he recovered his balance. He bent to give her a hand up, and she was astonished at the change in him.

He truly does not remember, she realized.

Ragnar laughed and swung her back onto her feet. "I should not have thought that you would fear it," he teased her. It was easier—and far more pleasant—to accept his laughter than to explain what had almost happened. She would have to tell

Audun, and guard herself and her own guards in the meantime. Her ribs grew more painful as she walked. She had
never, in a sheltered, palace-bred life, had to walk six miles;
to walk them with bruises the size of Ragnar's hands on both
sides was agony. At least no Petchenegs attacked.

They conquered Nenasytets two days later, days in which
she had no chance to talk with Audun, who directed the portage; nights in which she slept only fitfully, afraid that Irene's
face, Irene's voice would possess her while she slept.

Thereafter the river narrowed until it was no more than the
width of the polo ground at her home. Barren islands rose in
the middle, stubbornly enduring despite the terrible force of
the water relentlessly dashing against them. She would have
thought it quite terrible had she not seen Nenasytets first. Es-
supi, it was called, meaning "do not sleep." She could well
believe it.

But beyond clear water rolled in wide, strong swells.
Ahead lay Kiev, and all the towns of Gardariki. And beyond
them was the Bearmaster's domain.

Chapter 4

☆

Weeks later, earth and river, the ease of sail and the sweat of
portage, brought them to Staraja Ladoga.

Sails taut with cool wind, *Hvitbjarn* sailed past stands of
birch and dense forests of pines. Here the river broadened as it
rolled tranquilly between forested banks. Though the sun was
bright, from time to time clouds scudded overhead and cast
brief shadows across the river, ship, and forests. At the horizon shone a narrow glint of silver, the lake by which Staraja
Ladoga had been raised. Though Alexa was not especially

cold, she huddled into her cloak. In the past weeks, she had become used to her shipmates, and they to her. But a townful of staring strangers, each gifted with Audun's ability to look into her heart . . . she forced herself to remain impassive. Otherwise she would have hidden behind many cloaks.

Audun had told Alexa they would arrive by sunset. She would have little more time to fear or worry. Hearing his footsteps, Alexa laid down the copy of her grandfather's Strategikon that she had found among the "accounts" Audun had given into her care. Its description of the best ways to build and defend catapults blurred into meaninglessness.

Her evening discussions with Audun had turned into arguments over history and armies; she had been amazed to realize that he weighed her words with the care that any ruler might give to an ally's counsel. Had she become Empress, she would have expected it. But who would listen to an exile with anything but scorn for the bad judgment that put her into that plight?

"It will be good to be home," Audun said, and glanced narrowly at her. "Ragnar told me he thought you were uneasy."

"Ragnar thinks too much," Alexa replied. Her eyes strayed over to the big, braided man as he coiled rope. As if sensing her attention, he looked up, grinned at her, then nodded at Audun, salute and confirmation. Alexa flushed, knowing herself under observation.

"Ragnar thinks right," said Audun. He eased himself down onto his haunches beside Alexa and sat there in silent contentment as the afternoon waned, the shadows lengthened, and they drew ever closer to the Aescir town.

He was like one of his bears, Alexa thought as she had done a thousand times: quiet, patient, and waiting—for what? For some outburst of mad activity on her part? "Do I look uneasy?" she finally felt herself driven to ask.

Audun shook his head slightly and smiled. "Terrified is a better word. No, child, don't glare. I know your courage. If you weren't brave, you'd be cowering some place where no one could find you. Tell me, Alexa, what do you fear?"

Because he had not called her coward or weakling, she

risked a reply. "At Staraja Ladoga, Bearmaster, what shall I do?"

"What do you want to do?" There it was again, her dreams and uncertainties thrust back into her face.

Alexa sighed. "I know what I was born to do—but cannot."

"When Osiris was slain, Isis gathered the pieces of his body and dared hell itself to bring him back to life, then bore her brother's child, Horus, as savior of the world. A heavy burden . . ."

She nodded. "And one I am unfit to bear. Do you know, it is almost a relief to know it?"

"And your brother?"

"I comfort myself with your words: if he had died, I would know it. I think I would die to save him, though what use that would be, I cannot tell you. Marric . . ." her voice trailed off as she thought of him. When she was a child, he had seemed only slightly less godlike than their father; the splendid older brother who coaxed or scolded her, who always protected and taught. She had never thought of a life in which that would not continue. He would not succumb to Irene, whether she tortured or cajoled him. Where was he now? She glanced into the water as if his image might appear there.

There was nothing she could do to help him, no way to get word of him. And harming herself? as she had said, it would not release him from danger or undo the attack on him that resulted in his death or capture. At best, death would bring her extinction or the chance to try again; at worst . . . she pushed the matter to the back of her thoughts. She had promised Audun that she would not kill herself, except in the last resort, should Irene's power reach out to devour her soul. If she were wiser than she had been, she might cobble together a life of sorts in Staraja.

She shuddered, as if she had suddenly brushed through a door filled with cobwebs. Tingles flashed from her spine to her fingertips, and she was simultaneously hot and chilled. She shook her head to clear her sight of a sudden mist . . . no, it was not mist, but a veil of faint rainbows that danced on the *Hvitbjarn's* planks, stained its colored sails with mosaic splendor, and made the high prow gleam as if some master craftsman had inlaid it with gold and garnets.

"We will be through the barrier soon," Audun assured her.

"You knew of this?" she demanded, and saw him nod. She had heard stories of the shivering lights that the Northern sky wore like the finest gauze veils, but to find them here, used as protection! It took more than bears, more than a mastery of wind and wave to wield such power. The Aescir were not the barbarians that Irene had called them, nor the exuberant primitives that most Byzantines considered them. What were they? The priests might have answers for her—or the town that lay ahead.

Alexa spread her hand out across her knee. Colors played and faded on the pale skin while the amber bracelet she wore clung to the green wool of her tunic. Her hair seemed to stand out from her skull. *Hvitbjarn's* prow moved out of that realm of light. The wood lost its gemtones and diminished once again into weathered pine.

"You wanted to see how I would react," Alexa accused. "What if I had been unable to pass through it?"

Audun laughed. "I should have been much surprised. The veil is our first defense. Think of it not as a wall, but as a warning. Those unfriendly to us see it and know that we are masters of no little power. And we . . . just from passing through it, I can tell that others have dared. Still, it is good that you did not faint or become ill. No evil dreams recently?"

She shook her head. "None that I remember." Did Irene's powers hold firm this far from Byzantium—or was it simply that the Red Empress regarded her as too trivial to crush?

"Try to remember all of your dreams," Audun told her. Alexa nodded, and watched as the lake ahead of them grew larger and larger, and only a narrow spit of woodland and fields separated them from it.

A shout from a mounted man rang out over the water. Several bears emerged from the trees, rose onto their hind legs, and bellowed a welcome to which Audun's own bears roared answers. Ragnar answered it, and then, with several others, began to pull down the sails and unship oars. Ahead of them, the forest gave way to a long, flat shore on which ships were beached. Ahead of them, Alexa saw a curved wall of wood

and rammed earth, surmounted by a palisade studded with
towers. Beyond the walls were mounds near which stood
carved stones like the one at the rapids on which Alexa had
etched runes with a knife and her own blood. Not only man,
beast, and barriers protected Staraja; Alexa sensed it had a
magic of its own.

Inside its walls, Staraja was like an active child squirming
in too-tight garments. It was like landing at Khortitsa, only
worse. The center of town teemed with people who laughed
and called out to *Hvitbjarn's* crew as they passed. As a
stranger, Alexa came in for much staring and whispering, but
not as much as she feared. Suppressing an unworthy impulse
to hide herself behind Audun or Ragnar, Alexa strode into the
lane—paved, to her astonishment, with wood—that led into
the center of town.

It was even more crowded here. Wooden houses and small
workshops were crammed so close together that their steeply
pitched roofs almost met. On one roof hung an ox. Beneath it,
a man wearing the robes of an Arab stood writing.

"Ibn Fadlan! Not you again," Audun shouted at the smaller,
darker figure. "Have you decided to make do with writing
about animal sacrifices, then?" He bent closer to Alexa and
muttered, "We always have one or two of this kind up here.
They say they plan to write histories. Actually they're always
a-prowl for scandal and tales of human bloodshed."

Alexa found herself laughing. Hearing her voice in an assembly of men, the Arab turned to look at her. His dark eyes
widened at seeing a Greek woman in the crowd, and he
bowed ironically. But Alexa was not, she realized, the only
woman here. A horse-drawn wagon clattered by, driven by a
middle-aged woman whose shoulder brooches and heavy
bunch of keys proclaimed her of some importance. Two other
women jolted alongside her in the wagon; others strolled
through the town, gossiping about the motley crowd of
traders. Alexa recognized Khazars and a few fair-haired people she thought must be Celtoi. The woman who drove the
wagon halted it and stood. When she saw Audun, her face
reddened, and she cried his name.

"Gerda, my wife," Audun said. Catching Alexa's elbow, he

drew her through the crowd, almost oversetting the three women who carried laundry and the chessboard that two old men had set out by the street. Audun came to a stop by a larger building set back from the central lane and protected from the crowds by a fence.

Gerda was waiting for him there. They smiled at one another, then hugged with such back-thumping vigor that Alexa winced.

"It is good to see you, husband," said Gerda, whose round-cheeked face, only slightly lined, was rosy with pleasure. She was a tall woman, though still half a head shorter than the Bearmaster, and she wore the long, pleated tunic and twinned aprons of Aescir matrons with great dignity. Her cloak, of blue wool bordered with Persian brocade, fell over her shoulders, and her brooches shone. Over her thick, graying braids, she had tied a silken scarf shot with golden thread.

"Have we been attacked?" Audun asked. "The veil was disturbed; I saw that when we sailed in."

Gerda shrugged. "A black bear or two," she said. "Just in case, I ordered meat and honey set out for them. But if they *were* Jomsborgers seeking a quarrel, they went away without it. The second attack was worse, though. A hawk with red wingtips swooped down and tried to steal Ingebjorg's baby son."

Audun frowned, his bushy eyebrows contracting fearfully. "Why was a child left unprotected?"

"How could you think he would be?" said Gerda, and raised a hand. A younger woman, wearing red and brown, stepped out of the wagon and greeted the Bearmaster. She too wore her hair twisted into a scarf; a second one served as a sling for her right arm. "Ingebjorg was with him. She drove the bird off with her knife, though it fought her and broke her arm."

Hawks had sharp talons and beaks, Alexa thought. The woman might have lost an eye, or been battered to death by strong wings. Audun patted the woman's shoulder. "Well done," he said. "Now, tell me about the hawk."

"Bearmaster, I think that the Red Empress sent it," Ingebjorg's voice was low and fearless. "The hawk has ever been the Empire's sigil, and the red—that is Irene's mark. Another thing: when it struck me and broke my arm, my sleeve fell back and its feathers brushed me." Very cautiously, she pushed up her sleeve. Bandages stained with salve covered the broken arm. "I could have gotten no worse burn had I put my arm in fire."

Alexa looked down at her own hands, remembering the fire she had summoned. It sounded like Irene. She would wait for a time to speak alone with Audun and tell him. It added up: Irene sought alliance with Jomsborg and attacked Audun's people to support the Jarl.

"Foolishness!" sniffed the third woman, eldest of the three. "Why would the Red Empress attack us? Miklagard has ever been our ally." Her eyes flickered constantly, scanning the people who clustered about Audun until they found Ragnar. Seeing him, she tensed, and her taut face seemed abruptly to sag. As if anticipating no pleasant task, he came up to her, assisted her down from the cart, and drew her aside. Moments later, she wailed, and he hugged her hard against him, his hand pressing her head against his shoulder.

Audun followed Alexa's gaze, and sighed. "That was Einar's mother, child." Then he turned back to his wife. "We have the reason for Irene's attack here," he said, and beckoned Alexa closer. "Several weeks ago, Prince Marric and his sister Alexa tried to leave the City for Tmutorakan, where he had an army waiting. Their plan was to retake it. It was premature, but we did succeed in bringing out the Princess."

Alexa stood as straight as she could, allowing Gerda to examine her: shorn hair, Aescir garments, and all. She could feel her face smoothing out into that expression of imperious calm that she had been schooled to for her few public appearances; it would enable her to bear Gerda's greetings or abuse with equal dignity.

"This child should be in bed!" Gerda announced. "From the way she moves, I can tell that she was wounded—and to go upriver after a battle! Child—Princess, I should say—you are welcome, and I shall prove it once you enter my house. Consider it your own for as long as you wish."

The woman standing with Ragnar's arm about her gave another wail. Ragnar clutched her, one hand pressing her head against his shoulder. "I will be a son to you now," he promised. She broke free of his embrace and, wringing her hands, pushed through the crowd.

"Halldis," Audun held out a hand to her. "I regret Einar's death as if he had been my own lad."

The woman Halldis pulled off her headcloth, wiped her face, and walked over to him. She drew herself up into a semblance of her former pride, but she did not accept Audun's hand.

"Ragnar has already told me how my son died," she said. "You tell me the rest."

"What else is there to tell?" asked Audun. "At Dnieper-mouth, Einar was guarding Princess Alexa. She and I walked on the shore. Petchenegs came, we fought, and he died." He spread out both hands in a gesture of frustration and finality.

"*You* will tell me," Halldis ordered. Inflamed from weeping, her eyes were the color of smoke, and they glared at Alexa. "You tell me, Princess, what are you?"

"An ally," Alexa said, falling back on the old relationship between Byzantine and Aescir.

"And do you think that you, with your pale face and puny limbs, and your hair cut short as any thrall's, are worth a man's life, my son's life?"

Gerda shook her head furiously at Halldis, and tried to lead her away. Though she was taller, broader, and younger than Halldis, the woman shook free, and glared at the Bearmaster's wife.

"By the Bear of Hropt, I want an answer!"

In the Women's Quarters of the palace that had always been her home, this degree of rage would have been expressed with feline quiet, probably with poison to follow. Alexa stopped herself from taking a step backward. She lifted her hand from the hilt of her dagger. Halldis meant precisely what she said. She wanted an answer. If she did not get one, Alexa would have made an enemy of the older woman, and she desperately did not want to make enemies so soon.

She shook her head. "I am worth no man's life."

"Then why did my son die?" asked Einar's mother.

"For the *var*," Alexa blurted, without thinking. "The Bear-master ordered Einar to guard me, and he obeyed, as he would have obeyed any lawful order. He died fighting; if he had not fought, I would have died. Perhaps, the Bearmaster would have died too—and he is worth . . . more than I." Her voice threatened to break, and she swallowed a sob.

"What blood price can you give me?" Halldis asked.

"I helped cut his runes into the rock," Alexa said, "and spilled my own blood in the doing. I will do all I can."

"And if I say it is not enough?" She shook off Ragnar's clumsy attempts to lead her away and stood watching Alexa, challenging her to prove herself. A sizable crowd had gathered. At first it had been noisy, good-natured. But as word of Halldis's loss and her challenge to the Bearmaster's guest spread, it quieted, waiting for Alexa's words.

"Then I will try to do more. But you must tell me what you require."

Halldis stared her up and down, then turned. Ragnar put his arm about her and led her away. When Alexa would have spoken, he shook his head. *Not now,* he mouthed.

There was one obvious answer. Perhaps the Bearmaster would permit her to join the *var,* the company of pledged Aescir. They were not born all one people; she had seen Lapps, Finns, even people from the Misty Isles and the Middle Sea among them. She would swear allegiance to the Aescir and make her home here. That was not just a possible future; it was a fine one. She opened her lips to demand the terms of the oath. . . .

Hail, Princess. The words rang inside her skull, and she whirled around.

"Greetings, Bearmaster," came a well-pitched voice from behind her. A man strode forward, a harp in its leather case hanging from his shoulder. Throughout the Empire and beyond, bards were used as emissaries and spies, but this one —Alexa had seen that expression before: half-ruthless, half-visionary—on the faces of priests. Though she had never seen a Druid before, Irene having banned them, she suspected that she was looking at one now. He looked very young for a man who had studied and been tested as she knew Druids were. His hair was dark, and his eyes darker. But there was nothing at all dark in his flashing smile or the respect with which he greeted the Aescir chief.

"Pwyll," the Bearmaster acknowledged him. "What news from the West?"

He cocked his head after the retreating Halldis, shook it, then replied. "That Queen Blodeuedd of Penllyn has passed within the nemet, and her daughter Olwen wears the black dagger. Queen Olwen bade me ask you, 'where is my bear?'"

"Be assured, Pwyll, I shall bring it before the winter. In a few days, I go to Finnmark. Once I return, we shall speak of this again. But come, man, come home and feast with me. I would hear of your journeys West. You passed Jomsborg, I think?"

The Druid Pwyll nodded once, his mobile lips twisting into a grimace of disgust. "This is no fit place for my news," he said. "I fear that no such place exists. But tell it I must."

Most of Audun's people ate quickly, then, subdued by Halldis's grief, withdrew to their own houses or to beds within the Bearmaster's house. The bard Pwyll remained, however, and sat by the central hearth in a heavy chair almost the equal of Audun's own. Across from him sat Gerda, her bowls and ladles idle for the first time all evening. At her side, Alexa reclined on a wolfskin, and tried to listen, though the warmth, the firelight, and her own fatigue made her feel as distanced from surroundings and the Druid's tale as if the veil she had passed earlier that day lay over them.

These Jomsborgers: once kin of the Aescir, they now bore as much relationship to them as Irene did to the priestesses of Isis. They did not so much as tame beasts as subjugate them. Where a beast killed from fear or hunger, the men of Jomsborg killed for sport. The "men of Jomsborg"—that was another custom that Audun and his allies regarded as barbarous. Penllyn in the Misty Isles was ruled by a queen, Byzantium by the representatives of Isis and Osiris on earth, and the Aescir by the Bearmaster and his wife. But two things the Jomsborgers forbade to enter their island fortress: fear and women.

"It is dangerous to rule out women," said Gerda. "Something twists in a land which silences half its folk."

"It has indeed twisted," said the Druid. "While even the Reiver Jarl himself will not break the ban on women, one of my brothers has learned that among his chief counselors is his grandmother. I believe it is she who has urged him to ally with the Red Empress. Small wonder: she herself practices *seithr*."

Alexa started. She had never heard that word before, yet it stung her the way cold stings a rotted tooth. And yet another part of her longed to hear more. She started to rise, to remove herself, but Gerda's hand squeezed her shoulder.

"She was kin of ours. Before I hear such ill spoken, I'd like some proof," rumbled Audun.

"One of my brothers traveled near the Island, and sought shelter at a farm. They gave him shelter in a barn: no great hospitality for a Druid, but we have learned to expect that. He said that the place smelled wrong."

Audun and Gerda nodded.

"That night, he left the barn, went up to the house, and peered in. The mistress of the house was weaving with her maids. It is no strange thing for women to weave, but at night? He pressed closer and saw more clearly. Their loom was set up, but in place of weights, they used men's heads. Entrails were for weft and warp, a sword for beater, and a black Jomsborg arrow for the shuttle."

Alexa, who had lifted her cup to drink, thought better of it, and set it down on the floor again.

"And they were chanting:
'Blood rains
From the cloudy web
On the broad loom . . .'"

"Enough!" ordered Audun, and brought his fist down on the arm of his chair. Across the room, a half-grown bear raised its head, groaned, and sank back into well-fed sleep.

"I agree," said the Druid. "Any messages that reach you from across the North Sea must pass through such spells. We have not heard from several of our brothers for months. The Goddess grant that they are dead by now."

"And to the South?" asked Audun.

"The last message I heard was that we would try to find the Prince."

"I heard that when I was in Byzantium," said Audun. "One of your brothers saw him the night he returned there; since then, I have heard only rumor: prison, perhaps, or slavery."

A moan broke from Alexa's lips.

"His sister," explained Audun. "It may be that she needs a safe harbor for a time. Would Queen Olwen—"

Pwyll stared narrowly at Alexa, who forced herself to meet his eyes.

"I sense power there, but . . ."

"That is indeed the problem. Power, but little discipline, and much, much remorse. We shall try to heal her ourselves, but the bears . . . they fear her. Penllyn, now, has a cleanliness that she might need."

"I can ask," said Pwyll. "The moon will be full soon. But Bearmaster, if this continues, I fear that from now on, you must mistrust any tidings that our messengers bring. The Reiver boasts that before he dies, the Black Bear will fly from his two lakes—the North Sea and the Middle Sea. And should that happen, there is no hope for us. Already some few among the Saxons in our land mutter about finishing what was stopped by Arktos Warleader; the Reiver calls them kin and sends them rings. As for you and yours, you must withdraw into your own fastnesses up by the White Sea, and sleep until the weather of the world changes."

"That is despair speaking, not hope," said Audun. "And I am resolved not to despair."

Chapter 5

☆

In the days that followed, Alexa timidly began to adapt to her new life. She no longer suspected that every eye glared at her in condemnation. For one thing, the people of Staraja Ladoga were too busy; for another, she herself was busy too. The bard Pwyll whose tidings had turned homecoming into disquiet set out West several days later.

"Tell the Queen she will have her bear before winter," Audun said. "Fortune granting, I shall be there—" he had glanced at Alexa appraisingly and she sighed. If she could not adjust to Staraja Ladoga, she supposed she would be packed off to Penllyn. The Isles of Mist: she had scoured the chests of books in Audun's storerooms for more about them. They were distant kin to the Rhomaioi, as some Byzantines still affectedly called themselves, through common ancestors who had survived Troy; and there had been unions since then between the Empire and the kingdoms of the West. Her own brother's name of choice had been that of a man of Gallia, who had struck East and married a noblewoman.

She had read until her eyes were swollen and her head ached. Then she had discovered another advantage: if she read, she was quiet; if she were quiet, the people of Staraja let her pass by unnoticed. Halldis was far from unique in voicing every thought and emotion in public. Used to the deadly silences of Byzantium, Alexa found the verbal brawls of Staraja unnerving at first, then useful. If one kept quiet, one listened and learned. And *that* was a skill she had perfected just to survive. So it was that she overheard Audun asking the bard to alert "the net" (which Alexa privately thought of as a magical version of the Byzantine civil service) to seek out her brother; and so it was that she heard Audun telling Gerda about his proposed trip into Finnmark.

"Foolishness!" Gerda had snorted. "Soon the snows will fall there, and what if you must spend the winter there? Do you think that I enjoy running this town as if it were my own holding?"

They had both laughed then. The Bearmaster's house was simply where he ate and slept. His home was anywhere the Aescir roamed.

"I must fetch Queen Olwen's bear," Audun said.

Gerda had snorted again.

"In normal times, she might wait until spring when the Lapps come down from the White Sea. But these are not normal times. I must warn our brothers in flesh and in fur. And then, there is Alexa—" the voices dropped low, but Alexa sensed concern and affection in them.

Audun held to his word to take her into Finnmark, but the

bears still were wary around her. The elder males watched her
and gave her a wide berth; the cubs fled, and their mothers—
Alexa knew better than to approach them. And these were the
bears most used to human beings, who lived among Aescir as
beloved kin. How would the great wild bears of the far North
react? That made for grisly imagining.

Had the times been calm, she might have risked it. But
now, with the black bears of Jomsborg sniffing at Staraja's
borders, and Audun perturbed for the more peaceful far
North, now was not the time. So the next dawn, Audun
headed North without her.

She herself had promises to keep, notably to Halldis, whose
grief and anger had simmered down into a narrow observation
of everything Alexa did. A kinswoman of Gerda, she was
often in the Bearmaster's house. *An enemy is behind this
door!* Alexa quoted the Aescir proverb to herself each time
Halldis entered the house. She knew what one did under a
hostile woman's scrutiny: one listened and learned, tricked her
into underestimating oneself if possible, and bided one's time.
But in Staraja, listening and learning were not enough. She
had to *do*. Accordingly, she did. After Audun left, she accompanied Gerda on her rounds. She heard messengers, traders,
priests, soldiers, and common scolds, consulted with her upon
her judgments, and learned gradually to sift rumor from truth.
And she moved constantly from walls to markets to farms and
into the storehouses.

They were crammed not just with the trade goods of the
Aescir—amber, silver, weapons, and furs so soft that hands
and face were caressed as if by silk—but with the results of
years of trading and salvage. Alexa's books had come from
that trove; she saw sapphires from the Land of Lions near
Hind, emeralds, brocade woven in Persia, even bolts of fine
silk stamped with the angular letters of the Land of Gold, and
fine cotton that could only come from Alexandria. Other storehouses held cheeses, casks of wine and beer, smoked meat
and fish—enough food to last three winters, or a siege. And
in a third were weapons: swords, spears, shields, arrows,
wood, ropes, weights, sword blanks, and—"Those," Alexa
said, walking toward massive, heavily sealed ceramic jars,
"those are from home. She blew at the dust that covered them,

read the lettering on them, and then, involuntarily, took a step back.

"Sea fire!" she cried. Prized allies the Aescir were, but no one, no one but the Empire should possess the treacherous, deadly stuff, which would burn friend as readily as enemy, and which could be doused by no normal means.

"Quiet!" hissed Gerda. "Do you remember hearing of that army outpost slain by some plague? The traders who found the bodies found this too, and brought it here."

"Only the Empire..." Alexa began. She remembered one afternoon when her father was alive, and they had sailed out into the Horn to watch the ships shoot sea fire from bronze tubes. She had been appalled, but it had not stopped her from watching—or listening.

"Would you prefer the Red Empress have this—or the Reiver Jarl?" asked Ragnar, who had been examining one of the catapult's ropes. The raised voices had drawn him, he said, an excuse that produced even louder laughter. He greeted Gerda and Halldis respectfully, then turned to Alexa with a smile.

"Have you come to choose weapons?" he asked Alexa.

"I have my knife," she said, and patted its hilt. She wore it now as Aescir women did, hanging from a long chain about her neck.

"Did you remember to sharpen it?" he asked, as he always did.

Alexa sighed. "Among my other tasks, I tend it every night," she said. She had set herself those duties. Should she come to live here, it would be as a princess with hordes of servants and slaves to spare her any labor.

"How do you find them?" he asked her.

"She... is adequate," Halldis put in, in the tone of one making a vast concession. Halldis had taken particular care to make certain that Alexa was spared none of the most boring or arduous tasks customarily allotted the younger women, and had been irritated when she realized that Alexa asked for no favors or exceptions. In fact, the one time Alexa scrambled toward the rooftree while the much taller Halldis looked on, tapping her foot, Gerda had reproved them both.

"You should not tell me that," Alexa put in dryly. "Is it not truly said, 'praise not the day till evening has come, a sword until it is tried, ice until it has been crossed, and beer until it has been drunk'?"

Gerda burst into laughter. Halldis raised her brows. "It is also said, 'praise not a woman till she is burnt, a maiden until she is married,'" she capped Alexa's proverbs in a low voice. Her glance, cold as sea ice, flicked between Ragnar and Alexa.

"The Bearmaster told me that I should show our ally the walls. How about right now—that is, if you are finished?"

Gerda smiled and waved Alexa away, as the other women laughed.

"Quickly!" Ragnar hissed at her as he propelled her back into the crowded lane where she stared, dazzled by emergence into the sunlight and by the sight of two Lapps passing in tunics lavishly trimmed with red and blue braid. He tugged her by the wrist toward the outskirts of town, stopping only when she pretended to be out of breath.

"Does Halldis always scold you?" he asked her.

"Usually. I don't think she is doing it because of Einar..." she glanced up to gauge the impact of her words, "but because of the *var*. She as much as told me that whatever tricky, idle ways I'd learned in my home, Staraja Ladoga had no place for them. Do all the Aescir see us as so corrupt?"

"I don't. And the Bearmaster doesn't," Ragnar said, distressed. "What about the other women?"

Alexa shrugged. "Ingebjorg told me that she doesn't blame *me* for the hawk that broke her arm. The rest—Gerda likes me, so they leave me in peace. Half of them are so much taller than I that they treat me like a child, anyhow. It is no matter. Where are these sites I am supposed to see?"

"It matters to some of us," Ragnar. "Look over there." He pointed. "You should probably see the lakeshore as well."

In Byzantium, that would have been a reason to summon litters or wagons, to waste much time... it was pleasant to walk out beyond the walls here, through fields of yellowing grass, marked here and there with birch trees. From time to time, they passed guards, who raised hands or nodded at them.

"Over here," Ragnar took her hand and tugged her toward one of many mounds circling the town.

"Are these shrines or tombs?" she asked. If ships attacked from the lake rather than the river, the mounds would be good defenses, ideal for mounting catapults, unless it were blasphemy to use them thus . . .

"The Bearmaster's father is buried in this one," he said. "All around here . . . there is a belief that if any enemy passes through this field, those lying here will rise to defend us."

"And it is true?"

Ragnar laughed. "I would rather rely on my own sword, my friends, and our bears." He gestured widely, and Alexa marked a spot where men might lie in wait for raiders. Two armed men emerged and waved to him. One called out something she could not understand, and both men laughed.

Ragnar still held her hand. Now he pulled her up an incline. At the top, it sloped downward onto the beach of Lake Ladoga, which stretched out, gray and placid in the afternoon sun. "Do those women make you unhappy?" he asked.

No more unhappy than I deserve, she started to say, then closed her lips on it. "I think," she chose her words carefully, "that they mean well. But they are . . . very forceful. All our histories say so." Mischief bubbled up in her. "Do you think that that is why the Reiver Jarl will not permit them on his island?"

Ragnar shouted with laughter. His warm grip on her fingers started to tighten. Laughing unsteadily, she withdrew her hand. She understood Halldis's barb now: *praise not a maid before she is wed.* She had lost one son; would she now have to share her son-by-courtesy with the woman whom she distrusted? Rumor spread as rapidly in Staraja as it did in Byzantium. Alexa had no doubt that if she lacked Gerda's strong support, Halldis would seize any chance to make her look bad. She might even agitate for Alexa's exile as a sorceress.

That would be truth. Weeks ago, she would have sworn that it was no more than she deserved. But now, she found herself wanting to adapt to Staraja. With the Empire closed to her, how bad would it be to belong here? Half the people in town had seen Ragnar pull her through the streets. She found herself studying him. He was at least as tall as her brother. But

where Marric's skin was olive-toned and tanned to the color
of bronze, Ragnar's was ruddy; where Marric's dark eyes
could flash with anger or narrow with craft, Ragnar's blue
ones seemed open and friendly. She trusted him—somewhat;
and he made her laugh. Knowing her future set, she had never
looked at any man. Her face felt hot, and she struggled to
speak of something else.

"You could set up catapults there and there." She pointed.
"Another good location would be right after the veil. Enemies
who broke through would not expect them there. I can tell you
how to build them; it was in one of the books Audun Bearmaster gave me." Ragnar nodded, never taking his eyes from
her face.

She was different from the women he knew. For all she
knew, he might see her as weaker because of her size, or the
magic that had tainted her. Or he might think of her the way
men in Byzantium regarded women from Persia or Circassia.
Granted, that wasn't likely, seeing how meager she was, compared to the women here with their robust blond beauty, or
Irene's dark lushness. *Why* did Ragnar want her to pledge
loyalty to the Aescir?

"I am cold," she said. He moved to stand between her and
the wind. Against her will, she relaxed into the warmth his
body created, then backed away before he could lay an arm
over her shoulders.

"Princess Alexa?"

She looked up. Beneath his beard, Ragnar flushed. He
started to speak, shook his head, smiled, and started again.

"Don't let them bully you," he told her. She would have
wagered gold that that was not what he had started to say.

"We should go back," Alexa said. Her voice trembled
slightly, and she despised herself for it.

He was reaching for her hand again, when two men strode
upslope toward them, a young boy, flushed and out of breath,
with them.

"I was sent to bring the lady back!" he panted.

"Why?" asked Alexa. "Gerda herself told me I might go."

"It's Heidi . . . the *völva*," the boy said. Seeing her uncom-
prehending, he went on. "She is from Finnmark and has the
Sight. She has offered to See for the women . . . *all* the

women. She says she will not start until all the women of the Bearmaster's house are present. Halldis asked if that included you, Princess; and she said it did."

Possibly a barbarian sorceress who practiced women's magics. It would be best to avoid her, to make certain that she did not See anything about Alexa that might harm her—and that Alexa was not tempted to draw on forbidden magics herself. If she asked Ragnar, would he hide her? But wait: if she could not face the sorceress, that in itself could be an admission of guilt.

"How did you know to find me?" she asked the boy.

"Lady Halldis told me."

Alexa stifled a groan as she felt the trap close about her. "Isis, blessed mother, grant peace and rest, if it pleases thee, to my adversities, for I have endured enough labor and peril," she murmured. Perhaps this time, the goddess might even hear me. Then she turned to Ragnar.

"Go on ahead," he told the boy and the other men, then scowled at their smirks.

Before Alexa could follow them, he had both her hands captured in his. "Listen to me, Princess," he said. "I have seen this woman before. Each year, ever since I was a boy, she has come to Staraja Ladoga at this time. She stays as long as Audun is away, helping Gerda ward the town. I tell you, there is no harm in her."

A wild priestess, Alexa lamented silently. A priestess whose magic was not for health, or protection, but instead, a celebration of what was within one, for good or for ill. Perhaps she was sufficiently healed to confront such a one and go away unmoved by magic that she dared share.

"Wait," Ragnar said. From about his neck, he lifted a chain from which dangled an amber bear. Awkwardly, he draped the chain around her neck. The talisman dangled beneath her breasts.

"Don't let Halldis see you wearing it," he warned, and chuckled. Alexa bunched up the chain and dropped it beneath her long tunic.

"Do you want any help?" he asked. Alexa found herself laughing a little breathlessly. She started down the slope so he might not see how she flushed. But when he offered her his hand, this time she took it gladly.

Who opens a door, Alexa thought again, *must be on the watch for an enemy behind it.* Sure enough, Halldis, rather than the warm, motherly Gerda, opened it for her, as if she had been waiting for just this opportunity.

"I understand I have you to thank for this chance," Alexa said silkily.

"The *völva* would not See until *all* the women were gathered. You delay her," Halldis replied.

Well parried! Alexa darted a glance at Ragnar, who shifted from one foot to another, then smiled back at her. "Perhaps you will tell me what she says," he hinted.

For a moment both women's eyes went blank as they joined forces to quell improper male curiosity. Until the closing door blocked out the sound, Alexa could hear him chuckling as she entered the darkened hall.

It was filled with strange youths, boys and maids with the narrow eyes and flattened cheekbones of the Northerners. Each tended some sort of instrument: a small drum over which hide of an unhealthy gray was stretched, a bone rattle decked with feathers, a crude flute, the shrill whistle of which pierced her ears. They flanked the woman who sat eating at the head of the hall, in the place of honor usually occupied by Audun.

Without looking up, the woman beckoned. Alexa shrank back into the shadows, wanting time to study her. Though the sorceress was young, little older than she herself, her hair was white, practically the color of the fur-lined cloak and hood she had thrown back onto Gerda's own chair. Under it she wore, not the pleated linen and wool of the Aescir, but a long tunic of dingy leather and fur, banded with strips of snakeskin, and embroidered with bone beads and shells. To her left lay fur-lined gloves, each finger tipped with a long claw. It was barbarous garb, though crafted with great skill. Alexa suspected that each piece had as much meaning as the leopard skins of the Osiris priests or the circlets of the servants of Isis.

Then the seeress raised her head and caught Alexa's eyes. All thoughts of hanging back were driven out by that gaze, which drew her as a cobra might draw a bird. The women in the hall murmured in satisfaction as Alexa started forward. The *völva's* eyes were slanted, almost hidden between high cheekbones and heavy lids, but they were very bright and fierce, and her lips were red.

Alexa glanced down at the seeress's dish, of some gray, unglazed pottery unlike anything Gerda would permit on her tables. From it rose a flat, sweetish smell. A blood smell. The small gobbets of meat left on that plate . . . "those are hearts," Alexa whispered, and swallowed bile.

"Hearts of warm-blooded beasts," replied the seeress. "Of all that have life, save for man." She smiled, and her teeth were very bright and sharp. "Though I am told that that is the sweetest of all." She laughed, and it was the equivalent, in sound, of a cat toying with a mouse it had no plans to kill, at least not yet. "I smell power in you, stranger. Sit beside me."

Alexa felt her gorge rising. She pressed one hand against her throat, and her fingers brushed the chain from which Ragnar's amber bear dangled. Amber had power, she recalled, and cupped the amulet through the folds of her garments. Restored even by so slight a thing, she met the seeress's eyes with more confidence.

She meant her no harm. Gerda was here, and Gerda would not permit her to be hurt. It was just that here she faced magic that ran wild, not tamed by thousands of years of temples, rituals, and priests. The temples revealed an Isis who wore the moon as a crown, the gracious lady and kindly mother. But she had a wilder side: the shameless power that stripped herself at the gates of hell, gathered up the pieces of her brother's body, healed him, and bore him a son. Shameless, yes, perhaps more powerful than the well-tested rituals she had been trained in, but without the salt fascination of the dark sorceries. As well ask a bear to eat at table, she thought, and sat down.

"Do you think that I am a savage?" asked the sorceress, and smiled with those thin red lips again.

"I think," Alexa began hoarsely, "that you are unlike anything I have ever known." A sibyl, a Circe, perhaps, with knowledge of man and beast, that could set someone on the path to the underworld and, if her teachings were followed, return him safely. She was afraid. It was wise to be wary when dealing with the wild. But she could master her fear, rise above it to learn as the Aescir learned from the bears they met by the White Sea.

The seeress leaned forward. Her breath was like that of a cleanly beast: hot, but clean. She set her hand over Alexa's.

"You are a stranger here. You have suffered much, and will suffer more," the woman began.

It took no powers to see that, thought Alexa. She closed her eyes in aggravation. Then the seeress's hand clasped hers, the claws sewn on the gloves she wore pricking her fingers.

"Well, would you know more?"

No, Alexa wanted to say, but the other women in the hall were rapt. If she refused and dashed from the room as instinct told her she should, they would hold her in more contempt than they already did. She raised her head as she used to do in the palace when her will was crossed.

"You may proceed."

The seeress smiled ironically, then gestured with her free hand to her servant. One girl threw incense on the fire, while a boy beat a small drum in the rhythm of a human heart. The others began a low chant. Though Alexa understood none of the words, the chant insinuated itself into her awareness and twined with the drums, the incense, and the music. All the women in the hall were bright-eyed, and they swayed in unison as the music took them. She was swaying too, back and forth to the rhythm of drums and voices.

But the seeress still kept silent. Halldis brought her a small brazier. With her free hand, the seeress groped into a skin pouch and brought up a pinch of some sort of powder that she hurled into the brazier. Orange flame, followed by dense smoke, puffed up into her face, and she leaned forward to breathe in the fumes. They made Alexa's eyes sting. She closed them, and dizziness made her sway further. She could not fell the bench beneath her; she was rising in the air, she was floating sideways. . . . Only the seeress's strong little hand kept her from toppling.

Then the woman began to chant, long strings of sharp, barking words that ended with the question, "Well, would you know more?" "Yes!" one of the other women would gasp, and the chanting would start up again accompanied now by gasps, mutters of amazement, or low cries of protest or joy.

"And you, would you know more?" Once again, the shaman's nails pricked Alexa's hand. "Would you?"

Alexa started to refuse the visions. She had not dared venture near power since her disastrous brush with it at Dniepermouth. And here it was, heavy in the room, waiting for her to consent. If she shook her head, the dizziness would return. If she tried to stand up, to flee on feet that felt like lead weights, she would sprawl, perhaps into the firepit itself.

"Ahhh," the shaman's sigh was echoed by the other women. Then she raised her voice in the chant again. Why could she understand the words this time? "Look you here, stranger, princess that you are; traitor that you call yourself . . ."

The reek of the heavy incense grew stronger as smoke from firepit and brazier rose and twined closely around Alexa and the seeress. She felt a trickle of heat run up her spine and down her arm, to flow into the other woman's hand. Abruptly, she ceased to hear. The floating sensation she'd feared earlier grew more acute: now she hovered over billows of smoke that darkened, thickened, transformed themselves into waves on which galleys sailed. She could all but smell the brine, overlaid with the acrid stink of the galleys.

Then she seemed to board one such ship, to sink past its deck into the foul hold where men lay sprawled awkwardly to ease the wrists or ankles bound by rusting chains. At the end of a row lay one man, wrapped in bloodstained bandages. Though his wrist was unbandaged, save by a metal clasp, it too bled, so fierce had been his struggle to break free. That was the only sign of fight in him; now he had collapsed beside a smaller man who turned him with surprising care and dabbed at his brow with a rag. As the man took the rag away, Alexa gasped.

"Oh my brother . . ." She had imagined him dead, imprisoned, subjected to Irene's magic; she had never dreamed that he might lie in a slaver's hands, wounded and sick. Her pulse quickened with her rage, and the smoke wreathed more and more thickly about her. The slavehold was fading, and her brother with it . . .

"Marric!" she cried, but felt the word snatched from her lips. Now, she floated, cast adrift in time and place. Her only anchorage was the seeress's grasp, and she clung to it. The woman's voice grew louder, more urgent and faster, then cracked and turned hoarse. Finally it died away. In this tranced place, princess and shaman floated motionless, hands clasped as its emptiness filled with a faint thrumming that grew louder and louder.

A flash of deep crimson slashed down among the clouds, and the thrumming intensified, thinned and rose into a shriek. The shaman screamed too and pulled her hand from Alexa's so she could cover her ears. Now they were spinning across vast spaces. The crimson lit the sky again, color solidifying into a hawk, its beak dripping with blood. It cried out, shrilly, in an accent Alexa knew.

She had not called on magic, but had consented to its use. And Irene had sensed her presence in the no-world of magical workings; sensed it and strove now to draw her back, in soul, if not actually in body. Tumbling head over heels toward unthinkable dark was the shaman. Irene had no use for her, and thus would discard her. Even as Alexa watched, appalled and terrified, the woman's form faded.

"No!" she shrieked, and hurled herself after the seeress. One hand caught the hem of her garment, and she wadded her fingers in it desperately, tightening her hold, moving handhold by handhold until, once again, she grasped the shaman's hand. The woman started to chant, but her voice lacked power and authority, and it was soon overpowered by Irene's strength. The red hawk swooped down upon them. Alexa twisted away, taking the shaman with her. But in its next pass, the raptor could easily tear them apart. And then, Alexa would be Irene's to deal with as she pleased.

"Bring us back," she found a wisp of voice somewhere and forced herself to look into the seeress's face, ashen now with exhaustion and horror. She shook her head, her eyes wide and angry at her own helplessness.

Abruptly the same rage heated Alexa. Magic was about to destroy her, and yet she still bound herself to scruples about using it for her own protection.

And if you die, Alexa, what happens to the shaman, Gerda,

all the women who watch? Irene would have no qualms about flicking them out of existence.

She held out her free hand and tried to summon the flow of fire. Power trickled through her nerves, then ceased. Overhead, the hawk screamed. She had done no magic, let alone the evil spells she had sworn never to use again, but because she had been close to power, in an instant, Irene would seize her. It was not fair. Fair? What is fair? She remembered a lesson from the tutor she and her brother had shared. "For the strong do as they will, while the weak suffer what they must." Dubious morality, she had called it then; now that she was the weak one, it seemed damnable.

If she died for it, she was not going to let Irene snatch her back to torment. She was tired of weakness, tired of being the pawn or the victim. Beside her, the shaman began a hesitant chant. That was wild magic: impossible to call it good or evil. She had learned magic that was, unquestionably, evil; had been able to learn it because of the power that was her birthright. Not magic, then: power. It ran in her veins, inherited from the gods that were her first ancestors. She would demand her inheritance, demand it now, in flame or wind or light or whatever form it took.

Light crackled about her and flung her above the clouds, which dissipated as she watched. Now earth itself lay beneath her: the blue of the Middle Sea, the golden sand of North Africa, the dark forests and rushing rivers of Germania . . . a flash of malice at the mouth of one river, a roaring as of an enraged bear, and a hag's cackle. She slashed out with her own power and heard the hag scream in rage, but not before a blow struck her and strength ran from her like blood. They had marked one another. It would not do to leave a wounded enemy, who would heal and seek revenge. She started to swoop down, to finish the battle, but she had passed that place beyond hope of return, was soaring north . . . and found her attention claimed by islands that gleamed and pulsed as if they were wrought of living emerald. Warmth and vitality flooded her as she gazed.

She wanted to go there, but "farther," whispered a voice inside her skull. And farther she flew, the shaman with her, faster and farther until she looked down at a white wilderness in which a tall, fur-clad man and an even taller bear faced one another until the man cautiously reached up to stroke the bear's jaw and the great beast lowered her head and rubbed his elegantly pointed muzzle against the man's shoulder. Man and bear walked through that waste, and Alexa trailed them until a storm struck. She saw them hunch their backs against harsh swirls of stinging whiteness, and then the wind snatched her and tossed her back south.

Now she hovered, staring at Staraja's tiny houses set near the gleaming gem of a lake. Then she was sinking down, the seeress with her. They sank down through the rainbows and warmth that were the Veil, and the seeress sighed with relief: only when the Veil was rent, or they soared above it were they at risk from other magics. Alexa found her gaze drawn to one house in particular. She could look through it, down upon ranks of tranced women and two others who writhed on the floor . . . they were dropping, descending—slowly there— melding with those agonized, twisting forms . . .

The last thing Alexa saw before the wind tossed her from that odd space back into her own world was a flash of light that altered, even as she glimpsed it, into the form of a standing woman wreathed about by a rainbow and crowned with silvery light.

The rough planks bruised her cheek, but that pain was nothing compared to the anguish that lanced through her temples and down her spine. Someone—other than she—was moaning. She scrambled onto her knees, suppressing a whimper to do it, and leaned over the shaman. Kneeling opposite her was Gerda, who pulled off the woman's gloves, chafed her hands, and issued one order after another for warm furs, hot drinks, and aromatic herbs.

"Why did you save me?" asked the shaman.

"That was my enemy," said Alexa. "If I had the strength to oppose her, I could not permit her to destroy someone else."

"Your enemy is my enemy . . . sister," the shaman told her, and held out her hand to grasp Alexa's. As she took it, she felt a spark of power flash between them. Exhausted, she slipped sideways and found herself upheld by strong, motherly arms —by Isis and Hathor; it was Halldis who was raising her, asking tenderly if Alexa wanted something to drink.

"Water," she whispered. Cool water for her dry lips, her parched and thickened tongue, her aching temples; water that splashed onto her wrists like a promise of the joys at the Horizon. She yawned until her jaws stretched, then felt herself lifted and carried to a bed of furs she recognized as her own.

"Sleep," said Gerda.

She did. But for the first time since she had come to Staraja Ladoga, she woke screaming.

Chapter 6

☆

Leaning against a birch tree, Alexa tilted her head back and looked up through yellowing leaves at the deep blue sky of an autumn afternoon. This far north in the summer, several hours of full daylight still remained. The fresh, crisp wind brought her sounds of hammering and men grunting with effort as they lifted the catapult onto its base and twisted its ropes into place.

The day had passed like most days since she had snatched herself and the seeress from Irene's magic. Released—at the seeress's urgent words—from indoor tasks, Alexa roved the markets, the riverside, and the outskirts of the town, running alone, her skirts kilted up like a little girl, or in the company of some of the younger men as they built the catapults she had suggested to them.

The women seemed determined to make these autumn days carefree for her, if not for anyone else in Staraja Ladoga. Autumn . . . though no more ships from Byzantium would dare the rapids until next summer, some ships still sailed upriver from other towns, or across the North Sea; that would con-

tinue until the autumn turned wet with the first of the storms
that heralded winter.

By that time, all the supplies Staraja needed for the winter
must be stored. The perimeter guards doubled their vigilance:
since winter came earlier in the North, Audun had to have left
Finnmark weeks ago. Moreover, autumn was the last time that
raiders might strike before the spring thaws. Winter meant
isolation and cold, perhaps even hunger; but, for a few
months, it meant safety too.

So did daylight, at least for Alexa. She stretched and
yawned. Perhaps she could sleep. She hated to sleep at night.
The nightmares had grown so bad that Gerda's women had
thought to try out all their potions on her, but Gerda and the
seeress had both forbidden it. If they suppressed Alexa's will
enough so she could rest, there was no telling—or rather, it
would be too easy to predict—what evil might snatch at her
mind and soul. So night after night, she napped and woke
sweating with dread. But in the sunlight, she could still find
rest.

The sunlight cast gilded patterns on the thin leaves, lulling
Alexa into a light doze. The sounds of building seemed far-off
and pleasant, like the roar of the sea as heard in a conch shell.
But a cheer snapped her back to alertness, one hand snatching
at her dagger as the dry grass crackled near her and a shadow
fell across her face.

"The catapult! It works, just like the ones in Miklagard,"
Ragnar told her. He gestured to her dagger. "Did you draw
that to sharpen it?" he asked, teasing her, as usual.

Alexa yawned, then turned it into a smile. The men had
decided that if this catapult worked, they would build others,
perhaps larger ones if the sketch Alexa had found in her books
could be expanded. Ragnar wiped his hands across his
breeches, and stretched out beside Alexa.

"I'm sorry I woke you," he said, intent on the long grasses
he was pulling and plaiting. "Did you dream again last night?"
He tore one blade of grass, and cast it away.

Alexa shook her head.

"Was it very bad?"

"They are getting worse," she said softly. "Last night, I
didn't just see the bloody hawk; I saw the hag again, the one

that Heidi the shaman says is Jarl Grettir's grandam. They were looking for me. I will be thankful when Audun returns." The less sleep she managed, the less strength she had; the less strength she had, the less power to fight off dreams. Soon, her dreams might create a pathway through which her enemies—Irene, and now that hag—could strike at her, and through her, at Staraja. It was a terrible spiral that would end in her surrender. Before that happened, she would wander off into the forest first, or use that sharp little dagger on herself. Unless, of course, Audun returned and could add his strength to her waning endurance.

"The shaman—is there nothing she can do?" Ragnar tossed the plaited grasses away.

"Nothing. Hers is a different sort of power. She can dose me . . . occasionally . . . but nothing more. Audun, perhaps . . ."

"He will return any day now," Ragnar assured her. His hands opened and closed against the remaining grasses. "He can help you." *Please call that the truth*, his eyes implored her. *Let him make you well: be well*. He glanced at her dagger with the beginning of a new fear, and Alexa regretted every time he had found her honing it to a razor edge.

She nodded wearily. The sun played on Ragnar's reddish hair and the beard that seemed to flow into it. His eyes were very blue and earnest in his tanned face.

"I wish I could be with you when the nightmares hunt," he said. His hands worked, as if he fought from taking her in his arms right then.

Alexa blinked, swallowed, and tried to speak, but no words came out. She was spared having to reply by a white bear cub, which scampered up to Ragnar, butted him in the arm, then scampered off again.

"I am raising that cub," Ragnar told her. "If the Bearmaster approves of my work, he will reward me. I could put the gold toward a morning gift for you."

Alexa started, then relaxed under his steady gaze. *Why not?* something murmured within her. Why not indeed? Ragnar was kind and steady. He had guarded her when she could not care for herself, had helped her make a place for herself here. He cared for her. His arms and shoulders looked so strong. If she could seek shelter in them, perhaps she would find rest. *I still might not get any sleep,* she thought, and suppressed a sly smile. She had abandoned what she thought was her destiny: ruling as Isis on Earth, her brother's queen and consort. Now, please Isis, perhaps she would find compensations.

"You have a face like a cat, do you know that?" Ragnar said, his voice low. "In Miklagard, have you not a goddess who is a cat?"

"Bastet."

"So tiny you are, with your cat's face and eyes; so different from the women of Staraja." He rolled onto his side and held out his arms, to draw her into them. She yielded, scratching her cheek in sleepy contentment against the rough wool of his clothing. She liked the smell of him, compounded of sweat, the river water in which his clothes were washed, and some oil she could not identify. His arms closed gently around her, and his big hands rubbed up and down her spine, easing the tension she had lived with since her father's death. She purred then, and he laughed, freeing one hand to tilt up her chin.

"Cat-face," he said huskily. "Say you will have me. Say it."

"Ragnar, you talk of a morning gift to a woman who brings no dowry but ill luck."

"Such foolish talk for my wise princess. Hush then." He glanced about—*checking to see where his comrades are,* Alexa thought with a hidden crow of mirth—then bent to touch his lips to hers. They felt warm and a little uncertain. He moved closer, tightening his arms and she felt his breath roughen. For an instant, he pressed her against the length of his body. She wanted to go limp in his embrace, to accept the comfort he offered; yes, and more than comfort. She whimpered a little against his lips and flung an arm around his neck. Their kiss deepened, and she opened her mouth beneath his.

Then he sighed and, very reluctantly, disengaged their mouths. Hands on her shoulders, he held her away from him. "No, don't look away from me now," he whispered. "I want you. And now I think you . . . you could be happy with me, Alexa." It was the first time he had called her by name without hesitation or apology. "Tell me that when Audun returns, I can speak to him."

She opened her mouth to say the words that would surrender herself. But in the instant before she spoke, she heard footsteps and pulled away. "They're coming. Don't you hear them?" she hissed.

"Let them." But he sat up, and helped her sit up too, leaning once again on the birch tree just in time to arrange her hair and her expression to meet his friends' banter without a blush.

She had learned from Marric how to talk with young warriors. The thought of her brother brought its usual pang. So certain she had been that he was her destined mate, that she had never thought of another. She would think of it now. She needed joy in her life, and caring. Gerda would be glad. Perhaps even Halldis would not mind. She would marry Ragnar, pledge to the Aescir, and be as happy as she could.

"When Audun returns," she whispered in half-promise.

The autumn passed in a sunlit blur, like a happy dream from which the dreamer, upon waking, remembers only a few scenes. Her hair grew longer, and now, she knotted it up in a scarf like the Aescir women ... the *other* Aescir women, Ingebjorg teased her with a knowing smile. She had a place now, beyond Gerda's and Audun's charity to a sickly exile: she was Ragnar's intended wife. It brought her much attention, some petty spite from other women who wanted him, and wary acceptance from Halldis. Still, she wished she might forget Gerda's face when she sat beside her that first evening to whisper her news. "Princess, you are certain that this is what you want?"

She had nodded vigorously then and passed from fear into happy dreaming. There was so much to learn until Audun's return, and so little time to learn all the minutiae of women's things among the Aescir. She knew much of courts, much of intrigue, of vast staffs of servants, and protocol—but of tending trade goods or an Aescir hearth, of nursing sick men and beasts, nothing at all. But she had the quick, wily intelligence of her breed, and when she turned her mind to learning something new, she learned fast enough to win praise.

She did not always stay within doors. Women of the Aescir walked where they would, worked where their needs took them. And there were still hours when she wandered Staraja. Though the catapults were in place and tested now, there had been no raids on Staraja this summer, no attempts to penetrate the Veil beyond the ones Audun had seen when he brought Alexa North. Despite her protests, Ragnar's friends regarded her as a sort of mascot and oracle. They would not hear her talk of ill fortune, and after awhile, she stopped trying to convince them.

She looked forward most to the time she spent with Ragnar. Despite the frank gossip about hot-blooded southerners that sometimes, but not always, was stifled in her hearing, he had not asked to come to her bed. That kiss in the birch grove was far from the only one, but he pressed her no further. She came to welcome his caresses and, occasionally, invite them.

Twisting a spindle, Alexa stopped briefly and shut her eyes. The spindle dropped onto the floor, but the women about her did not scold. Yesterday, Ragnar had strained his shoulder lifting timbers. As any Aescir woman would, she had sought him out after he bathed and insisted on rubbing his back and neck until he growled with satisfaction. Then he had rolled over and clasped her close. She had run her hands up and down his back and sides, happy to be kissed and fondled. He had her half undressed and wholly roused beneath him before he drew a deep, shuddering breath, and moved away from her.

"I am not going to be an unwilling wife, am I?" she had murmured, raising one hand to push back her hair, the other to stroke his face.

"Not reluctant at all," Ragnar agreed. "But not dishonored either." He kissed her palm, but kept his eyes averted until he was certain that she had reluctantly closed the side fastening of her tunic once again.

So the historians were right when they rambled on about the chastity of the people whom they were stupid enough to term barbarians. (Most women in the place had dismissed them as satires on womens' morals in the Empire.) The revelation was fascinating, though she ached now with longing. In Byzantium, chastity had posed no problem for her; the only man who had dared approach the future Empress had been her half brother, whom she had murdered for his presumption. Her temper had let her know that she had inherited hot blood from her ancestors. Now, for the first time in her life, she knew desire, and wanted to know more.

The nights grew perceptibly longer and colder, and the people of Staraja began to draw together, as they did every winter, for songs, chess, and above all, feasts. On one night, after the many guests in the Bearmaster's house had left platters of beef and mutton, loaves of barley bread, and alehorns looking like the sack of a town, to lean back, replete, against the walls, Ragnar rose and stretched.

"I need air," Ragnar had announced. "Alexa, will you walk with me?" Giggles burst out from the women who slowly cleared away the wreckage, accompanied by deeper-voiced laughs from the men who tried to convince them not to move just yet. The skald, in his seat of honor near the hearth, ran fingers over the strings of his harp in the beginnings of a song usually reserved for wedding nights. Ragnar glared, then glanced at Gerda, who nodded.

Alexa laughed and broke free of the women who tried to detain her with advice or cosmetics. Ingebjorg pelted her with her new cloak, lined with sables finer than any ever sold in Byzantium. She was grateful for it the instant they left the overheated, smoky hall. A draft of arctic wind swirled about them, tugging at the heavy folds, until she took a few involuntary steps forward.

"Don't run away!" Ragnar drew her back against his side and rested an arm contentedly over her shoulders. "There's snow in that wind. Do you smell it?"

Alexa breathed the cold, sweet air that burned in her throat like unwatered wine. Winter in Byzantium was an enemy. It meant gales howling out from Scythia, cranky furnaces and hypocausts, and bone-deep chills in thin but fashionable garments and whatever few furs Irene had not purchased for herself. She had always hated winter.

She tested the air again. "I think I can smell snow. But Ragnar, how still it is!"

"Audun has to come back soon, or he'll have to winter up by the White Sea. And I don't want that at all," Ragnar said. "But let's walk. There's something I want you to see." He led her past the close-packed houses where only a torch or two lit the darkness, past the storerooms, out of the town itself toward the rammed earth of its encircling wall. Their footsteps creaked on the ground. There would be frost, perhaps snow too, by morning.

"What should I look for?" Alexa asked.

"On nights like this, you can see—ahhh, there!" He pointed at a pale rainbow glow that fell in transparent folds. Isis herself, or Nut, who overwatched the night sky, would not scorn such a veil.

Though the air was still, those folds shimmered like gauze curtains blowing in a wind. Alexa's hair and the sables of her cloak crackled with energy. Though the air in the hall had made her drowsy, suddenly she felt strong and alert again. She leaned against her companion and watched the lights dance in the dark sky. Then the wind blew again, and the rainbows vanished. She returned to herself, let out a long sigh, and felt Ragnar's chest move in a chuckle.

"Let's move out of the wind." As he turned, his arm tightened around her, and she warmed with anticipation.

"It is so still!" she said again. From the journey she and the seeress had taken, she remembered her "glimpse" of the vast tracts of land and sea to the north of them. If she blotted out the rushing of the river, the whistle of that sharp wind... there was nothing, no footstep of guard or crackle of brush.

She stiffened, and felt Ragnar tense.

"Too still, do you think?" Alexa nodded.

He whistled softly, the summons most Aescir used for the bears, but nothing huge and white lumbered up. Not even his bear cub answered. He muttered to himself, almost a growl of disquiet.

"Alexa, get back to the hall," he ordered, and gave her a push to start her off.

"I'm coming with you," she hissed. "Don't tell me I can't fight. I know it. I won't get in your way. But if I go with you and we both see something, then I can raise the alarm." No Aescir woman would let herself be treated like fragile glass. Neither would she.

He glared at her, then nodded. "Keep behind me, though. And when I say run, you run!"

She walked quietly, surely after the Aescir, glad of all the times she had prowled the outskirts of the town.

"The bears," Ragnar whispered. "The guards. Something should be moving." He led her past the fenced enclosure where the bears often came for food and water. Many lay sleeping there, as they would not normally have done. Their breathing came harsh and forced.

"No attack all autumn. I knew it was too good to last." He drew his sword with a hiss of iron and leather. Alexa reached for her dagger.

"They look drugged," she whispered.

"Something got past the guards. I want to check one more place, and then you are going back . . ." He stopped before he stumbled across what looked like a log.

"Goddess!" Alexa breathed, and knelt for a closer look.

Lying across their path was the seeress. Her neck was twisted at a crazy angle, and her eyes glared in sightless fury at the sky.

A coughing grunt made them both whirl around. A foot above even Ragnar's head glared evil red eyes. A black bear with froth dripping from its jaws roared, then charged, forepaws outstretched for a deadly embrace.

"Run, 'Lexa!"

Ragnar pushed her aside and brought up his sword. She saw him sidestep the bear's first rush.

And then she fled. The furred cloak broke her stride, so she flung it off, hoping it might confuse or trip anything that pursued her. Behind her, she heard Ragnar scream a war cry, and heard the bear scream back. She ran faster, sweating with terror and exertion, and gasping for breath. The cold air stabbed into her throat. She was going to cough, to fall to her knees retching from that cold—no, she wasn't! Her knees felt like melting butter, but now she could see the steep roof of the Bearmaster's hall, and she staggered toward it. She slammed against a doorpost, steadied herself, and flung the door open.

The skald stopped playing so abruptly that one harp string snapped and twanged as he cast down the instrument. All around, men and women leapt to their feet.

Alexa reeled and brought up against a wall. "It's Jomsborg," she gasped. "No guards . . . the seeress . . . she's dead."

She sank to her knees but waved away offers of help. "A bear . . . he's out there . . . oh, help him!"

She couldn't draw enough of the hall's hot, smoky air into her lungs. Red flecks swam before her, and she felt herself fall. Footsteps pounded past her, and she rolled into a ball to avoid them. Then her consciousness fled.

"Wake you!"

Someone shook and slapped her. Alexa moaned, then snapped back, to full awareness. "Ragnar!" she screamed. She leapt to her feet and would have run out again, but Gerda caught her and used her greater height and weight to pin her against the door. She slapped her again.

"I've got to help him!" Alexa cried, then started to sob.

"You already have," said Gerda. "They won't let him fight alone. Now come along and work."

The hall was almost stripped of people and of arms. A few of the eldest women remained. They had water and eye-watering herbal brew boiling, and cloth laid out—and knives and swords close at hand. "Three of you," Gerda ordered, "take down those spears and get to the bears. Wake them. Alexa, you come to the storehouse with me. We need to get out more spears."

Even a small woman, Alexa thought, might be able to bring down a bear with the greater reach a spear would afford. Might. A blow from one of those mighty paws would shatter a spear shaft. The women hurried out, cloakless despite the cold so they would run faster. Now Staraja Ladoga was as clamorous as it had been silent before. Bears grunted, men shouted or screamed, and from the outskirts of the town near the lake came hammering and whistling noises.

"Your catapults," Gerda panted. "They use them . . . against boats." She flung open the door to the storehouse, touched flint and steel to the nearest torch, then ran for the racks of spears and filled her arms.

As runners pounded up to the unbolted door, she rushed forward and began to pass out the weapons. Two women pushed into the storehouse and reached for bows: among the Aescir, even the women would fight. These archers would climb onto the roofs of their houses and shoot down into the battle.

"Get more spears, Alexa!" Gerda ordered.

She started toward the spears. Then the light of the torch fell upon some ceramic cylinders she had glimpsed once before. Sea fire, taken by the Bearmaster from a Byzantine settlement that had been overrun. Audun thought sea fire too vile a weapon for use—but Audun was not here.

She heard a cheer from the direction of the lake, and she knew that a catapult there scored a hit on a Jomsborg ship. The catapults hurled stone; it would take a very lucky shot to sink a ship. But what if the catapults hurled sea fire instead? She looked for what must be nearby: sheets of leather, and skins of vinegar. She dashed vinegar over the leather, and the acrid smell brought Gerda around.

"The spears, Alexa!" she shouted. "Leave that alone."

Alexa shook her head. "For the catapults. We can burn their boats." Before Gerda could protest, she wrapped the leather about her and lifted down two cylinders of the deadly sea fire. Gerda started toward her.

"Don't come near me." Alexa, holding the jars, backed away. "If I drop these, and they break . . ." Sea fire burst into flame as it was hurled, and could not be doused. Once it touched flesh, the only way to save its victim was to cut away the burning skin. And Gerda knew it.

"Alexa . . ." Gerda held out both hands. She wasn't going to try *that*, was she? Alexa knew she was terrified and overwrought, knew how close she was to the sort of frenzy that turned her toward the dark. But Ragnar was out there fighting, perhaps dying . . . she backed a few steps further.

This wasn't the mad rage she had felt before, but a kind of fierce coldness in which her eyes saw more keenly, her hearing was finer, and her mind worked more swiftly than she had ever dreamed possible. No footsteps! Then she could leave without fearing that someone might run into her and send the sea fire toppling to the ground.

She started out the door.

"If you fall, Alexa . . ."

"I burn. I know it. I do not plan to fall, Gerda." Then she turned her back, heading as swiftly as she dared toward the

lakeshore. Several Aescir loaded the catapult, wound it, and
shouted as a rock sped toward the massed boats heading toward the sand. Several had touched bottom already, and men
leapt from them, ran toward the catapult. Two Aescir lay
dead, feathered with arrows.

Another rock flew and struck a Jomsborg ship. But even as
the catapult crew cheered, the ship disappeared. The cheers
changed to curses, and the men's voices went taut with fear.
They had no Audun and no shaman to protect them against—
what? *Illusion?* Alexa thought. *How many of those ships are
real, and how many illusion? They are closely ranked. If we
used the sea fire, we can burn them all.*

One man spotted her and started toward her, sword out before he recognized her. "Keep back!" she cried. "I have sea
fire."

She bent low to avoid arrow shots and ran to the catapult.
"How good is your aim?" she asked, and heard the men laugh
grimly.

"Good! Load this with the next stone," she ordered. She
laughed too, and shuddered at the sound. "Come on, come
on," she whispered. It seemed an eternity until they could fire
again. Rock and sea fire whistled through the air. A gout of
flame exploded in a Jomsborg ship, darted down the oars, and
splashed across the next ship. It disappeared. But a shred of
flaming sail from the first struck the next boat's sails, and they
roared into flames as towering and bright as signal beacons.
The men cheered once again.

"Sweet Isis," whispered Alexa. The boats that burned were
not large, splendid ships like the *Hvitbjarn*, but cruder,
smaller things that looked as if they had been hastily knocked
together. The map! she thought. There was no direct way
from the Gulf of Finnmark to the Lake. They came by land
and were divided.

"The real threat comes by land!" she screamed. "Half of
you, back to the town! Tell them!" To her astonishment, they
obeyed as quickly as if she had been the Bearmaster herself.

The men remaining reached for the second cylinder.

"I can get more," she whispered.

"Do that!"

She started back, running this time, wrapping the protective leather sheet around her in a place of a cloak. The storehouse was empty. Gerda must have gone to hand out the spears. She took down two other jars and started back toward the shore.

"Stop there! A prize!" By some miracle she stopped herself from falling. Ahead of her were three men whose dark bearskin cloaks and bloody swords marked them as Jomsborgers who had gotten through the lines of defense. There were unsteady footsteps behind her too . . . help perhaps?

Alexa screamed because they expected a woman alone to scream, and that expectation might give her, or a rescuer, precious instants more in which to act.

"Get down!" She knew that voice. As Ragnar reeled toward the Jomsborgers, she flung herself to one side. His cloak was shredded, and blood dripped down his arms and shoulders. But he yelled defiance at his enemies as he charged.

Alexa darted by. One of the catapult crew met her halfway and reached for both cylinders of sea fire. "Not both!" she gasped. "Fire at the beach!" she ordered. With any luck, the invaders would panic and rush back among their fellows. Let them all burn. She wanted them to die.

She hurried back toward Ragnar, her fingers chipping at the wax that sealed the jar. If she fell, or could not hurl the sea fire with enough strength, the jar might not shatter and the devil's brew that made it would not ignite.

"Ragnar!" she screamed. "Get away from them! Get away now!"

Even as she watched, he took a thrust in the side, and crumpled. The Jomsborgers leapt over his body and ran toward her.

"I warn you," she hissed at them. "Get away from here."

She waited until they laughed at her, then hurled the sea fire.

The jar's stopper flew out, and the sea fire exploded into gouts and tendrils of flame that splashed against the men's long hair and beards and furred cloaks, and fed. Alexa flung herself back to avoid the explosion. But she could not avoid the screams and the vile sweetness of burning flesh. She tugged her leather cloak over her head and crawled past the men, who ran back the way they came, streaming fire, their flesh charring as they fled. A few small fires lingered on the barren ground, and she dropped the leather over them. Then she ran toward Ragnar.

He lay curled in on himself, his knees up, his hands pressed against the wound in his side. Alexa gagged. The stink of burning lingered on the air, and Ragnar reeked of blood and sweat and his own waste, released when the shock of his wounds stripped him of control. With a wail, she threw herself on her knees beside him trying to roll him over. When she touched his face, his skin felt clammy, frigid. She tore off the long aprons she wore, wadding them and trying to staunch the blood flow that poured over her hands.

"Ragnar?" Her voice trembled and broke. "I raised the alarm. I think we may win."

"I killed the black bear. When it died, it . . . turned back into a man. Glad you . . . did not see it." She tried to hush him with a hand to his lips, but he kissed her palm, then went on talking.

"You fought well," he muttered, then gasped with pain. Blood trickled from his mouth. "Audun will be angry you used the fire."

"Let him!" Alexa cried. "It may have saved his home. But you, Ragnar, they're tending wounded in the Bearmaster's hall. If we get you back there . . ." She reached for his left arm. If she pulled it across her shoulders, then heaved, maybe she could struggle back onto her feet and steer him toward help. But when she tugged, he screamed in such bestial agony that she recoiled, crying, "I won't try it again, oh Isis, forgive me, I hurt you!" She tried to soothe him with her hands, but he jerked away, curling in on himself.

In the firelight, she could see tears tracking through the blood, sweat, and grime that had turned his familiar face into a horror. She wiped it as clean as she could. He shuddered, both from the cold and his wounds. She longed for the fur cloak she had tossed away, to lay over him so very gently. Lacking it, she tried to warm him with her own body, huddling over him while men and beasts fought around them. Something butted against her arm, and she started.

"It's your cub, Ragnar," she told him. "He wasn't harmed."

" 'Lexa," his voice was reedy and faint, "you look after

him. I wish . . . I won't be able to give you that morning gift now."

"I don't care about it. Just don't die!"

"My little love . . . since I saw you, there was nothing I would not do for you. But I can't do this, 'Lexa." He drew a long, shuddering breath that ended in a wet gurgle. "Sorry."

His teeth were chattering. Alexa flung her arms about him, trying to warm him.

"Is your knife sharp?" he asked, and she froze. "I know it is. 'Lexa, would you give it to me, then run away?"

She shook her head. He raised one hand to pat her, but it fell before it could touch her. "I don't have the strength left now anyway." He yawned. To her amazement, his breath came more easily. "The pain's going now. It won't be long till dawn. They will come looking for us then. Stay with me until they do."

"I'm here, Ragnar. Try to rest."

He yawned again, and the bear cub raised such a howl of anguish that Alexa cursed herself silently for a fool. Wiser than she, it knew that such a yawn meant death, not sleep. But Ragnar wanted her to be fooled, and so she would be: it was the last she could do for him.

Cheers erupted on all sides. She stretched up and kissed his cheek. "Victory," she whispered. "Your victory, my dearest. They'll find us soon, and see me lying here with you, after all your care not to dishonor me. Oh, I hope Audun returns soon."

There were more cheers. Now she could hear a troop of men approaching from the town's walls. Ragnar made a sound.

"What's that, my love?" The sound came again. After a moment, she realized that Ragnar was laughing. His chuckle faded into a gurgling sigh, then into no sound at all.

"Ragnar? Ragnar?" She sat upright and tried to shake him. His head lolled on his shoulders, and his hands fell limp. When she let go of him, he fell back onto the bloody ground.

Alexa buried her face against him. She heard a high, hopeless keening, and realized that the sound tore from her own throat. Though it seemed like hours later, it was actually but a few minutes until the defenders of Staraja Ladoga found her, crouched protectively over a dead man, a white bear cub whimpering at her side.

With them came Audun Bearmaster.

Chapter 7

☆

One hand braced on Ragnar's shoulder, Alexa rose to her knees. The bear cub butted at her shoulder, whimpering. She lifted a hand to soothe it, but it yelped and recoiled from the blood coating her fingers. Bleakly, she studied Audun, then bent over the dead man. Though his eyes were already closed, she brushed fingertips over their lids and down his stained cheek. The first light of dawn glinted off his hair.

Mutters rose with the smoke from burning trees and charred bodies, then were choked off. Audun must have stopped them, she thought. He started forward to raise her, but she dodged his hands and levered herself up. The folds of her garments clung to her, sodden with darkening blood.

Halldis cried out and hurled herself to her knees at Ragnar's side.

Alexa looked down at herself, and slid a hand over her body where the stains dyed deepest. "None of it is mine. He fought the men who would have seized me . . . till I burned them with the sea fire from your stores. Mistress, I fear that you have lost another son. I would offer you a daughter's services instead, but I know better." She turned to Audun Bearmaster. "Sir, it is good that you are back."

The Bearmaster unpinned his cloak and draped it over Alexa's shoulders. She shrugged out of it, then bent to spread it over Ragnar's body. He had been a tall man, but the Bearmaster was taller still; the cloak covered him from face to knees.

Finally the Bearmaster spoke, and his words came haltingly. "Alexa, a storm delayed us by the White Sea . . ."

"I know. The shaman and I saw." Still she stood, looking down at Ragnar's shrouded body. Dark stains were already soaking through the Bearmaster's blue cloak.

"He will rest in honor," said the Bearmaster.

"We were pledged," Alexa murmured. "Did Gerda tell you? I wish I had been the one to die."

She turned on her heel and walked past the Bearmaster. Halldis stretched out a hand to her, but she shook her head. Her eyes burned, but the rest of her felt encased in ice. Even the blood—his blood—that soaked her garments was chill now. She walked through the twisting streets of Staraja Ladoga, as men dragged out the bodies of their enemies and women struggled to mend wounded bodies and cleanse the town.

A cry of horror woke her from a stupor of exhaustion and guilt, and focused her attention on a knot of men. As she stumbled over to them, they opened their circle to show her the creature—half man, half bear—that lay hacked on the ground. Its smell was foul, yet familiar from her dreams. "Berserk," muttered one man. "They are skin changers, those of Jomsborg."

Alexa walked on. The men of Jomsborg became beasts when they fought. She, too, when she was enraged, became something monstrous; something that had kinship with Jomsborg, perhaps, if to anything that walked above the earth, but no relationship at all to the health and sanity that were the Aescirs' birthright. They were staring at her now. If they were not so kindly, they would stare at her with loathing. If she stayed here, she would only poison them, soil their cleanliness with her rages and tricks. She would have to leave this place—now.

She turned toward the heaped earth of the town's wall, where a tangle of rope and a pile of hacked wood still remained. Three men lay nearby. If she bent to look, she would recognize them as Ragnar's friends, who had laughed with him and accepted his strange choice of an outland wife. Their blood, too, must lie on her head. Beyond the wall stretched only the forests. There would be quiet, forgetfulness in the deep woods' heart.

Claws scrabbled beside her, and she looked down to see Ragnar's bear cub. "Go back to your dam, little one," she whispered. There could be no comfort in her, whom the great bears shunned, for this young one.

The cub hooked claws in her dress. "Go on!" she cried softly, and gave its round head a push. Reluctantly, the bear cub started away. Then the scratch of heavier paws made it halt. Cub and woman alike stared up at its mother, who emerged from the trees, and weaved back and forth.

Go ahead and strike, Alexa thought at the great bear. *I unleashed the burning, which might have killed your forests. I went into a killing rage, and cared nothing for how I dealt death.* She bent her head. If fortune were kind, the creature would smell the blood on her and kill her with one mighty blow to the neck.

The cub ran to its mother's side and whined. Then she cuffed it very gently, sending it scurrying back to Alexa. It appeared, then, that the bear would not kill her. But when she started toward the forest again, the great beast growled and reared up. So the woods were forbidden her? The cub tugged at her skirts and turned her back toward the town, guiding her when she faltered or turned aside. Clinging to her sodden clothing, it drew her toward the Bearmaster's hall.

They cannot want me there, she thought. Though a few looked up and whispered to one another, no one barred their way.

Alexa walked up to Gerda. "Tell me what needs doing," she asked. All about her, men and women twisted and moaned in pain, while those able to move scurried from pallet to pallet, trying to ease them.

"Bring hot water," Gerda called. She put an arm over Alexa's shoulders. "Is Ragnar . . ."

"Dead. Defending me. I'm sorry." Gerda's face twisted as she steered Alexa toward an inner room. "At least the Bearmaster's back, thank all the gods. Where are you taking me?"

"To my own place. First, we will get you clean. Then you

will rest. And then, we must decide what is to be done with you."

"How can I rest now? I must help," Alexa muttered and began to push against Gerda's encircling arm.

"You can't help, not as you are now," said the older woman. "Do what you are told! Right now, that's all you are good for."

If I'm ever good for anything. Alexa stood, docile and exhausted, as Gerda and Halldis stripped her clothing from her and bade her kneel in a wooden tub. They scooped dippers of steaming water over her tangled hair, and it trickled down over face, shoulders, breasts, and thighs to form a troubled mirror, that revealed the trembling lips and blank eyes of a woman who looked as if she had been yanked from the Dnieper rapids. Water poured out of her hair and down her face, making her seem to weep. The amulet—Ragnar's gift—was cold against her skin.

Gerda handed her a rough cloth. "Here *is* something you can do. Help clean yourself."

She scrubbed at herself until her skin chafed and they took the cloth away from her. Then she began to wring her hands.

"Cry if you can," whispered Gerda.

Alexa shook her head numbly. She did not deserve to feel better. Halldis brought her a steaming dipper of some dark, pungent brew. Her nostrils twitched, and she turned away.

"Swallow!" ordered Halldis, and pressed the dipper firmly against Alexa's lips. It pinched. At least she could avoid that tiny pain, she thought, and swallowed. The fumes of the potion filled her eyes and nostrils, and she coughed, protesting its acrid taste.

"Now, let us rinse you." Both women helped her from the tub to stand on a floor that rose and fell like the deck of a ship. "Here, lean on me, child. A moment more, and you shall sleep."

Alexa slipped sideways and felt herself caught in a strong hold. The floor lurched again. "I had them brew it double strength," she heard Halldis say before she concentrated her attention on keeping afoot in a strange place. Was this a strange place? Surely, there were names she could remember, familiar, friendly ones . . . at least, she thought so. She clung

to the arm that supported her while a thin woman, her face
white and streaked, wrapped her in a warm cloak. Ragnar? He
would not be with her, not in a bath with Gerda and Halldis—
that was three names she knew!—present. She tried to call his
name, but her lips were so thick, so sluggish that only a croak
came out.

"We can talk later, child," Halldis said, then gulped. Alexa
blinked. That sounded as if Halldis were crying. "In the morning."

"'S dawn already," Alexa mumbled as they walked her toward a pallet. Gerda gave her a little shove, and she found
herself lying on her back, looking up at dark wooden beams.
She felt a weight settle beside her and nestle close. Ragnar?
He would not be with her unless—she had a brilliant idea.
Perhaps this was her wedding night. But then why was everyone so sorrowful? There should be singing and bawdy jokes
designed to make the most stolid bride blush and hide beneath
the bed furs.

The carven beams above her started to spin, and she shut
her eyes. Had she drunk too much at her own wedding feast?
Why weren't they laughing, then? Ragnar would be disappointed, she thought; and so would she. She sighed and curled
around the warmth next to her.

She could not think or remember. Perhaps sleep would
help.

"Let the bear stay," Gerda whispered. "Take the tub out
quietly, and burn those clothes. I don't want her to see them
again. I'll be out to speak with Audun when I'm sure she's
asleep."

That sounded like no wedding song Alexa had ever imagined. What did it mean? She stored the words away. Perhaps,
after she slept, they would make sense.

Warm furs were tucked in around Alexa's chin. Then the
room gave a terrific lurch and toppled her into blankness.

*She was floating in a warm place where endless waves
seemed to lap a quiet shore. Was this the Horizon to which the
Sky's Boat came with souls who were now at peace? And
she . . . was she at peace? . . . in her drugged sleep, Alexa*

groaned and tossed. Seated beside her, Gerda frowned as she recognized the onslaught of one of Alexa's nightmares...

Alexa opened her eyes and glanced up. Sand and sky were the color of mother-of-pearl. Even as she watched, a gold flash of splendor streaked overhead, and a feather drifted down from it, to float on the water in which she lay. "Cometh Horus upon the waters..."

Had the Hawk come for her? Surely not. Alexa sighed and reached languidly for the feather. At the exact moment when her fingers touched the feather, a shaft of light pierced the sky and struck it. Though the feather burned like molten gold, she could not release it. The light grew fiercer and, moving within it, she saw the tall form of her brother, the Falcon of his sigil flying overhead. Ahead of him were two figures on which Alexa could not bear to look. Moon-bright light blazed from the crown of the Woman, while the Man wore grave wrappings and the crown of Empire. Her brother knelt before him. Alexa had never seen him abase himself before anyone, even their father. But this seemed right. She could see her brother clearly now. His mouth was twisted in pain, his back and sides scored with many bleeding wounds.

Marric was dying! No wonder he bowed before the Lord of the Dead! She whimpered... and Gerda steadied the girl whose body twisted on the bed, and held her steady, calling for help. "This is the worst nightmare yet! Halldis, help me hold her! I know Ragnar is dead, my precious, but he's at peace now..."

Alexa flung herself onto her face, clutching the feather tightly. Don't die, my brother, don't! The feather burned into her flesh, and she transmuted her pain into a great cry for help. Marric! Come back! The figures blurred before her eyes until the pearl that was land and sky vanished. Now she saw her brother driving a chariot in the Hippodrome as he had so loved to do before their father sent him to his own command. He had but two horses, a dark, troublesome stallion and a moon-white mare, responsive to the slightest touch of the reins; and they drew his gleaming chariot across the sky in a blazing arc... Alexa drew her breath in wonder, then choked as she saw the darkness twist itself into a snare to snap his horses' reins or splinter his chariot's wheels.

"My brother! Look out!" At the instant he drove over the blotch in the sky, his face twisted with fear, his eyes widening until, for what seemed like one eternal moment, Alexa gazed into her brother's eyes. Then he went sprawling, away from the Two who shone at the Horizon and back into a world that promised him pain if it promised him any life at all. He had not seen her, she knew.

But he lived.

"He lives!" she cried out in triumph.

"And what if she goes mad, my husband?" Gerda asked the Bearmaster.

"She will not go mad. The blood of Byzantium is potent: too much so, at times for those not destined to rule. I shall take our princess to the Misty Isles, as I should have done in the first place. I know that when she renounced her crown, she hoped she would lose her powers, and sometimes hope and belief make for truth. But the powers of her line are in her. Blood and soul, they are in her; and when Irene seeks her, or danger strikes, she responds. The choice is no longer hers, if ever it was. She must be schooled in her powers, will she, will she not. Or—if her Goddess is merciful—she will die, and the health of two kingdoms with her."

"When will you go? In the spring?"

"She—and her Empire—cannot wait until then. Nor, I suspect, can the Misty Isles. I'll leave as soon as she can travel. The North Sea is safe for a few weeks more."

"From storms, perhaps, husband, but from Jomsborg?"

The Bearmaster shrugged, an oddly helpless gesture for so huge a man. "Can you wake her, Gerda? This sleep gives her no peace, and I must talk with her."

Gerda nodded and reached for a phial made of heavy blue glass. She poured an astringent drop upon Alexa's tongue. Even in her fitful sleep, she choked and gagged, flinging out a hand to forestall a second dose.

"What's that?" Gerda asked, and prisoned the small hand in her own. Scored red across the palm as if branded there was the mark of a feather. Even as she gazed at it, the brand faded.

Alexa coughed and opened her eyes. Beside her sat the Bearmaster.

"You!" she cried. "Where were you when I needed you? If you had been there, Ragnar might be alive, and I would not . . ."

She let out a low wail. As the Bearmaster, his face sorrowful, reached for her, she cast herself into his arms.

Her sobs shook them both, but her mourning was tearless and brought her only dizziness and an aching throat. Audun's hands were heavy and reassuring on her hair and back. Finally, when she had achieved the quiet of exhaustion, he loosened his grasp. She drew a shivering breath, and he handed her a small beaker.

Not caring whether it was another noxious potion, she drained its contents. A strong taste underlay the honey flavoring the drink, but it had not the heaviness of poppy, nor the bitterness of Halldis's brew. It steadied her, and she met Audun's eyes frankly.

"I beg your pardon," she said, her voice low.

"I think I should beg yours. For being gone so long. For underestimating your strength."

"What strength?" Alexa asked bitterly. "Do you mean the thing that causes me to leave a trail of blood and death wherever I go? For the rest of my life, Audun, wherever I go, people can say, 'A corpse? Alexa must have passed by.' I used the fire, Audun. You forbade it, you locked it in your armory, but I used it. I didn't even think that it might set the woods ablaze."

"Alexa . . ." Audun's eyes were very sad and patient.

"I kill with rage and without pity," she went on, feeling a hot rush of guilt melting the chill in her bones. "I cannot say I kill like a beast; they kill cleanly and without hatred. I kill like a skinchanger of Jomsborg, with malice and relish . . . and we call them barbarians. I too . . ."

"Quiet!" Audun's voice was low, but it stopped the torrent of accusation and self-hatred that poured from Alexa's pale lips.

"If you can stop rending yourself for one moment, Alexa, let me point out that you discovered the attack and cried the alarm. You defended yourself as best you could, with what weapons you had to hand. And you saved Staraja Ladoga."

"For other people," Alexa muttered. "I can never live here again, never meet people's eyes."

"And why not? If you walked out there right now, I promise you that most people would be too busy tending wounded or rebuilding to do more than nod or ask your help. A few people might even thank you for a battle well won."

"I used the fire," Alexa's voice rose into a wail.

Audun grabbed her by her shoulders and shook her. "You used sea fire, Princess. You did not use the magics Irene taught you!"

Alexa gasped and reeled back, her hands covering her mouth.

"You did not summon the burning. You never even thought of it. Remember how quickly you turned to it at Dniepermouth?" Audun smiled joyously at her and pulled her hands down from her lips to hold them firmly.

"Speechless, little Princess? Well enough that you are, if all you can do is confess crimes you have not committed."

"Then this . . . this means . . ." Alexa began.

"This means that you have grown stronger," Audun interrupted. "Your dreams are nightmares, you are vulnerable to attack—but you yourself, Alexa: you are clean again."

She made a faint sound of surprise, then shook her head. "Don't ask me to change my mind about power," she told him. "I am not worthy."

"I will not ask you to change your decision to renounce the Crown of Isis-made-manifest; it is too hard a burden to be borne by the unwilling . . . as, I believe," he said, with a mischievous grin, "your priests and priestesses could tell you, far better than I. I stand for Law, not coercion. But though you renounce a crown, power you cannot renounce. You tried. You tried with all the power in you. For a time there, it even seemed that you might succeed. But your attempt to join the Aescir, to sink yourself in the cares of a household, a husband, and a town must prove to you that you cannot escape what is in you."

Alexa shook her head. "The instant there is a fight, the first thing I do is take command. I tried not to," she added so plaintively that Audun laughed.

"So you did. Now you must try to harness your power, use

it to protect yourself and the people who will be drawn to you. Your brother is not the only one with the gift to sway hearts and minds, you know."

"I dreamed he was dying," Alexa said. "I saw him at the Horizon Itself. But I am tired of my dreams. I would like to be rid of them all." She yawned, then eyed Audun suspiciously. "I am also tired of being drugged," she remarked.

"I will tell Gerda you said that. But we bury Ragnar tomorrow, and she thought it would be best for you to sleep as much as you could. And no, that is neither pity nor dislike."

As Alexa sank down against the furs again, the bear cub lying among them grunted a brief protest, then nestled against her side and sank back into sleep.

"You see?" Audun asked softly. He lifted the soapstone bowl in which oil flickered and smoked, and his immense shadow danced across the wall. "That cub accepts you now. He will accompany you when we leave here."

"Leave?" She levered herself up again. "Where do we go, then?"

"Why, Penllyn, of course," said the Bearmaster. "You are going to the Misty Isles, to be healed and to learn the ways of power."

She opened her mouth to protest indignantly, but a huge yawn swallowed her voice.

"Sleep well, Princess," Audun smiled. Taking the light with him, he left the room.

Chapter 8

☆

The next day, Staraja Ladoga buried its dead. Men she would have thought too weary to do aught but sleep had dug graves and assembled grave goods by torchlight. Alexa, heavily cloaked, her face all but covered by the nearest thing Aescir women had for a veil, walked out from the Bearmaster's house between Audun and Gerda to the open graves. Silently, the townspeople watched them pass, then fell in behind them. The sky was gray, heavy with the promise of a dismal, cold autumn rain.

There stood Ingebjorg, whose child Alexa had helped save and whom she had called friend. Tall and fair, she looked ashen now. Though Ingebjorg consented to meet Alexa's eyes, when her son would have run forward to Alexa, his mother caught him up in her arms, and pressed his round head against her breast. Alexa thinned her lips and tried not to wince. As she passed, Ingebjorg shook her head in guilt and sorrow.

So that was the way of it. The Aescir would respect her, even as Audun said. Some might even love her. But mixed in with their respect and love were awe and the remembrance of spilled blood: such things made for bad neighbors. Had Ragnar lived, Alexa might still have pledged to the Aescir and been welcome, her strangeness blotted out by her oath. Now, however, for the rest of her life, the Aescir would see her as outside their ken, more isolated from them than even their shaman. She could not violate their peace, then plead to remain among them.

She tossed the heavy, dark cloth back from her hair, which hung loose down her back, the way she used to wear it in

Byzantium. Let them see her face. The autumn wind whipped it back like a mourning banner. But its chill was soothing to her eyes, and the sound of it, caught by the rustling trees, was better dirge for the dead men and women than any clamor of drum and sistrum from the temples of Isis and Osiris.

Her mother's death was little more than a memory of wailing, and of her transformation from baby princess to living statue, so stiffly robed she could barely totter, clutching her brother's damp hand as they walked in the procession to the Necropolis behind the spirit-boat that would bear Antonia to the horizon. Her father's death . . . she had been as fearful as she was heartbroken, though Alexander had faded, mind and body, long before his spirit left him. And the interval between death and funeral had been a protracted anguish of grief, fear, and meticulous preparations: embalming, prayers, the final touches to his tomb. They had lasted for months, though still not long enough for Marric to lay down his command and return home, Horus-on-Earth, and rightful heir.

The Aescir dead would lie in mounds such as the ones she and Ragnar had wandered by, hand in hand. Green would cover them, and the rocks used to outline their graves would weather. Beyond lay the trees; behind them, the taut silver of the Lake. It was a kinder thing than eternal rest in stone tombs that would have weighed down their spirits.

"Over there," whispered Gerda, and gave Alexa a little shove.

Halldis waited for her by Ragnar's grave, a chamber dug in the sandy earth, kept out by boards and pegs set up like the foundations of a house. In it lay Ragnar, wrapped in his finest furred cloak. A shield stood at his head, bow, arrows, ax, and blade to his right. The ax blade, severed from its haft, glittered in the sun. Alexa had watched as Audun had broken it and snapped Ragnar's sword, "killing" the blade so it might accompany him into the Forest in which leaves never faded and blight never came. At his feet lay a statue of a bear: it was unthinkable that they sacrifice a live beast.

A cold, wet nose nudged at Alexa's hand, and she stroked the head of the cub Ragnar had hoped to train, thus earning the morning gift of husband to bride. "You and me, alone now," she murmured to it. "We will miss him."

"Say farewell," Halldis murmured.

Dutifully, Alexa moved forward, her hand at her throat. She tried to think of Ragnar: his humor and warmth, his courage, the eagerness of his desire for her. And hers for him, she thought. Desire had never meant much to her, trained as she had been; yet she had desired Ragnar, and his love for her had made her . . . she *cared* for him, she thought carefully. If she admitted more than that, she might crumple into his grave and disgrace herself and his memory. His death had meant more than the loss of a man she loved. With Ragnar gone, she had to surrender the illusion that she could escape into a life that was merely human. As Audun said, whether she wanted it or not, the power was in her; and her attempt to retreat into the life of an Aescir woman had ended in blood. Her hand tightened on the folds of drab cloth at her neck. She felt a familiar weight of metal, and drew off the amulet, warm from her flesh. She kissed it, then let it drop over Ragnar's heart.

She turned to face Audun, who was chanting. The place where the shaman might have stood at his side was empty. Audun raised one hand and gestured to her; if Alexa dared to take it, that place was hers. She stepped back, and flung a fold of her cloak over her head once more. No, she thought.

Not yet, came a second, treacherous thought. A deep sigh rose from the assembled Aescir as their white bears emerged from the dark trees and sank to their haunches in a ring about the burial field. Beyond them, as if drawn, other animals stole from the forest and watched.

Audun's chant rose higher and louder. Now the Aescir joined in for a brief measure, but soon fell silent. Then the bears themselves raised their long muzzles and began to wail in mourning for the dead. Their howls, broken off by occasional staccato barks, melded with Audun's deep voice. As if the animals' grief freed them, laments and sobs rose from the Aescir, twining about the music of man and bears. Tears prickled at Alexa's eyelids, which itched as if hot sand had blown beneath them, but her cheeks remained dry.

Hand on her arm, Halldis drew her back from the grave. Three strong young men came forward and began to heap earth over it. When the mound was finished, they would arrange stones about it in the shape of a boat. On the rocks might be carved runes, images of bears and ships: Ragnar's story. There were many such shapes hereabouts.

She stared unseeing at the grave as it filled. "You need not watch," said Halldis, but Alexa did not move. Many packs lay waiting in the Bearmaster's hall, preparation for the journey west. To her astonishment, one such pack belonged to Halldis, who had asked to tend and guard Alexa on the trip.

That had been another argument she had lost only that morning.

"It will be winter shortly," Alexa had warned Audun as she saw provisions—including sledges, ready for assembly—stacked in the hall. "The shaman is dead. There has been a battle here. Should you not stay here for a while to guard your people? If Queen Olwen has waited this long for her white bear, can she not wait till spring? I know I can."

"Princess," Audun had growled at her, "I have not spent time and lives on you only to lose you in nightmares during the winter dark and snow."

"But you should not be risked!" Alexa protested.

Audun's fist thumped down on the table, overturning drinking horns and setting bowls to clatter. "Saving your fears for me, Gerda can lead. Should she choose, she can summon one of our sons, or all seven, to aid her. You gave up your claim to rule, child. Do not tell me how to rule my own people."

She had been stupid to object. This was Gardariki, the land of towns, each of which would aid Staraja. And they would travel down the Neva to the Gulf of Finnmark, from there across the Baltic to Birka, and south and west to the other trading towns where Audun had kin. Their need would be known, if it were not already, the message borne by the bears who trod the wilderness with the ease of Gerda in her own home.

And the Misty Isles had other means yet. Even now, despite Irene's hatred of all magics not hers, gray-robed Druids hid in Byzantium, part of a network of spies and sorcerers that spread its subtle grid over the civilized world. Soon she might know more of that than she wished. For the first time, Alexa thought about living among the Celtoi of the Islands. They were kin, she knew, from both sides of the Trojan War. Alexander, whom her line revered, ancestor of Cleopatra, claimed

descent from Achilles. The Rome that bred her consort, the
Emperor Antony, had been founded by Aeneas, Prince of
Troy, while exile drove another prince to the Misty Isles
where he too built a kingdom. Since then, the occasional
westerner had married—or not married—into the Imperial
family, Marric's namesake being one of the more recent.

The chant ceased. All around her, Aescir wiped their eyes,
drew deep breaths, and began to put their mourning behind
them. The bears had fallen silent. Alexa glanced at the raw
grave mound, numbly wondering how long she had escaped
in thought from the funeral. Already men began to lay stones
around it.

Audun and Gerda passed, and Alexa joined the people who
thronged behind them, Halldis to her left side. She felt her
right hand clasped, and turned to see Ingebjorg smile timidly
at her. Her grief behind her, she could be kind to Alexa, who
would be gone tomorrow. Then Ingebjorg and all the other
Aescir would have their peace back. They were like the bears:
they killed quickly; they felt keenly; and mercifully, they
could forget. They were innocent.

It was different for someone like Alexa. She remembered.

Ever since they set sail, Alexa woke before dawn, the time
that Aescir songs weighted with mourning and memories.
This dawn had been different. Blending with her nightmares
had been a sense of longing, not just her own . . . someone,
something longing for her? It had beat like a pulse through the
usual regrets, and waked her with its utter unexpectedness.
She had been glad to huddle into her heaviest cloak and
clamber out of her tiny aft cabin.

Balancing on the slippery planks, Alexa shivered, and drew
the cold air gratefully into her lungs. The night before, frost
had rimed the ship's mast and ropes. Sea and sky gleamed
pale silver, shrouded in wisps of icy fog. She shivered. Growing up on the Golden Horn had accustomed her to the brass
and blue collision of light on water, not this endless silver,
broken occasionally by rushes of foam-crested green on distant shores. They seemed to sail endlessly between two halves
of a gigantic silver shell, in which the smallest sound echoed.
Paradoxically, she felt shut in and exposed at once.

She strained her eyes toward the shore. She missed the forests, with their dark, towering trees, and the soft, silent footing, fragrant with many years' fallen pine needles: a quiet place, but rich in life, sheltering. There was no shelter here on the Baltic. Just the rush of waves, and the rhythm of the oars. She found no trace of any longing but for firm land.

The ship came about, turning into the fjord that concealed Hedeby from invaders.

Halldis came up behind her and laid a second cloak over her shoulders. Alexa smiled at its warmth, then glanced up at the older woman.

"Hedeby," Halldis said, pointing. "We will be as safe there as at Staraja. There we have kin. Even the Druids come there and carry messages."

Alexa shrugged off the mention of those priests of the Western Isles, with their network of messengers: some men and women; and some magical, rather than human. She would be glad to sleep in peace.

Despite its sheltered position on a lake, its hill fort and terrible cliffs falling a hundred feet from beneath the citadel, Birka, their first and greatest port, had been half-consumed. The landward wall lay ruined, at least one gate tower toppled. Smoke reeking of burned flesh still coiled up from the disaster that had been the jetties and beaches that once housed a merchant fleet. Not even one guard met their ship. Finally Audun had had to leave the ship, a half-grown bear pacing nervously at his side, his hands outstretched in sign of peace. Only then would the battered survivors of the town sneak from burned-out houses or charred, toppled carts to stand before him.

They asked no coin for food, lodging, or fresh water; Grettir's men had seized their food and destroyed their lodgings. The water was theirs for the taking, but they would be grateful if the Bearmaster and his crew would help bury Birka's dead, those carried from the desperate defense of the town's walls, those washed up on the rocks, and those found later on amid the ruins. The blood eagle had been cut on the back of one man. Though bodies were too few, and the spoor of black bears like the one Ragnar had fought was too much in evidence, Birka's burial grounds swelled. Alexa had had to fight not to hide on board ship, her face buried against her bear cub's snowy fur. Audun had watched her, kept watching for the few hours longer that they were compelled to remain at Birka.

South they had sailed. Night and day, no one had slept. For their next port lay in what Alexa's old maps called Germania, too close to the Jomsborg fortress at Wolin for them to relax their guard. Finally, Audun had ordered half the crew to rest, but he had allowed Alexa to remain. She shook with cold and exhaustion, then passed beyond them into a kind of trance, her eyes wide and staring until she shuddered convulsively. Her hands came up, fingers clawing. Her eyes bulged, and faint sounds croaked from between pale lips. Before she could scream or fall, though, Audun had caught her and held her.

"Have they guards out? Do you see them? Tell me!" he had demanded.

The stars and swirls behind her eyes were bursting out to overwhelm her, but at his question, she had pointed to that one spot on the horizon from which the horror had emerged to wake her. Then, as Audun hissed orders, she had sagged against his shoulder. She had a quick glimpse of the Aescir, boots shed so they might move noiselessly, turning the ship, and fleeing on muffled oars until they came to safe harbor.

Hugging the coast for protection against Jomsborg ships rather than to eat and sleep on shore each night as they would have liked, they fled toward Hedeby. Audun had kept watch on Alexa, who spent hours huddled by a brazier, never quite warm enough, watching firelight pour redly through her thinning hands.

She had bent her head on her knee and slept until he woke her, then staggered toward her cabin until she waked, as she always did, before dawn.

"Hedeby!" cried a sailor. Now Alexa could see its forty-foot earth wall, broken only on the south and north by gates. Low rows of rammed-down piles formed piers, and armed men were among those waiting to help them anchor and make fast.

The town was large and well-protected, Alexa was relieved to see. A stream ran through its heart. Alexa averted her eyes from a thriving slave market, as they followed the shore guards along a wood-paved street toward one of the largest houses. Though it was built of wattle and daub, gabled, and roofed with reeds, inside, however, the walls were all of wood. Audun sat with its headman at the great central hearth, shook his head over the damages inflicted by the Jomsborg raiders at Birka, and traded, more because it was expected, than for serious profit: furs, amber, a finely carved chess set, and wrought-silver rings—gifts for the new Queen of Penllyn. Around him clustered close and far kin: men from Wendland, tall Sviar, Danes, even one bard from Eire, whom Alexa studied from beneath her eyelashes. A Druid, perhaps?

She had no time to speculate. Alexa and Halldis had been taken into the women's rooms. Guests though they were, they were immediately offered distaffs. Halldis spun silently, as if glad to relax. Alexa was drawn into chatter with the younger women of the household as they worked. Her dark hair and olive skin made her a novelty, even in this market town.

They spun until summoned for dinner, mostly ale, bread, cheese, and boiled meats. After dinner, Alexa drew apart, and sat with her arms wrapped around her knees, staring into the hearth fire. The leaping patterns formed pictures: a slave market; a rocky field and a shining spring; golden faces; a battle.

Several of the young women invited her to join them on a walk to the nearest storehouse to bring in silvery, silken fox and marten pelts, but she refused. Though Hedeby had not yet been assailed, the very earth underfoot quivered in dread.

A woman whom Alexa could not see clearly hurled a handful of seasoned wood into the flames, which crackled into sparks as sap exploded and the smell of apples filled the air. Alexa had exclaimed in instinctive delight. "So that makes you smile!" the woman's voice was warm and sure. "Then you will like the Isles of the Mists, too. Wait until the spring when the trees flower; no scent was ever more sweet." She came around the firepit to where Alexa might see her. She wore a cap and carried a staff. As she sat, she smoothed the folds of her shaman's garb about her. For a moment, before remembering how the seeress at Staraja Ladoga had been slain, Alexa leapt up in welcome.

The shaman shook her head. "Not I, sister, but my kinswoman. I am pleased to see that you remember kindly. Welcome to you."

"How did you know?" Alexa asked, still on her feet, wishing she had gone outside with the other women.

"Druids have brought me word. Welcome, sister."

Sister. Alexa sat down, and when the seeress held out her hand, Alexa took it.

"Tell me of your journey," said the shaman. Long into the night, Alexa spoke while Audun examined first the fox, then the marten and the amber and the fine wool cloth that Hedeby boasted.

"Bearmaster!" the shaman called imperiously, and he dropped the strand of amber he had held up to the light, rose, and approached her.

"What have you done to this child?" she demanded.

To Alexa's astonishment, Audun crouched at her side and took her hand.

"Forgive me," he muttered.

"For what?" she asked sharply.

"For using you," he began. "I know your fears of the power you bear. Yet I too have awakened it prematurely, using you to give me warning of my kin and enemy Grettir and his skin changers. You are the lamp I carry into a dark place . . ."

"I do not want this power," she interrupted. "But it will not leave me. If it serves you, then that is the first reason I have to welcome it."

"Well spoken," said the shaman, "half-trained, quarter-trained or less though you are. Soon you will sail north from Hedeby. Who sails with you?"

"I," came the deep tones of one of the men who had traded with Ragnar.

"Stjerne-Oddi," said the shaman. "It is well. He is skilled with sun-board and sun-stone; he will guide the keel of your ring-prowed ship on its road . . . where, Stjerne-Oddi?"

The navigator's voice took on the chanting tones that the Aescir used either for ritual or for remembrance. "Two days under sail from Hedeby though the islands, Jutland, Sillende, and their sisters, and west on the open sea for three more, and beyond that, five days north to Kaupang."

Well and good, Alexa thought. *But what protects us as we sail?* In the shaman's eyes she found her answer. Just as Stjerne-Oddi knew the sea roads and his instruments, Alexa herself, with her knowledge of the dark things, would have to ward them.

"You can refuse," the shaman said, testing her.

Certainly, she could. Refuse and endanger the man who had saved her life, who was probably the only reason that on the day—Isis grant it be far hence!—her soul was weighed against the Truth of Maat, it would not be devoured by crocodiles for eternity. Absolutely, she could refuse. The idea was as preposterous (though similar, to her way of thinking) as her returning to Byzantium, flinging herself at Irene's feet, and pleading to become her apprentice.

"I cannot refuse," Alexa answered. But, as it stands now, I probably have not the strength to do what I must. So you must show me. You have me, and you know it." She laughed shortly, but without bitterness. "Do you know how long I have fought against asking for the magic?"

The shaman smiled thinly. "Our nets stretch wide, even into the Golden Horn, little sister. We know."

She held out her hand for Alexa's, then drew her aside into a darkened room. Herbs and gums burned there, and Alexa remembered the sweet, flat smell of a dish of animal hearts. This time, however, she shared it. She expected to gag on the meat, but found herself eating hungrily, welcoming the strength it gave her, strength intensified by the incense smoke and the song that the youths of the household began to sing.

"Lie down, sister," said the shaman, and Alexa stretched out on a white, silky pelt.

The room faded from her sight. Alexa felt herself rise from the thin body lying in that darkened room, and she turned. She held out a "hand" and saw only light. Another light glimmered nearby, if "near" was a word she could use in this strangeness. The shaman? she thought, and felt warmth was the woman drew closer.

They are close.

The light that was Alexa shook: agreement.

Let us scout, sister.

The two motes of light cast themselves forth, soaring over a gray simulacrum of the islands and waters Alexa had heard Stjerne-Oddi describe. Abruptly, they were battered by sleet and gales. Their light flickered and weakened; it took no shaman's warning for Alexa to know that if her light died in this place, she would die in the waking world too. With the shaman supporting her, she fought for strength, drew on her memories of temptation and endurance. To her astonishment, the sleet died, and they floated motionless in the grayness.

If she stood here in her actual body, she supposed, she would lift her head and gaze about to get her bearings. She had no referent for any equivalent actions that a beam of light might perform, but she did them. To the east . . . close by she sensed foulness, a whine, a hissing, and a sullen red light that reminded her of . . .

Give no names in this place lest you summon what you most hate! warned the shaman in the instant before Alexa thought of the woman who had usurped her place, and her brother's in Byzantium.

That must be the Reiver Jarl's fortress. It lay behind them. But a similar glow, like rot on the hull of a battered ship, clung to some of the islands they would pass on their way north to Kaupang; Alexa marked each in her memory. Stjerne-Oddi would know them and avoid them.

Oh he will, will he? Little fool, little lost soul! The voice that snapped into Alexa's consciousness was familiar from the ritual in Staraja that had shown her the magics used by the Reiver Jarl's grandam. Since she had no name, the thought of her caused her ancient, hunched form to coalesce in Alexa's thoughts. As before, she stood beside the blood-drenched loom on which murders and spells were woven. Weather workers crouched at her feet, awaiting her command to call up the next storm. The hag laughed as she pointed to pattern after pattern: this one was her brother's torment, this her lover's death; this picture the rape of Birka, this next one a vision of future destruction, Staraja and Hedeby, Kaupang and then the Isles of the Mists themselves. They glimmered in her consciousness, pulsing like a beating heart . . . like the source of the welcome of which she had dreamed only that morning.

She would be damned if the witch would have them! Alexa felt the light that formed her body contract and heat. In an instant, it would explode into flame . . . *yes, and in that instant, the hag would send sleet and snow upon her, and snuff out her life. Steady, Alexa,* she warned herself.

No. You shall not pass, she warned, and heard savage laughter.

Join me and share my feast.

And what stops you, then, from turning on me, too?

Why should I not, if you are the weaker?

Now what? Alexa questioned the watching shaman.

Do you know her now? asked the shaman.

If she had been able, Alexa would have snorted at the folly of that question. In any guise, in any voice, she would know that woman as her enemy.

Well enough, then. Mark her; harm her if you can, and let us return. Audun will want to sail soon; and you will need to sleep. Draw on me for what strength you need.

Once she had seen Greek fire sprayed from a copper tube into a wreck to destroy it. Now Alexa took her own anger and revulsion and directed them against the hag just as if they had been such fire. The woman screamed and writhed. One claw-like hand flailed out and grasped a weather worker by the hair, while the creature howled for release, and then just howled until he was consumed.

Strength restored, the hag turned again toward Alexa and the shaman. *Now,* said the shaman, *take strength from me.*

Power flowed into her, intoxicating as health after long illness, and she lashed back. Fires played about the woman, scarring her wizened face and body, and smoke rose from her garments as if from the pyres of Birka. She screamed again and devoured the second weather worker.

Again! ordered the shaman, but her mental voice was faint.

Not if it means your death, Alexa protested, and turned to retreat. The hag was marked; she could find her again, and, she promised herself, she would.

She found herself held, then drawn ineluctably closer into that chamber with the loom and the withered husks of the hag's slaves.

But if it means our souls? asked the shaman. She was much weaker. In this war of wild magic against wild magic, it was the user who did not scruple to steal another's strength who had the advantage.

But there were other magics, Alexa thought, and cast about frantically for them. Isis, Goddess and Mother—that was a power she had profaned. She dared not call on her, at least not yet. What if she died before she learned how to address the goddess she had profaned? Strength borne of rage and frustration flooded her, and her light blazed up.

Beside her, the shaman exulted. But Alexa feared, even as she fought more fiercely. She had seen runners gather their energy for one last dash, then collapse. Though the wild magic of the shaman thrived on just such energy, she was but its foster daughter. The power to which she was born now: that was a matter of thought and ritual as much as feeling. Sure enough, the rage-inspired strength ebbed now, and her light ebbed with it. A howl of victory rasped across her consciousness, and her light trembled, an unshielded lamp in a harsh wind.

Think, imbecile! she demanded. The hag flung out her skinny arms, gesturing boastfully at her loom. Its bloody pattern changed again. Now Alexa saw violence beside which the wreck of Birka was a mere tavern brawl: white bears, their entrails clawed out by skin changers; Audun himself, the blood eagle cut on him, his ribs shown white and bloody red, and the raw lungs heaving; a hill-fort spurting flames like a volcano while people fled, trailing sparks from burning hair and cloaks, and a crowned man and woman sat in a blazing hall. It was the Misty Isles Alexa saw, dying in fire. After that, the lights would die out forever. Wolves and black bears would rule until they had stripped the land. Then they would seek other lands and other prey . . . such as her lost home. She had a brief picture of it, Huns stalking the Middle Way of Byzantium, the priestesses raped, the walls in rubble. The Misty Isles would crumble to overwhelming force, and the Empire would rot from within, and thus be easy prey.

Not so. The light-focus that was the Misty Isles impinged upon her consciousness, glowing green, like an emerald wound in wires of gold, pulsing like a loving heart. That was the true vision, Alexa thought, and her heart leapt within her.

You offered me welcome, Alexa thought at it, a frantic shout of emotion. *Now give me strength!*

Power cascaded into her. She had a confused impression of golden harvests and green groves, fragrant with apples, and deep, cold springs teeming with fish. The land was peopled with men and women she knew she would see one day: robed men, a warrior with bright hair, and, crowned with emeralds and gold, her hair like a harvest itself, a tall queen whose smile gave her courage. On the witch's loom, they had been among the people burning, but now they laughed.

Alexa took the strength they lent her, slashed fire across that damnable loom and over the hag's face. In the instant before she recoiled, Alexa's strength drove deep into her twisted thoughts and marked her. Whatever guise, whatever works bore her mark, Alexa would know. The foulness of that touch was like bathing in a cloaca. Even agonized, the hag sensed that and tried to hold her. Now horror fueled her strength. Welcoming the last spurt of emotion, she used it to tear free . . .

. . . and woke to the sound of her own screams and panting breaths, the shaman crumpled beside her on the white fur. Spittle dripped onto her chin. Struggling up to lean on one elbow, Alexa tried to wipe her face, but Halldis forestalled her. Around them knelt other women, men clustering behind them, shouting questions. The plate from which they had eaten lay broken on the stained floor. The shaman blinked and stirred.

"We'll both live," she said, and drained the horn of ale held out to her. At the same time, Audun offered Alexa a silver cup full of unwatered wine. She gulped it, welcoming the biting sweetness in a dry mouth and a raw throat. Then she sank back on the fur, blinking at him. For the first time since Ragnar's death, she felt like crying. No tears came.

The wine raced through her, making her exhaustion into a pleasure that was almost sensual. She was floating, free from the need for battles or prophecy. Perhaps once they let her sleep, she would escape into dreams of such pleasures as she had never known. But Audun's hand was on her shoulder, he was shaking her gently and asking something. Through a haze of wine and sleep, she read, rather than heard his words.

"I can guide you now," she promised.

Chapter 9

☆

Because they were compelled to race the Jomsborgers across the North Sea to Penllyn and probably elude them too, Audun decreed that *Hvitbjarn*, in which they sailed up until now, would not serve. It would be safer to make the five-day dash across open sea in a craft as closely resembling the Jomsborg ships as possible. Alex took one look at the hundred-foot-long ship with its single vast sail hoist on a yard half the ship's length, and shivered.

In such a ship one fled or fought with equal success—assuming one were brave enough to board the thing in the first place. Built of heavy oak, it drew shallowly. Its vast sail, side rudder, and oars gave it maneuverability in calm or storm. It was as weather-tight as any such ship could be during the turbulent crossing so near the end of sailing weather. Special lids closed the oarholes when not in use; shields hung on a rack over the side provided added protection to its fifty oarsmen and gave evidence that the ship was ready for battle.

Unlike *Hvitbjarn*, which was luxurious even for a merchant ship, this one was stripped to the bare oak. Even the ornamental metal vanes that would ordinarily rattle and shine on the mastheads were removed. The crew rowed, seated on their sea chests. At night, they slept two each to the vast skin bags that by day stored their gear. Since there was no aft cabin, Alexa and Halldis shared a similar bag . . . when they were not bailing, creeping along a narrow catwalk to distribute rations of beer, water, and salted fish, or keeping out of the crew's way during the storms that threatened to double the five days the trip was supposed to take.

The sky was overcast: for the past two nights, they had been unable to see a star. When an unexpected gust had ripped the sail from the yard, taking a man with it, and all but toppling the mast, Stjerne-Oddi shook his head and proclaimed it witch weather. He glanced hopefully at Alexa, and Audun beckoned her out of her sleeping sack.

The wind freshened as she struggled over to where he and Audun balanced near the ship's high prow. It had already licked most of the bright paint from the serpent head that adorned it; now it licked and tugged hungrily at her, sending her stumbling into their arms and almost hurling her into the heaving gray waters.

"Islands up ahead!" Audun bellowed. But the wind snatched his words, forcing Alexa to read the shape of his lips.

She knew what he was asking. Could she tell which islands would be safe to pass among, and which might harbor Jomsborgers? She tugged at him to bring his face down to a level with hers.

"I must see them!" she shrieked.

The two men nodded. Taking her with them, they stumbled and weaved aft, at times toppling into rowers or gear as they headed for the side rudder. Audun relieved the steersman and beckoned Alexa up. She tightened her lips, and caught up a coil of hide rope, which she handed to Stjerne-Oddi. Then she wrapped her cloak firmly about herself and took hold of the side. "Lash me to something!" she screamed at him. She could not withstand the wind, but if she were tied down, she could see the islands without risk . . . if anything about this journey were without risk. She glanced behind her at Halldis and the bears, their eyes bright and watchful.

Then Stjerne-Oddi pointed at a darker mass amid the driving rain and waves. Alexa studied it, then shut her eyes. The saltwater made her lashes stick, and she blinked while trying to summon the undersight that had come so clearly in the shaman's company. Water: cold: rock . . . nothing. She shook her head, and Audun held his course.

The pounding grew worse. Alexa rapidly became soaked even through her cloak, and the hide rope began to cut into her. But that next island—her scream and the bears' sudden eruption from their hiding place came together. Not only Jomsborg-held, that island, but—"A ship, do you see it?" Alexa cried, pointing. "There!" In that moment she would have sworn that she could hear the hag's laughter.

"Harder, brothers!" Audun shouted at the rowers, and leaned on the rudder. They came about, and Alexa felt herself tilting far to one side. A wave dashed into the ship, setting the stored gear awash in foam and icy water. And still the ship tilted, further and further.

"We'll overturn!" shrieked one of the younger rowers, his voice scaling up and cracking grotesquely as he panicked. Halldis flung herself to his side and clasped her hands about his on his oar.

"Steady . . . steady . . ." Audun's lips moved. Alexa shut her eyes and breathed out prayers to the stormy gods who commanded the primal sea. Another wave sluiced over her, and she squeezed her eyes shut. They were all weary. She had heard that drowning did not hurt, but "No," she whispered to herself. "No." She delved into her memories, seeking for her vision of the Isles of the Mist as a perfect green gem, energy rising from it in time to the beating of her heart. Ahhh, there it was now. She flung out a hand shriveled with its exposure to water and grasped Audun's fist as it clutched the tiller. He must feel it too.

Audun nodded. He threw back his head and bellowed out some oath or plea, and then, miraculously, the ship righted itself. The wind and waves were still fierce, but "can you see them?" Audun shaped the words at Stjerne-Oddi, who shook his head.

They had evaded their enemy. That night, the winds died, the rains stopped, and they could see the waxing cold silver moon of autumn and, finally, the stars.

Stjerne-Oddi glanced down at the sun-stone, then up at the glittering stars. "That way," he croaked. The crew staggered about, making repairs, bringing the ship onto its new course. Crouched beside Stjerne-Oddi, blessedly free of the ropes, Alexa drowsed until she heard a new roughness in the clamor of wind and wave. It brought her leaping up with what would have been a cry if she had had that much voice left. "What's that?" she husked.

Even before she could look over the side, she had her answer. Within her, the Isles' welcome pounded, and she felt their energy reach out to touch her, body and spirit. Audun bowed his head, with its matted beard, on his chest. "The tide," he told her. "We've come to land."

They drove the ship onto a quiet beach that it shared with chests and spars from a ship less fortunate. When the men would have staggered over to them, Alexa flung herself into their path.

"Jomsborg?" asked Audun. At her nod, he croaked out orders for them to hold. Praise Isis, they obeyed. Alexa knew she could not move another step. Halldis kindled a fire beside her. Then, though Alexa protested that Halldis too needed rest, she covered the younger woman with her least wet cloak, then stripped her of her torn garments, pummeled the stiffness from muscles bruised by the battle with the storm, and helped her dress as if she were an infant. Only then would she accept help in making dried meat and grains into a hot soup and bullying the crew into eating it.

Then Audun had pulled out salt-stained leather maps. "This is Lindissi country," he declared. "And we too have kin. Several generations ago, three boatloads of Sviar settled here. They have lived in peace . . . until now."

"Eat!" Alexa had ordered, and refused to listen to another word about the various kingdoms held by Celtoi in these isles until Audun obeyed her. She sank down by his side, arms hugging her knees, almost too stupid with exhaustion to take the bowl from his hands when he was finished. He raised his head, and his reddened eyes gleamed. Snuffling grunts made Alexa twist around to see the bears weaving about him, and he growled to them in what seemed to pass as speech.

"They will guard us." He nodded with satisfaction, then yawned. "Nor are they the only guards. There is power here. Don't you sense it?"

When he continued to watch her, clearly demanding a reply, Alexa shut her eyes. Reluctantly, as if testing bathwater with a toe, she reached out to sense power as she had learned to do.

"Old," she whispered. "It isn't just the Jomsborgers. There is something old here, a temple perhaps?" She almost giggled at the idea of a shrine—pillars like the temples in Byzantium, out here among the barbarians—but did not. There was power here: immensely old.

Audun nodded.

"Shall we find it?" she asked, yawning. She wanted nothing more than to sink down beside Halldis on fire-warmed sand and escape into sleep from all talk of power or enemies.

"Likelier," said Audun, "that it will find us. Go to sleep now. We will fret about it in the morning."

Alexa stumbled over to the small fire Halldis had decided was theirs.

"Here, Alexa," said Halldis, taking a bone comb from a pouch. "Your hair is all matted, and I am too tired to sleep."

Alexa leaned against Halldis as she combed her hair, gentle as a mother with her daughter. Tears came to her eyes. She started to speak, but Halldis laid her free hand on her shoulder.

"When you first came among us, I was harsh, I know. But he was my last son, who died serving you. And then there was Ragnar, and he turned to you too. I remember your face, when you said you would have offered me a daughter's service in their place, only you knew better than to think I would accept. Child, the time when I would have refused is long past; and the daughter I would not have accepted has grown into a woman any mother would be proud of." She pressed Alexa's shoulder, easing her down onto their outspread cloaks. "Though you were not born among us, and are not to remain with us, you have been as loyal as if the words of our pledge were the first you ever spoke."

She smoothed Alexa's long hair, free now from its tangles, and laid the comb beside her. "You keep this," she said.

Alexa knew that Halldis treasured that comb, and the knowledge brought her awake. "Why?"

"A gift," said Halldis.

Alexa eyed her narrowly. "A gift," Halldis repeated firmly. "Just a gift. Do you still not trust your friends?"

As always, Alexa woke early. The beach looked like the field of some lost battle, men sprawled this way and that. Even Audun and the bears slept. The sun had not yet risen to burn away the night's mist. She rubbed her eyes and looked for a rock or some other sheltered spot. It would be wonderful to wash, to tend herself in privacy. She forced herself to her feet and stretched the aches from her back. Sometime during the night, the dampness had turned to frost. She cast an approving eye on the wood washed up on shore. Some of it might even be dry enough to burn. When she returned, she would build up the fire once again. She walked past the ship, away from the beach, and behind a large tree.

Then, smoothing the damp folds of gown and cloak back around her knees and ankles, Alexa glanced about. Not far from her, the sand yielded to coarse grass, then to a dark forest through which cut a narrow track. The forest drew her attention. She would tell Audun, she decided, when he woke.

No time, no time! A sense of urgency overpowered her even as the morning mist thickened. Alexa crouched, hand on her dagger. If she hastened, could she make it back to the shore and her comrades before the mist grew even darker? She drew her blade, and water immediately splashed onto it. Soon she could scarcely see it, or the hand holding it.

Witch weather again? It had none of the foulness Alexa associated with the hag. She heard footsteps in the mist. Very well, then: let someone think her easy prey. "Who's there?" she called, trying to sound young and frightened, then darting noiselessly to one side. The footsteps neared. *Just a few steps further, fool!* she thought. *If you came to loot, I swear this is the last time you will try it.* Her lips set in a fighting snarl, and she padded forward, her knife up, then poised to spring.

"Drop that knife, Princess Alexa." The blade fell from her fingers onto the coarse grass and sand.

The mist faded, a few last wisps haloing the man who approached her. He wore a long, coarse robe of yellowish white wool and a braided belt. And the sight of the man's eyes, unafraid, tolerant, even a trifle amused, as much as the golden sickle tucked into his belt told her that she was looking at one of the Druids of the Isles of the Mist.

She had known of Druids before, of course: spies within Byzantium, or wanderers along the Northern seaways. But they had been hunted men. This man stood before her on his home ground, confident of his powers.

Though she sensed he would detect a lie, she forced herself to look surprised, as if he had misnamed her.

"Pwyll told me. A brother whom you met in Staraja. Don't waste time trying to lie to me, Princess. You probably spent your entire journey here dodging Jomsborgers. But two nights ago, three shiploads landed. They are headed this way."

"Help me wake the camp!" Alexa demanded.

"You dare not fight them," said the Druid. "Not now. Once they pass farther into the land, however, we have defenses. But first we must lure them."

She ran at his side back to the sleeping Aescir, sliding down the slope to the frosty beach. The bears were already stirring; the cub yelped a welcome that drew moans and complaints from the men. Alexa flung herself down by Audun and tugged at his shoulder.

He came awake in an instant, huge arms thrust out to grapple his assailant until he blinked and saw her and the Druid. At once, he came fully awake.

"Pwyll got through," he said, more a statement than a question.

"No. But his message pierced the barriers they set."

Audun shut his eyes in brief pain. "He was a good man."

"He was that. Now, unless you wish to follow him, hurry!"

"Jomsborgers—they are here?"

"And have been. Last night they attacked a village to the North. Lindissi and Sviar both lived there. Not a one was spared."

Then how did you learn of this? Even as the thought flashed into Alexa's awareness, the Druid lifted a hand. As if struck by lightning, she reeled from the blast of fear, anguish, and rage that assailed her, streaking from his mind as it had raced from the dying townspeople, leapt across the conduits of power that she had once envisioned as embracing the Misty Isles as wire enfolds a gem. But that power waned in their presence, flickered toward silence and the dark. Though the land itself cried out beneath its invaders, its voice faltered.

Alexa opened her eyes. From that instant of revelation, she had learned something else. "This is no raid," she said.

"No. Three boatloads landed. We suspect that that is just the first wave of an invasion."

"Wake you!" Audun shouted. About the camp, men leapt up, grabbing for axes or swords even before they were on their feet. The Bearmaster swore. "Ever since Arktos, we of the Aescir have lived in peace with the kingdoms of the Misty Isles. *All* of the kingdoms."

"That is why we need you. You go freely into realms in which men of a hostile tribe, even though they be Druids, might not be welcome."

It was like the Empire, Alexa thought. Weakness at the core caused the edges to crumble; a flaw at the heart of a gem soon sent fissures throughout its depths.

One of the bears barked harshly. The Druid lifted his head as if testing for scent upon the wind.

"Your bear is right, Audun. I sense them upon the road. Hurry. We have horses ready for you outside the grove."

The word he used—"nemet"—was an ancient one that made Alexa shudder. She slung a bag onto her shoulder and followed the Aescir inland. In a few moments, what looked like an earthwork such as guarded Aescir towns loomed up before them. The Druid skirted it, and each Aescir, as he passed, averted his eyes. Alexa, however, glanced within and caught a glimpse of oak trees, their bare branches shadowing gray stone. Power crackled along those branches, casting a faint glow that became immediately swallowed in mist.

Beside her, Halldis gasped. Alexa saw her lay hand to an amulet at her throat. "The night of the dead," she whispered hoarsely.

"Samhain," agreed the Druid. "Tonight the spirits walk: ours and theirs. And tonight we shall fight them."

He raised a hand in greeting to the other robed men who watched a herd of small, shaggy horses. "I shall set you on your way," he said.

All that day, they rode west, up from the shore and past swampland now hardening with the first heavy frosts. As the shadows lengthened, and the pallid sun of afternoon reddened and sank, Alexa found herself glancing over her shoulder.

The Druid's keen eyes met hers. "It . . . stirs," she whispered.

"The Princess has an instinct for the dark things," he observed to Audun.

The Bearmaster nodded even as Alexa winced and colored with shame. "She endures it well. But she needs mastery."

"So you plan to bring her to Amergin? He should be able to teach her mastery, or control her."

That suspicion again! Alexa let her horse slow its stride, and dropped back to ride beside Halldis.

Their shadows furled out behind them like huge cloaks through that afternoon of flight. They began to climb, their pace slowed by the now-flagging horses. Three times Alexa caught the Druid, Audun at his side, staring narrowly at her. *It wasn't fair!* she thought in a brief spurt of rage. *The land quivers with magic here, yet they watch me as if I were a spy or a witch. Audun promised I would find healing, not imprisonment here!* Curiously, her anger seemed to refresh her, and she straightened in the saddle. The twilight stroked her senses to high pitch, and she almost trembled with eagerness to see what lay beyond the next bend in the road. Ahead of them the sun bled down into the horizon, while the sky darkened toward nightfall.

It was long past the time when the Aescir would have chosen a campsite and kindled fires. But "ride!" ordered Audun and the Druid when the men looked at the roadside longingly or rubbed aches in their backs and legs. The wind grew chilly, then subsided altogether. Halldis touched Alexa's shoulder and pointed.

The road over which they thundered, little more than a track rutted with many hooves, had started to glow.

At the crown of a hill, by a tumble of stone and earth that might once have been a fort, the Druid signaled a stop. Alexa glanced down into the valley. What looked like a gleaming web stretched over it, the filaments of light stretching upslope to the place on which they stood. If she could see into the next valley too, she would probably see the same thing. The night was very still. No horse stamped, restive, eager for grooming, a warm blanket, and grain; no bear complained; and even the skeletal hands outstretched by long branches of trees along the track were motionless.

Stealthily, the Druid dismounted, then stretched himself out full-length along the damp ground. He lay still so long that Alexa thought he had fallen asleep. Then he rose, shook himself, and gestured to Audun.

"Tell your friends not to touch their weapons," he ordered, and the Bearmaster nodded as if he had been the most junior man present.

Alexa winced. *I do not want to fight. I do not dare,* she told herself. It was not that she feared killing in battle; it was the manner of the deaths caused wherever she was—some by fire, and some by beasts; some, even, by magic and treachery. She reached for her dagger, to toss it from her, then reconsidered. *Best keep it, lest I fall into the raiders' hands.*

Mist began to pool in the valley beneath, causing the lights Alexa sensed to twinkle, then blur into a pale haze. The silence stretched out, became well-nigh unbearable. The mist grew, and the light with it. Overhead, a ring encircled the moon of Samhain. Again the horn sounded.

"I hear hoofbeats," came a whisper.

"Aye," said another man. "Whose?" Then Audun hushed him.

Halldis brushed Alexa's arm. Now she saw movement, clots of shadow against the whiteness of light and mist. Those shadows clung to cover. Then, as if realizing that concealment was impossible, they strode out boldly, up toward the hill on which they waited. Alexa reached out to study them, then recoiled. The Druid nodded. Jomsborg, all right. She shut her eyes and recalled the evil she had sensed the way she might recollect the savor of a red wine: the bloodlust and greed were there, but the worst she knew of Jomsborg—the insensate longing to destroy, the cackle of laughter over funeral pyres ...those were lacking. The hag was lacking, she realized suddenly.

"Soon," whispered the Druid, a shape of the lips, only.

Waiting for a battle was the worst part of it, Marric had always told her. What battle did her brother fight tonight she wondered. She glanced up at the moon. "Goddess, hover over him," she breathed.

A yell of triumph broke the silence. The Jomsborgers had seen them, waiting at the crest of the hill. They quickened their pace. Was it a trick of the darkness, or did Alexa really see some of them shamble from two feet onto four paws, and back upright again? Again that yell sounded, mingled now with jeers and obscene challenges to battle. Audun held up his hand, signaling for quiet.

Now their enemies fell silent, even to the pad of their feet as they hastened toward what they thought was prey. The fire began to stir in Alexa's belly, and she forced herself to patience.

Then a long horn-note echoed out over the valley. It was not the horn of the Empire's armies, but something older and, Alexa suspected, simpler and darker. Its sound made her want to cower in despair or kick her horse downslope into some battle, illusory or actual. Again that horn-note sounded: aching and lonely, lamenting years of solitude, and promising vengeance for each one of them.

The mist thickened, wreathing around each of the Jomsborgers as they raced toward the Aescir. In an instant, men and bears raised weapons and paws against thick wisps of white cloud that rose and fell. Screams rising from within the mist made Alexa see that this was a very real enemy. It solidified now into the shapes of riders clad in leather, shining with phosphorescence, bearing rusty swords and spars, and wearing bronze helms that were almost green from age, like something unearthed from a grave.

"The Wild Hunt," Halldis whispered. Her eyes distended with fear and exaltation. "It comes to take them. But there is a price on its services . . ."

The troop of wild riders began to close in on the Jomsborgers. In the next moment, their arms did not look as old as they had, and their bodies seemed younger and more substantial. The rider who led the van wore a magnificent bronze helmet etched in gold. Mounted on its brow were long, twisted horns.

"Ride now, for your souls' sake!" cried the Druid.

Alexa drove spurs into her horse's flanks, and the beast jolted forward, broke stride, then forced itself into a run. A wisp of the mist drifted toward it, and it burst into a panic-stricken gallop. Alexa clung to the saddle and prayed that the beast would soon—but not too soon—exhaust itself. Behind them, the mist was tinged with red as the Wild Hunt encircled its prey and moved in for the kill. The screams behind them scaled up into madness and past that, into silence.

Now other hoofbeats pounded behind them. Alexa's beast screamed and would have bolted if it had the strength. It was very close, she knew, to bursting its heart from sheer terror. She crooned to it, hoping to calm it. A fall now would leave her to be trampled by the Aescir or prey to the Wild Hunt.

A cold wind and a sense of ancient hungers tore at their backs as the Wild Hunt gained on them. Then their horses balked. The Wild Hunt divided and swept around them, enveloping them in an ever-moving circle.

"What do you seek, brothers?" cried the Druid.

The Hunt's leader rode forward, lowering his spear until it pointed toward the Druid's breast.

His voice, when he spoke, was husky and cool, almost bloodless. "You know what we seek when we ride abroad. Vengeance. To rid the land of our foes. Blood. And warmth. We slew your enemy. What will you give us?"

They were asking for a sacrifice! The bears moaned and swayed back and forth. Audun's hand went to an amulet at his throat Alexa had never before seen. Halldis, so distraught earlier that day, appeared serene. The Huntsmen's leader unhelmed, and swept his eyes about them. Alexa gasped when his eyes met hers.

She had not expected him to be so beautiful: hair the color of weathered bronze, gleaming pale eyes in a proud, high-cheekboned face; long hands careful on the reins of his horse and caressing the shaft of his leaf-headed spear. For a long moment, he studied her, and then he smiled.

Will you not join us? his voice whispered inside her head. *Here are heroes, riders risen from their grave mounds because of a vow to protect their lands, or when they died, thwarted of their rightful vengeance. Here is power and strength forever, if you have the heart to claim them. Come to me!*

Alexa glanced down their ranks. Heads adorned many spear blades, trophies of the night's hunt. Their faces and bodies flickered in and out of focus, then solidified into men and women whose trappings and weapons were so different that

surely they must be drawn from thousands of years apart.
Here was a warrior-queen on whose chariot wheels starlight
glittered; and here, a man who looked much like any of the
Aescir who sailed with Audun. Far to the rear, as if guarding
it, strode a huge man, an even huger bear pacing by his side;
and he was laughing. If she looked further, would she see
Ragnar, or someone like him, balked of his vengeance? And
her brother: what if she were wrong, and he had died . . . Fear
and bile rose in her throat.

No need to fear us, whispered the gleaming prince who led
the hunt. *Come to us and share, as sister, consort, and beloved.* Desire quivered from that voice and kindled her blood.
It would be a solution, of sorts. Among the hunt, her power
would be powerless to injure people she loved; and her genius
for destruction would only be an asset. She pressed her legs
against her horse's lathered flanks, and it sidled forward a
step.

But Halldis sawed on her mount's reins and cut across her
path.

"The Hunt needs a sacrifice," she said. "Someone cheated
of vengeance to ride with it. But not you, Alexa. I have lost
my son and a man as dear to me as he was. And I have seen
you tormented."

"Halldis, no!" Alexa whispered. Audun started toward the
Aescir woman, his face anguished, his arms outstretched.

"I tell you," she cried, "that one life is not enough to slake
my hatred of these people! They need a companion. I am
willing."

"Halldis," rumbled Audun. He pressed closer. In an instant,
Alexa saw, he would have her horse by the bridle; and then
they would see about this nonsense.

"Let me pass," Halldis ordered. "Or, if you do not, I swear
—" Swiftly, she snatched her dagger from its sheath on the
chain about her neck."—I shall kill myself before your eyes
and the sacrifice will be to provide all over again."

The Huntsmen watched her. Slowly, their prince dismounted and walked over to her trembling horse. He stretched
out a hand and aided Halldis to dismount. Then he bowed.

"Welcome, lady; thrice welcome."

Like priest and priestess in a rite, they returned to his troop.

A rider through which Alexa could see starlight shining led up a horse, and the prince himself assisted Halldis to mount.

"Like the royal sacrifice," murmured the Druid. "She gives herself for the good of the land." He stretched out his arms and began to chant.

"The Druid asks the Hunt to swear not to harm us." Audun whispered to Alexa.

The Huntsman's leader left Halldis's side and came forward. Alexa thought he smiled at her—but was that smile lips curving over warm flesh, or the death's-head grimace of a skull? Then he spoke. "You may pass. I and mine shall not harm you, and if we do, may the sky fall and destroy me, and the sea overflow and drown me."

The Druid nodded. "The gods witness it."

The Huntsmen helmed themselves once again, turned their horses' heads, and began to disperse. And the sound of their passage changed from a troop of horsemen riding, harness a-jingle, to a wind whistling down into the valley, slashing through the mist and bearing it away into quietness.

Then the moon shone over the road once again. Not even a bone showed where the Hunt had been.

Chapter 10

☆

Unwilling to sleep where the Wild Hunt had revealed itself, they rode a few miles farther by moonlight: slowly, for fear of roads that were little more than rutted tracks marked with a jutting stone or mound. Alexa's spine felt like a column of fire; long ago, and mercifully, her thighs had ceased aching. In the Empire, the roads would be evenly paved and guarded; and she might have had a closed litter or carriage to ride in.

When they finally dismounted, there was no Halldis to glare at her for weakness, then tend her. That loss was like a new wound: numb at first, then building into agony.

The grief leapt upon her when she woke to a sullen, gray day. Mists roiled in the valley beneath them, licking up from a river with an unpronounceable name to the equally hard-to-say hill on which they had slept. For an hour, her aching muscles distracted her. A chill rain began to fall, and she huddled into her cloak. Her horse stumbled, then plodded on, head down, behind Audun and the Druid. The bear ambled up beside her horse and moaned.

"I know," she whispered. The track wound on, mile after mile, and ever upward, twisting along the sides of rock-strewn high hills, with rivers and streams running in the valleys below. When, from time to time, the wind lifted the mist, she could see fields marked out by earthenworks or rock walls. Mounds such as those in which Ragnar had been buried studded one such field, and the Druid raised his hand in blessing over them.

Halldis would have no such burial, no such peace and honor. She would ride these vile roads, thirsty for vengeance, until the seas dried. Which, judging from the way the rain fell, did not seem likely to happen any time soon. *I should have gone with the Hunt, not Halldis.* The prince had smiled at her, inviting her to ride at his side. *Why did Halldis spare me?*

Audun reined in, turning to study Alexa. She looked up at him and shook her head. She could not rely forever on his comfort. One of these centuries, they would arrive in Penllyn, and there he would leave her. *It might have been some comfort if Halldis had stayed. Not that she wanted to leave me, but she wanted vengeance more.*

Wood smoke rose from firepits in the houses below, a tempting reminder of food and shelter. At noon—or as close as they could gauge it in a sunless sky—they rested, huddled in the overhang of a rock ledge from which rivulets fell, splashing, to turn the earth into mud. It was dark. It was cold. It never seemed to stop raining. Ragnar was dead, and now Halldis was gone.

The rain soaked through her cloak. Her hair fell straight, in dripping strands, onto her shoulders. Fat drops of rain spattered over her lashes and down onto her cheeks. They were cold, and they stung. Her eyes burned suddenly, and tears ran from them. Her bear moaned again, and pressed his head against her knee. Alexa reached down to scratch the rain-spiked fur behind one bedraggled ear. Ragnar had left her the cub to raise, and now she would have to yield it to Queen Olwen, if that were the right name. And if she had the name wrong, she would have to learn it and all the other names. She wept harder, out of self-pity, while the bear butted against her, and the rain fell.

And then, finally, she laughed. Laughed until her cheeks ached, and the others turned around to stare. Audun tilted his head at her, an expression so bearlike that she laughed again. She was not responsible for Halldis, any more than for the rains or the bad roads or the mists. If she chose to make herself miserable—*any more miserable, that was*—she was free to. But it would be a waste of time. Audun had had her healed, brought her here, at considerable risk, and he would not have done that unless . . . perhaps she could even be . . . well, happy seemed presumptuous, considering that it was Alexa, but content. Safe, or reasonably so. Perhaps she might even find a focus to her life to replace the crown she had fled. She was free to try.

Late that afternoon, the rain ceased, and the clouds rolled back. The Aescir began to sing as they rode, Alexa to look forward to the promise of a fire and dry clothing.

Suddenly, her bear yelped and struck Audun's horse's haunch. The beast screamed in fright, and dashed forward while the spear that would have spitted him like a chine for roasting quivered in the mud beyond.

The men roared their anger at the dishonorable attack from ambush. Weapons were drawn, though the Druid tried to stop it. He stepped off the path, held out his arms, shouted, and was answered. Another spear flew, narrowly missing him.

Then, out of the cover of rocks and scrubby trees crept men wearing the heavy tunics and breeches of the Isles, their hair either clubbed back or bleached and limed into high, ridged crests like those on ancient helmets. Some were warriors; others carried knives, hoes, even clubs.

It might be that they feared the Aescir, Alexa thought. She thrust forward to stand at the Druid's side. She looked harmless enough; perhaps that might convince these tribesmen to lay down their arms.

Their headman mumbled words she could not understand.

"No feuds!" shouted the Druid, shocked from his usual calm. "Not *galanas*. You must not feud with the Dobunni: not ever, but especially not now. Or against the Picts. I tell you that the Jomsborgers have landed. If they will laugh, they'll thank you if you swear *galanas* against your own blood! You do their work for them!"

Alexa's bear scampered toward her, growling at the men he thought were her enemies. Two lifted their weapons. "No!" she shouted. The Druid leapt down from his horse, his arms upraised. "I put peace between you!"

To Alexa's astonishment, they laid down their weapons.

In a dizzyingly short time, Alexa, Audun, the Druid, and the Aescir went from the status of enemies to that of honored guests. Soon they were settled in the largest house. Mutton seethed in a cauldron that was the obvious pride of the village, and trout, pulled moments before from the nearby stream, sizzled over the central fire. Alexa was glad to shed her wet clothing for the long plaid tunic and skirt of heavy wool a woman about her age shyly offered. She rubbed her hair dry and let it hang loose, since many of the women she saw either plaited their hair back or wore it hanging down their backs, and gave one of her silver hair clasps to the woman who had loaned her dry clothing.

Then, with a poignant memory of Halldis, she allowed herself to be drawn into the knot of younger women who spun or helped with the food. Aescir methods were not so different from those of the Celtoi, she started to decide. Then she realized what a mix these villagers were. Some were as small and dark-haired as she, while others looked like the Aescir, Wends, and Sviar she had seen on the trip west. The children who tugged Audun's chain and beard were a similar mix: here the tribes and peoples had blended.

Hot water, pungent with crushed herbs, steamed before the

Druid as he tended a steady stream of villagers. He gestured at Alexa, who laid down her spindle with a polite show of reluctance, then hastened over.

He pointed at an herb, and Alexa realized he expected her to name it. She closed her eyes, trying to remember her Aristotle, and said its name in Greek. To her surprise, he nodded approval, then repeated its name in the language of the Isles. Her tongue twisted over the unfamiliar sounds, but she managed . . . as she managed to hold the child whose boil had to be lanced, or reassure a woman, barely out of girlhood, in her first pregnancy as the Druid patted her belly to see how the child lay within.

The Druid kept up a running stream of comments and observation, much to the awe of the people waiting for his services. *Another mystery cult,* Alexa thought. As a baby, she had been presented to Isis, then initiated into the lesser mysteries once she began to bleed. But arcana were for priests and priestesses.

"Do you mean for me to become a Druid?" she dared to ask. "Caesar wrote that all the Druids are men."

The Druid laughed. "You are years too old to begin," he told her. "Look at it this way," he said, handing a screaming child back to his mother, then reaching for a plant. "This one buds in the spring. I can force it to bloom in the winter, but then I must accept the consequences. There was power latent in you. For whatever reasons, it was forced into manifesting. What matters now isn't why it was forced; but how we can harness it. Or, if you prefer, how we can teach you not to endanger yourself and those around you. For, of a certainty, you cannot return to what you were."

Alexa glanced down at her hands. *Or remain as I am,* she thought. "Amergin, the ArchDruid in Penllyn, is a noted teacher. If he accepts you, then you will learn the ways of your power."

"And if he does not?" she asked, in sudden fear. To have come all this way, only to be refused . . .

"If he does not, then you will be taught how not to use it. But you will not be abandoned, and we will not let you falter."

Alexa sighed.

"Now," said the Druid, "name me these herbs, in order."

She was clever, had always been too clever, she was told. It had been a long time since she had been absorbed in learning, had stretched her memory as the Druid demanded. Boredom. The women's quarters in the Palace had been boring. Perhaps that was why Irene had gained such a hold upon her.

She would not be bored here, she vowed. There was a whole new kingdom—or cluster of kingdoms—to learn: from the lands of the Picts to the far north, where the people were smaller than she, and far darker; the kingdoms of the Iceni, the Cornovii, the Catuvellauni, even of various Saxons and Danes. There was no Emperor, or as they might say, High King. Or Queen; for some of the lands were ruled by women: the Iceni and Brigantes, for example, and some of the Picts. In Penllyn too, the old ways were strongest. There the Queen was the Goddess's favorite daughter. She brought abundance to the land, and had the power to heal with a touch. It was her duty to bear children, to lead her people in battle . . . as long as she was fertile.

Two children ran up, carrying a pitted stone that they presented to the Druid with rough ceremony. Alexa strained to follow their rapid speech, half-proud, half-embarrassed: that this rock had fallen from the sky, and that they had followed its trail, scooping it from the riverbed where it had steamed.

"And when she is no longer fertile?" Alexa glanced at the rock, then turned back to the Druid.

He traced along the stone, his long fingers running over dark, slick portions of the rock.

"You see these dark streaks and knobs?" he asked. "They are iron, cast in the heart of a star. The Queen of Penllyn has a dagger made of such iron. When she no longer bleeds in the manner of women, then she must enter the nemet—a hawthorn grove such as the one you saw—and turn that blade upon herself. The land needs blood. One way or the other, it will get it."

Alexa laid the chunk of star-borne rock aside. As a cry to come and eat went up from the women at the firepit, she ran to help, glad of the distraction.

* * *

Stretched out on a clean skin in the sweet-smelling straw, Alexa accepted a second beaker of the mead brewed in the village and gazed up through the vent in the roof at the stars, wreathed in smoke from the firepit. The mead was potent; soon she forgot that her body had ever ached. She blinked over at Audun and the Druid, also seated in places of honor. The Druid was explaining regretfully that he was no bard, but a healer and judge: if the villagers wanted music, they would have to provide it. He had only news and warnings. The Hunt rode forth; let every man and woman cease from raiding their neighbors, abandoning kin-strife to prepare their weapons against the Jomsborgers, whether they came as men or as skin changers.

Cheers and boasts went up. One man gestured into a corner, toward what had looked like pots stored on shelves. They were not pots, but heads, Alexa realized, taken in battle and preserved as trophies. She shuddered.

Feuds? If there were no overlord, she supposed they were to be expected. It would be—or might have been—as if Alexandria, Rome, Byzantium, and even the frontier provinces were each ruled by a kinglet, with no emperor to oversee all. But that way also lay an open road to invaders ... as had happened in Empire and was apparently happening here. At one point—the reign of this Bear of whom Audun always spoke—Prydein had had rulers who commanded all the lands: Arktos and his Queen. Trained to sacrifice her life as she aged, she had failed at the test, and betrayed him and her lands. Thereafter, there had been only small kings or queens: and no overlord.

She had fled the Empire to find a similar situation here. She took another sip of mead. It felt splendid to be warm, fed, dry, and as safe as could be hoped for. She stretched out, shutting her eyes as hoarse voices attempted a praise song about the Queen. They had learned it from the last traveler to guest with them. Daughter of a queen supposed to have been made of flowers, Queen Olwen was so lovely that white blossoms sprang up wherever she walked.

I would like to see that, Alexa told herself.

The song shifted to tales of Olwen's brother's exploits, his one-handed leaps onto his horses, his raids, his fast chariots, and Alexa raised an eyebrow. Isis and Osiris; sister and brother—how else could it be? She had seen them in a shaman's dream: soon she would see them in the flesh and witness the unity that she had denied herself and her brother.

She yawned, smiled muzzily at the people around her, and gazed into the fire. Patterns formed in the dancing flames and sparks, a veritable sea of fire, in which an island floated. That circle of flames gouting from a charred place on the fresh long: it took little imagination—or mead—to envision it as a circle of standing stones. The firelight and heat grew overpowering, and Alexa shut her eyes, like others at the feast.

Abruptly, she stood outside her body. *Why now?* she asked.

I summoned any who might hear, she was answered.

Show yourself. She cast her awareness west, toward her vision of the island she had seen limned in flame. A hawk called as she floated in her thought over land and sea. Then, to her astonishment, she was the hawk. It winged out over the island. Alexa could see standing stones there, cut and set by human hands as long ago, she imagined, as the pyramids themselves. They were sites of immense power, though: unthinkable that they be left unused. A man in Druids' robes emerged from beneath one such stone and gestured a welcome to her.

I am Amergin, ArchDruid in Penllyn. I will await you . . . Seeress.

She started to wing toward him.

Abruptly, the hawk was assailed by ravens, each cawing in rage. Their eyes glittered with hatred, not just the hatred of creature against creature, but that particular venom that some women reserve for their enemies. One beak slashed her left wing. She cried out, and twisted her head to avoid the others . . . she was a hawk; she could soar, could elude them until she learned how best to fight them.

High over their heads she flew.

And woke, panting, on the sheepskin.

Abruptly, she was too hot, too full. Her left arm ached, and the sleeve of her borrowed overdress was dark with blood. She jumped to her feet and ran outside. The Druid followed her to a small stream. She slashed at her shift with her knife, bound her arm roughly, then crouched on the ground shaking, trying not to be sick. She had no energy to speak with him.

He laid a hand on her right shoulder, and she jumped. A tremor ran from it down both arms; her wounded left felt as if it had been cleaned with wine.

"Seeress," he murmured. "Amergin will welcome you. It will be interesting to see whether all Penllyn will share that."

By the time they reached Penllyn, the raven's bite in her arm had eased from constant ache to a dull throb each time her horse stumbled on the road.

"We will travel more easily once we reach Sarn Elen," the Druid told her as she cradled the wounded arm against her breast in a brief rest halt.

Alexa nodded and drank thirstily from a water skin. She pretended to eat, and shook her head at the Druid when he came to tend her. The wound was clean. What she needed now was rest, and she preferred rest inside a house, preferably at the end of their journey. Clouds had been shifting and massing all afternoon; if they hastened, they might be indoors before the inevitable storm.

"Sarn Elen?" she asked, hoping that a request for knowledge would distract the Druid. It usually worked on priests, she had learned as a child.

"Elen was a princess, who married an emperor," the Druid said. "She was as wise as she was beautiful. And hearing of the roads in the Empire, she ordered roads like them built between Penllyn's major fortresses."

"A sensible woman," Alexa murmured automatically, her mind working on the Druid's words. *A princess who married an emperor!* She had asked for decent roads; now it appeared she would find some. She knew that the Celtoi were kin, several times over; head-takers or no, perhaps they would not be the savages she had feared.

"You will hear that story in Queen Olwen's hall," the man promised. "It is a long one, and requires better than my voice to do it justice."

By the time they reached Sarn Elen, though, Alexa was too weary to notice how smooth the road suddenly was. Her arm

was swollen, and it felt hot. Any sudden jolt sent shooting
pains up into her shoulder, and she kept her lips thinned
against crying out. Audun looked narrowly at her and started
to shout for a rest halt. She shook her head at him, wincing at
what it cost her. He nodded, and rode on.

Sarn Elen wound through field and forest, once past a field
of barrows in which a single standing stone pointed like a
finger at the rising moon. Though the woods were leafless,
they looked very deep. The temptation to turn off the road and
ride into them, losing her way and herself and her pain, was
very strong.

Nemet, something whispered into her consciousness. But
the Druid's face, when she turned to ask him, was shut.

Now the way led past a cluster of huts and well-kept
houses. "The Queen's maenol," someone told her, and she
spared it a glance. They rode through, Alexa too tired to pay
attention to the children who clamored at the sight of the
bears, then up the crest of a hill. Mist filmed it, or she would
have seen the men with spears who guarded the earthworks at
its crest. She heard greetings, sighed a little in relief, and
tumbled off her horse. Pride helped her keep her aching back
straight.

Not much farther, she promised herself, and followed a
middle-aged man who called himself *fychan* (which she interpreted as similar to a palace cubicular) into a hall wider and
more richly furnished than anything she had yet seen in these
lands. A huge fire burned at its heart. All about gleamed burnished gold and bronze and the luster of well-polished wood,
a good setting for the people who lounged in the hall, eating
and listening to a man with a harp. He wore a violently pat-
terned checked cloak and sat in a place of honor beside . . .

Alexa saw the Queen in her high seat and stopped short. If
she had been any younger, her mouth would have fallen open
in astonishment. The songs had been tame: Olwen was more
beautiful than any woman Alexa had ever imagined. She was
a head taller than Alexa, and that head was crowned with
red-gold hair that framed her face and swept thickly down her
back. Against that hair, the slender circlet that bound her
brow almost looked dull. She wore an overtunic of bright
green, and a gown that fell past her feet. Her body was full

and looked splendid in repose. Massive bracelets clasped wrists that looked delicate in comparison, and a torque shone at her throat, above long strands of pearls, clasped with green stones, that must have come from the Empire. At her waist shone a belt wrought of leaves intertwining, and on it gleamed a dagger in its sheath.

She forced her fascinated gaze upward to Olwen's face: warm eyes, a straight nose, and a generous red mouth that smiled at her.

Other presences were there, at the Queen's back: a tall man in the plaids of a warrior; a keen-eyed man in Druid's robes, who seemed but slightly older than the other two; hovering at the side, a thin, tall woman who moved with restless, angry grace. But Alexa stared at the Queen as years ago she had stared at her mother. Olwen was young, perhaps only a few years older than she herself, but she seemed ageless. She looked serene, but Alexa thought she might be quick to laugh or to anger.

Audun, his men, and the Druid had already made their way into the hall. Now Alexa forced herself to totter further inside. The sudden warmth, and the rich smell of roasting meat brought tears to her eyes, and she swayed. She heard her name, and saw the Queen raise one golden eyebrow.

Drawing a deep breath, Alexa sank down in the court prostration reserved for emperors and their queens.

"Kinswoman, no!" Olwen's voice rippled out in alarm. In an instant, the Queen ran in a flurry of skirts to Alexa's side. She raised her and enfolded her in arms that were strong for all their grace; a fragrance of flowers and herbs rose from Olwen's very skin. The Queen's body was warm and full. Clasped to her like a long-lost sister, Alexa brushed against the swell of her belly: in four or five months more, perhaps, the Queen would bear a child. She was like a tree in bloom, beautiful, fruitful, and innocent.

It was pleasant to be held as if she, too, were a babe, but Alexa compelled herself to push away. "I brought you a white bear. Of my own training," she stammered out.

"Poor thing, you are weary, cold, and wet. Hungry, too, I wager. Not a word about why you came here until you bathe and eat," Olwen crooned. "But what is this?"

Her hands were busy on the bandage that sheathed Alexa's left arm. The raven's bite looked red, inflamed.

"This is no natural hurt," she said, and looked at the young Druid who had joined her at Alexa's side. The look gentled and kindled. Then she gasped, for Olwen had laid cool fingers on the wound itself. Alexa expected pain, but felt a sudden tingle, a warmth, and then ease. She glanced down at her arm and saw only a red mark, as of a fading scar. It disappeared even as she gazed at it.

Alexa glanced up at the taller woman in wonder. She opened her mouth on gratitude, but . . . "Not one word more, cousin!" Olwen interrupted her. She laid an arm about her shoulder and drew her toward the fire. A rapid stream of orders produced roasted pork, bread, herbs, and wine drawn from the amphora resting in its wrought-iron holder. "Last spring, merchants brought this from Massilia," Olwen told her. "Since then, no more merchants have come. We are grateful to Audun for risking the storms."

Alexa took a careful sip of the wine, and choked on the fiery, unmixed stuff. She looked about for water to thin it, and found none. She laid the cup aside. Tired and wet as she was, it might make her drunk, and she would not risk it in this haven of warmth, before its friendly queen.

"And so you scorn the Queen's wine?" came a sharp voice. Alexa, her mouth full of bread and meat, looked up, blinking, at her accuser. The woman was taller even than Olwen. Her magnificent braids were deep red, and they flowed down over a russet checked gown stitched with shining thread.

Olwen was shaking her head at the woman and glaring, but she spoke again. Her lips, Alexa noticed, were very red against white skin, and her eyes were amber. "No, Olwen. The wine was dearly bought, and is the best you have. The Goddess only knows when those cowards of merchants will be back with more. And this scrawny 'kinswoman' looks about for water to drown its taste."

Alexa swallowed quickly and glanced around. Audun nodded encouragement at her. Over in the corner, the Druid she had ridden with argued heatedly with a younger man in white robes. Footsteps pounded in back of her, and a warm hand pressed her shoulder.

"She is twice kin to me, Bodb," Olwen said in a voice doubly sweet after the first woman's outbreak. "As both the *penkerdd* and *bardd teulu* can tell you." The two bards, seated in positions of honor, looked up. The elder man reached for his harp, but Olwen shook her head. "Once through the folk who fled Troy and founded both our lines; twice through Elen herself and the prince from the East whom she wed. And were she the meanest waif, I have called her my guest."

Olwen turned to Alexa. "Kinswoman, if the wine does not please you, would you prefer ale, or perhaps mead?"

Alexa caught up her cup and glanced at Bodb. It might have been tempting to hurl the acrid stuff into that pale, bitter face. But she would make her home here and needed to be liked. She drank again, and felt rapid fire kindle in her stomach. Only *barbaroi* took their wine unmixed, yet she thought she could become used to it. "It is long since I have eaten, kinswoman," she told Olwen. "I feared to become drunk."

"It is the custom to the south," came a voice behind her. "Folly perhaps, and hard to believe, but it is true. They mix water with their wine." A handclap and a quick order brought a scurrying woman in the gray of—a slave, Alexa thought—to her place with water. She topped off the cup with it, swirled it to mix the wine and water, and drank with a careful show of appreciation.

Across from her, Bodb suppressed what, clearly, she meant to say, and forced a glittering smile. Alexa smiled back. Halldis had given her the rough of her tongue, then become a staunch ally. Perhaps Bodb could be won over too. The red-haired woman raised her eyes to whomever it was had pressed Alexa's shoulder.

"Gereint, do you come to greet your kinswoman?" she asked in a gentle voice.

"Of course, if she will claim that name from me." It was the same man who had spoken before.

Alexa turned, looking up at the newcomer, and almost dropped her wine. Like all of the Celtoi in this hall, he was tall. Not as fair as his sister, he had hair and brows the color of burnished copper, and his eyes were a deep blue, fringed by black lashes. He wore a tunic of red checked with blue over darker breeches, with a thick blue cape flung loosely over his shoulder, where a huge, intricately wrought pin caught it into deep folds.

"Are my clothes that strange, kinswoman?" he asked, laughter rumbling in his deep chest. "Or did my face alarm you?"

Defiantly, she brought her eyes back up to meet his, and almost drowned again.

She had seen his face before. In her dream of the king and queen she would meet, and again, as the king who led the Wild Hunt—and had held out his hand to her. Her memories of Ragnar were a frail shield against those dreams and the blue, deep eyes she now gazed up into. "Be happy, dear heart," she knew Ragnar would bid her. He had tried to make her happy, had succeeded for a time and in a fashion. But this man—it was good that Ragnar had waked her to desire, or the weakness in her knees, the heat in her belly and loins, and the trembling in her hands would have thrust her, bereft and in terror, from his presence.

It was good that she knew, for now she would have to live with that desire until she could kill it. The man was very beautiful, and from the way she had taken his arm, he was all Olwen's.

"Your consort, cousin?" she asked Olwen.

"Her brother!" Bodb told her, as if that should settle that. It did. Sister and brother; queen and king—once she had had a brother at her side, too. Her eyes flickered down to Olwen's belly, where the child had begun to bulge out her gown. Prince Gereint laughed.

"Cousin, you are three times welcome. I have heard of your brother since I was a child. But you must have been born after my father Aillel left your father's guard."

Alexa reached for her cup and drank. "Ask him to sit down!" hissed Bodb. Alexa jumped up, startled. Surely a prince might sit where he pleased? But he stood above her, clearly and patiently waiting for the invitation that—just as clearly—Bodb would have loved to give. Alexa gestured, and he sank down beside her.

"Aillel?" she repeated. Marric used to lull her to sleep with stories of a golden Westerner named Aillel, who shone—so her brother said—like Horus himself, and who was almost as brave as their father. He had worshiped that guardsman, who treated him as a foster son. But he had left, pleading a family in the West.

With Aillel gone, Marric was lonely. Then I was born. No wonder he stayed so close to me. Tears filled her eyes, and she shut them.

"Then you've heard of my father?"

Coward, speak up! she scolded herself. "My . . . brother spoke of him often. He thought of him as a second father."

"Ah, your brother!" laughed Gereint. "Always when I was growing up, 'Prince Marric never flinched in training; Prince Marric learned his letters.' At first I hated this Eastern boy he was forever holding up as a model. Now I would like to see him. We had heard your father . . . what is the phrase?" he asked politely. "Olwen, do you remember?"

"The Emperor Antonios went to his Horizon," Olwen recited in what Alexa, to her astonishment, recognized as Egyptian. Then she repeated it in Greek. "Gereint didn't resent the part about your brother's not flinching in training. It was learning Greek letters that made him angry."

So at least nobles among the Celtoi, for all their wild looks, received a civilized education. That would help Alexa master this new tongue.

"Aye," Gereint said. "I always wanted to be out and driving my chariot, until Olwen took that over too. Aillel said your brother loved to drive. Does he even now, when he is Emperor?"

"He is not," Alexa's voice failed her, and she repeated the words, trying to copy Olwen's accent. "He is not yet Emperor. That is why I am here. There was a revolt . . ." She shook her head and turned away. "For my part . . ." The accursed tears, which had eluded her all those weeks after Ragnar's death, were coming now, and they stung as they rolled down her chapped face. "I failed, turned against my brother. And we will never rule together. Our House will have no heirs, will die with us . . ." Olwen patted her shoulder.

"Brother with sister?" Bodb's voice pierced her grief and shame. "The Sin, and you boast of it openly?"

Alexa blinked at her, then glanced at Olwen and her brother

Gereint. No wonder Bodb was resentful; she wanted the prince for herself. Well, Alexa could understand wanting him.

Olwen embraced Alexa, laughing until she had to lay her head on Alexa's shoulder. Concerned—should a woman who bore a child laugh so long or so hard?—Alexa stroked her hair. It was like amber, drawn out into incredibly fine strands that curled and glinted intriguingly about her fingers. The flower scent was very strong. "Ah, I understand now!" she cried once she got her breath. "So that is why you looked so sad, sister!" Olwen whispered into Alexa's ear and laughed mischievously. "I wish you good luck!" Olwen brushed tears of merriment from flushed cheeks and spoke to Bodb. "Aillel also told us that the customs in the East were different. It is no sin among their kings and queens for brother and sister to marry and so preserve their line."

"Isis and Osiris were brother and sister," Alexa said, somewhat stiffly. Their Goddess Modron, had she not a brother, a consort? What of that king who led the Hunt? But she shook, overwhelmingly relieved that this far away from Byzantium, customs were evidently so different. They would not blame her for shirking her duty to produce an heir.

Bodb thinned her lips and looked away.

"Your father Aillel: what became of him?" Alexa changed the subject with practiced skill.

Olwen thinned her lips. "He vanished on a great journey from Eire . . . *west,* if you can believe it. Shortly thereafter my mother, Queen Blodeuedd, passed within . . ." she broke off. "There are better times and places to discuss this—or other angry matters." She raised her voice, calling over to the Druids who still disputed in the shadows of the hall. "Rhodri bring your guest over to the fire. Or must he freeze and starve, as well be argued deaf?"

The younger Druid, Rhodri, broke off what he was saying, and led his companion to the Queen. "Lady, may I present to you the Druid and bard Kynan?" he asked.

"Of course," Olwen said. Her eyes warmed and she held out her hand, not to the Druid who had ridden so far with Alexa, but to the younger one. Like so many among the Celtoi, he was tall, finer-featured than Gereint, with intense amber eyes and a full mouth. His hair was dark and worn long, flowing down over his robes. He took the Queen's hand. Pressing it affectionately, he leaned over her and stroked her hair and cheek with his free hand.

"And were you well today, my heart?" he asked Olwen. "You and my daughter?"

The words leapt out before Alexa, worn from the ride, the wine, and meeting so many strangers, could stop herself. "You chose a priest as the father of your heir?"

Olwen nodded serenely, but Bodb rose to her feet, overturning her cup, which sent a runnel of deep red onto her gown. "First she boasts of the Sin. Now she insults my brother. Is there any limit to which this unmannerly brat will not go?"

The hall's heavy door burst in to admit newcomers. A raven flew over their heads and perched in the thatch of the roof.

"No, Olwen, I *will* speak my mind for once."

"Just this once," murmured Gereint.

"The Bearmaster comes here, bringing this castaway and a tale of war in the Empire and war among the Northerners. I say, what are these Northerners to us?"

"For one thing, lady," said Kynan, "they kill your kinsmen on the eastern shore, seemingly for sport."

"I disagree," the Druid Rhodri said. "How can they obey our laws if no one has ever taught them?" His voice was as resonant as a bard's and so intense that Alexa could see the resemblance between him and the virago Bodb.

"My brother is right. And besides, who else will tell this story? This waif from a fallen house, who sneers at an honest Druid and flaunts her corruption in our faces? We women of Penllyn consort openly with the best men, while you *Roman* —" she spat out a version of the old name for the Empire— "women let yourselves be debauched in secret by the most vile."

I am still virgin. Can you say as much? It was all Alexa could do not to fling an angry response or the dregs of her unmixed wine in Bodb's face. She forced herself to sit calmly, with what she hoped was a dignified expression on her face.

"She could be a traitor, a spy, but you take her to your

hearts. My brother even tells me that the ArchDruid will welcome you, will teach you secrets that even I—"

Gereint was on his feet too, his voice raised to drown out the woman's. "What would you use them for, Bodb? Choosing who will die every spring when you and your wild women build that ghastly hut over on the island?"

"Blasphemy!" two or three people shouted. Alexa forgot to be insulted, forgot, almost, to be afraid that she was insulted and challenged in what looked like her only chance at a home: these Celtoi seemed hot-blooded and argumentative to a fault. She listened, fascinated, as Bodb and Gereint shouted at one another. Gereint seized her shoulders, started to shake her, and she raised her chin to stare defiantly into his eyes and leaned against him.

"Ah, you would like that!" he said, and released her so quickly that she almost overbalanced and fell to the floor.

"Gereint!" Olwen reproved him.

"Let there be peace between you!" Rhodri cried, but the resignation in his voice spoke of many such quarrels.

Alexa glanced over to where Audun sat, placidly eating and drinking his way through the dishes that everyone else ignored. He flung a bone to the bear who crouched beside him, and grinned at her. Abruptly, she wanted to laugh too. Perhaps, she thought, one hand over her mouth to hide her smile, if the fight went on much longer, she would simply find a corner and go to sleep. Clustered shadows in the corner showed her that some people had already done just that.

She yawned. Overhead, the raven chose that moment to cry out.

"Do we bore you?" Bodb rounded on Alexa.

Alexa stretched. Bodb's rages reminded her of Irene's; and she knew just how to provoke Irene. "Of course not. But you seemed to be managing this scene very well without any help from me." She smiled at Olwen. "I mean no insult to your brother. I am not a spy but precisely what the Bearmaster has told you: a woman who needs teachers and a refuge among kind and civilized people, which most of you seem to be."

"Can you prove that?" Bodb flung at her.

"Take my oath on it," Alexa said. "We have two Druids to

witness it. That ought to be good enough, even for you. I swear that I mean no harm to you and yours," she said, struggling to recall the oath sworn by the leader of the Wild Hunt. "And if I betray you, may the sky fall and destroy me, and the sea overflow and drown me."

"I will witness that," Kynan said.

Olwen looked at Rhodri. "And I."

"And I say it is not enough!" spat Bodb. "Prove it, *Princess!* This spring, come to the island with the other women, and help us build the Goddess's house. If, as you boast, you mean no harm, you should take no harm from it. But if you lie . . ."

"No!" shouted Gereint. "I have heard that the Goddess does not judge. Instead, you choose an enemy, or draw lots. Then you trip your victim as she carries thatch and reeds to the shrine . . ." The raven shrieked again, and the hall was awesomely still. Gereint's angry words trailed into silence, as if he realized he had said far too much.

Bodb flashed a triumphant glance at him. "Do you dare to come with us?"

Alexa glanced around the hall. All about her, clansmen muttered and nodded. Olwen and Gereint might like her, but they would hardly alienate their most influential subjects for a woman they had barely met. The muttering grew louder; Bodb, Alexa realized with a sinking heart, had many sympathizers.

She sighed. Overhead the raven screamed and mantled like a hawk. Alexa felt herself forced into a corner.

"Well, will you go with me to the island?"

She would have to hope that by that time, she had enough mastery over her strength to protect herself. The raven flew about the hall, swooping in arcs that drew nearer and nearer to Alexa. *Unless it pecks at your eyes, don't you* dare *move!* she ordered herself. Bodb wore a triumphant smile as Alexa opened her mouth to reply.

A crash and a gust of wind that made the fire dance in its pit made her whirl around.

His head wreathed in green leaves, his white robe fresh and shining despite the mud and rain he must have come through, an elderly Druid stood in the door. One hand held an oaken staff. The other rested on a golden sickle. He met Alexa's eyes. *Seeress.* He had welcomed her once, in a dream. Now he nodded agreement at her.

"She will not!" said Amergin the ArchDruid.

Chapter 11

☆

The ArchDruid's superb voice echoed through the room and dismayed the raven, who shrieked one final time, then flapped out through the open door. Alexa stared up at him. He was tall, even in this race of tall men, even despite the many winters that had stooped his shoulders. Thought, as well as power, gleamed in his eyes, and Alexa thought of Divitiacus, the Druid whom Caesar, her ancestress's first husband, was proud to claim as friend. No culture that could produce such majesty could be called barbarian.

Giving the man the respect she would have accorded the high priest of Osiris, Alexa rose to her feet.

"You," said Amergin, pointing to Bodb, "have your mysteries. I do not scorn them; but you, when you seek to use them to trap the unwary, come close to having them turn upon you. Be careful, lady, lest you fail and fall when next you build the Goddess's house."

In a face white with rage, Bodb's lips looked like a bleeding wound. She nodded sharply, then strode from the hall in a whirl of heavy skirts. In its corner, the white bear growled unhappily. As the door slammed behind her, an outcry of ravens was heard overhead.

"And you, Princess of Byzantium," the ArchDruid's voice was scarcely less harsh, "shall cease to regard yourself as a victim, lest, in your folly, you become one. Open your eyes and cease to need protectors. What you need instead is schooling in power. Eat, bathe, and rest; your lessons begin at dawn."

The ArchDruid held Alexa's eyes for a long moment. Did she see a smile quiver at the corner of his eyes and mouth, or did she merely hope to? She bowed, and was relieved when he turned away to greet Audun with a restrained embrace. Audun looked over at Alexa and gestured to the corner. *Present the bear*, he mouthed.

It weaved its head back and forth as she approached, then ducked its muzzle into her hand and butted her shoulder, almost knocking her over. She started to lead it forward, and Audun joined her, stopping them long enough to throw a strand of amber over the bear's head. It caught on the neat, small ears, and Alexa twitched it free. Her eyes were smarting. The bear yelped and tried to catch her in a powerful hug. "She will be a good mistress to you," Alexa whispered. "Go, with my love."

Olwen smiled as man, woman, and bear came toward her. As it crossed into the circle of firelight, the bear reared up on its haunches. "My gift to you, lady," said Audun. "But not only mine. The Princess helped to train him."

Gereint rose to his feet, and the Druid Rhodri was close at Olwen's side as she walked toward the bear, one hand extended for it to sniff as if she introduced herself to a large dog of uncertain temper. She carried a child! Alexa remembered with a stab of fear. How would she fare if the bear hugged her too hard? But the white-furred creature sniffed Olwen's hand, then ambled closer to nudge at her shoulder with its round head.

Laughing in delight, Olwen removed the amber necklace and placed it around her own neck. When she returned to her seat, the bear followed close behind, and sank down near her feet with an almost human sigh of relief and pleasure.

"You trained that bear?" Gereint whispered to Alexa.

"He lived with me," she replied. "I never taught him tricks."

He was shaking his head in admiration—for the beast, the beautiful, wondrous beast, Alexa reminded herself.

"Take good care of him, lady," said Audun. "And take good care of the Princess I have brought you. I think she will surprise you in many ways." He saluted the Queen.

"You will have the winter to see what care I take of them both," Olwen said, but Audun shook his head.

"I must race the storms back to my home, and ready it to weather war or winter," he said. "I leave at dawn."

Audun couldn't abandon her in this strange place where already she had made one mortal enemy, could he? Alexa ran over to him. "I had hoped . . ." she began, then faltered. She had hoped that he would stay here, to ease her way, to protect her: precisely the things that the ArchDruid had ordered her to renounce. She shook her head, unashamed, for once, of the tears that poured down her cheeks, and began again. "I had hoped that you would stay, that you would see me become what you have seen in me." She hugged him as if he were one of his own bears. "That is the only way I can ever thank you!"

Audun stroked her straggling hair. "Little Princess, little daughter, trust yourself. Trust the Queen, her brother—eh, I see that you more than trust him already!" his chuckle rumbled through her body. "Listen to the ArchDruid and his people. Rhodri—the bear accepts him. But protect yourself from . . ." he glanced sidelong at the door through which Bodb had stormed out.

Alexa nodded against his chest. "She . . . reminds me of Irene."

"You will always have an eye to the dark things, I think," said Audun. "And you grew up in a turbulent court. Do not let anyone persuade you that you are a babe. Now I must rest, if I am to leave at daybreak."

"I'll see you off," Alexa stammered.

"How can you?" Audun grinned at her. "You heard Amergin. Your lessons start at dawn." He kissed her on the forehead as if she were a favored daughter, then tramped forward to take Olwen's hand. "My best wishes to you," he said.

She started to thank him for the bear, but he held up a hand. "I have brought you a bear and a sister," Audun told her. "They will serve you well. Thank me when they do."

He turned and left the hall, his face somber. Alexa returned to her seat. Gereint filled her cup with wine, then turned tactfully away as she swallowed it and blinked her tears away. When she was certain she had her voice under control again, she thanked him.

"You are most welcome," Gereint said. "I always envied my father his travels. Had I another brother, I might have followed in his path, but I am needed here as war leader. Now," his voice hushed and darkened, "more than ever. You have seen the men of Jomsborg's works, Alexa. Are they—"

"Terrible," she whispered. "They came as black bears. They killed . . ."

The prince patted her hand. "Someone you cared for, is that it?"

"Others, too. Whole villages—you could see the fire and smoke of their trail from the sea roads." She remembered the death that Audun had called the blood eagle, and shuddered. "They obey their lord and his commands, but have no other law but chaos and their joy in it."

"Then perhaps, if they were taught law," Rhodri the Druid cut in, "they would abide by it. As does that white bear." He gestured with a long-fingered hand at the beast where it crouched, staring up worshipfully at the Queen. His own face changed, the sharply defined features growing with a version of the same worship.

"These are not beasts," whispered Alexa, "but men turned beasts. Turned to *mad* beasts. You cannot teach them law, or Audun would have tried. Is he not their distant kin?"

Rhodri shook his head. The same light that seemed to follow Olwen gleamed about him. They were innocent, Alexa thought. They had never blundered as she had. How could they fathom the darkness in people's hearts, let alone what the Jomsborgers might do if they were set loose here? She thinned her lips, determined not to stain that innocence.

Still, Rhodri seemed gentle, and Olwen loved him. "I wish," Alexa ventured, "that your sister were not so angry."

"So do I, lady," said the Druid. "When we were children, we both petitioned to join the Druids. Though a few women are admitted to the nemets, Amergin refused her and chose only me. It was the first time we had ever been divided, and she has never forgiven him. Or, I am afraid, me. Now, you appear, and she feels like a daughter who has been refused her rightful inheritance, and sees it lavished on a stranger. I pray that one day her rage will cool."

Gereint grimaced behind the Druid's back, and Alexa stifled a laugh. *Innocent*, she thought again. *The ArchDruid was wise to reject her. Let us see if his wisdom extends to me.*

She turned to answer some merry comment of Gereint's, yawned instead, and turned instantly crimson. Gereint slapped his leg, laughing. "Olwen!" he cried. "Your guests are weary." He rose and pointed at the bear, who was snoring. The laughter that rose then woke him, and he shambled off, looking offended, into a dark corner.

Olwen leaned over to shake her head at her bards.

"Quickly!" Gereint said. "Before this one snores too, and I must carry her off to bed."

Appalled, Alexa buried her hot face in her hands. She was not sleepy now, but mortified. However, the laughter that rose about her was kind, and she suppressed her desire to run over to the sleeping bear and hide.

Olwen rose lithely, one hand to her belly. "Gereint, who told you that Beltane came in the winter? Or is this a special holiday, just for you?" She walked over to Alexa and held out a hand to her.

"Sister," she said, "let me show you where you will sleep. And Gereint, I am certain that our guest can walk to her bed." She held up a much-ringed, warning hand. "Without your help."

As the days waned and snow lay heavily on the bare boughs of the oak trees, Alexa entered the Druids' groves and learned. Not to be a Druid, of course: she had started late (she accepted it now without blaming herself) and made bad choices. Once there had been Black Druids in the fellowship, Amergin had said, then refused to say more. When she had pressed him, he sent her to listen to the bards who sang outside. They were a mixed lot of Celtoi, men of the North, even a few Picts.

By now, Alexa was accustomed to the Druids' temple, if

that was the proper word for this square-built house of wood and stone within a round earthwork. She no longer averted her eyes from the skulls enshrined by the doorposts, nor shuddered at the knowledge that their bodies were surely embedded beneath them in the walls. "Do you sacrifice men often?" she had gasped the first time she had seen the discolored, staring bones.

"Not often," said Amergin. "And sometimes, too often, it is not a man whom we sacrifice." Horrible, she wanted to think, but it lay in her own past too. The god Osiris had been sacrificed that the Two Lands might flourish; and, she knew, the barbarians far to the East had other such tales. She remembered how she and her brother had wept over the funeral of Patroclus in the *Iliad*—and had not Achilles sacrificed heroes to him?

The danger lay not in the sacrifice, but in the spirit that inspired it. Perhaps that was why Amergin had rejected Bodb. Undeniably she had power, enough to make Alexa shudder. But if ever a woman had strength without judgment and a passion for the dark, it was Bodb. She made a formidable enemy. The tall, magnetic, red-haired woman was the daughter of a Deceangli chief with powerful ties to the nearby Brigantes; her friends pointed out that she was descended from the same great-grandmother as Olwen and thus . . . Alexa paused to consider that. Thus, if Olwen died, in childbirth or any other way, Bodb was likely to be chosen Queen. As Queen, would Bodb be willing to pass within the hawthorn nemet and yield up her life?

Not as long as blood ran in other women's veins. Women like herself.

A dangerous woman, Alexa calculated, her mind running in familiar paths. And Rhodri, Druid and judge, Olwen's lover, was her brother. Would Rhodri betray his Lady? She pondered the question for the hundredth time and came up with her usual answer: Rhodri did love his sister, but he had two passions—the Law and Queen Olwen.

The novice Beda (who trained to be an historian and judge) nudged Alexa back to attention. For the tenth time, a bard sang the genealogies of Olwen's family, with the praise songs of the bard Gildas thrown in. As usual, she had missed a century or so. If only she could write down the endless lists of names, the herblore, the system of time-keeping laws that dinned into her ears, day after day, week after nine-day-long week. But it was Druids' law that nothing might be written down . . . assuming one could force this language into Greek letters in the first place.

She was disgracing herself with a faulty repetition of the lists she had but half heard when Rhodri beckoned her out of the circle. Cautiously, Alexa followed him outside, wrapping her heaviest cloak about her.

"Amergin asked that you be told. Word has come from Kynan, who heard from our brothers far to the south, in Egypt." Ice seemed to form in Alexa's belly, but Rhodri's eyes were kind, almost humorous.

"Your brother has escaped. One of ours, Taran, son of Iolo, took him in and helped him find refuge with the priests of Osiris."

Alexa clasped her hands.

"Ah, that pleases you!" Rhodri smiled. "The rest of my news is less pleasant. The Jomsborgers on whom were invoked mist and Hunt are being avenged. A full ten ships landed and promptly sacked an Iceni village. They may be heading west."

"They travel in winter?" Alexa marveled.

"It is said," Rhodri went on, reluctantly, "that they may winter here."

Then there would be no seasons free of attack, no time to prepare defenses. "Gereint must call out the levies, send to the tribes roundabout," Alexa muttered to herself. If it came to war—and she saw no other way—Gereint would lead. Perhaps the Druids would let him use the net of power that girdled this land and sent tendrils of power down into the realms of the south. Alexa's mind's eye described that net to herself as winged words, flung across the miles from standing stone to standing stone, and into the willing consciousness of their priests.

Gereint would have to lead. Even now, Olwen's pregnancy

was too far advanced for her to ride in her chariot to battle, even though it was her privilege as Queen to lead her armies.

"We can pray that there will not be war," said Rhodri.

Alexa shook her head. She knew that he would think she disagreed. In a society of warriors, he was used to disagreement. As a Druid, he had no need to bear arms, and he liked it that way. No, it was impossible that Rhodri would back Bodb against Olwen.

Alexa dreamed that night, and most of the nights that followed: dreams of Byzantium, the harbor chained against pirate raids; of the Hunnic tribes encamped to the east. Irene would come flying through such dreams, or, at times, the wizened face of the hag at the loom. But now she could compose herself, create a form of spirit armor that protected her, yet permitted her to use her dreams. Increasingly, she realized how right Amergin had been to call her seeress.

As she grew stronger, the compulsion to use her dreams grew. Gereint would go up against the Jomsborgers with a small force, he would be captured, be slowly, agonizingly slain, and she could not help. She dared not set foot on a battlefield ever again. The atrocities at Staraja had proved that, along with the inadequacy of her knowledge of a general's art. If only her brother could advise her!

For the first time in weeks, she woke crying and in a cold sweat. Olwen knelt at her side, chafing her hands; Alexa was glad to bury her face in the taller woman's shoulder. Olwen stroked her hair, comforting her as if she were the infant to come.

"Do you miss your brother?" Olwen asked. "If Gereint were stolen from me, I think I would want to die."

Lulled into calm by Olwen's flower scent, Alexa roused and started guiltily. Gereint's humor haunted her daytime thoughts as much as the shape of his mouth, the breadth of his shoulders, and the narrowness of his hips. They spoke often, and laughed more—much to Bodb's aggravation. ("Bed with that mad vixen?" he had asked once. "Never!" Seeing that her brother would be Queen's Consort once the babe was born, his dislike of Bodb augured a difficult family relationship,

Alexa told him once. Because she was an expert at such relationships, he should heed her warnings.)

"I miss Marric." Alexa nodded. No need . . . yet to tell Olwen how desperately she feared for her. "But it isn't that. I need to *know!* What Amergin and Rhodri tell me isn't enough. I need to see for myself."

Never mind the fact that each time she saw for herself, either Irene or Jarl Grettir's grandam attacked her savagely. Ignorance and fear could be just as deadly as magical assault.

She said as much later that day to Amergin, who sighed. "You couldn't possibly restrain yourself until Beltane?" he asked. "By spring, you will be ready for the first degree of initiation."

"I will?" Alexa's eyebrows went up. "You trust me that much?"

"Let us say that if . . . when you emerge from your trance, we can trust you fully. I can tell you that it would be safer for you if you waited."

"And for you?" Alexa asked. "Do I put you in any danger?" Amegin smiled thinly.

"Then it is my risk," said Alexa. "The first night I was here, you warned me not to seek protectors, but to use my own strength. I need to see."

"Then so be it," Amergin said. He pulled off his cloak and started outside the maenol. "Come with me. No, leave the cloak."

"It's the middle of winter!" Alexa protested.

"You cannot control your own body heat, yet you dare to summon visions of the present and future?" That was a challenge. Oh, he was *very* like the Osiris priest who had served her and her brother as conscience when they were too young and too lawless to have one of their own.

The cold air bit into her unprotected fingers until she remembered the breathing and the quick phrase that sent the blood thrumming hotly in her veins. Gereint, muffled in his brightest cloak, drove his chariot around a corner, and shouted at her. At another time, she would have been tempted vastly to run like a wild girl beside the chariot until he swept her up onto the oak and wicker platform for a dizzying ride with dogs barking and the children of the maenol dashing out to watch.

Instead she followed Amergin out past the maenol, past the oaken grove where the Druids harvested mistletoe with their golden sickles, stealthily, as if in theft, past even the circle of hawthorn trees into which she had not dared to venture. The snow crunched and scuffed up beneath her thin shoes; she had neglected to wear leg wrappings beneath her shift, and yet she was not cold. She drew a deep breath of the frosty air and gazed in delight at the peaks.

Beyond the hawthorn nemet, Amergin turned into a narrow path, little more than footsteps half hidden by snow. They followed it for a time, then emerged in a clearing. A white burial mound rose to the left of a standing—or rather, Alexa put in irreverently, a leaning—stone that was reflected in the pool at its ice-rimmed foot.

"Why hasn't it frozen?" she wondered.

"You have heard, have you not, of the *gorsedd*, the throne mound? Who ever surmounts it will either see visions, or suffer blows. The time will come when you too will test your fate upon it. Then, if you live, you will spend a night in the chamber below." He paused as if to let Alexa understand that if all went well—*well*, for sweet Isis's sake!—she would be buried alive in an ancient barrow.

"Stop trying to frighten me," she said. Her voice carried very far in the stillness, and she hushed herself. "You have succeeded."

"Good. Perhaps it will teach you caution. Do you wish to proceed?"

Alexa gulped and nodded.

"It will not be necessary for you to climb the *gorsedd* now. Simply look into the Water of Vision. Turn your will to what you would see."

She knelt by the pool, unfrozen despite the ice and snow all around, and dared to touch the water, then raise her fingers to her lips. The water tasted strongly of iron, and the ripples her touch caused fanned out, then, abruptly, ceased. There was power here, as there was in Byzantium, and in the great shrine, the *omphalos*, or world's navel, in Egypt. Alexa adjusted the folds of her robe to cushion her knees, then began the deep breathing that brought on trance. Thanks to the

Druids, she no longer needed the smokes and drums of the North that had always helped her before.

The water rippled, then cleared, and Alexa saw herself reflected: small, thin, with enormous eyes fringed in dark lashes, dark hair pouring down her back. Save that her eyes were green, and the shape of her face ("you have a cat's face," Ragnar had loved to tell her), she could have been one of the people whom bards said still lived far to the north, in the hollow hills. There was a look of wariness and endurance to her, fining down her features to the beauty of a dagger blade. She met her reflection's eyes unflinchingly. What crime she had committed had long since been atoned for.

Safe in that knowledge, she bent and breathed on the water. "Show me," she whispered, "what I hold dearest." Using this pool for vision was like riding an immensely powerful horse downhill. The water rippled fast, then cleared... *and she looked on more water, the brilliant blue of the Middle Sea. Merchant ships, watchful Eyes painted on their prows, cut through the water...* "No," she whispered in horror. *There, on the horizon, were other sails. Pirate dromonds! Like a hawk, her vision swooped down on the merchanter leading the fleet. Its oars dipped and rose like immense wings, but it was heavily laden, unable to outrun the pirates. On its deck, small figures came and went; she heard chanting; saw light crackle and wreath about the tall man at the prow. He trembled under its force, which grew and grew. Then thunder pealed out, and the skies and seas rose to fight one another...*

The Water of Vision rippled again. *Now she could see the man at the merchant ship's prow. Priests surrounded him, almost "touched earth" in the old bow to Pharaohs before him, but he ignored them to gaze out at the rainbow that arched at the horizon. A golden hawk flew overhead. The man was dark-haired and burned by the sun until, almost, he resembled a pirate himself. That was no pirate, she thought. Wouldn't she know her brother anywhere? That was his height, the shape of his eyes—though the lines of pain endured and mastered that squared and bracketed his mouth*

*were new to her. His knees buckled, but he caught himself on
a smaller man's shoulder. Blessings on you, brother!* she
wished him.

The water rippled and was still again until a hot tear fell
into it. For a moment, Alexa crouched beside the pool. He
was alive; she had seen him herself. Then the water welled
up from the pool, and she recoiled hastily. When it subsided, she realized that she gazed upon . . . *the mountain
trails through which she had ridden with Kynan and Audun
months ago. Only this time, black bears hunted along them,
and men almost as bestial savaged the villages as they
passed. She saw the huts in which she had been a guest
burn and fall, saw blood slick against the ice, freezing into
a purplish black.*

*Nor were the men of Jomsborg alone. Three of the
strongest held short lengths of chain from which iron nooses
secured tiny, dark men: iron, trapping the men of the hollow hills!* Alexa's anger and fear almost destroyed the vision, but her need to look further steadied her breathing.
*Though Jomsborgers were men of all ages from eighteen
to fifty, in a closed cart rode . . . even through the furs
that sheathed it, Alexa could sense the presence of the
hag.*

Pain burst in her temples. *I have read the bones, the hag*
cackled at her. *You are not destined to kill me, lostling. More
pain . . . no! The hag had always managed to attack.* But not
this time, Alexa decided. Not this time! *She drew on all her
strength, pulling energy, as she had been taught, from the
centers all along her spine, letting it build behind her eyes
. . . and then releasing it, to sear into that cart like sea fire
. . . a scream . . . then the water rippled, and there was
silence.*

Alexa toppled over onto her side, inches away from falling
face-down into the pool. Instantly, Amergin was at her side,
raising her. "What did you see, Alexa?" She moaned. She had
used all her strength to burn into that cart, overturning it and
—please Isis or Modron or whatever other power might suffice—delaying the men of Jomsborg until Gereint might call
out the warriors. Amergin slapped her face rhythmically, right

cheek, then left. She welcomed the pain, which forced her to speak.

"Jomsborg," she told him. She lowered her head, lest she see despair and fear upon his. "They come in full force. And they are marching west."

Chapter 12

☆

Apple wood burned in the firepit, but no fragrance could sweeten the war which Olwen and her twenty-four advisors wrangled. Not were they the only speakers. Alexa flicked her eyes from one excited warrior to the next, and over to the Druids and noblewomen who interrupted whenever possible. Did all Celtoi always shout all at once? She had peered in on her father's councils: a matter of speakers in order of precedence, and total hush after her father had spoken. Or so it seemed.

"These are our lands, our herds," Bodb cried. "We must not let these southern invaders steal them!"

Cheers went up and warriors of her tribe brandished knives in approval. Rhodri shook his head at his sister.

"You need not lead the Deceangli, brother," she said. "When I knew you would refuse to bear a sword, I took myself to Eire and trained six summers with Scatha's heirs. I shall lead them myself. Gereint shall ride out, like Arktos himself, our warriors at his back!"

Gereint closed his eyes in resignation. Bodb was too eager to fight, Alexa thought, too eager to cast Olwen's brother in the role of the ancient hero, and herself? What did that leave for her?

"No," Bodb went on triumphantly, "the bards will have no need to make satires on the women's courage. The Queen will have her chariot, and I shall have mine. But what of you, Princess? Do you ride with us?"

"No," said Alexa. "May I pass living through a lake of crocodiles before I set foot ever again on a battlefield."

Bodb tossed her head contemptuously. "It is a wonder that your Empire has survived this long."

"We have not survived by folly," Alexa said, low-voiced. "But by law."

Rhodri and Beda had spoken quickly and urgently together. Now Rhodri rose and raised a hand for attention. Olwen nodded and leaned forward. For the first time in hours, the verbal brawl ceased.

"By law," Rhodri repeated. "By law. We live by law, but do the Jomsborgers?"

Nothing anyone could say diverted Rhodri from that argument for long. For a foul moment, the stink of sea salt, burning flesh, and ash at Birka seemed to overpower the sweet burning wood. Alexa swallowed bile and a desire to scream that the Jomsborgers were beasts of prey, lawless and hungry. But this was not her council. If she spoke, Bodb would twist her words to call her a coward yet again.

"Indeed, they do. They swear an oath to their lord and to one another. They forbid flinching in battle, and—for better or for worse I do not say, my sister—ban the presence of women in their stronghold. Yet they honor one aged priestess, I have heard. Thus, they indeed have laws that they respect. Perhaps they do not know that we too have laws. If our laws were explained to them, they might respect them, and leave us in peace."

Alexa flinched as the screams of protest and approval clashed like two armies of screaming Celtoi. Sweet Goddess, what an insane idea!

"Let me finish!" Rhodri shouted his kindred down. "What harm does it do for one man to try? I am not even a warrior whose sword you need. Let me go to them and tell them of our laws."

Olwen's face went white, and her mouth spasmed.

"This may work. At least, I pray it does. If it does not," he went on, "I have bought us time, time in which Gereint can send to all the neighboring tribes for more warriors."

"Don't throw your life away for a point of law," Alexa cried. "They'll carve the blood eagle on you."

Rhodri smiled at her. "If they do, I die. I am not afraid to die, Princess. Death is but a matter of an awakening, a judgment, and rebirth into a nobler life."

Alexa might have been back in Byzantium, listening to an ancient priest from Hind discussing rebirth with the high priest of Osiris. It wasn't the idea of rebirth that she disliked; it was the painful interim between one life and another. She opened her mouth to say so, but Olwen spoke first.

"What," she asked, her voice harsh to keep it from shaking, "could possibly be nobler than what you are now?" Her hands clenched against one another over the gentle mound of her belly to keep from reaching out to him.

"Let me go, Queen," Rhodri asked softly. "If we do not try to reason, how are we better than beasts? And if I fail, what do we lose?"

"You!"

Alexa rose stealthily from her seat and went to Olwen.

Rhodri held out a hand to her, and she carried it to her cheek. "You will never lose me. Or," he whispered, "my love for you. Let me go, Olwen."

Olwen glanced about her hall. Bodb and Gereint, in rare agreement, called Rhodri's proposal madness. A warrior from the hills near Sinadon shouted a war cry, inflamed by the honor of the idea. Alexa laid a hand on Olwen's shoulder and felt the Queen tense as her eyes met the ArchDruid's. He stroked his beard and nodded.

Olwen kissed Rhodri's fingers. A tear fell onto his hand and sparkled like an emperor's ring. Then she released his hand and drew herself up.

"You shall go," she decided. "I shall send a troop with you."

"No warriors," said Rhodri. "Just myself."

Suicide, Alexa thought. No Byzantine would order a man to commit suicide. Byzantines were prudent, sober strategists. But these were Celtoi, and, as Strabo the geographer had written, "at any time or place, and on whatever pretext you stir them up, you will have them ready to face danger, even if they have nothing on their side but their own strength and courage." She looked at Rhodri's fine-cut features. A nimbus of light seemed to hang about him; his brow and hair shone

No warrior, Bodb had reproached him. But certainly no coward.

At the Queen's decision, Bodb's eyes flashed, and Gereint stirred. Though she surely had no illusions that she would ever see Rhodri alive again, Olwen stared down the assembly. Then she rose.

"When will you leave?" she asked, almost as if they spoke of his riding to the next village.

"At dawn."

Kynan's fingers swept his harp strings, and he sang a praisesong of Arktos made by the bard who had borne his name to Olwen, as she sat with Alexa and, reluctantly, Bodb, whose amber eyes were deep and dream-filled from the music. Olwen toyed with her long amber necklace, polishing it with a fold of her green cloak. She had worn that cloak the morning Rhodri rode out, had stood in the snow, a splendor of green and gold, until women whispered to her of her child's well-being and gently compelled her to sit by the fire by which the white bear lay dozing.

That had been several weeks ago. Now, no hooves rang on the frozen ground outside the Queen's maenol without "He's back!" But it was never Rhodri. Gereint, at times; at other times, a warrior-woman of the Brigantes, a prince of the war-ravaged Iceni, a Druid from far to the south, all bearing the same word. Winter was no time for war. Let the spring come, and they would march at Penllyn's side. No civilized people fought in winter. *Who says they are civilized?* The one time Olwen had not been present to hear, Alexa had cried that at the back of a departing tribesman's head, and the man had turned around again.

"Then, if they are not civilized," he replied, "we shall fight them as we must."

Alexa listened to the song. As they must. As Arktos had. As she herself had done.

Kynan struck a discord so abruptly that Alexa's head shot up in surprise. She was in time to see Olwen go pale. She swallowed hard, one hand going to her belly, the other to her back, as she too often did these days. The white bear growled.

Hoofbeats, sharp in the cold wet air, but somehow uneven,

unsure . . . the Queen levered herself to her feet and waved off Alexa's offered arm. She all but ran outside.

The usual crowd of farmers, craftsmen, and children thronged the area outside the Queen's Hall. But there was nothing usual about their silence, or about the way that the bay horse . . . Rhodri's bay horse . . . thin and scarred of side now, stood trembling, pink, ropy froth dripping from its jaws. Or the body lashed across its heaving back. The cold had preserved it. Purplish rivulets of frozen blood bound it a second time to the worn-out horse. Even as men cut the ropes that held Rhodri to the horse's back, the beast collapsed.

The white bear growled again, then reared to its full height and brandished sharp-clawed paws.

"Don't look!" Gereint swung his cloak over the body, but not before Alexa saw frozen meat and a terrible gleam of bone, like the wings of a grisly eagle. In the instant that Bodb started a keening wail, Alexa flung herself between the sight and the shining Queen. But Olwen, taller than she, had seen already.

"My Goddess!" Olwen screamed. Her eyes rolled back. Then she doubled over and fell to her knees.

Overhead, ravens shrieked and dived toward Bodb where she knelt, her face turned up to the sky. Her strong hands tore at her clothing and bared her breasts. The ravens swooped down. Three circled the white bear, which batted them off, crushing two, broken-winged, into the snow. More flew toward the dead man, and Gereint drew his sword to beat them off.

"Do not touch them!" Bodb shouted hoarsely. "They will avenge us, avenge my poor brother . . ." she drew the last word out until it was almost a howl.

Ravens tried to peck at another warrior's face, and he too raised his blade. Before he knew, Bodb was upon him. She tore the blade from his grasp and brandished it so that the sharp iron whined in the cold air. "Who rides with me?" she cried.

"Stop it!" shouted Gereint.

Bodb's face twisted. *"Galanas,"* she hissed. "We of the Deceangli swear feud against these Jomsborgers."

"We cannot fight them," protested Kynan. "Not now, not until spring when the other tribes will aid us."

"What will they aid?" cried Bodb. "A land of men who look like *that?* Or her?" She gestured at the ruin of her brother's body, then the Queen, who twisted and moaned as Alexa and Kynan tried to make her stand. "Ride with me!"

It seemed as if no one would be left, Alexa thought, as the tide of blood-maddened tribesmen fled past her toward their homes and the stables for weapons and mounts.

"No . . ." Olwen whispered. "Not to fight." She gasped, then struggled onto one knee. "Not without help."

"Let me stop them," Gereint begged. Tears streaked his handsome face. "I can take my men, ride behind them until they cool off, then bring them back."

Olwen shook her head and winced. "My . . . chariot," she said. "Bring it."

"You must sleep now. You cannot ride like this," Gildas told her. "What if you miscarry? Bodb is your heir until the child is born. Is that what you want?"

"What is an heir without a land?" Olwen whispered. "Or me . . ." she sobbed convulsively. Then, as loudly as Bodb had screamed before, "Bring me my chariot!"

"Could we drug her?" Alexa asked over Olwen's bright hair. The flower scent seemed fainter and tainted.

Gildas shook her head. "Arm her. Let her ride. Soon, she will need to rest, and may forget this frenzy."

Olwen leaned on Alexa, then rose to her feet, breathing deeply, heavily, as women brought her a cloak lined with wolfskin, the Queen's torque, and the wrought metal belt from which her dagger hung in its black scabbard. Unable to fasten it, she hung it over her shoulder. Then, leaning on her spear, she struggled up into her chariot. Her drive cast a despairing look at the Druid and Alexa.

"Drive gently," she whispered.

"No!" Olwen ordered fiercely. "I must catch them. Faster!" she screamed at the driver.

Moments later, Alexa stood alone in the maenol. Gereint had taken his closest friends to trail Bodb's army. Gildas and two other men carried Rhodri's body to the shrine.

Now what? she asked herself. It seemed as if all the Celtoi had gone mad at once. Now what? *Now I too must do some-thing. It will probably be the wrong thing to do. But it will be something.* She was thinking like a Celt (horrible thought!). What was it Strabo had said, besides praising their courage? "The whole race is madly fond of war, high-spirited and quick to battle, but otherwise straightforward and not of evil charac-ter. And so when they are stirred up, they assemble in their bands for battle, quite openly and without forethought, so that they are easily handled by those who desire to outwit them."

To outwit them. Yes. Alexa could do that, or try.

Women clustered about the Queen's hall, children hiding in their skirts. Alexa stalked toward them. Not one of them was less than a head taller than she.

"How many of you," she demanded in her most imperious Celtic, "can use a sword or spear?" Almost all could. The others were either pregnant or old.

"Good! You will guard the maenol. The rest of you—" she took a deep breath, trying to order her thoughts as effectively as she was bullying these women, "boil water, fat, cooking oil . . . oh, anything. If anyone comes, you can pour it down on them." The old women cackled at the idea. *Gods,* Alexa thought.

She strode inside the hall, hunting for thick boots, a warm cloak. She had seen some furs . . . a whine made her spin around. The white bear she had raised crouched outside. She knew she had needed fur. Not just fur, however, but a beast: a white bear to counter the black beasts of Jomsborg; a bear such as Audun gave rulers sworn to protect their lands.

"You come with me," she whispered at the bear, as it butted against her. "No, don't knock me over." Cloak, dried meat and meal, a packet of herbs and cloth, knife, short-stabbing spears (not that she would ever be able to use them): she snatched them up and ran for the horses. She had seen them saddled often enough to have an idea of how to do it herself; she used a nearby rock as a platform to climb into the flat saddle. The stirrups were hopelessly long. She hoisted her skirts up over her legs so she could grip the horse's barrel with knees and thighs, then rode off, the bear padding at the horse's side.

* * *

By the time the day bled down into dusk and a spattering of fresh snow covered any tracks that might have guided her, Alexa admitted she was thoroughly lost. It disgusted her. *You are not a warrior, not a Druid, not a tracker,* she raged at herself. *You are a fool who is about to freeze to death if you do not speedily grow wise!* This was no country for a stranger to prowl about in without a guide.

Being alone, she could travel fast. But she frankly preferred to freeze rather than join Bodb's army—and she distrusted the reception that the woman would give her. Gereint's band had ridden cross-country to head Bodb off before she engaged the Jomsborgers: if she met them, they would doubtless send her back . . . with an escort they could not afford to spare. Olwen? The Queen knew the land—that is, if she were thinking at all, she knew it—and so did her charioteer. But Olwen should not be traveling without another woman, not at this time. Alexa had not liked the way the Queen had looked: the thinness of her limbs against her thickened body; the waxy skin about her mouth; the shadowed eyes. She had herbs and a woman's comfort to give, but how could she find her?

The sky grew darker and colder, and in it, the stars glittered like ice. The stars. Assuming she had managed to listen to some of Amergin's lessons, she had a guide! She oriented herself swiftly, took several deep breaths, and tried to summon a vision of the network of powers that bound this land. It quivered, frayed in some parts almost to breaking; and in one place was a great hole, as if moths had gnawed good wool. That would be the Jomsborgers' camp. The others would head toward it.

Light coursed out before her in a great straight track. She turned her horse toward it, and the bear followed. She had found herself a guide, and the bear was the best protection she could have. Perhaps she was not quite the fool she had called herself.

The moon rose, and the light it cast let her ride safely for hours longer. When she had enough strength only to topple from the saddle, cover the shivering horse warmly, and wrap herself in her cloak, Alexa stopped. Though she dared not kindle a fire, the bear pressed against her side and warmed her.

She awoke in the grayish violet light before dawn. She had always hated that light before. Now, she saw only light to hasten her journey. She fed her horse some of her grain, and tossed dried meat to the bear, lest he stray from her path to hunt. A fallen tree trunk helped her mount, and she rode all that day. No snow fell. By late afternoon, she spotted the ruts of chariot wheels and horse droppings. If she rode hard, perhaps she would camp with the Queen that night.

But somehow, Alexa missed her. Calling herself every word for imbecile that she knew in at least four languages, Alexa made camp for the night. Greatly daring, she scooped out a hollow, lined it with stones, and built a tiny fire. Time ran out, and she must have a better guide. She would need warmth while she went into trance, trying to see the people she must find. The bear whined, and she held its face between her chafed palms and ordered it to guard her. Then she scattered a meager pinch of herbs over the tiny fire, and lay beside it.

The fumes that rose from the flames made her head swim. She thought she might be sick. Then, abruptly, she was warm and composed. She stared into the flames, which bent and crackled into the semblance of a map: she seemed to look from a height at the land itself, on which motes of gleaming light wandered and clashed. There they were! For what seemed like half the night, she stared at the fiery map, memorizing it. Then, with a blow of her fist, she scattered the embers of the now-dying fire, and the pain woke her. She eased it with snow, and rode on.

The third and fourth days passed in a blur of cold and hunger. Even though she knew where she was, even though the bear guarded her day and night, she was badly frightened. Twice in one afternoon, she hid in the undergrowth and wished she had a Druid's ability to summon that lethal mist. (She even thought longingly of the Wild Hunt. Halldis would scold, but would fight for her. And as for the prince who led it! At the thought of him, Alexa felt anything but cold.) But each time she hid, staring back along her track, terrified lest

Jomsborgers spot her, she saw animals: deer once; the second time, a wolf with its cubs.

She rode through what seemed a land empty of people. She had never known such isolation before. Somewhere behind her were people guarding a fortress; somewhere in front of her were friends and enemies. She knew that, but it seemed unreal . . . so unreal that when she heard screams, she reined in and wondered, bemused, what made the noise.

Ravens whirled overhead. Ravens . . . now that she understood. Ravens circled where they found battles. Battles! "Sweet Isis, I've found them!" Alexa gasped. She checked her weapons, pulled her clothing about her tightly, and kicked the weary horse into greater speed.

On opposing ridges above a snowy field crouched cloaked Druids who shouted curses down at their enemies. They had been fairly successful. Jomsborgers in leather furs, and black bears bled and died on that field. The Celtoi stopped in their advance. In the van strode a figure cloaked in red, who flung back the cape to reveal a splendid woman's body. It was Bodb. She turned back to where her chariot awaited, and brandished a spear from which, tied by matted hair, dangled a head. Her warriors cheered.

The wind blew and flung Bodb's words into the brush where Alexa crouched, hand on a spear. "She sent my brother to his death . . . cannot, no, will not fight . . . should make a satire . . . let her die here or pass within the nemet . . . proclaim the next heir Queen." Bodb flourished her spear with its gory prize again, and the warriors clashed their weapons against their shields.

"Go back!" Gereint's clear voice rang in the air, as powerful as the beast-headed carnyx that one man carried. "More of the damned shape-changers are headed this way!"

He must have heard Bodb's plan to make herself queen. He must have. Yet his first thought was not to protect her crown, but her people. Bodb gestured, and her chariot rolled toward him. Though the treacherous wind devoured their words, Alexa knew that they spoke and that their words caught fire. Bodb screamed and then, to Alexa's horror, she lowered her spear and flung it at Gereint.

Overburdened by the dripping head, it fell short, of course. But in that moment, and as the two bands of warriors paused, appalled, Alexa saw a flash of wheels and a gleam of golden braids. Bodb whirled in her chariot, and snatched up a second spear. Though usually warriors dismounted to fight, she gestured fiercely at her charioteer, commanding him forward, against—

"Olwen!" Alexa cried, and started forward. Bodb's charioteer gestured back at his lady. Surely, that was a refusal, for her spear thrust forward, and the man fell onto the snow, his blood steaming in the cold.

Now Alexa saw that Olwen drove unarmed and alone. She rode forward in her chariot, thinly clad, displaying herself to friends and enemies alike. "Go on, brother!" Alexa urged the bear. "Save her!" The beast whined at her. "No! I'm not your mistress," she told it. "I raised you, but you belong to the Queen. Help her!"

The bear lumbered downslope, its powerful hindquarters bunching, building up speed with every stride. Bodb screamed at her horses for greater speed. Now, she drove straight at Olwen, her spear leveled to impale her.

"Bodb!" Alexa shrieked hoarsely, and kicked her horse into a gallop. Sweet Isis grant she could stay mounted *and* grasp this accursed spear long enough to distract the madwoman while the bear—Bodb's damned ravens dived down at her, pecking at her eyes, and she buried her face in the horse's mane.

Olwen, posed shakily in her chariot, turned toward her and saw Bodb. Her mouth firmed, and she halted her horses. Closer and closer Bodb came. Her spear was leveled, her eyes were wild. Gereint galloped toward the women, screaming like a Druid himself, but he would never reach them in time to save his sister, who threw back her cloak, proudly exposing her swollen belly to her people and to the woman who wanted to rule them.

"Stop her!" Alexa screamed in despair. Her horse stumbled but recovered. Alexa dropped her spear, and reached for her dagger, useless as it probably was. She would never reach Bodb in time.

Then like an avalanche, a rush of white roared up at the woman and caught her in a fierce embrace. Her death shriek rang out, then was muffled. The sharp sound of splintering bones rang out in the cold, clear air, and the white fur of the bear's chest and massive forepaws reddened.

Then it screamed too, and fell, pierced by four spears at once.

Tears poured down Alexa's face. But she had reached the center of the field now. Deliberately, she drew up in front of Olwen's chariot. The Queen swayed, then caught herself with one hand against the chariot's rim. She looked dazed and sick. All the blood had drained from her face.

"*Galanas!*" Alexa cursed as she heard Bodb's tribesmen raise the howl for blood feud. Then Gereint rode to her side.

"What are you . . . ?"

No time to explain herself now: there was a feud to stop! "By all means kill your enemies!" Alexa screamed. "A bear killed Bodb. And the sign of Jomsborg is the black bear! Kill them all!"

"There they are!" Gereint stood in his stirrups and gestured with a spear. Black bears growled and shambled over the ridge. Alexa gasped for breath again, and pressed her hand against her heaving ribs. Runnels of sweat poured down her sides and stung in her eyes.

"I'll let them," Gereint said. His face wavered in and out of focus. Now he was young and handsome, now older, battered, looking much like Audun . . . *or the man he must have been once, lifetimes ago*. He glanced over at the dead white bear and his face twisted with grief. "Sister?"

Olwen turned slowly, trying to bring her attention to bear. "Alexa, you get the Queen off the field. Hide somewhere with her. I swear I will find you or may the . . ."

"The sky won't need to fall on you, or the sea drown you if you don't start fighting!" Alexa told him. She leapt from her horse onto Olwen's chariot and snatched the reins from the Queen's lax hands. They were very cold. Once, years ago, her brother had adjusted Alexa's hands on the reins of his own team (and just before she could drive, the officer assigned to watch him had caught up with him). She breathed a quick prayer that the beasts were well-trained, and turned them back toward the underbrush. For a miracle, her own horse trailed them.

"We should move away from the chariot," she said to Olwen. "Can you walk?" Her own sides were heaving, and she thought she might faint. But Olwen, who did not answer her, was a worse case. "I didn't follow you here and bring you off the field to lose you now," Alexa muttered. "Forgive me, sister." She brought up a chilblained hand and slapped Olwen across the face.

"My white bear," Olwen spoke. "It died. A terrible omen. Rhodri died." Agony stitched itself across her face, and her eyes rolled up. A spasm rippled across her belly, and Olwen fell to her knees. "I should die too."

Alexa ripped off her cloak, wrapped it about the Queen, who writhed now in a terrible parody of labor pains. She knelt by her, thinking frantically of fires and hot water and herbs to staunch the bleeding, then put all of them out of her head to grasp Olwen's hands.

"The baby?" Olwen finally met Alexa's eyes, her attention as faint as that of a dying woman.

She shook her head. "I promise I'll try my best to help you." Then inspiration struck her. "Can you heal yourself the way you healed me?"

Olwen arched her body and bit her lip to stifle a scream, then fell back. Alexa smelled sweat and withered leaves. "Not this. My child's dead. Barren. I should be dead too, and the crown pass to the next heir." She reached for the knife belt draped over one arm, but Alexa flung it out of reach. "Blood. One way or the other, the land needs my blood."

Alexa fumbled flint and tinder from her pouch and scrabbled for loose, dry brush. Tears put out the first sparks; the second ones caught. At least Olwen would be warm. She brushed matted hair out of her face, and seized a leather bag. If she were very, very fortunate, she could melt snow, and steep herbs in it. She tried to remember every word she had ever heard from the Aescir women about childbearing lest she lose Olwen along with the child.

Chapter 13

☆

Alexa wiped her bloody hands on her cloak, then laid one on Olwen's brow, too white under straggling ruddy hair and smudges. At the last, as the child thrust forth, she had finally fainted. Alexa gagged, then shrouded the tiny body in linen torn from her undershift. She tramped away from the unconscious Queen and grubbed out brush and rock under which to lay the child. It should have been a daughter, and Olwen's heir.

For the first time in hours, the scream and clash of battle reached her, fainter now, as if during the battle she had waged for Olwen's life, one side had gained the advantage. Alexa crouched lower and held her breath, listening. She darted a glance over toward the cloak-wrapped bundle that hid the Queen.

The underbrush crackled and rustled under booted feet. She had been stupid to think she could hide herself and Olwen. Anyone could smell the blood shed here. Wild energy crackled along the nerves in her fingertips, tempting her. Surely, just this once, if she hurled the burning at the Jomsborgers, she would be forgiven. Wouldn't she? Olwen had accepted her, cherished her—but if the burning consumed this underbrush along with the Jomsborgers she wanted to destroy, Olwen too would die at her hands.

Drawing her dagger, Alexa raced back to the Queen. The underbrush tore and crackled underfoot, betraying her approach, but she did not care. Perhaps she could draw off the men, the enemies who approached.

But one man already knelt at Olwen's side, and he had his hands out to touch her. Knife out, Alexa flung herself forward . . .

. . . and found herself caught, trapped in strong arms. She writhed and bit, trying to kick her way free, but the arms were too strong. "Sweet Goddess, just look at her. Like a wood-wose or something out of the hollow hills!"

"Light a fire, or we'll have every wolf for miles here." Another voice. *No fire,* Alexa whimpered, but only creaking sounds came out.

"Where's the . . ."

"I'll wager she buried it. Why else do you think she would have left the Queen's side?"

"Talk to her, Prince. Make sure she knows she is safe now, and that we will get her and the Queen home."

"Alexa . . ." The hands holding her did not release their grip, but they gentled and held her at arm's length. "They're gone for now. We won. You're safe."

She tried to divert all her strength to her knife-hand. "Someone take this from her," ordered her captor. Strong fingers pried her fingers apart. She whined with pain and hated herself for it.

Then she felt herself drawn close, held against someone's shoulder while he stroked her hair and murmured of safety over and over again.

Gradually the words and the warmth and arms made sense. Not Jomsborgers, then. Not an enemy. She raised her head. "Gereint?"

"Aye." His face was streaked; grime and clean spots smeared across the blue of his war markings.

Her own tears came then, but she blinked them away, and tried to push free of the man who held her. "Olwen . . ."

"A healer rides with my men," Gereint said. "Praise the Goddess, my sister will live."

"You did well," the healer turned on his knees and looked up at Alexa. "She would have died without you."

Then they were in safe hands For this moment, no black bears stalked her and her sister-friend. Alexa shivered and felt Gereint's big hands rub down her back. "She won't stop shaking," he muttered. The healer rose and laid a hand on her cheek, turning her so she had no choice but to look into his eyes, darker than the forest depths.

"Your part of this is finished. Let it go now. Rest, like flowers under snow. Weep if you must. Then sleep, like, your sister."

Tears ran down her cheeks and might have frozen there if Gereint had not wiped them away. She knew when someone wrapped her in warm furs and laid her down beside the Queen.

Olwen's eyes flickered open. "A girl-child?" she rasped.

Alexa closed her eyes in pain. The blood in her temples throbbed, drowning out Gereint's answer, but not Olwen's exhausted sobs.

"They say you will bear other children," she whispered, but the Queen shook her head.

"You cannot have two springs in the same year," said the Queen. "Or restore apple blossoms withered by a frost."

"Both of you, rest!" ordered the healer. "Or, may the Goddess strike me if I lie, I shall brew such a potion for you that neither of you will wake until you are in your own beds."

A yawn threatened to crack Alexa's skull. She opened her mouth, and found a hot, steaming drink held against her mouth until the beaker pinched her lips.

"Is this your potion?" she asked. "I could sleep that long without it."

"No potion," said the healer. "Just something warm for you."

Three gulps warmed her belly. Then the rest spilled over slack lips.

Did he lie to me? she mused in the warm darkness beneath her eyelids.

No, it told her. *This is Penllyn. This is Prydein. No one will lie to you here.* The darkness was very comforting, and she let it sweep her away.

Alexa's strength returned fast that winter. There was even one week when she bet Gereint she could eat as much as a warrior—and did.

"You almost starved," he told her ruefully. "So you must gain weight. If a warrior gains that much weight, we fine him until he fits back into his belt again." He handed over the armlet that he had lost, and she slipped it onto her right arm. The wrist was still bruised from where one of Gereint's warriors had wrenched it when he took away her knife.

The prince stared down at the bruise. "It seems I owe you my apologies as well as a knife to replace the one I made you drop," he said.

A knife. That forced Alexa's thoughts again to the blade that Olwen kept beside her even now. Metal. Sharp and glittering and harsh. Halfway back to Penllyn, childbed fever had almost killed Olwen. She raved until her voice failed about hawthorn and death, and her words had sent all of the men, and most of the women, rapidly out of hearing. Once they were alone, she offered Alexa the black blade of her queenship. "Amergin will bring it to you once I pass within the nemet," Olwen whispered. "Promise me to wield it well."

Alexa was kin here by courtesy, only by courtesy. She had no wish to be Queen, here or anywhere. Olwen would heal, she would rise, gain strength . . . over and over, Alexa murmured those words and thousands like them to Olwen until she found her own mumbling waking herself from uneasy sleep. She was profoundly relieved when the healer-Druid forced her out of Olwen's shelter at night and took over her care.

Though Alexa healed quickly. Olwen mended slowly. By the time days and nights grew to equal length, she sat upright and walked short distances, her movements unsteady as a crone's where once they had been lithe. Her body seemed to droop, and her golden hair hung flat and lifeless down a back that looked to frail for her height. The scent of flowers that always clung to her flesh seemed dried, autumnal now. Though Olwen said little about it, Alexa knew that her monthly courses were slow to resume.

I do not want to be Queen. That much was true. But if Olwen could not peform her duties, someone must; and Bodb was dead. Still, as Olwen grew stronger, Alexa gladly gave back her tasks. Once again, Olwen heard her council, and rendered judgments. The familiar duties steadied her, and she gained weight and confidence. But the scent of bruised flowers never left her and, Alexa noticed, she never attempted the sort of healing once wrought on her to cure the raven's bite. Before her miscarriage, Olwen had been innocent and joyous; and Alexa had loved her for it. Now . . . she feigned cheerfulness for any small progress Olwen did make, and returned to her lessons with the ArchDruid. As if she had passed beyond some barrier of fear or despair, she now learned quickly and well. Amergin began to talk of her initiation at Beltane as if it were a settled thing.

Beltane: there was much to do before then: weapons to ready, nearby allies to coax, and far-off ones to warn. Alexa herself wrote the message to be sent to Audun; and she wept when she told him how the white bear had sacrificed its life to save a queen. Flocks and fields were less than fertile that spring; and many of the flowering plants were blighted.

The pace of her training quickened, absorbing first her waking hours, and then even her dreams. She even slept in the Druids' precincts, much as their youngest students did, as their elders weaned them from their families. What was she being weaned from? Power? Olwen's need for her help, a need that might, in time, cripple the ailing Queen? Alexa had no idea. She had needed training; she had found it: it was enough. Had it not been for Olwen's weakness, she would have been content.

Each day, dawn came a little earlier. Though Amergin pressed her hard, Alexa rose willingly each dawn and found herself thriving under the discipline. She could not remember having felt so well since she was a child. Her happiest time in Staraja Ladoga was a holiday, she decided; this was—or could become—a life.

One morning, she woke smiling. Her body felt supple, light, and new again. She remembered that day. A week later, Amergin brought her word that Irene was dead, and her brother wore the Double Crown of Empire.

"You could go home, you know," said the ArchDruid.

"My home is here now," she insisted. She thought of Marric, her brother, ruling in Byzantium, the place beside him empty. She felt brief shame: she had not deserved to fill it. Now, when, perhaps, she might have been worthy, she knew that it was not her place, and no longer her choice. "If I am shirking any task that is rightfully mine, I will pay for it," she told Amergin. "But I cannot return there. Not while Olwen is ill, not Jomsborg survives: probably not ever. I offended it too greatly."

"And what if he—your brother—comes to claim you?"

Alexa laughed long and merrily. "I will worry about that when I see him. We do not even know if I will survive initiation," she told the ArchDruid. She would enter the tomb beneath the *gorsedd*, and be sealed within. She didn't know which made her more afraid; entry into the chill, dark tomb, or the sight of her brother, his strong hands outstretched to claim hers.

"I know," said Amergin. "But you must know too."

What Alexa should have known, she grumbled later, was not to take her fears to the ArchDruid. Amergin ordered her to spend the nights before Beltane in meditation beside the chalybeate pool near the *gorsedd* itself. If she were in truth a seeress, rather than gifted only with scraps of power like a grandam with the Sight, then she must see clearly.

But even this late in the spring, the highland nights were chilly. She had only her white robe to warm her, and the spring winds were brisk. Alexa sighed, then turned her face up to the moon that had waxed to fullness during the nights of her meditation, and shivered in the silver, achingly pure light. The moon's disk was huge, and the clarity of the mountain air made it seem very close. As above; so below: the moon reflected in the Water of Vision was huger and closer yet.

On such a night, Alexa thought, Isis had walked up and down at the Horizon, seen the moon, and, being female, coveted it for a jewel. Being a goddess, she could stretch out her hand and take it. A little drunk from nights without sleep and meditations as labyrinthine and strange-formed as the goldwork that Celtoi loved, Alexa stretched out her hand . . . and sent ripples flowing out the width of the Water of Seeing, pale as hammered silver. She brought her hand up dripping with the water, which seemed to glow in the doubled moonlight, and splashed the droplets over her face. To her astonishment, the water felt warm. Again, she dipped her hand in the pool, and the ripples danced. In the water cupped by her hand trembled a tiny moon. She laughed and drank it.

"I have drunk the moon!" she boasted to the night sky.

Earth and air quivered like harp strings plucked in a dancing tune she could not resist. Her dance drew her around and around the pool until she sank down, gasping for breath, and a thirst too great to slake by dipping her hand in the pool. She crouched down and drank her fill.

The air hummed again. Surely, on such a night, the Horizon was very close. Alexa's white wool robe suddenly became far too warm. Its presence on her body was intolerable; her skin felt so sensitive that even the finest silk would scratch like bramble. She stripped off the robe and flung it to the earth.

The Water of Vision beckoned her and she slipped into the pool. Though she had never heard of anyone's bathing in it, the idea struck her not as sacrilege, but as utterly, absurdly right. The water was warm: more fragrant than heated water in a marble bath into which rose petals had been strewn; more soothing than lying on cushions and being rubbed with warm oils.

She rose from the pool. The water glistened on her skin. A night breeze made her tremble, and she brought up her hands to cup her small, high breasts with their stiffened nipples. The touch made her acutely conscious of her own flesh.

It was near Beltane. All over Penllyn, men and women would build towering fires, then, lying beside them, kindle other fires that only their bodies could slake. Alexa looked down at herself in the water. The moonlight limned her silver, like a statue of the Goddess. She was lovely, yet she was alone. Unfair, she lamented: so unfair.

Again the breeze came, as if drawn to caress her. Suddenly, she heard hoofbeats in the wind. Perhaps she need not be alone. She remembered the prince who led the Wild Hunt, and how he had looked at her. Louder and louder grew the hoofbeats. Then they stopped.

Footsteps padded toward her, avoiding the nemet, taking the path to the tiny clearing with speed and sureness. Abruptly fearful, she darted to the top of the *gorsedd* and peered out over the trees.

Dappled with moonlight and leaf-shadow, a man emerged from the shelter of the trees where no man not Druid-sworn should walk and tossed the last of his garments away behind him. Darkness hid his face, but Alexa saw horned shadows, such as antlers might make, jut from his temples. She drew a deep breath and stood proudly, waiting for him to approach.

He entered the clearing and gazed up at her, his hands rising in supplication. She was the Goddess, and he the Horned God: he wanted and needed her—and she desired him. Majestically, as if she wore the moon crown of the Goddess, she inclined her head.

And then she *was* the Goddess, welcoming Her Consort, Her brother and love as He woke after the winter's chill and came to Her to be restored. Slowly, His every movement like a dance step, He climbed the mound of the *gorsedd*, then slowly sank to His knees at Her feet and laid aside His crown. She reached out to touch His face, but He bent to lay it against Her silvery feet. Then He rose, His hands sliding over and between Her thighs until She warmed and cried out as fingers hunted out Her warmth, and He pressed a heated cheek against Her. He rose still further and cupped Her breasts as She had done just moments before. He kissed them, then embraced Her and kissed Her lips, swinging Her up in His arms so that Their mouths could join thirstily and Their hips press together.

Finally He drew back from Her opened lips. She nodded once, and He laid Her down on the pale grass that covered the *gorsedd*. As He had before, He explored with tongue, lips, and fingers until She moaned and tried to hold Him with arms and legs. Though He could not be held, He could be seduced. Carefully, He covered Her with His body and parted Her thighs; and the drunkenness of the moonlight washed over Them both, and They were One. Beneath Them, the grass that was Their bed softened, and the earth sighed and eased. The harp strings a woman had heard earlier sounded again in a sweet shrill note in the instant They cried out together, and Their bodies tensed, then went limp.

Alexa shifted under the weight of the man who embraced and filled her, his head pillowed on her breasts. She put out a languorous hand to stroke his hair. He raised his head.

"Gereint!" she whispered.

She had seen him as the Prince who led the Wild Hunt, and seen better than she had known.

"I was asleep," said Gereint, "and I dreamed of you, naked under the moon. And I thought that I would not live if I could not, at least, see you and tell you how I desire and cherish you." He bent and kissed her deeply, and she arched beneath him once again.

Then he moved away, and she whimpered as his flesh left her. Instantly, he was cradling her. "I am too heavy for you, little love, little heart. So many weeks, and I did not see you. Then the dream came and I knew I would find you here." He stroked down her side and over her thigh. There he paused, his fingers probing intimately, until he brought them up before his eyes.

"Blood?" Gereint asked. "Alexa, are you virgin?"

She flung her arms about him. "I was," she told him happily.

His face twisted guiltily. "I hurt you. Forgive me."

"You didn't hurt me," Alexa whispered it against his mouth. "I was the Goddess, and you were the God. How could that hurt?"

Gereint turned aside, leaving her body. He rose, then padded down the slope of the *gorsedd*. The water trickled from his palm back into the pool as he scooped up some and returned to her. Gently, he bathed her thighs with the Water of Vision. Again his fingers strayed, probing and rubbing high within her, and Alexa moaned.

"Do I hurt you?" he asked. She shook her head.

"Then *that* was for the gods. This," he moved above her again and pressed himself against her, "is for us."

When she woke to her senses again, she lay with her head pillowed against Gereint's heart, and the moon was near its setting.

"Did I sleep?" she asked, and felt his laughter against her cheek.

"I wish I had not," she said, and moved her hips in a rhythm that she was sure they must have invented.

Even as Gereint's body quickened, he moved aside. "I cannot be found here. You know that," he told her.

Alexa sighed. She drew one finger slowly, consideringly, down the arch of his chest. "Now what?"

"Now what? Now I return to my bed. Alone, which is a pity, And you must perform whatever tasks and rites they command of you. But once you do, Alexa; once they release you, call me to your side. Meanwhile, I shall beg the Goddess to let you conceive." He rested a hand so gentle that Alexa could not resent its possessiveness on her belly. "Then we can wed, and Penllyn will once again have an heir."

"What?" Alexa started to question him, but Gereint left her side and retrieved her robe. Lovingly, he spread its folds over her bare body, caressing her through the cloth.

"I must not be here. You have a vigil to keep, remember?" He kissed her lips lightly. "Keep it, but think of me."

Then he padded downslope and was gone. Alexa heard footsteps, an interval of silence, and finally, hoofbeats.

All the rest of that night, she lay covered by her robe, staring raptly at the arch of the sky where slowly the stars wheeled, then faded and went out as dawn drew near. Memories and dreams flickered before her opened eyes. She had no questions now, neither of the truth and power of her visions, nor the strength of her commitment to this place. When she tried to think of the weighty rocks and mounded earth of the *gorsedd* that would soon cover her over, her thoughts heated, and she saw Gereint, his fire a mate for her own, his body pressing hers against the grass. Impossible, she thought, to snuff such a flame.

Alexa stood before the *gorsedd*, facing west and squinting in the violence of the sunset. On either side of her, fanning out about the Water of Vision, stood a tall, white-robed row of Druids. Behind them, she knew, was wood and tinder. The fire would be kindled at sunset.

She knew she would not see it, for even now the ArchDruid was opening the mound, scraping away at the grass with a flint knife until it scraped and rang against stone. He signaled, and two of the youngest Druids came forward and lifted away the slab. Alexa braced herself for a gush of foul air but felt only coldness. She gazed at the entrance into the ancient tomb, then, deliberately, gazed away. The reddish sunlight of late afternoon poured down upon the barrow. The grass that covered it was greener now than it had been the day before, and strewn with tiny red and white blossoms.

Red: green: white: the brilliant oranges and scarlets of the sunlight—Alexa devoured them as if they were the last colors she would ever see. They deepened into an imperial splendor of purple and indigo, then faded into ashen tones. The sky darkened. Behind her, she heard the rush of fire kindling, and she knew by the roar someone waved a firebrand.

It was time for her to pass within, to enter the burial mound and meet whatever visions would confirm her as a seeress. Or her death. Though she would be shut away from the air, from the light, alone in the ancient blackness, she did not expect to die. Still it was best not to think of it. Amergin gestured her forward toward the pit, and Beda came forward, holding a firebrand to show the way. The ranks of Druids chanted words so old Alexa understood none of them. At the Horizon, the last ember was snuffed out.

Almost imperceptibly, Amergin nodded at her. She firmed her lips and went forward into the tomb. She had to bend double to crawl through a stone passage that led into an arched, central chamber. Beda thrust the torch in after her to show her the bends in the tunnel.

Her breathing came fast; already, she could feel the roof of that chamber press down upon her. A stone slab lay before her, and she stretched herself out on it. She had time for one frantic glance at the walls—splashed or etched with pictures of beasts—before the torch was withdrawn. She heard scraping and knew it for the stone as it was rolled back over the entrance.

Darkness. Her breath rasped in her ears, and she squeezed her eyes shut until eerie lights rolled beneath her lids. *Sweet Isis, guard me*! she whispered to walls she could not see. *Hermes, guardian of souls, guide me*. Some candidates must have failed this test. Abruptly a vivid image occupied her mind, of the stone being pried away, the Druids waiting outside, and then, reluctantly, entering the tomb to lay a cloth over the whitened hair and maddened features of the youth who had lain clawing at the pitiless stone until the air failed.

It possessed her mind with the certainty of vision, then was replaced by another tomb: her mother's, with its splendid

murals and the gilded boat in which she lay, heaped with all
the treasures that her *ka* would require in its new life at the
Horizon. She had no doubt of that, nor of the chiming sound
she heard. Was that her ears ringing as the air went bad, or the
music she had heard last night, lying in Gereint's arms?

It had to be the music. The air would last until she could
escape into trance. Abruptly, she was certain of that. She ar-
ranged herself again on the bier, and drew the rhythmic
breaths that would free spirit from flesh.

She could see now. She was floating above her body, which
seemed to possess a beauty it lacked when she was actually in
it. A transparent strand of silver still connected her to it.
There was nothing else in this place for her; it was a gateway
to a test, she understood now, not the test herself. She would
have until dawn to complete it: best to make haste. Her spirit
rose through the roof of the mound, above the waiting, chanting Druids and the brilliance of the needfire that glinted in the
Water of Vision. Similar fires rose all over Penllyn like a
garden of red blooms. Past earth, water, and air into the
sphere of flame she rose. For what seemed like hours, but
(judging from the movement of the stars in their dance) could
only have been seconds, she hesitated, remembering the burn-
ings she herself had unleashed. Then she heard the chiming
music that played eternally at the Horizon, and passed through
the flames that swayed the strands of her dark hair like a
summer breeze.

She found herself in a realm of pearl and crystalline silver.
Was this the realm of aether? Where was her test? Would she
wander here until the silver cord that linked her to her flesh
gave way? Wings beat high above her, a flash of gold, and
she followed it, quickening her "pace" to try to catch up to her
guide. It was a falcon, and it led her forward to stand before a
high platform, separated from her by a gulf. She glanced
down into that gulf and recoiled. Crocodiles and worse monsters twined in its bottomless depths. A giant balance appeared on the platform. In one cup rested a feather she knew
to be the Truth of Maat. Then the tiny figure that stood
upright in the other cup must be her soul. If feather and soul
balanced, or her soul rose up, she would be free. But if her

soul sank down, weighted by its sins, it—and she—would fall, to be gnawed by the crocodiles for eternity.

Here were no *ushabti* to plead for her. "Hear me," she began, then fell silent. She had turned against a brother; had lied; had killed—she could not speak the confession that would free her, not without lying again. The balance wavered, her soul began to sink, and over the chiming of the music came mocking laughter. She would be damned. The jackal materialized and reached for her, to draw her down, and she shrank back.

Irene had told her once that she could never escape the dark. That must be her laughing. But Irene was dead. If Alexa looked, she might even see . . . no! She had done all the things of which she was accused. But she had grieved for them, tried to atone for them, been willing to sacrifice her life to set the scales even. Men and women were alive because of her desire to try to change.

I *have* changed, she whispered to the Scales. I have.

The laughter rose up. No, that was not Irene's laughter.

It was her own, her own fears, her own hatreds, her own anger at a self who, being human, had made mistakes and made yet another by not forgiving and loving herself. Oh, she thought she had, but she had been wrong yet again.

Here I am, my soul weighing in the balance, and I am blaming myself for yet another sin! she realized. *I am not only consistent, but consistently stupid.* There was a kind of grace to her stupidity, she decided. She was so determined to atone that if damnation were the price of her expiation, she would pay it.

And that, of course, was absurd.

The scales wavered before her, and the jackal floated toward her. She caught its thought—that she was adding cowardice to her other crimes. In the instant that it caught her arm in its paw, she looked at it, looked at the scales, and laughed.

Laughed for her own folly, for her strength, and the wonderful, ridiculous stubbornness that was simultaneously her curse and her salvation; laughed with joy at the strength of the love that had let her redeem herself.

The jackal vanished. In the scales before her, the feather

and her soul quivered, then poised: of equal weight and value. Then they disappeared.

She was back in the sphere of aether, the hawk flapping overhead. She glanced down, and obligingly, the "floor" cleared, and she could see the stars far below. The tiny fires that marked Penllyn burned brightly, but the moon had set. Time to complete this test and return, she thought. She looked up at the hawk. *Now what?*

It turned and flew in a different direction, so quickly that Alexa could not track it.

What I need, she thought ironically (laughing at herself for the excellent absurdity of irony at the Horizon), *is a better guide.*

Perhaps I could serve, came a gentle voice, soothing as spring water.

Alexa turned and saw a tall woman, somewhat older than she, if she could assume age counted for aught here, who held out a long-fingered hand in which she held a red, red rose. She smiled at Alexa, her blue eyes and gentle face kindling with it. Alexa found herself smiling back.

I would be grateful, she thought at the newcomer. *I am Alexa.*

I know who you are. I have been waiting for you, the woman told her. *Now you have come to me, and I am so glad!*

The woman seemed to shine with the joy of it. Even her coronet of silvery braids took on a brighter luster. No one had ever been so purely glad of Alexa before. She moved forward impulsively.

Who are you?

The woman shook her head. No name, then? For some people—or spirits, apparently—names were too precious to be given out. Alexa spread out her hands in a gesture of apology.

Your sister. Your friend. Your guide, if you will have me.

Now it was Alexa's turn to glow. *Yes!*

Her guide turned and led her out of the realm of aether, and Alexa gasped at the splendor revealed. The stars below were only twinkling points: paste gems as compared to the stars that bloomed here in the true heavens. The music Alexa had heard the night before was but a tinny echo of the hymn that rose into almost a shout of joy. And above the stars, shone a light that drew her . . . it was the Goddess Herself! If only Alexa had the strength to leap over those stars, she might be able to hurl herself into the Goddess's arms. She had to try.

Wait!

Abruptly she was plummeting, batted away from that light with a casual strength that robbed her of breath, and almost of what passed for life here. But her guide launched herself upward, effortlessly catching her and steadying her. Alexa caught the scent of roses, heard the woman's gentle laughter.

I failed.

Did you? Those heights are reserved for perfected spirits. Are you such a one, sister?

Alexa shook her head.

No need to be downcast, the woman said, shaking her head at Alexa and looking at her affectionately. *I am not such a one either, even though they say I have passed beyond the need for a body.*

Not this time, Alexa mused. *I know what I did. Because of it, I have to forgo the full power this time. That is just.*

The taller woman smiled, and Alexa knew that she had read her thoughts.

When I had a body, I too was a seeress. Now I shall guide your visions. Call on me when you need me. She started to drift off.

Wait! She had so many questions she needed to ask.

The woman shook her crowned head and pointed to where the sun began its slow climb above the Horizon in the east.

You must return now. Let yourself be drawn back, Alexa, sister. Farewell, but only for now.

Her voice grew very faint, and then was gone. Alexa became aware of the tug of the gleaming cord that joined her soul and her body. As long as it was unbroken, it would draw her back to her body where it rested beneath the *gorsedd*. She had to go back, she realized. The joy in her had to be shared with the Druids who had trained her. And with Gereint and Olwen. Gereint loved her and Olwen—perhaps she could return to the Queen some of the faith and trust that Olwen had lavished upon her.

She was sinking through the spheres. Now she could scent the dawn air. Her body lay before her, she had reunited with it, and she exulted in the warmth, the tingling, of flesh and blood. All around her was darkness, but it was the darkness before birth, not of annihilation. She drew a shallow breath of the close, stale air and wondered how far away dawn was. Ahead of her she heard scraping.

The Druids were drawing back the stone! she realized. Alexa rose to her feet, astonished at her body's suppleness after a night spent flat on a slab of rock. Brilliant light flooded through the narrow passage into the round chamber. Alexa bent and climbed back into the light.

She had expected to be blinded, but after the brilliance she remembered, mere dawn light was bearable. It was Amergin himself who stepped back, averting his eyes from her face, even as he held out a hand to her and drew her from the mound.

"Who are you?" he asked solemnly.

There were words she should say now, words and gestures that she had been schooled to recall. Other words, drawn from her own heritage, leapt to her tongue instead. "I am the lady who sheddeth light in darkness. I have come to give forth light in darkness, and lo! All is lightened and made bright. I have illumined the blackness and have overthrown the destroyers. I have made obeisance unto those who are in darkness, and I have raised up those who wept and who had hidden their faces and sunk down."

Deep within herself, she felt her silvery-haired guide smile.

Omitting his own ritual response, Amergin drew Alexa into a formal embrace before he conducted her from the *gorsedd* out to where a crowd of people waited. She caught a flash of bronze and her heart leapt, for bronze was the color of her lover's hair.

"But what is this?" asked Amergin, looking down at Alexa's hand, where it rested in his own.

She stared down in amazement at a full-blown red rose on which dew glistened. Then the people waiting to hear of her life or death caught sight of her. They cheered, and, breaking custom, Gereint ran toward her like a boy, not a warrior and prince. Laughing with relief, he caught her up in his arms and carried her to where the Queen sat. Alexa placed the rose in her hand, and Olwen smiled.

PART II

☆　　☆　　☆　　☆　　☆　　☆　　☆

The
EMPEROR

Chapter 14

☆

Thick black smoke roiled above the trees and disturbed the great hawk in its lazy circles. It swooped away, and soon became only a speck against the summer sky. The man hailed variously as Lord of the Two Lands, Autokrator, and Great Horus, but who thought of himself as the fighting Emperor Marric, reined in and signaled to his Hetaeria guardsmen. As the command to halt rang back from the cavalry banda to their baggage trains, the honor guard ahead of him halted too, then turned as if to meet someone. The Varangians nearest him tensed and reached for their great axes.

Marric, standing in his stirrups, braced himself against his lance, the ten-foot kontos used by all cavalry, and shook his head. "That should be scouts, not bandits," he reminded his men. "Have them report to me with their officers."

A town lay up ahead. Its original citizens had intermarried with the natives generations ago, but it still was one of the few places this far west that remembered its old allegiance to the Empire, even in the teeth of the Jomsborg fortress down the coast. Months before, he had sent word ordering ships prepared for his journey west. Had the town been burned for its obedience?

With luck, the scouts would not be too overawed at the presence of their Emperor to speak clearly, he thought. He stretched, shrugging his shoulders under the heavy scales of his armor and padded garments, testing his strength as he did every day since he had recovered from a beating in Alexandria that would have killed anyone less bent on surviving to regain a throne. The lash had bit deeply, and he was scarred. To the end of his life, he knew that he would test himself, to protect him against some betrayal by his flesh of the Empire he now lived only to serve.

Today brought another reprieve: no pain, apart from the usual aches and saddle-galls that any soldier learned to discount. He glanced downslope toward what should have been the friendly lowlands of what even now, a thousand years after the Caesar who had been Divine Cleopatra's first husband, the Empire still called Gallia Belgica and which held, however precariously, to its imperial loyalty. Which was more, he thought with the usual glowering anger, than he could say of the lands through which he had ridden. Formerly, they had been imperial themes, but they were gone now, picked off during Irene's Interregnum.

At some point, he promised himself, Thracia and Dardania would once again prostrate themselves at Byzantium's throne. But not now. The Persians were quiet now or as quiet as that race of traitors and spies ever got, and the Arab pirates who had grown wealthy off Byzantine shipping were either dead or licking their wounds. This year, for the first time since he had won his father's throne back from the witch, he had won peace—for his Empire, if not for himself. Though some of his patricians thought this might be a good time for reconquering the lost themes, he preferred to ride through them on the way to the Western Isles. He could reconnoiter now. Time enough to reconquer after he had reclaimed his sister and made her Empress and his bride.

Go quickly, if you go at all, Audun Bearmaster had told him once. It had taken him two years of fighting to bring the City to health enough that it could be entrusted to Caius Marcellinus, his regent, and ride west. Thus, much as it galled him, he had asked leave and safe-conduct of the various Avar and Bulgar kinglets who cluttered highlands and the Danube valley alike. Audun was one of the few men alive whom he trusted enough to postpone reconquest and follow such advice.

Marric ran a finger along the mail draped in a cowl at his throat and cast an eye back along the line of his army, the ten thousand or so Hetaeria and cavalry who had ridden out from Byzantium, and the troops he had acquired along the way. The banners of each moira, or thousand men, flourished at jaunty

angles; no officers had allowed the men to fall out. Safe-conduct through Avar country could be no safe-conduct at all: the
men who were incautious had died early that spring.

The smoke ahead was growing thicker. That was no fire set
by lightning in a dry wood. The spring had been wet, and, in
any case, the smoke was black and heavy, the kind of smoke
you got when you fired an oil supply.

What was keeping the scouts? Set take them, they were
light-armed so they could move with haste! Marric would
have liked to spur his horse toward the cluster of slow-moving
men who struggled uphill, but he controlled himself. He was
general and Emperor. He could not afford to chafe at delays,
to display impatience toward his men, or to let them think that
anything might take him by surprise. And above all, he
thought with a grimace, he dared do nothing that would de-
prive his men of their leader. He cursed under his breath in
four languages. The man nearest him, a blond Northerner,
heard him and grinned with delighted respect.

Marric grinned back and felt the muscles along the back of
his neck relax somewhat. He had always been more comfortable on campaign (even if his army seemed half baggage train
and that half, so richly laden that it was a dangerous impediment to safe passage) than in a palace; and he was more comfortable with men considered barbarians than most Byzantines
would have said he had a right to be. If, of course, he gave
them that chance—which, as Emperor, he need not.

Blowing heavily, their heads hanging down to their knees,
his scouts' horses toiled uphill toward him. One stumbled to
its knees. That decided Marric. He held up a hand, and started
toward the scouts. Three men were wounded, and two rode
double. One saddle was empty, and Marric thinned his lips.
The rest of his scouts and the foragers, weapons drawn,
formed a wary circle around two men—mounted on horses
that belonged to other scouts (damn! that was two more dead)
who did not wear the heavy cloaks and armor of the armies.
Both were battered and leaning against one another for support.

They were tall enough and light-haired enough to have been
one of the Varangian guardsmen. But their hair, worn in the
braids of Aescir freemen, was darkened and slimed with

blood. The guardsman nearest Marric growled; he too was
Aescir, and all of them regarded one another as some type of
kin. As the younger of the two slumped into a faint, Marric
swung down from his horse, shouldered past a scout, and
caught him.

"Get the medical corpsmen!" Marric ordered as he swung
down from his horse. Two axmen and aides scrambled to keep
even with him. "Call my surgeon, too."

Now that they saw their Emperor in action, the scouts
moved to ease the older man to the ground too, loosen his
clothing, and unwind the hacked and stained cloak from his
left arm.

"What is it?" Marric demanded. He reached out a hand to
shake him by the right shoulder, then thought better of it.

Even as those nearest him muttered that the Aescir should
speak up, and answer the Emperor, the man moaned. Gently,
Marric laid a hand on his shoulder. Then he recoiled, staring
at the hand that had touched the Aescir as if it were tainted.

"This stinks of sorcery," he spat.

The Aescir shook his head. "Not sorcery, friend. *Seithr*.
The blackest, damnedest evil." At a gesture, Marric's guardsmen, about to resent the merchant's calling their emperor
"friend," fell back.

"Is it Jomsborgers?" Marric asked. Out of the corner of his
eye, he saw his surgeon kneel beside the younger man and
shake his head, then call for fire and water.

The elder merchant saw the surgeon's gesture and his face
paled under the grime and blood. "Jomsborgers, aye. They
came a month back and offered to buy ships—your ships,
Majesty!" He looked at Marric accusingly. "Claiming loyalty
to the Empire, the shipwrights refused to sell. So two nights
back, they came back to take or burn what they could not
by . . ."

"Easy, lad, easy, easy," the surgeon's sure voice interrupted
as the man he tended writhed. "If I don't burn that wound . . ."

Marric and the Aescir merchant both shuddered.

"Jomsborgers," groaned the man. "Like at Birka. The black
bears . . . they come in the night . . ."

Black magic and bears. Audun had warned Marric that he
had no power over Jomsborg and its pirate-jarl Grettir. Worse

yet: during the Interregnum, Irene had made overtures to the man. That meant that now he saw Byzantium and its allies as easy picking.

"Help me hold him!" snapped the surgeon. Emperor though he was, Marric leapt to obey as quickly as the youth's kinsman. Hands on his shoulders, Marric tried to will strength into the wounded man. *You are none of mine, but I would heal you,* he thought. A man could be drawn back from death if there was will enough to hold him. He met the merchant's eyes, and saw his own pain reflected there.

The surgeon drew the iron from the fire. Marric nodded and tightened his grip. "Not long now, lad," he whispered, carefully gentle, and looked away as he heard flesh hiss and smelled the stink of the cautery.

The youth screamed and thrashed, pulling one arm free before he fell back.

The priest-surgeon covered the youth's face with his bloody cloak. Marric laid his hand again on the uncle's shoulder, willing himself to accept closeness to the taint of magic.

"My sister's son," whispered the Aescir. "He went back . . . there were women, children he helped escape, but . . . the bears mauled him."

"We will help you avenge him," he said, and the surviving man sobbed.

Marric got to his feet. "See to his wounds," he ordered the surgeon. He walked away from the stink of fire and seared flesh and death, his embarrassed guards trailing him. He sniffed the air. The sun of late afternoon blinded him, and he shut his eyes, then sniffed again. Blood and sweat, horses, leather, and the green smells of the woods: those he expected. But dark and shadowy as the smoke was the smell he had learned to fear: magic, and magic, at that, born of dark power.

"Make camp," he ordered. It was early to make camp yet, and the army would be surprised: easy was not a word they used to describe Marric's discipline but he knew something they did not. "Black bears," his men called the Jomsborgers, because of the sigils painted on their sails and shields and the shaggy black hair that distinguished them from their cousins of the Aescir. They were vicious fighters, to be avoided until an army had all the advantages on its side. And one of those

advantages was daylight. Marric had no desire to pass the
night in a forest where skin changers and Isis knew what other
sort of evil magic roved.

"One more thing. Have the Osiris priests ward the camp."

He walked back to where the surgeon still knelt and shook
the surviving Aescir gently. "The town is gone, then."
Sacked, for trying to aid me, he thought, but did not say.
Spies had brought him news of the Jomsborg raid on Birka,
once a prosperous trading post, now a frozen charnel house.
This last outpost of the Empire would be another such grave-
yard. *No, it won't!* he vowed. *It is my town.* First he would
see to its refugees. Then he would help them rebuild, he decided, just as a junior officer ventured to speak.

"Majesty, shall we send out quartering parties to bring in
any survivors?"

Several hours remained until dusk. "Good man!" Marric
nodded at the man. "Not these men, however. They have
served us . . . served *me* well today." Wounded and tired as
they were, the scouts glowed at the praise and tried to hold
themselves proudly. "Choose fresh men. Make sure they have
torches, in case they find themselves slowed down. Yes, and
pass the word for the priests of Ares-Montu to go with them."

The entire army was priest-ridden. They might as well earn
their keep, Marric thought sardonically. He wouldn't want to
hear any excuses from the warrior-priests about how it was
beneath their dignity to accompany mere scouts. Not when
there were wounded to rescue. And, by the Hawk! as long as
there was a priest in this army who could shield them, Marric
was damned if he would expose his men, unprotected, to
Jomsborg magics.

"He knew," muttered a scout. "Even before we told him, he
knew it."

"Quiet!" rapped out an officer.

Medical corpsmen aided the wounded to the rear of the
army, officers came and went, and, behind Marric, the organ-
ized clamor of soldiers, grooms, and servants pitched camps.
Even after his staff told him that his quarters were ready, he
remained with Thorbjorn, the wounded Aescir merchant, who
refused the poppy that the surgeon would have had him take
until his sister's son was buried.

* * *

One last troop of scouts had yet to report, and Marric's guards had orders to bring their leader to him the instant they reached camp. That order given, he glanced at the books and maps spread out by his sword on his table and sighed. He had hoped to quarter part of his army in the town that the Jomsborgers had destroyed, and, with the remainder—largely companion cavalry—take ship for the Western Isles. But that plan, like the town itself, had gone up in smoke.

Refugees who straggled or staggered into camp brought the news that not all the ships—theirs and Jomsborg's—had been destroyed. Some had been hidden. Marric sighed. He could leave a moira of his troops here under his deputy to help with burials and rebuilding, then order them to join him in Prydein.

He and the rest of his troops would have to ride farther west. For the second time that day, Marric thought of Caesar, who had not lived to wear the crown he had earned. Caesar, first of all Romans, had tried to take the Isles. He had been greeted by war, by magic, and by storms that had delayed his cavalry and cost him many ships. The land was too strongly guarded for easy conquest, and later emperors had not even tried.

Nor would Marric himself. Let the kinglets—or the ruling pair he had once seen in a vision—keep their realm! He had a bigger kingdom! All he wanted was to recover what was his: Alexa, his sister whom he was destined to marry and who would rule the Empire with him, Isis on Earth, as he was Pharaoh and Emperor.

Marric smiled fondly at the thought of his sister. Never mind the fact that the last time Marric had seen her, she had turned on him with fire and spell. He had mourned her as dead. Then—as always, Marric winced at the memory—he had seen in a vision that Alexa lived; and Audun had told him that she had turned away from the magic that had almost damned her and cost him a year as a slave in Alexandria. She was alive, she was his, and he was coming for her now. His baggage train (preposterous as an emperor's baggage must always be) was further encumbered by gifts for her: silks, perfumes, jewels such as she could not have seen in her years so far from civilization. He would be glad to have his sister at his side again, to regain their old closeness. As a little girl, she had been enchanting.

If he were to see her again, however, he must follow Caesar's path. He grimaced, having hoped to spare his men a march that far west. He sat himself down in the battered camp chair he refused to allow servants to replace with something suitably elaborate. Laboriously, he began to twist sense out of the Latin text of Caesar's campaigns.

Lamps flickered and were replaced as Marric read. Night was the time for planning, for thinking. He had learned that years ago—about the same time that he had learned to think. It had been that or die; and even at that, the choice had been a close one. A mention of provisions caught his attention. Caesar had been separated from his train, and his men had had to raid nearby fields. Marric thought, briefly, of calling a scribe, then grunted and scrawled notes that provisions should be carried on each ship.

As he read on, what troubled him was his growing suspicion that the storms that had beached Caesar's ships had been more than the usual gales of autumn. Prydein, as its natives called it, was warded as surely as this very camp, by the priests called Druids. And they were strong magicians, as he had reason to know.

More priests. Marric twisted his neck to ease the ache that too-long reading and writing invariably gave him. A hanging quivered in the night wind, and he smelled hot water and oils. Doubtlessly, his body-servant was hoping that Marric would bathe in the near-Persian luxury that he suspected took ten horses to lug from Byzantium to here, before the water grew cold and all his work had to be done again. It would be pleasant to soak out the day's soreness, but he had work to do yet. Best dismiss the man.

As he rose and laid his sword on the map of the Western Isles to keep it from curling up, he heard guards snap a challenge outside his tent. He whirled and caught up his sword just as he heard the challenge answered.

"Who is it?" he demanded.

"The last scouting party, Majesty."

"Admit them!" Exhaustion—and his bath—could wait.

The tent flaps parted, and three men, the dekarch of a quar-

tering party, one of his aides, his own surgeon, assisted a
stranger to enter and salute him. Marric seated himself in his
favorite chair, pushed a stool toward the physician, and nodded to the other men to sit, or stand at ease. His body servant
edged in with wine and a look of resignation.

Even as Marric heard his men's report and, with one part of
his brain, calculated the drain that several hundred refugees,
including women, wounded, and children, might be on his
supplies, he was studying the stranger.

He was tall, almost as tall as Marric himself. But where the
Emperor was tanned and dark-eyed, kept his dark hair short
and his face shaven like a Roman for comfort beneath a helmet, this man was light-skinned from years spent in misty
lands. His eyes were light, his face bearded, and his brownish
hair hung in a draggled tail down his back. The surgeon
pushed him down upon the stool and cut through his tunic,
which was checked in shades of blue and green, a garish con-
trast to his breeches and heavy fringed cloak, which was
woven in many shades. Though gold glinted on his neck and
arms, he was unarmed. Unless, Marric thought, the bag that
swung at his side counted as a weapon, as well it might: it
held the man's harp.

A bard then. Only one type of bard went thus unarmed,
too. The stranger whose wounds his physician now cleaned—
and who ignored the pain of that treatment—had to be a
Druid.

Marric drained his cup of wine to cover a sarcastic laugh.
Had he not just thought of Druids? What a pity he could not
dismiss it as coincidence; he had known for years that he was
as priest-ridden as his army. He had wished to be general,
was determined to be Emperor, and hated the notion of being
priest as well. A familiar anger began to churn in him. By
now he would have demonstrated amply just how unfit he was
for the greater magics of kingship. But they still clustered
about him, priests and priestesses alike, and their very presence made demands on him that he wished he could avoid.
What would this new one want?

"Hail, Emperor." No further salutation. Marric stifled another smile. When he was a boy, he had admired one of his
father's guardsmen, a man named Aillel who came from Pry-

dein or Eire or some such place. Aillel too had been scant of
courtesy, though he could be eloquent when he chose, such as
the time he had found Marric, at age fourteen, in a taverna.
(Though, to give him credit, Aillel had waited until Marric
had brought matters to a moderately triumphant climax.) He
had taught Marric rudiments of his own language, which
he had been practicing with those Celtoi among his army on
this trip west. Now, he greeted the man in his own tongue. To
his chagrin, however, the bard almost laughed.

"Emperor, you speak like a man of Eire," the bard observed, smiling. "Hibernia, as you Romans call it. And if
your hair and beard were properly long, you would look like
one too."

Marric ignored his surgeon's and body-servant's scanda-
lized looks. "I knew a man once from Eire. But he had light
hair. As, I thought, had all your race."

The bard shook his head. "Some of us are dark." He stared
at Marric. "And one of your names . . ."

Marric nodded. "You are right. There is western blood in
my line," he said. Like all priests, the Druids were well-
informed, and probably knew more about him than he wanted
to know. He offered this one wine which, to his surprise, he
drank unmixed. "You know my name," he observed.

"I am Kynan," the bard said. Possibly from the same land
as your ancestor. Not all of the Celtoi crossed to the Misty
Isles, you know."

Marric knew. Cleopatra's ancestor Alexander had met them
in his travels too. They would talk and drink all night; as this
one, wounded though he was, seemed likely to do.

"What were you doing this far from home, Kynan?" he
asked bluntly.

"Singing," said the Druid. "Singing—and listening. Waiting, as I was instructed, for the Hawk."

Another not-coincidence, Marric thought. It was wonderful
how all these priests knew his business and turned up to discuss it with him.

"Never mind that for now. What do you know of the Jomsborgers?"

"What all the world knows. That they are hungry for blood
and land not their own. They cast eyes on your Empire and

failed. Thus they sacked Birka and now turn their eyes west. The land you call Gallia, Prydein itself . . . they have begun to raid." He paused and drank again. There was a bluish shadow of pain about his mouth. The surgeon took his cup to refill, and, Marric suspected, drugged it before he handed it back.

"You go to gain a bride," said Kynan, and drank deeply. "Ah!" he said to the surgeon-priest. "That potion would not have deceived a child." He yawned. "Quickly, Emperor, before I sleep. You go to gain a bride. We Celtoi have songs of such wooings. But see that you seek the right lady." Again he yawned, and struggled against it. "Shall I sing you those songs, Emperor?"

"Later," Marric said, amused despite himself. "When you are awake."

Kynan toppled forward. The surgeon caught him, hauled one arm about his shoulder, lifted him to his feet, and helped him wobble, unsteady as a boy on his first debauch, out of Marric's quarters. "Help him," he ordered his servant, and laughed.

Overhead, a hawk shrieked.

Once the men were out of his tent, though, Marric ceased to laugh. "See that you seek the right lady," Kynan had said. Alexa was destined for him according to the custom of the Pharaohs, since Isis and Osiris Themselves were wed. He could not rule without a consort of his own blood. They were the last of their line. So he had come for her, with presents such as girls liked. He remembered, then dismissed, the Alexa he had fought with, imperious, passionate, and much more mature than he had imagined, in favor of the little girl he had tended so many years ago. When they were children, they had adored one another.

Now that Stephana was dead, that childhood sweetness would have to be enough.

He felt the usual pang at that, and grimaced. Some losses never stopped hurting. He grimaced and threw off his clothes and headed for his bath, tepid now, after the incursion by scouts and Druid. The water lapped at the scars on back and sides, soothing him as he had Stephana, the night his spirit quailed within him. She had called him coward and forbade him to die. Then she had healed him, body and soul.

Now she was dead, murdered by Irene the night Marric moved to win back his Empire. He had won it, but at the cost of a curse and the loss of a seeress who had loved him.

He rose abruptly from the bath and reached for a robe. Silk, and smooth as a caress. Damn. Nights were the worst, he thought, pacing like the leopards Alexa had loved to watch when they were little. During the day, the thousand details of the Empire or his army distracted him. If he were fortunate, they helped him achieve exhaustion; and that helped him sleep, however lightly.

When sleep eluded him, however . . . he pinched out the lamps, then lay alone on his bed, burying his face in one of the pillows. Stephana had escaped the prison of her flesh and the threat of rebirth. How should he dare to dream of her and risk summoning her. He thrust his memories of her, silvery-haired, blue-eyed, slender and pliant in his arms, away. "Go free, beloved," he whispered into the pillow, as he had whispered the night she died.

Then he had had no time for tears, only for vengeance and power. Later, when he had the time to weep he lacked the power. Irene's curse, that as long as he wore the crown he would not know peace, lay on him. He could not weep, he could not forget, yet he dared not remember too clearly either. It tore at him sometimes, and drove him into rages.

To try to exhaust himself, he had thrown himself into his campaigns until the rumor that the Emperor rode on the battlefield or sailed on the flagship was enough to set soldiers screaming in terror. He smiled thinly, remembering a man in tattered finery thrust at his feet. Marric knew that man. He had sunk a ship that transported Marric into slavery, taunted him with choices he could not accept, then sold him in Alexandria. Marric had sworn to hang him. The year after he became Emperor, he had swept the Middle Sea for pirates and caught him in his nets. At his Triumph, he had had the spear at his throat, ready to kill him, but he had honored his vow and hanged him instead.

Be proud of me, Father, Marric whispered to the darkness. *I have not failed you. If I had had as little self-control as you thought, I would have broken my vow then and there. Tell me you are proud of me.*

But the darkness had no answer for him. Emperor, he was. Horus on Earth he was not: but unfit, afraid of the magic that would link him forever with the eternal gods on the Horizon. He had failed the test of initiation that would have made him priest and King. That failure had driven him to desperation. He had worn the mask of a god, had ridden in triumph on men's shoulders while his love took a knife in the heart . . .

Marric jerked himself upright before he could moan with grief. He fumbled to light the nearest lamp, and his hand shook. Fire . . . the last time he saw Stephana's face, the fire in the Temple of Isis made her look like she was alive.

He had taken another vow. When the Temple was rebuilt, the statue of the Goddess would bear Stephana's face. Though he might never see it again, she would always be there. They would see to it for him, the few friends he had left, whom he had left behind in Byzantium. At least that much would come right.

Marric Antonios Alexander, Lord of the Two Lands, Emperor of the Romans, Autokrator and Great Horus, hurled himself back into his camp chair. Turning his back on the shadows, he turned to his books and maps as if they were amulets with which to ward off his memories.

Chapter 15

☆

The next day Marric led his army, slowed now by a draggled train of refugees, back into the charred ruins of a riverside town and cursed that he had not arrived earlier. With its fallen walls and blackened rafters, the town looked like a lost battlefield. A warm wind stirred the broad green leaves that cast ironically peaceful shadows on the ruins. It had been part of the Empire, in his charge; he should have been able to protect it. He wanted to grieve but knew he could not weep. At times like this, the lack of tears threatened to drive him wild. The beginning of one of his worse rages made him tremble. At times, he thought his anger would drive him mad.

In their own fury, the Jomsborgers had attacked even the trees with ax and torch, but the forest had ruled here before ever a town rose, and would doubtless survive long after it crumbled into mold. The buzz of insects and the abrupt cries of birds were very loud. Burial parties, Marric thought. The sooner, the better. Perhaps they might build pyres on the riverbank where the Jomsborgers had beached their treacherous fast ships and where burned-out hulks now lay toppled.

He gave his deputy general his orders, then turned his horse's head so quickly that the beast reared in protest, and rode away from the ruined town, west, always west.

Behind him, the army followed at speed, drawn up now as if it expected battle. And all that day, Marric spoke no word beyond what was needed to order the march. He knew that his men watched him. He knew his duties, set down by the Strategikon his own ancestor had written: not to look downcast or worried, but to ride jauntily and keep his troops in heart. He had a duty not to isolate himself from his troops.

But what of his duty to that murdered town? A thousand men and a few priestly mumbles had not honored it, not to his way of thinking. No: Irene had made overtures to the Jomsborgers. When their jarl had rebuffed her, she had outlawed the Varangians who had served Byzantium loyally. Many had died, and Marric had vowed to avenge them. Now Jomsborg decided that the time was ripe to attack the Empire, and its friends. An intolerable state of affairs: Marric was tempted to regret that he could not march against their fortress and burn it as they had burned his town.

It was too much for any one man to do. That was why he needed Alexa, why he hastened west and forbade hunting parties to follow the spoor of bear that they saw in the forests. He would teach Jomsborg the lesson it had earned, but in his own time, when the advantages were on his side.

In the meantime, the battle he had to shirk made him bit-

terly unhappy. He was aware when his men muttered sympa-
thetically behind his back. He was even aware when his Varangians adopted the wounded Aescir trader Thorbjorn and
Kynan the bard. Shortly thereafter, the bard began to watch
him speculatively, fingers tapping out the rhythm of one song
or other. Bad enough that his own men made up songs about
him. He had heard some of them, good ones, fierce or ribald
by turns. Marric had not asked to be a legend, but if that was
what his troops chose to make of him . . . he shrugged his
shoulders and rode on.

A glint of water caught his attention. In a few moments, he
would know whether scouts felt it might be safe to pause by
the riverside to water their horses. It would be good to ride
beside the river until they reached the seacoast. Born beside
the restless glitter of the Golden Horn and the blue of the
Middle Sea, Marric longed for the sea after months of riding
inland. And a longing, keen as anything that set Alexander
riding east, drove him: sail to Britain, find Alexa, bring her
home: make an end.

Not peace: Irene's death curse denied him that. But whatever satisfaction he might win.

The riverbank was safe. The army watered its horses, then
rode on.

The next day made Marric aware of his shadows; Thorbjorn
and Kynan, riding close behind him, and the brilliant speck
that flew high overhead. *Hello, brother,* he thought at it. *Do
you want to come to me?* He felt a familiar tingle, half anticipation, half fear: whenever his sigil, the Hawk, soared overhead, he could expect change at least: adventure, probably;
and almost certainly, danger.

By late afternoon, his guards had seen it too and began to
talk among themselves with a mixture of awe and pride. They
thought of Marric as a lucky general and, please Isis, he
meant to keep on being one. He heard Kynan speaking of the
land roundabouts, telling his men of a nearby . . . what was
that word? Temple? Grove? He would tell the scouts to search
for it.

He glanced around, looking for the scouts and officers
whose report he expected. They were overdue, and he did not

know why. That uncertainty galled him. No general should
have to say, "I did not expect that." He signaled his guard to
move in closer. A shadow fell across him, and he knew that if
he looked up, he would see the Hawk.

In the moment it screamed and swooped down out of the
sky, the bard screamed, "Look out!" and Marric's legend,
such as it was, nearly ended right then and there.

His horse reared up, then screamed in pain and lurched to
one side. Marric hurled himself from his mount's back just in
time to avoid being crushed by the heavily armored animal.
He hit hard and rolled, his armor bruising him. Half-stunned
by his fall, he looked up as his horse fell, and a huge black
bear with outstretched paws and open jaws dripping red
turned away from it toward him.

No bear, unless maddened by fire or hunger, would wil-
ingly attack humans. Yet, judging from the screams of men
and horses behind him, bears—no, Jomsborgers, had done
so. The damned things must have tracked them all the way
from the shattered town. He had seen no ships; they must
have divided their force. They must feel very sure of their
prey to stalk him and then attack by day. He would have to
teach them . . . Marric tried to roll clear, and cursed as he felt
himself move far too slowly. Overhead the sky was spinning.

Kynan's grove! Perhaps, if they could reach it, whatever
power lived there would protect them until he could plan a
successful attack. "Bard!" he cried. "To me!"

A big Varangian swung at the bear with an ax, but it batted
him aside and headed straight for Marric. He could feel the
thing's hot, fetid breath on his face from here, and it made
him frantic. His lance lay several feet away, and he hurled
himself toward it. If he could reach it, bring it up, he could
spit this beast.

In the next instant, it stepped between him and his weapon.
All around him, men tried to force their mounts in to defend
him, but they reared and plunged. In desperation, Marric
drew his knife. Somehow he got his feet under him, and rose
unsteadily. The smell of blood and foul magic on the skin
changer's breath was enough to turn him even dizzier. Unfair,
unfair to die in a forest skirmish, he told himself, and the
thought drove him wild. The bear grunted, then lunged, and

Marric lurched aside. He could see the glint of the ten-foot kontos behind it.

"Hai!" he challenged the beast. Another feint, perhaps, and he might get at the lance. But the bear, a wicked intelligence glinting in its tiny eyes, rose to its full height and, quite deliberately, blocked Marric's path to his safety weapon. Then it pounced down toward him.

And in that instant, the Hawk struck! It slashed with bill and pinions, then darted away as the skin changer roared and brought up one massive paw to crush it to the earth, then circled, striking at eyes and ears until the intelligence of the man-turned-beast was quite lost in a bestial frenzy. The bear danced and wove on its stocky hindquarters, and Marric dived for the lance with a force that took the wind out of him.

"Now, winged brother!" He rolled, bringing the kontos up in the instant the Hawk attacked once more. The bear whirled, and impaled itself upon the lance. Its claws batted at it, trying to break it and kill the man who held it. Blood burst from its mouth and nose and spattered Marric's face and hands. It stung like acid, but he held his weapon as firmly as he would a boar spear. If he wavered—please Isis, let the shaft not snap!—the beast would dislodge the lance and grab him up in a hug that would snap his ribs and spine, whether or not the bear had taken its death wound.

All around him, he was dimly aware of other men bringing lances into play against the beasts. He heard screams and cries of pain, but he had his own battle to fight. The bear's struggles grew weaker. Then it toppled. For a moment, it looked as if it would fall. But its staggers dislodged Marric's lance. The bear roared and started clawing toward him. Marric leapt back and drew his sword. In that moment, Thorbjorn leapt between him and the bear.

"Get back, man!" Marric shouted. His footwork was unsteady, and the ax too heavy for him. As he swung, the bear struck the ax, then caught him such a blow that Marric could hear ribs crack. The merchant fell, and as the bear bent to seize him up, Marric swung his sword down on its neck. The bear kicked a few more times against the churned-up ground, then died.

Overhead the Hawk screamed. Leaning on his kontos, his

head resting against the splintered wood, Marric braced himself and held out his left arm for the Hawk to perch on. He staggered as its claws pricked deep into his padded garments and snicked against the mail. The bird mantled once, then stared into his eyes, a fierce, golden stare that drew him.

"I thank you," Marric said, and bent his head as he would in a temple. The bird belled once in satisfaction, then mantled, rose, circled him three times, and flew away. Once again, Marric sagged against the battered lance. It would be easy to collapse to his knees. But his soldiers might think he was hurt.

"Never mind, I'm not hurt," he told his men. "Look to the trader there." Men could die from blows like that, unless they had good reason not to. He wondered if vengeance would keep Thorbjorn alive.

"It is your duty," he heard his old armsmaster Philo's rasping tones, "not to take part in the battle, for whatever you may accomplish by spilling your own blood could not compare with the harm you would do to your own interests if anything happened to you."

Wonderful, thought Marric. *What if you have no choice except to fight a skin changer? What, no answer for me? All those years of education for nothing.* He grunted and dashed his hand across his brow, cleaning it of the bear's blood. The sun was sinking. He wanted his men safely lodged before night.

"How many dead?" he asked.

"None," came the report.

"Thank the gods," Marric said hoarsely, wishing he could weep in relief. There would be cauteries, though: but men usually survived that. He gestured for a fresh mount, then gestured for Kynan to approach.

"How far are we from this shrine of yours?" he asked.

"I can bring us there before dusk," said the bard. He shrugged. "A good thing for you, Emperor, that it is a hawthorn nemet. That is a death nemet," he explained as Marric lifted an eyebrow. "Iron may not be brought into most nemets, but you may not enter a hawthorn nemet without it. Even profaned as this grove is, I could not let you and your men enter it if it were not a death nemet."

Then the Druid gasped and moved his hand in a gesture to avert evil. "Goddess, avert!"

Beneath their eyes, the bear Marric slew was changing, its form shrinking, altering into that of a naked man, his face set in a snarl of rage, his scarred body twisted into a ball about the wound that had killed him. Then the man's form blurred too, flesh seeming to seethe from it until only a barren patch of ground showed where a skin changer had died.

"Bring us to this nemet of yours," Marric ordered him. "But bard, if there is any trickery..." Probably he should not have accused a priest of treachery, but he still felt dazed and sick. His surgeon materialized as if out of the air, his clever fingers probing for breaks or burns, but Marric pushed past him, mounted somehow, and gestured for the Druid to lead.

Somewhat later, three men, cold sweat beading on their faces, reported to Marric that they had found the scouts. Dead, of course. The men's eyes were wide with horror and their faces were gray.

"Can they be moved?" Marric asked. It was an important question. He could neither abandon his dead scouts unburied nor risk additional men by ordering them to bury their comrades, then catch up. He leaned against his horse's arched neck, waiting for them to speak. His brow burned, and his dizziness had not abated.

They laid the scouts' bodies across packhorses, and pressed on, Kynan leading the long, wary column of men deeper and deeper into the trees as the shadows lengthened.

Marric's companions drew in around him protectively. Several of the Varangians fumbled for amulets, and one man pointed out what he thought were signs of a holy grove.

Gesturing the others to keep back, the bard pressed forward eagerly. "Don't go in if he says not to, but keep an eye on him," Marric murmured. He had no desire to profane some rustic shrine but he would be very glad to dismount, to disarm, and to rest. He sighed, and then his nostrils flared. Despite the flashes of dizziness and chills that he had suffered ever since the bears' attack, he could smell...no, it was not an attack, not a trap by the bard. Something, however, was wrong, and he would have to find it out.

The bard emerged from a stand of hawthorn trees, his face grim, and his eyes wet.

"That is truly a nemet of death now. My brothers," he whispered. "All the Druids here. They killed them and heaped their bodies in the grove." All his humor and independence was gone, and he looked up at Marric as if he could somehow make it right.

This time Marric followed his mens' example as their fingers moved to avert evil. "Summon the priests," he said hoarsely. "We need a camp, and that shrine must be cleansed."

As a token of respect, even Marric shared the labor of digging a grave for his scouts and the Druids who had been killed. He was sweating profusely by the time he finished and could look around. The sun was setting in layers of cloud that looked as if they had been stained by blood.

The shrine that had been profaned was part grove and part something else, a number of roughly hewn stones, several fallen on their sides, all circling a massive trilithon beside which they had buried the dead. Marric started to ask what the rocks were for, then thought better of it. They were a mystery and now, they were a tomb. Around the perimeter of the circle, he could hear the priests chanting, smell the incense with which they sought to sweeten the air of the violated grove, and feel the nature of the space change as their wards took effect, sequestering them from the outside world.

The Druid knelt beside the heaped earth of the fresh grave, and Marric walked over to him. "May we build a fire?" he asked.

The Druid shrugged. "Emperor, it is beyond my power to purify this place," he said. "So do whatever you must."

Finally Marric was free to disarm. Then he faced attack by his physician and body servant, who stripped him of his armor, salved his face where the skin changer's blood had seared it, then insisted on rubbing him down with oil. Under their hands, he fell asleep.

His enemies, alive and dead, stalked him there; Irene's cold rage, the pirates he had slain, and faces he had never seen. Then a sense of power being used to summon those who could feel it drew Marric's thoughts toward one man in particular. A dark beard covered much of his face, except where it was scarred; and his black hair was shaggy and streaked with gray. Even as Marric watched, he beckoned to men Marric could not see. Standing beside him, one skinny hand on his thick shoulder, was a wizened hag whose look of malice made Irene seem almost benign. The summoning power emanated from her, though she channeled it through the man's body.

Despite their differences in size and age, and the man's scars, Marric could see they were close kin. He thought he could put name to them too: it was well-known in the Empire that Jarl Grettir's grandam was a witch and his chief advisor.

No names! he reminded himself. Even a man as incapable of magic as he should have remembered that simple rule. He had recognized the Jarl and his grandam, and that woke the hag to awareness of him. She glared, then gestured at him. "So brave you are, and so foolish!" she cried.

Her laughter rang out and she gestured toward a shadowy blot that coalesced, into a framework that seemed built of bones, little more than a butcher's stall. He tried to look away from the grisly thing, but found his gaze fixed upon the patterns that formed and re-formed on the loom's bloody strands: Marric alone; Marric fighting, his mouth squared in a silent scream of battle-rage; and, over and over again, Marric lay twisted on a battlefield, his face vacant and lifeless while a dark-haired woman knelt screaming above him.

"Be more foolish, then, and know yourself fated to die!"

No. Marric shook his head from side to side as might a hunted animal, then started toward the woman.

"No!" he snarled, his hands catching hold of the tunic of the man who stood over him, one hand outstretched to wake him.

He gaped in fear at Marric, who released him, and shuddered. "You should know by now not to sneak up on me like that, man," he warned his servant, and reached beneath his pillow toward his dagger. Best not let the man know that his master had dreamed of a death-curse; it would be all over camp by noon. Soldiers tended to create omens on the least excuse, and he didn't want them creating bad ones. "Well, what is it, now that you've waked me and almost got strangled for your pains?"

He swung his long legs down and began throwing on his clothes. "The priests, Majesty, they need you."

Marric permitted himself a short, mordant laugh. The priests always needed him. "Do you know why?"

The little man looked blank. Marric laid a hand on his shoulder, silent apology for frightening him. It was probably a matter of rituals. They would do their best to reconsecrate this shrine, he would make more gifts toward the rebuilding of Mother Isis's temple if . . . no, best not ill-wish himself, *when* he returned safely to Byzantium, Alexa at his side.

He had to assume he would succeed. Swinging a sleeved cloak like those the soldiers wore over his shoulders, Marric hastened toward the trilithon where the priests, his Hetaeria, and various other officers and priests gathered by a fire well away from the one around which the wounded lay.

They heard his footsteps and turned. Waving aside their salutes, he strode into their midst. Even though it was the height of summer, the air was cold this deep into the forest. He stood chafing his hands, waiting for their report.

Finally, Kynan the Druid gestured at the perimeter of the grove where the standing stones gleamed with a silvery light. Beyond them were blots of shadow that lurched and re-formed in a manner that reminded Marric of his nightmare.

He swallowed.

"Can they reach us?" he asked.

The priests shook their heads. Torchlight glinted off the shaven skull of the Osiris priest. Marric shrugged. Breaking out of the circle was *his* work, not theirs, he thought.

All around them gathered soldiers, eager to watch their Emperor, to speak to him, or simply listen, drawing their reassurance from him. He could feel it, like blood draining from a wound.

Over by the healers' fire, a man groaned, then shrieked, and Marric suppressed a shudder. Lest the men bitten or clawed by bears sicken, their wounds were burned. What of Thorbjorn? No one could sustain burning along one side and live. He would turn feverish and die—and Marric had promised him vengeance. The priest wearing Thoth's symbol about his neck closed his eyes in shared pain. "I must get back," he said.

The priest nearest him, who wore the robes of a senior adept of Osiris, nodded respect. "We must meditate on this tonight, Majesty."

"What of the rest of the army?" Marric demanded. Meditation was fine; battles were won by soldiers.

"Those who camped outside the grove, Majesty? Warded, to be sure, but . . ." the officer shrugged, unhappy at the report he had to make.

It isn't the army they want, Marric thought. *They want me.* "Can we signal to them?" he asked.

"Show His Majesty," said Merikare, chief of the priests who had marched out with him from Byzantium. Kynan stooped, picked up a rock, and hurled it at the space between two standing stones, and it recoiled upon them.

"We may not be able to break out," said the bard. "If so, they will hold us until our food and will to fight give out."

"Well," Marric said slowly, "for now, we are at stalemate. They cannot get in; we cannot get out. Is that any reason for us to lose sleep? Double the guard, and, the rest of you, turn in." He whirled and headed back toward his own bed, walked two steps, paused for effect, then turned.

"Except for you. That's right, you. The bard. Come with me, and bring your harp. It has been a long time since I have heard music."

The bard unwrapped his harp from its leather case and cocked his head at Marric with wry humor. "Do you really want me to sing, or was that just to put your army in heart?"

Marric glowered at him, then sank down on a camp stool and pointed with his chin at a second. "Yes," he said, and waited to be obeyed.

"Emperor, if you keep on like this, you will be more Celt than Hellene," he commented, watching Marric carefully for signs of affront.

Marric fixed his eyes on the harp. "You told me there was a song I needed to hear. I need to hear it now." The bard was watching him with that priest-look that saw too deeply into his motives yet humored him, for reasons Marric could never fathom. "If you must know," he admitted, "my sleep is troubled."

The Druid nodded. "All over the camp, men dream ill. You, their leader . . ."

"I dreamed of Jomsborg," Marric said, low-voiced. "Of a hag—Grettir's grandam, as I think—and her loom. She spoke to me and showed me myself dead, with a woman kneeling above me, mourning." He could not suppress his shiver, and wrapped himself more warmly in his cloak.

The bard nodded. "So you would have a tale of marriage and power, would you, to put yourself back in heart? Well enough, Emperor. Listen, then, to a tale of your own family."

He drew his fingers across his harp, which glittered with goldwork and garnets, and the sound of the harp strings shimmered like firelight on the harp's gems. The bard smiled, some tension in him easing with the sound of the music:

"The Emperor was greater and more powerful than any Emperor before him, but he grieved because he had no heir. One night, as he lay troubled, he slept and dreamed, of tossing water, high rocks—an island rising from the sea, facing his home, crested with mountains. Shining on the highest of the mountains was a river and at its mouth was a hall, fairer than any he had ever seen. In his dream, he walked within. The hall's roof was all of gold, its walls studded with precious gems, glimmering in the sun. At golden seats, warriors feasted at silver tables. Chief among them were two young men who played chess before an old man who sat in an ivory chair, backed with the figures of two golden hawks. White was the old man's hair, and he wore a diadem. Though he was old, he was yet unwithered. Rings and bracelets were upon him, and he wore a mighty torque. And as he watched the youths play chess, in his hand was a file; and he was fashioning chessmen.

Beside the old man, in a chair of shining gold, sat a maiden brighter than the sun. The Emperor could not bear to look upon her, yet, for his very life, he could not bear to look away. She rose and came to him; and the smell of flowers followed her; and white blossoms fell at every step she took. He put his arms about her neck. Yet, when he had her in his

arms, his cheek pressed against hers, he heard the barking of
dogs, the clashing of shields, and horses neighing.

And he awoke."

The bard's voice fell silent, as he played the Emperor's
grief and bewilderment and, despite his power, his awareness
that alone, he possessed nothing worth the keeping. "Is this
the song you wanted, Emperor?" asked Kynan the Druid.

Marric nodded, and sank back, chin in hand, his eyes
hooded.

"Well, then," sang the Druid, "the Emperor grieved until
the wisest men of his realm said, 'Send messengers to test the
truth of thy dream.' So they journeyed and came at last to the
isle of Prydein, to Snowdon, and Arvon. There they saw
the youths, the white-haired man, carving his chessmen, and
the maiden.

"And the Emperor took his army and sailed to Prydein to
conquer it that the maiden might be his. Castle after castle he
took, until, at last, he camped beneath the fortress of Arvon
and prepared to take it too. But the maiden came out to him,
and of her own will, laid her arms about his neck and became
his bride that very night.

"The next dawn, she asked her morning gift, to have and to
hold Prydein itself and its castles; and the Emperor, right willing, granted it in return for a great gift: the lady's name,
which was Elen.

"Now Elen was wise as she was fair, and she made high
roads such as were in the Emperor's lands from one castle to
another; and these roads are yet called Sarn Elen, the roads of
Helen of the Hosts.

"Seven years did the Emperor stay in Prydein with Elen,
and they had sons and a daughter. Then the men of Rome
made a new Emperor. So the Emperor left Prydein for Rome,
and sat before the city. And at the end of a year, he was no
closer to taking it than he had been on the day he had arrived.
Then Elen's brothers sailed with an army from Prydein, and
each man had the strength of two Romans. They set their
ladders and engines against the walls of Rome, and blew the
carnyx; and the gates opened.

"Then the Emperor sat on his throne, and asked his
brothers, 'What lands shall you have?' And Adeon went home

to Prydein, but Kynan chose to remain and dwell here . . . and his sons and sons' sons live here even till this day. This is the dream called the Emperor's dream; and here it ends."

The harp strings shimmered one last time into sound, then subsided as as fire burns up the moment before wood collapses into embers. Then the bard fell silent.

Marric drew a long, shuddering breath, his first, he realized, for many minutes. "What else?" he asked huskily. "What of the lady Elen? What did she look like? And did the Emperor ever see her again?"

Kynan smiled at him. "Ah," he said. "Now you know all that I do." He rose. "Dream on this, Emperor, not on horrors or the battle to survive past tomorrow."

He rose, saluting Marric with deep respect, and left the tent.

Chapter 16

☆

Though the Druid's song eased Marric into dreamless sleep, he snapped alert to the overpowering conviction that he was needed. Physicians and mothers, he understood, felt just such compulsions to rise in the night and look in on their charges. The Empire was his; and until he could make the marriage that would heal it, he must watch over it. It was chilly within the dark tent. The wool tunic he threw on was cold on his scarred shoulders. He chafed his arms to start the blood flowing. His hands and face, where the man-bear's blood spattered them, felt hot.

He slipped outside, and the sensation of need came to him even more strongly. He was not at all surprised when an under-priest padded up to him and asked him to speak with the priests and augurs who had assembled. The man wore the jackal's insignia, and that did alarm him. Marric's own patron was the Hawk; the jackal—and the priests of Anubis—had more to do with death and darkness.

The priests sat about a fire. Most wore tunics and cloaks much like Marric's own; except for their shaven heads, they looked like most officers . . . until you saw their eyes, Marric mused. In the firelight, their eyes gleamed like cats' eyes. What they saw was nothing of this world. Those eyes watched him approach and pierced him. He almost raised a hand to ward off their hungry, glittering stares.

Place was made for Marric, and he sat beside Merikare, the priest of Osiris whom he had known since Alexandria. He nodded respect to the priests.

"'We haven't the power to break the magic that the Jomsborgers cast around the grove," Merikare told him.

They could not break out; the Jomsborgers could not break in: stalemate—until their food ran out. Marric thinned his lips. "You didn't ask me here to give me a death sentence," he said. "And I will not accept one. What else is there?"

He looked at the Osiris priest, but it was the priest of Anubis, eldest of those who followed the army, who spoke. "This is a hawthorn grove. Do you know what that means?"

Here it went again: questions, portentous pauses, and answers, until the priests thought they had Marric maneuvered into doing their will. He raised a hand to his brow. Could he have a fever from just a few drops of blood? If the priests would finish with him, he could wake up his physician. He sighed and gave the priests the answer he thought they wanted. "The Druid explained it to me. It is a nemet of death, of blood sacrifices. Not only can you bring iron into it; you must."

"There is power in the very earth of such nemets." High overhead came the thin scream of a hawk. Marric shivered and looked up at the night sky. He thought he could see a faint shimmer in the air, a dome of power that sealed them from their enemies. But the power he sensed came, as the priest said, from the earth itself. The land hereabouts was rich; and this grove's soil was richer yet, he realized, because of the sacrifices—centuries of them—that had taken place in them.

"Centuries ago, the Empire tried to outlaw the Druids for such sacrifices," Marric heard himself retort.

"And we, are we any different?" asked the Anubis priest. "Perhaps we no longer bury men beneath tombs, but we understand sacrifices. You, better than any man alive, should understand."

Angered, Marric rose to his feet. The earth beneath him seemed to quiver with power. Had he been priest as well as Emperor, he might have known how to channel it. But he had failed at that test, and they all knew it.

"What is it that you want?" he snapped. "Shall I offer myself as sacrifice, or simply hold the blade? What is enough for you?"

Merikare shook his head at Marric. "I beg you, sit back down. You know that you *are* a sort of sacrifice," he said in his unusually rich, beautiful voice. He laid a hand on Marric's arm, and the younger man was swept by a sensation of compassion for his losses, from Stephana herself to the scars on his back, even to such a small sacrifice as the chariot racing he had to give up when his advisors thought it was too risky. They all added up to the denial of self that made being Emperor as arduous a task as the most ascetic priest ever faced. And Marric, who undertook it, had been denied two consolations: the power of an Emperor's magic, and the power of any other man to weep or find peace of mind.

Marric looked away. *Cornered again,* a cynical voice told him, but he ignored it. His sense of being fevered abated. "What must I do?" he asked, more humbly this time.

The priest of Anubis approached him, a bowl of blackened silver in his thin, pale hands. A dark rainbow of oil floated within it. Many times Marric had watched his lover scry, and he knew what it cost her.

"Will you look within, Emperor?" he asked, in that voice that made Marric think of a salamander resting in its bed of fire. The rainbow shimmered, and started to re-form into high-prowed ships. It swirled into a storm, then settled into a meandering pattern of gleaming lines—*the road I must travel?* Then it blurred again. Marric glanced away. When he looked back, he saw a new vision: a hall, and within it . . .

Before he could bend closer to peer at the vision, the priest snatched the bowl away and emptied it into the flames that roared up into a pillar of blue-greens and red. Despite the chill of the night, Marric was sweating. His skin tingled with the awareness of spells about to take hold.

What price would he have to pay this time?

He was not aware he had asked that aloud until the Anubis priest answered. "To unlock the power of the nemet? There must be a sacrifice."

Marric shook his head. No. he was not going to select a victim, not going to execute him. Even if the Anubis priest had retreated to a bloody, ancient past, Marric had not. He was a Hellene, a man of reason as well as faith.

And what of the war at Troy, the Achilles you have always admired? Merikare nodded at him, and Marric knew he spoke directly to his mind.

Marric drew himself upright. "We will hear what you intend," he spoke as Emperor to the priests. "And then we will decide whether we will allow it."

The Anubis priest gestured, and a tall man limped into the firelit circle accompanied by Kynan the bard.

"Thorbjorn!" Marric exclaimed. "Man, don't throw your life away. I promised you vengeance, didn't I?"

The merchant saluted Marric, a gesture he had seen the Aescir use when greeting the Bearmaster. "Tomorrow, you must break out of this place. When the priests take down their wards, let me go first."

"What will happen if he throws himself against the power that the Jomsborgers cast up?" Marric appealed to the priests.

The Anubis priest shrugged. "He can break through for the rest of us."

"But not him." He shut his eyes for a moment, long enough for unwelcome visions of the Aescir crisping in blue flame, or being crushed by giant beasts to flicker in the darkness there.

"Do you know what you're doing?" Marric asked.

"Aye. You come for Law, Emperor. Like the Bearmaster himself. That's worth dying for. You promised me my vengeance, you said. This is my vengeance. Just before dawn, I will hurl myself at the barriers. That will give you a chance to escape. You will have the bears to face, but you've fought them before."

Marric looked about the circle of silent priests. "What other choices are there?" he asked. No one answered. He appealed to the bard, a true heir of such nemets and the magic they held. "Kynan, do you know of any other way?"

The bard shook his head. "I do not. I tried to contact my brothers, but that . . . barrier prevented me. When I failed to get help, I volunteered as a sacrifice myself but was denied."

The Aescir limped over toward Marric and touched his shoulder. "Look at me, Emperor. Oh, I can survive these cuts and scratches, but I don't think I'd ever be a fighting man again. And I don't want to die in bed."

Forgetting any thoughts he had of looking imperial, Marric paced, while underfoot the magic built up and throbbed in a rhythm that rose throughout his body. It was becoming harder and harder to concentrate as the magic rose to possess him. If he had been truly Emperor, he might have interceded, drawn the power into himself, channeled it. Wait . . . once, on the journey from Alexandria to Byzantium, priests—Merikare among them—had used him as a focus to draw down the primordial waters. When he reminded Merikare of that, the priest shook his head.

"This is a *death* nemet, Majesty," said the Anubis priest. "Such means will not work. Have we your permission to begin? The men will have to prepare to ride out soon."

Men had died for him before; he had never become used to it. Battle was one thing, but this willing immolation . . . *Stephana had accepted her own death*, he remembered. Some might consider his own necessity more cruel: he must accept, must submit to others' decisions to die, and must live so he might still rule, aware of the deaths his rule cost.

"Do what you must." He forced the words out. His eyes burned, as he turned and embraced Thorbjorn. "I promised your Bearmaster weregeld for the men slain in my service," he said. "I keep my word."

The man nodded and turned away, his eyes glowing and intent on the barrier that gleamed between the menhirs. Marric looked down at the ring of seated, silent priests. The fire around which they sat had burned down, and the sky was paling.

"If you will, tell our officers to join us in our quarters," he asked the under-priests. "We must arm."

The first rays of the rising sun pierced through leaf shadow and slanted over the great trilithon in the center of the grove. Light fell on the rough earth of the grave mound beneath it, then cast a fitful, somber magnificence on the dulled armor and weapons of Marric and his men.

Marric edged his horse forward to a position between the chanting priests and Thorbjorn, who wore armor and armlets donated by Guardsmen, and who stood at the perimeter of the grove, ax balanced in his hands. The wards, Marric knew, would dissipate just as the dawn sunlight centered on the trilithon. At that moment, when the powers of *seithr,* or Jomsborg sorcery, were at their weakest, Thorbjorn . . . he didn't want to think about it anymore, he suspected, than any other ruler who saw men go out and die for him.

At that moment, gold light blossomed above the great standing stones, the priests' chants rose to a climax, then ceased, and the sense of protection, of warmth that had ringed even this nemet ceased to exist. Now Marric could see outside the grove, where armed men—or almost-men—crouched over their weapons. He tightened his grip on his lance.

Thorbjorn turned around and, incongruously, grinned at him. Marric raised a hand in salute before the Aescir turned back, his hands eager on the haft of his ax. Marric heared him laugh.

Raising his ax, the Aescir charged between the standing stones. Light crackled from between them, wreathing his whole body. Then he was outside the circle, striding forward toward men (or were those furred things men?) swinging his ax.

At the moment they rushed forward and overpowered him, the Jomsborg wards broke. Marric had time to visualize a dome of glass thrust down from a table to shatter. Then he raised his lance, shouted his war cry, "Horus with us!" and spurred to meet that rush. His horse reared, spooked by the power that rose from the ground, then dashed forward. He impaled the first bear to rush him on his lance, then drew his sword. His horse lashed out with heavy-shod front hooves.

Screams of men and beasts—too many types of beasts—told Marric that his men fought as desperately as he did. Now the power he had felt in the land all night built to an overpowering vibration. Marric's horse screamed in fear as the earth shook. Over the din of battle rang Kynan's voice, "Let them into the nemet!"

Marric and his officers took up the order, drawing to one side as the black bears rushed from the forest, through the grove, and into the circle of standing stones.

Marric stood in his stirrups. "Now!" he screamed. At his command, the priests, with a clamor of horn and sistrum, began a new chant, and wards shimmered up again to hem in the standing stones with light. Now it was the Jomsborgers who could not escape the circle, within which the earth trembled and broke open. The fresh grave mound sank to the level of the ground, then was covered over. The huge stone pillars shook, then buckled, and the central trilithon collapsed.

When the dust subsided, Marric, accompanied by priests, rode forward cautiously. Nothing moved within the circle. This group of Jomsborgers would never answer the summoning of Marric's nightmare—but there were others.

A little later, the Anubis priest found what was left of Thorbjorn. Marric unpinned his cloak, and swung it over the body. Later that day, when they buried him in the hawthorn grove, it was his shroud.

Then the army rode west again. Marric sent out messengers to ride before them to the harbor, to arrange for ships, and to warn the town to defend itself well. Kynan rode, rapt in thought. At times his lips moved, and Marric thought he was communing with Druids far away. Then he drew his harp from its leather case, and sang of Thorbjorn.

It was a pity, Marric thought for the thousandth time, that he could not weep.

Chapter 17

☆

The water was gray and choppy. Marric flicked a glance over the harbor at Gesoriacum, comparing it unfavorably with the harbors at Byzantium, their sun-on-brass splendor awash with ships and boats of all sizes, or with Caesar's Portus Itius. When Marric had campaigned against the pirates of the Middle Sea, he had had a fleet of dromonds, each one's prow painted with the Eye, each one equipped with catapults for throwing Greek fire. When Caesar had launched his assaults on Prydein, he had had eight hundred ships, including supply vessels and troop carriers.

Marric had what—two moirae? Yes, with the third helping to rebuild farther east. If the gods and forwarding winds aided him, the third moira would meet him in Prydein. Caesar's attack had foundered for lack of cavalry.

Assault. Marric wrapped his cloak about him and started to pace, aware of priests' and soldiers' eyes upon him. Though it was early summer, he felt fevers and shivers at once. Gesoriacum, on the Gallic coast, was chill for a man used to the heat of the Middle Sea. His physician started toward him, and Marric shook his head. Last night, his dreams had been troubled—ruined towns; Jomsborg ships massing off a coast he had never seen. He had waked with a sense that desperate haste was needed. The news, coming at dawn, that Kynan the Druid had disappeared from the camp, had made him press harder. Kynan was no traitor, but his loyalties were not to Marric. If he had friends here, and they had a boat, the bard could reach Prydein before him.

He strode toward his tent, his officers half running to keep up with his rapid movements until orders detached them from his party. Behind him came whickers and panicked whinnies, crooned encouragement, and curses, as the horses were loaded. They had arrived in Gesoriacum a day ago, and found—Isis be praised for the miracle—ships in readiness (poor enough things, though he had to entrust his men to them) as he had ordered. All that day, he drove his army worse than any overseer—though without, he conceded in his favor, a whip—until now, Marric's tiny fleet was ready to set sail at midnight for Prydein.

Caesar's way again: sail at midnight; arrive in the morning to take advantage of the long days to choose the best landing site available. Best site for what? Merikare had asked.

Marric stretched hands out toward the brazier his servant had grimaced over but lit nonetheless, and asked himself the same question. *If you try to conquer, or even raid Prydein with three moirae, you aren't just as rash as Father said, my lad; you're insane,* he told himself. Well, there were times, he admitted, that he approached madness: when anger, grief, or frustration drove him to rages that tears might have quelled. For him, there was action, only action—and regret thereafter. He did not want to invade Prydein, which was a land of fierce and dogged warriors, the women (Aillel had told him) as well as the men. Caesar's misfortunes had convinced Divine Antony to concentrate his power in the south.

For Alexa, he told himself then. Alexa was worth a raid or two. She might even be worth a war, though she was no Helen. He shook off the thought of war, which had recurred since leaving the ruined town.

Restlessness drove him from his quarters to oversee the final loading of the ships. The moon was full and bright, and the priests had warned him that high tides might make landing in Prydein difficult on the morrow. The water had calmed from the turbulence of the afternoon: at least that would be easier on the horses.

You cannot pass. You cannot prevail. Go back. The thoughts struck him with the intensity of harp music breaking silence. Marric whirled, looking for their source—priest or spy or bard. He looked out over Okeanos toward Prydein.

Despite the brilliance of the moon, the night was obscured by a kind of dark cloud, forming into a cone, reaching toward— he shook his head to dispel his fancies. The night air stung the raw spots where the bear's blood had struck face and hands: a small matter. He thought of salve, then decided he was getting soft, campaigning west in the ease accorded emperors. His Hunnic allies would jeer if they saw him. The Jomsborgers already did.

When they embarked, he forced himself to go to his quarters. The salve that the physician applied felt blessedly cool. His sleep was shallow, disturbed by flickers of dreams that brought him no enlightenment; and he was on deck by dawn. Time was when he might have had company on deck; now no one dared disturb his Emperor's meditations. Time also was when he would have had reason to linger in his quarters: best not think of that. Soon he would find Alexa and his loneliness might not ache quite so much. The cool air was pure pleasure on his reddened eyes. Sky and water looked like two halves of the same shell.

Then huge chalk cliffs loomed up before him, like a seawall built by gods. Prydein was even better defended than Byzantium with its harbors across which a chain could be drawn. The island was a fortress in itself. They sailed northeast along the coast, looking for the harbor Marric's maps and sailors told him they would find.

One of his officers pointed. "That damned spy!" he said, and spat over the side.

Lining the coast was an army of Prydeins—if you could call a horde of men on foot, brandishing swords and shields, a troop of riders in no particular array, and a host of two-man chariots drawn by ponies an army. Interspersed among the warriors were men and women in pale robes, their arms upraised. The sun emerged briefly, picking out the gold of their heavy armlets and torques, glinting off the bronze and dark iron of their weapons. The wind rose and shifted, bringing Marric their war cries and—were those curses? He gestured for Merikare to station their own priests where the Druids might see. It was safe enough; they seemed not to have catapults.

The sensation he had felt the night before, in Gallia, of a

kind of power forbidding him to land, intensified until he perceived it as the most tenuous of black fogs. For a moment, it obscured his vision of the island. *I ask only my own back,* he told himself. *That land is beautiful. I have heard it is very rich. But I have lands of my own. I do not come to conquer— even assuming that I could.*

They steered toward a harbor at the river's mouth, and the men of Prydein following. The ships, too heavily laden for his liking, wallowed in the tides as they drew toward land, and the warriors drew nearer. Finally, a man flourished a standard bearing the Golden Hawk, Marric's own emblem, jumped over the side, and splashed onto the shore.

Marric flashed his hand downward, and to an orderly clamor of shouted commands, the first Roman force for a thousand years landed on Prydein.

Surrounded by his guards, Marric splashed through the water toward the Hawk standard. He clasped the standard-bearer's shoulder and saw the young man's face flush dark, his eyes widen. "Good work, Demetrius. I won't forget." Under his hand, the man's shoulder squared, and he lifted the standard even more proudly.

"Men coming," one of the Guardsmen gestured with his shield.

"Land the horses," Marric ordered. He would need both cavalry and foot if he had to fight an army, part of which used chariots. He heard splashes behind him but refused to turn his back on the people approaching him: Druids, two or three men wearing violently checked tunics and leg-wrappings and almost as much gold as courtiers, and two more in a chariot.

"We're outnumbered," someone muttered.

"We're not fighting!" Marric snapped. "We've come here in peace. Keep your hands away from your sword hilts." That would be hard; his own fingers itched for the reassurance of his familiar blade. He forced himself to study the chariot as it rattled toward him, its driver standing well out on the central pole; a man armed with javelins balancing behind him. It had not the splendor or the axle-scythes of the Persian-style chariots he himself had owned, and the horses—ponies, almost— lacked the fiery grace of the Arabian-bred horses that won cheers in the Hippodrome, but he thought he would enjoy driving it.

Another chariot followed, driven more quickly than Marric would have believed possible over the tangle of coarse grass and sand. Hand possessively on a case of javelins, a woman balanced effortlessly on the swaying platform. Marric blinked, then forced himself back to impassivity. She was very tall, with long hair that gleamed reddish in the fitful light, and she wore a queen's treasury of gold about her strong throat and wrists. Though Aillel had told Marric of the warrior-women of the Celtoi, he had not imagined this much grace, or strength—or arrogance as she became aware of his gaze and raised her chin proudly.

He forced his eyes back to the first chariot and the men in it; and the warrior nodded, as if acknowledging his interest. He dismounted and walked down to the strand toward the Byzantines, and two Druids joined him.

"You made excellent time, Kynan," Marric remarked ironically.

The Druids saluted with equal irony. "Most Sacred Majesty," he said, choosing one of the more absurd of an Emperior's titles. Behind him, the warriors started at hearing Marric speak in their own tongue, then, with ostentatious good manners, refrained from comment. They were barbarians, Marric thought; they would have no strategy worth recording, but they were obviously deadly for all that.

"I am Corio of the Canti," announced the man in the chariot, who then climbed down and gestured from one elaborately jeweled warrior to the next. Addedomarus of the Trinovantes, Comux of the Regenses. The revered elder there is Dylan, skilled in omens of the sea."

Marric raised an eyebrow at Kynan. Surely, he had told this gathering of tribal kinglets precisely who he was. They would be offended if he summoned a man to speak for him, he decided.

"Marric Antonios Alexandros," he announced himself. "Emperor of the Romans and Lord of the Two Lands." Grandiose titles, they were: but they were his. The Celtoi nodded, as if they had expected it. "We come in peace, my guard"—a flick of his fingers reduced his two moirae to a band of household retainers—"and I."

The woman had left her chariot and strode over to them. "Corio did not give you my name. As usual," she added, glancing sidelong at Corio. "I am Luned of the Iceni."

Marric bowed slightly, courtesy from Emperor to petty queen. "Surely," he said, "it is a queen's privilege either to bestow or withhold her name."

She smiled, and Corio permitted himself to look briefly up at the darkening cloud.

A brisk wind had started to blow, tugging at the dark, curling hair that brushed Marric's mail, sending his dampened cloak of scarlet billowing out behind him. His temples throbbed slightly, as they usually did before a storm in the Middle Sea. The weather of Prydein was treacherous, Marric remembered; that wind, combined with the moon and high tides, heralded a truly remarkable storm. He had a sensation of vast strengths arrayed against him, much as he had felt the night before when he thought he had seen a cone of force and heard voices telling him to turn back.

"You come in peace," said the Druid pointed out to him as Dylan. Older than Kynan, robed while Kynan wore the plaids of a young warrior, he had not spoken before. "But they do not." He pointed with his oaken staff, and Marric had no choice but to turn.

The water had turned choppy again at the shore, rising to deep, darkening swells farther out. But the swift, deadly Jomsborg ships knifed swiftly through the swells. "May the Gods grant that they sink," Marric muttered to himself, and added a few curses in Hunnic. But they did not. He raised a hand, and horns sounded. His men moved into formation, and he wished, briefly, for catapults or flame throwers. He hoped that he could fight alongside the Celtoi without his men and theirs turning on one another.

The black mist he had sensed before appeared to wreathe about the ships, rising and falling with them so easily but was turning choppy again. He shuddered.

The elder Druid watched him closely. "Emperor," he said. "You sense the cone of power we have raised, do you not?"

He dared not deny awareness of the power that now grew

rapidly, like a swift current in one of the rivers of the North, leading toward dangerous rapids. He allowed himself a curt nod.

"You cannot come in peace," the Druid told him. "For there is no peace in you; nor in this land, not as long as those folk think to take it and dwell in it. We face times fully as deadly as the Storm years before all peoples here learned to dwell together. For this time, our enemies will not be content to come, to fight, plunder if they can, and depart by winter. No: this will be a long campaign for the very rule of Prydein."

Why tell me? Marric thought. *I want to find Alexa and sail from here before Set unleashes all his hells upon this place.* The cone of force was darkening. Now Marric could practically see it, its base emanating from the Druids who shrieked and gestured on the shore, its tip pointing down toward the Jomsborg ships like a flamethrower. From the way his men spoke among themselves, fingering amulets as often as arms, they saw it too.

"Come to land, Emperor. Now is not a time to talk, but to fight. Once Prydein is safe for the time being, we may discuss your road north and west to Sarn Elen."

Marric felt sudden, furious embarrassment at his reaction to the name; he flushed up like an untried youth. Even as he scolded himself for lack of control, the Druid nodded. "You seem surprised, Emperor."

"I thought Sarn Elen a name in a song: a legend, nothing more." And which song? The dream of the emperor of his line who had come to Prydein and won a bride. Take it as an omen, he told himself. A good omen.

"And you yourself, Emperor, are you not also a name in a song? The Emperor of Rome, a man with a dream and magic's spoor about him?"

The wind blew even more strongly, but Marric refused to pull his cloak about him. The first splatterings of rain struck his face. It was going to be a truly remarkable storm, he thought; and he wanted his men sheltered before it struck.

"Could we not discuss old songs—and my presence here —elsewhere?" Marric asked. "The man who taught me your speech taught me many such songs. As I recall, they told of your hospitality to strangers."

He held very still, wondering whether they would accept his bluff for what it was. He didn't want to have to fight, perhaps retreat back to his ships in the face of a storm that could founder them all.

The warrior in the chariot laughed. "Roman he is, like the ruler who came here before—and whom the land and sea drove back—but for all that, he is a man! Come, let us call him and his men our guests, not stand here while the water rises!"

With a clattering of weapons and horse hooves, they headed for higher ground, their path winding away from wet sand to a land hospitable and fair even beneath this darkening sky. The Druid held up a hand for them to halt. When they obeyed, he left them, running with the speed of a much younger man back toward the shore. Even Kynan, a generation younger than he, was hard put to keep up with him.

The Jomsborg ships approached the shore. Seeing the Byzantine ships bobbing in the water and the Druids arrayed on shore, their crews screamed derisively and brandished swords and spears against the shields they snatched from where they had hung over the sides of their ships. A gust of wind caught the sail of one of the ships far to the rear, and sent it bellying out. It was blood-red, except for the raging black bear that blotted the center of the sail.

Marric turned toward the shore, his eyes wide. "Get down," he whispered hoarsely, just as the first lightning crackled from thick clouds into the water. The sky turned a sickly yellowish gray, which the water mimicked. Then mists wreathed about them, as the clouds lowered still farther, and the rain came, veritable walls of it. In an instant, Marric's cloak was drenched, but he raised it just the same about mouth and nose so he could breathe air rather than the driving rain, mixed now, despite the season, with stinging hail.

The wind howled like a barbarian warrior in a death-charge. From time to time, it stripped the mists away from the water, and Marric could see the Aescir ships attempting to reef their sails, to come about in a furious but doomed fight to stay afloat.

Memory struck him with the force of lightning: *waterspouts punched through the decks of the Emir's ships that would have enslaved him once more, sold his crew, and made of his love a toy in a woman's body. On the* Pride of Isis, *a tall man shuddered as the magic took him, and screamed like a death shriek,* "Ha'k i-ri!" *the cry of Osiris to be raised from his own death. Behind him, his priests chanted and muttered. As the power coursed up his spine and out through his hands, he swayed, but when he would have fallen,* not to be slain, not to be taken, never to be sold again, *he vowed; and withstood.*

Now, for a brief, treacherous instant, his thoughts winged to the pirate ships—Jomsborg or Arab, it barely mattered—and he felt the crew's baffled fury at losing game, battle, and life so close, so close to shore and the quarry; stifling fear, then a convulsive struggle for air, quickly over; and finally nothing at all. He ws gasping, choking, and he coughed and panted for breath just as the Prydein nobleman crouching beside him pounded him on the back. He was sputtering too, but he managed a whoop of triumph as the wind blew the mists clear of what had been a sea full of Jomsborg and Byzantine ships.

One of Marric's ships had capsized. The others floated on long, green surges of water, off which the sun sparkled merrily. Of the entire Jomsborg fleet only a few broken spars remained, sinking beneath the water, or floating idly toward land, and a few scattered vessels turning away from the shore.

"They're fleeing!" screamed a very young Celt, and began to pound sword against shield with a wet, clangorous sound.

Marric squinted out, glad that he had the farsight of his patron Hawk. Certainly, they had turned; but from the way the ships handled, it looked more like retreat than rout to him. The treacherous empathy of a moment past shook through him again, to be replaced by rage and a need for revenge, to tear and rend the land that had refused surrender. *Spying again, princeling?* The question, in a hag's cackle, shattered the moment and hurled Marric back into his own mind.

"They'll be back," he mused. Though he had kept his voice soft the charioteer heard him and nodded. "Aye, that they will," he said. "And this time they will come with men, with arms, and horses—and their families. Winter itself will not suffice to drive them back to their own shores. But we will be waiting for them."

The senior Druid leaned over one of Marric's guardsmen to speak to him directly. "You have the Sight, haven't you?"

Marric glared at him. "Do I look like one of my priests there?" he asked.

The Druid smiled and refused to be baited. "You look like one of ours. And the sight is common here in the Isles of the Mists, whether or not a man be priest, bard, warrior, or farmer." Marric could just imagine what he looked like: haggard from visions, drenched from the storm, and sadly in need of a shave and a bath. His shoulders ached abominably as he levered himself up from the mud into which he had flung himself. All along the strand, Greeks and Celtoi rose slowly and stretched. Grooms were already soothing the panicky horses. Three people down from him, the Iceni—what? chieftess? queen?—woman squeezed water from her hair and spoke longingly of hot water. Aillel had said these people bathed.

Jarl Grettir had been on board that ship, Marric thought. How had he known that—and why, for a terrible moment, had he betrayed himself to feel pity for men who would have laughed as they cut him down? Had the potential for magic in him, so long frustrated because of his unworthiness, finally festered and turned him toward the dark? Or was it a trick of the blood that had splashed him when the were-bear died? He didn't know—yet he must know let it betray him. *I'll fall on my own sword first!* he promised himself.

It would be war, he knew. He could tell himself that Prydein's war—or a war fought by Prydein's tribes—was none of his. But he would be lying. A war fought against the Jarl who had tested his Empire was very much his war. *But on my terms*, Marric thought, *and at a time of my choice, with an Empress beside me.*

He was these people's guest. Very well: for now he would be these people's ally. When he rode north and west to claim Alexa, he would ride as their messenger, warning them to arm against the Storm Year to come.

And then he and his sister could be gone from this place full of splendid barbarians and their unfamiliar, but deadly, magics.

Chapter 18

☆

During the ride into a village that clustered about Corio's hall, Marric rode with his weapons politely unavailable—all weapons, that was, except his mind. Byzantines, and Hellenes before them, had raised curiosity to an art. A military art, as well as a pure art form, Marric thought as he set himself to question his companions. They were not fools. They would tell him what they thought he should believe; and he would believe . . . well, some of it.

One careful glance at them told him that these people were not all Celtoi of Prydein, but the mixture of races he should have expected would result from generations of raiding, conquest, retreats, and migrations. Some were from Eire, and spoke with Aillel's accent. Others were Belgae and mainland Celtoi who had returned to Prydein after the Storm Years. A few men had the straw-colored hair, light eyes, and vast height of Germani, distant kinsmen to the Aescir. Probably they had come here during the Storm Years, and made peace with that Arktos whom they never called king nor priest.

The village was crowded, since Corio played temporary host to war bands from so many of the neighboring tribes. Their names were familiar to Marric from Caesar and later explorers: Canti, Durotriges, Atrebates, even—led by Luned —members of the tribes ruled by women, such as the Iceni. They were all tribes from the south and east of the island, who might first expect attack. Each tribe kept fairly much to itself. Judging from his experience among the Huns, Marric suspected that clan leaders hoped to avoid insults that might lead to blood, thence to blood feud, and a shattering of the temporary alliances that always wore so on barbarians. He marked which leaders spoke with cold formality to one another against potential need.

Then Marric found himself under attack both by his own servants and Corio's people, intent that he submit to their hospitality. Though bathing customs here replaced scented oils and strigils with rendered animal fat that his servants sniffed at, and handed back ("With courtesy!" Marric hissed.), he was glad enough to rinse what felt like half a beach from his hair and skin, then sink into a wooden tub of steaming water, replenished by a steady stream of matter-of-fact men and women. He was self-conscious at first about his scarred back and sides, conspicuous in this throng of lighter-skinned men, until Corio glanced at him and nodded approvingly.

He pointed to a livid weal on his own shoulder. "I killed the man who gave me this," he announced.

Marric showed his teeth in a grin and made the reply expected of him. "So did I." Never mind telling him that he had been a slave at the time, or that the heavy gold torques these men sported looked like slave collars. He was scarred, therefore a proven warrior: it was enough. Marric sighed, stretched out on the closest substitute his servants could find for a bench, and let them work oil into his skin. That, apparently, drew curious stares and whispers until a sharp reproof dispersed his audience.

Just as much to console his body-servants for this outrage as to impress his hosts, Marric did not protest when a tunic of purple so dark as to be almost black, embroidered with gold and pearls, was held out for him. It was more subdued than the plaids most of the tribesmen wore, in any case. He won a skirmish about whether to wear a lighter or a heavier circlet, lost a major engagement over how many necklaces he would endure weighing down his neck, and then stalked past a crowd of curious children to the hall. Jangling, no less, from the damned jewelry. At lest it would cover the growling in his belly. He had feasted with Huns; he expected better fare this evening.

Corio's hall was more Saxon than Celtic. It was built of wood and thatched, with a central space, such as one would find in a court above a rain-pool; benches and boards about a central firepit, with a separate seat for the king and honored guests on a raised dais. Not quite Marric's own dining hall of marble and mosaic, he thought, with its couches cushioned by silk woven on his own palace looms. A welcome change. He bowed to Corio's wife who was already wearing—among other jewelry—the amethyst clasp he had asked the king to give her. He sank down gingerly and accepted a wine cup, a huge silver thing that took both hands to hold and looked ancient.

He drank cautiously and raised his eyebrows in delight at the taste. Clearly trade with the mainland had flourished here if he could be served Falernian wine unmixed. He drank more deeply, then beckoned to one of his officers. "They drink their wine neat here," he warned the man. "Pass the word to the men to watch themselves. No knives out, and no byplay with the women." Then he attacked his meal—the oysters harvested from local waters, beef, and lamb—as enthusiastically as other men there.

Finally he stretched, ignored the lack of a servant to carry around water to wash with, and held out his cup to be refilled. The food here was better than among the Huns; and the wine! he had drunk mares' milk with Ellac and Uldin, but he would not pretend he liked it any longer than he had to. When bards and harpists came forward, he banged his cup on the table with the rest of the chiefs.

Very quickly, the songs outstripped his knowledge of the language. Something martial and loudly acclaimed, about Arktos, his ten great battles, and his tragic betrayal. *What Sophocles or Homer could have done with that story!* Marric thought with regret. *I must be more drunk than I thought.* He waved away the wine next time it was brought round, and sank back, ostensibly to listen, but actually to think.

He had thought he understood barbarians. His Strategikon, not to mention other texts, had long sections dealing with the proper tactics for conquering, pacifying, and flattering them. His Civil Service had special bureaus for assimilating them into the Empire. What he understood, he decided, was people like Ellac and Uldin: Huns proud of their craftiness, impatient of civilized restraint; or men like Audun, countrymen with a countrymen's sense. Though Audun—it was as hard to refer to a man as wise as the Bearmaster as *barbaros* as it was to call the hypercivilized and treacherous Perians that.

But in the name of Thoth, what did you do with barbarians who regarded themselves as civilized and *him* as the outlander, at least as decadent as a Persian and probably more volatile? He put the topic away for more sober meditation, and gazed into the depths of his wine cup where the firelight cast strange shadows. No visions, thank the gods. He might be priest-ridden, might even have the Sight, but he saw no visions.

As he leaned forward to strip a bracelet from his wrist and hurl it to Kynan the way Corio had, slender fingers touched his wrist. He turned and saw Queen Luned, who waved away his offer of help and pulled her chair closer to his. He rose until she was seated, and saw her smile.

"I understand," she told him, "that your men are behaving themselves. Too well, in fact. Did you order them not to seduce the local women?"

The fire and the press of bodies made the hall very hot. Marric grinned and admitted it.

"They are soldiers; they keep discipline."

"So are some of my women. Your men would not force them."

"If they are soldiers, then my men would take their lives in their hands if they tried, would they not?" Marric asked.

"Their lives—or something else," said Luned. She leaned forward to listen to the bard who sang a softer tune now.

"Is there really a queen so fair that where she walks, four white trefoils bloom?" Marric asked, laughing. His rules on "seducing native women" applied to him too, he decided. Luned would just as soon stab as slap a man who offended her. That would mean war.

Luned shook her head so that the reddish glints in her unbound hair swung and flickered almost as brightly as the garnets she wore on her wrists and in a wide necklace dangling beneath her torque. "They sing of the queen who rules the Coritani and Deceangli, to the north in Gwynedd. She is my cousin on my mother's father's side. He was one of the Brigantes. I have met her. When she was younger, she was beautiful. But as fair as all that? No woman is that beautiful . . . save as men see her. And the bards are all men."

She flashed a smile and dark eyes at him, and leaned a little closer. The garnets flashed in the deep cleft between her breasts. She was flushed, and Marric could smell smoke and fragrant oils on her, as well as a musk that heated his senses. He shut his eyes and tried to slow his breathing.

When she laid a hand on his arm, he started.

"Emperor!" shouted Corio. "You tell us a tale!"

Before all the gods, was he expected to play Odysseus now? After he had drunk so deeply? Marric raised his cup and toasted the petty king ironically.

"What will you hear?" he asked. "Of the dream that brought me, the Emperor of the Romans, here to your shores?"

That drew a roar of laughter and recognition from the crowd. Marric stood, stretched lazily, then walked down to join the bards. If this was a game, he would play it to the fullest. It reminded him of his months on campaign, long before he became Emperor, when he was still a wild prince—when, by all the gods, when he was still young. Then he could relax among his men and among their tame barbarians, drinking with them, riding with them, enjoying those women who offered themselves. Some of his senior officers looked shocked, which amused him. His Varangians, however, cheered lustily. They remembered that younger, more carefree Marric. He suspected that that was the man they had sworn to, not the Emperor, Lord of the Two Lands, and all the other titles.

He held up his hand for quiet.

"I am no bard, of course, but let me tell you of a vision I had once," he started. He heard his voice, trained to address armies, ring out into the hall. Though its tone was still true, it was too harsh now from shouting over the din of battle to be musical. "Once a prince, a scholar, and . . ." his voice faltered . . . "a seeress sought refuge from invaders who sought to make them slaves. They came to a Druid's home, where the mists clustered thick upon the ground. The mists changed shapes, and their enemies saw that which they feared most of all; and they broke ranks and fled.

"'Show me my future,'" the prince asked the seeress. "And she took out her silver bowl, and filled it with water and oil, and gazed into the troubled water. Now, the prince had a sister who was very dear to him. But she was lost: dead, he believed, and he grieved deeply. But the seeress blew upon the water, and when it cleared, there in the bowl was revealed a golden king and queen. The king was a man of strength and valor; the queen a woman of great beauty. We have a tale in my land of how the Goddess Hathor lives in a grove far to the west of us: that was how this woman seemed to the prince.

"But standing between the king and queen was a dark-haired lady, with a face like a cat. And seeing her, the prince wept. For she was the sister whom he had mourned as dead. The prince's tears fell into the bowl and shattered the vision. When his eyes cleared, and he could look again, he saw only oil, a rainbow floating on water. So he vowed that if ever he could, he would sail west and seek his sister."

For a long moment, Marric paused, struggling in Celtic for the words that would tell, yet veil, his story. *Fool, last time you played the actor, your concubine Stephana died for your pride. What will this night's foolery cost you?* His face heated, and the room spun a little. Stephana . . . she had not been concubine, but beloved. Within his skull, echoing, it seemed, within the bones, came a cackling laughter that he fought to blot out. He had to fight the Jomsborgers, not listen to them. And certainly he must certainly not let them strike through his defenses.

But his mood was shattered. He drained his cup, then drew a deep breath that came out like a sob. It would have been a sob, had he been able to weep. "I myself am the prince," he said. "And I have finally come here to Prydein to bring my sister home."

He nodded, then looked up at his audience. Save for the crackling of embers and the wind in the thatched roof, the hall was silent. The Celtoi on all sides of him were bright-eyed, rapt; a tear shone on Luned's cheek. Several of the Varangians were weeping, while his Greek-born officers sat silent, biting their lips. Marric wondered how many of them had been in the Hippodrome the night he had worn the mask of the God, then laid it aside. Revealing his love and his fear before that crowd had won him an empire. Tonight, might it gain him a queen?

Then the hall erupted in whoops and cheers, led by Corio and Luned. Marric walked slowly toward his seat but found Kynan blocking his way. He bowed, as he might salute a master of his art, and from his wrist pulled the armlet that Marric had tossed him only that evening. "You would not want to be a giver of rings," Marric told him. "Keep that one, in token of this night."

As the wine and beer went round still again, he sank into his chair and wished that the night were over.

Luned's hand was on his arm. "I may know where your sister is," she said.

Marric whipped around, grasping her shoulder. "Where?"

Deliberately, Luned looked at his hands, the strong fingers pressing in. He had to have been hurting her, he, who never willingly would harm a woman. He loosened his grip. "Sweet Isis, lady, where?"

"My cousin Olwen—ah, that is the name, isn't it?"

"That is the name Audun Bearmaster gave me," he said.

"Queen Olwen, the one the bards sang of earlier, rules in Penllyn far to the north, past Sinadon. Her land is near the isle of Deva where there is a college of Druids. I have heard of a dark-haired lady whom she calls kinswoman. But Emperor Marric, you should know that the lady is a seeress, much honored in the land. She may not wish to leave."

"She must!" Marric, intent on his own thoughts, hissed. Queen Luned raised a russet eyebrow.

"Must? Surely, she is a free woman, with the power to come and to go, not ask may she, may she not. She is not your slave, Emperor."

"Lady," Marric said, appalled at how husky his voice was, "I am not the one to whom you should speak of slavery. For I have worn chains and bear the scars. Today, though I wear a crown, and have chains of gold about my neck, rather than shackling my hands and ankles, I am yet a slave. To my Empire, for so I was bred. Alexa is my sister. How can she give less?"

Luned shrugged. "It will go as it must. But I can set you on your path. Still, that is a matter for the dawn. There is still tonight, though . . ." Her voice was rich, enticing as the wine Marric had drunk. And the hint of musk that rose from her breasts made him draw his breath sharply, then lose it.

He had not been celibate since Stephana's death. But such women as he had bedded were hetairai, skilled artists of pleasure who took his desire and his gold and brought him temporary respite from lust and, sometimes, dreams. They neither had, nor wished, more claim on him than patron owed hetaira.

This woman, however, was a queen. Strong, healthy, proud, she was simply unwilling to pass the night alone. What would it be like to lie with a warrior-woman? She would not shrink from his scars, that much was true. And he would not have to fear hurting her.

"Or," she looked away, with great courtesy, "is it true of you what is said of Romans?"

For an instant, Marric was at a loss. She put out a hand that was graceful and well-shaped despite its many scratches and calluses, and touched the silk of his sleeve. "I heard," she said. "In the bath, you use fine oils. And this cloth is very fine," she observed. "Far softer than our warriors would wear . . ."

For the first time in Marric's life he was tempted to curse his ancestors. Let Achilles or Alexander love a friend, and all their descendants were thought to be notorious lovers of boys.

"Have I the Persian trick?" Marric asked. He made himself laugh. "We have a saying in the Empire: never turn your back on a Persian. Lady, if I hesitate, it is that I feared to give insult in a land where I am a stranger." In Greek the word for stranger was the same as the word for enemy; judging from the way Luned's smile warmed, strangers here were welcome guests. Very warmly welcomed guests.

Why not accept Luned's welcome? It had been months since he had seen a woman whom he desired. This one was obviously willing, and would put no bonds on him.

His officers, obedient to discipline, clustered together, though now, thank the Gods, at lest they lounged, rather than sat stiffly erect. He had no doubts that they had spent part of the evening discussing siege engines; Marric himself had spotted at least two places where catapults could be used against Jomsborg ships, and his engineers probably had seen more. He caught a senior man's eyes, from which all disapproval had been carefully excluded, and shrugged. The Canti and their allies had fought these battles before; they knew their enemies. If they found it safe to feast, it probably was. To make ostentatious play of posting guards might even offend these barbarians, who had the reputation of being very proud and touchy.

Luned's hand brushed his knee, wandered slightly higher. Very touchy indeed. It could be a pleasant night. The hearth fire had died down in the hall, and they sat in shadow. Still, he could see her eyes gleam and her tongue flicker over her lips to moisten them. Her lower lip was full. He wondered what it would feel like to kiss. He glanced with appreciation down the long lines of her body, let his eyes linger on the thrust of full breasts against taut fabric, then met her own eyes so she could see him kindle frankly into lust. Her hand crept further up his thigh.

Marric drew a finger from her torque up her neck to her lips, tracing them gently. "Where can we go?" he asked. "My quarters?" She nodded. He stood and held out a hand to her. When she clasped it, he pulled her up against him, pinning her against his body with one hand against her buttocks so she could feel him rising against her. She flung her arms around him. Her hands were excitingly strong. Sweet Isis, he wanted to feel them stroking down his sides, holding his hips, urging him toward the center of her body.

Marric flicked his tongue tip against her ear. "You can ask me your questions about Romans again tomorrow. If you want to," he whispered in a voice experience told him made women shiver. This one proved no exception. He pressed his hips firmly against hers, and felt her body mold against him. "And if you are still able."

Luned's fingers played with the damp curls at the back of Marric's neck, tangling them even more thoroughly than her body lay tangled with his, then, with exaggerated care, smoothing them out. He tightened his arms about her and nuzzled against her breast, a motion of his lips, as her heartbeat slowed. The tiny room seemed very warm now, but her skin was warmer still.

For all their strangeness to one another, their bodies had been marvelously at ease. Marric moved one hand experimentally down her spine, and felt, as much as heard, her laugh in her throat. A pulse throbbed in it, and he kissed that too.

Luned shivered.

"Cold?" he whispered. *He*, born of a warmer climate, should have been the one to tremble; there had been times that night when he had. He rolled slightly away from the woman to pull up the fur coverlets they had kicked to the edge of the bed. Now that they were quiet, their bodies cooling for the moment, it was chilly. He tucked the soft furs gently about Luned's shoulders. Her breasts were magnificent, and he bent to kiss them again.

His lips brushed against a long, raised line, and he ran his tongue along a thin scar that brushed down the center of her body almost to her belly. Her hands tightened in his hair. When he looked up, her eyes were wary.

"If you hadn't been quick, this would have . . . " Marric shook his head, then traced the line of a scar that might have gutted the woman in his arms.

"Are your scars any different?" She smoothed one finger down his shoulder, across his chest, and lower. "You are going to tell me that it is one thing for a man to be scarred, another thing entirely for a woman. A warrior bears scars, Marric of the Romans. And I am a warrior."

Marric slid onto his back and pulled her down on top of him. "Since you have already said it for me, what reason do I have to open my mouth?"

"I can think of several." Finally Luned pulled away from his parted lips.

"You would protect me out of my strength," she told him. "As you would protect this sister of yours—whether or not she wills it. And that would not be right."

"Don't fight your war in my arms," Marric whispered. "Yes, I would protect you if I could. I would be wrong, but I would do it." He laughed. "Will you ever forgive me?"

She purred almost like the cats in the temple of Isis, and

stretched against the length of his body. "Would you like me to stay with you tonight?"

He and his forces were still in strange territory, and Marric liked to be within call. But it had been a good night, a fine night; he hadn't had this sense of well-being for years. He hugged Luned hard, savoring her response, her warmth. How long had it been since he had found a woman he wanted beside him all night? Since Byzantium? "They say that you Celtoi are a hospitable race. I ask you, is it hospitable to leave a guest to wake lonely in the night?"

"You? That isn't the only way that you would wake. That you are waking." She slid her hand lower down his belly to caress him. "I had heard about the men of the east, that they are . . . schooled, as a warrior is at arms."

Celtoi heard a lot of stories about the Empire, Marric thought. Conflicting stories. He snorted with incongruous laughter, even as his blood took fire from her touch. An exotic, that was what he was to her. The day had gone well: it had been a satisfactory storm, an even more satisfactory feast; and she was curious. She was not the first. He tried to contain his laughter but shook with it as much as with desire.

"Does this make you laugh?" She lifted her fingers, and he was sorry.

He caught her hand and firmly replaced it. "Don't stop that," he told her before they lost the capacity for anything but panted breaths and laughs.

Afterward, he drew her to lie with her head on his shoulder in a contented weariness. He was reminded of a hetaira he favored in Byzantium. That woman was no longer especially young or dazzling. Her breasts had even begun, ever so gently, to sag. But he always enjoyed her laugh and her warmth. They were veterans together. So were he and Luned.

As Marric waved on the edge of sleep, he heard Luned's soft voice, muted almost to a yawn. "I wonder what the truth is behind that story you tell of a sister. Well, they will find it out in Penllyn."

He tried to raise his head, to answer her, but she rubbed her face against his shoulder. "Quiet!" she ordered, with mock sternness. "Do you ever rest? Or are you waiting for me to

assure you that I no longer need to ask you again the question
I asked earlier?"

It was a fine thing to fall asleep laughing, Marric thought,
and then did it.

Chapter 19

☆

He had staggered through mists for hours. When had he become aware that something stalked him? Now he could hear
the pad of its feet, the rasp of its breath, so confident it was
that its prey could no longer elude it. It seized him, one
clawed hand over his mouth, the other on his heart, sending a
deadly chill into his bones. His knees gave out, and he prayed
death would come quickly. Instead his captor forced him to
stumble forward through the mists until his feet splashed into
something warm, and a loom rose up ahead of him.

He tried to hurl himself to one side, but the creature forced
him to lie with his back against the loom and bound him to it
with slimy tendrils, splaying out his hands and feet so he was
helpless.

"Welcome, Emperor," he heard on a wave of foul
breath. The hag stood before him, a flint blade in her hand.
Where would she strike first? He could feel the faint rush of
the blade as it descended, as it pierced through his entrails,
and he opened his mouth to scream . . .

"Easy, rest easy," Luned's arms were warm about him, and
her mouth on his was warmer still.

"Ah gods!" Marric whispered hoarsely. "Not again." He sat
upright, and wiped cold sweat from his brow. The lamps had

burned out, and he could see only the bulk of walls, or crude furniture, and the long curve of Luned's body.

She unwrapped herself from the wolfskins and knelt behind him, slipping her arms around him. "Again? Powerful enemies you have," she commented. "You should speak with the Druids . . ."

He would have pulled free, but her arms tightened. "No more priests!" he muttered. If he were what he should be, priest and king, he could banish these night horrors with a flick of his will. But he was only a warrior, so a warrior's courage must sustain him.

"So stubborn you are," she told him, though, for a mercy, she did not argue. "That is the Celt in you." She pulled him down to lie beside her. "But must you be sick as well as stubborn?" She took his hands and chafed them, cupping them between her breasts until they were warm again.

"I am sorry," Marric began, but she laid a palm over his lips.

"Hush," she told him. "Perhaps if you will not speak with the Druids, your sister can ease what troubles you. For now, though, sleep."

He rested his head against her breasts, but long after her breathing softened and steadied, he lay awake, longing for the pallor of earliest dawn.

Sunlight touched the wooden walls with a splendor like that of gold mosaic tiles when Marric woke. Luned was gone, but the room and bed still smelled of her. He stretched in contentment. Then he remembered the rest of the night and glanced down as if he half expected to see a wound where the hag's blade had slashed his belly. For a wonder, he was unmarked, except, of course, for the old assortment of scars and a new love-bite that he smiled over.

Hot water steamed from a jug in the corner, and he hastened toward it, shivering in the chilly dawn air. If even in summer, Prydein was this cold, he could understand why the barbarians wore trousers. He might consider them himself, he decided, chuckling. Dressing rapidly, he went in search of food and information. And, just possibly, Queen Luned herself.

Two of his officers sat cross-legged near a knot of Saxons, trying to talk in a barbarous *koine* of Greek, Celtic, and the Aescir tongue. Marric approached, holding up a hand to prevent his men's rising.

"Once he leaves Jomsborg, Jarl Grettir will not return there to pass the winter," one of the Saxons stated flatly.

"Is it not the custom?" asked a cavalry officer. "The bar . . . the Jomsborgers fight during the summer, then retreat at harvest? What makes you think it will change?"

"During the Storm Years, *we* did not," retorted the Saxon, pushing the ale toward Marric as he squatted down opposite him. "We took—"

"Arktos *allowed* you lands of your own—" interrupted a woman whose necklaces reminded Marric of Luned. She grinned, but not with humor.

"Surely that quarrel died with your great-grandsires," Marric cut into the conversation. "Is this the truth of it? You expect that the Jomsborgers will stay, and there is no Arktos to rule over you all and repel them."

Sullen nods answered him. Marric sipped his ale. He could help them, he knew it. Parties of soldiers and engineers, with, say, one or two scouts to serve as messengers, could be detached, could build catapults that could stop Jomsborg ships, or could contrive all sorts of military ingenuities that had always served before to frighten and scatter the barbarians. It could be his gift for the Celtoi's care of Alexa.

He glanced over at his own men.

"Any word of our missing transports?" he asked in rapid Greek.

The man shook his head.

A whole moira, vanished. Marric controlled his expression before he could frown. No: he would not whittle down his forces, Advisors could too easily become hostages, should the changeable Celtoi turn against them. Quick inquiries convinced him that he had a long ride northwest: it was best to go in such numbers and splendor as he could manage. The Celtoi were experienced at this sort of fighting, had done it since the days of Arktos. And they had the best advantage of all: they knew the land on which they would fight, knew it and loved it.

This was the pragmatic decision, therefore the correct one for a general to make. But ironic laughter rang in his ears. He barely restrained himself from clapping hands to them. Somehow his decision pleased Jomsborg, and that bothered him profoundly. He opened his mouth on a question about guides for the trip to Penllyn, when the way his men's faces changed alerted him. Careful not-grins stitched across their faces, then smoothed to bland courtesy as Luned approached. Today she wore a loosely bloused man's tunic and breeches. Despite the passion of their night together (and Marric knew that he had pleased her), her face was impassive. When Marric, rising to greet her, held out his hands to take hers and draw her close, she pretended not to notice.

"I know you must ride north, Emperor," she said. "Today my warriors and I ride for home. You and yours are welcome to ride with us for as long as our paths are the same. And then I can direct you how best to reach Penllyn."

This was what he wanted, was it not? No time to involve himself in battles for a land that was none of his. Simply ride north and west, find Alexa, and bring her home. The sooner he left this Prydein of terrible dreams and enigmatic barbarians, the sooner he would have peace—or as much of it as he could wrest from his stepmother's curse.

There could be no time, no need, even, to learn if the night he spent with Luned might lead to deeper feelings. She had been passionate and lovely, but, no doubt, appalled by a bedmate who woke screaming. *What woman would not? There was one once, who loved me*, he thought of Stephana with familiar grief. But magic and his own hubris had slain Stephana. If his nightmares were magical attacks, he knew he faced enemies whose magic was as evil as Irene's—and as strong. Luned would have a war to fight; best not complicate her life with magic that could end it.

I will not give in, Marric thought. Before I submit, I will fall on my own sword. Whether I have an heir or not.

At least, Luned had stayed the night, not put him to the

public shame of abandoning his bed for someplace more tranquil.

Meeting her formality with formality, Marric thanked her.

When they rode out, however, Luned rode at his side. Magnificent in her disdain for his soldiers' grins, she silenced the one Varangian who dared comment with a remark about the only need unweaned pups had for females. Marric would have liked to laugh with Luned's warriors then, to share in the ease that spread through the ranks and let Byzantine and Iceni ride peaceably together. But the sun soon vanished behind a haze of cloud.

Marric sighed, pulled up his hood, and waited for the inevitable drizzle. Bad enough to wear armor in the heat, but in heat *and* wet—no wonder Caesar had not pursued his campaigns into Prydein. He thought longingly of the splendor of the Golden Horn or the ferocious glare of sunlight on the Falcon's wings when it appeared to him in Alexandria or in the Middle Sea. Sunlight burned away illusion and slew demons. For as the mists thickened, Marric sensed the hag's presence more and more closely, and now he knew why. In his dreams, she had blooded him, strengthening the bond she had cast about him. It did not help to avoid thoughts of the hag; her damnable laughter followed him, and it was getting closer.

When had it started? Marric cast his thoughts back. That bear that had rushed him . . . somehow, it must have marked him. And now he must wait, test his spirit constantly for signs of betraying him to his enemy.

Sweet Isis, no wonder Alexa had broken. To live in the palace, to fear every day that Irene might devise a new spell, or find a new poison; and then, poor little one, to slip, just once, into curiosity, and feel her enemy seize that weakness and twist it into a rope to bind her. At least he was a warrior trained. What was Alexa? She had been very young, poor child, and very much afraid. No wonder she had turned on to him too. Empathy, painful as love, pierced him, and he was glad, for once, that he could not weep. Once he had his sister safe, he would have to take great care of her.

Luned had called her a healer, though. How odd. Still, it had been years, long enough for the girl to have become a woman. He could not imagine it. Perhaps her presence would heal him. That must be what Luned meant.

"I said, Emperor, that your men care about you. I had not known this of the Romans."

Marric jolted himself back to awareness of the woman at his side.

"We have a saying, that a general should be father to his troops," he told her gruffly to conceal his pleasure in her remark.

"It goes far beyond that," she murmured. "They sing about you." Marric smiled. He had heard some of the songs. The legions' song about Caesar, "Lock up your daughters," was nothing to them.

But Luned did not smile back. "The songs I heard say tell that when you took power, you received crown and curse."

Marric felt his mouth twist into a snarl. "Soldiers' tales."

"I saw the truth of them myself. Marric, I will repeat what I said last night," Luned's voice was soft. "You should talk with the Druids. If need be, go to the Druid Isle near Penllyn to consult with the healers there."

"Lady, I could surround myself with priests, and the curse would still be with me. I had it of the woman who stole my father's crown: that I would never know peace as long as I reigned."

Luned's eyes smoldered. "And your dreams?"

Marric shrugged. "I have dreamed before."

"What if your dreaming endangers your men?"

"Lady, you go too far!" With an effort, Marric kept himself from shouting at her. Cold sweat beaded his brow. Luned did not look away nor retreat. He had not expected that she would.

All that day and the next, their scouts found no sign of Jomsborgers; and Marric was relieved. Less pleasant, however, was the news that his ships seemed to have vanished. Losing that moira would hurt him terribly, and his enemies knew it. But if the Jomsborgers had destroyed them, the hag would boast of it. He forced his attention within, to the dark place inside him. For an instant, he had a blurred impression of ships with prows carved in the shape of bears. Then the hag's voice struck him like a slave master's whip.

So you come now to seek me? Do you think I am a pretty

*young thing, like that wench who calls herself a queen, yet
warms your bed, hot as any tavern slut? Or have you come to
bow . . .*

This is absurd, Marric retorted and withdrew his consciousness, retreating back to the outside world. It was worse than
absurd, it was dangerous to have any speech at all with the
hag. Her laughter rang in his ears as he blinked, relieved to
see rocks, trees, and the figures of warriors and horses. His
men were preparing to fall out and rest, but Marric raised his
hand to signal for greater speed.

Luned, of course, protested. "My people cannot keep pace
with your horses," she told him. "You will be crossing mountains. Do you wish to be worn out when you reach Sinadon?"

Marric shook his head. "They are closer," he muttered.

"And you must seek out this sister of yours, before they
land. Is that it?"

He nodded again. At the very least, messengers could be
sent out to warn the tribes, so that Jomsborg would not surprise them. That much he could—and must—do.

"*Why?*" she demanded, cross in her worry for her people
and perhaps even some slight concern for him.

"I have no heir," he told her. Luned's face twisted.

"You ask me to believe that you would seek out your sister . . ."

"It is the custom for rulers in the Two Lands." If he said
that distantly enough, perhaps she would be silent.

"There is no greater sin in Prydein than for close kin to lie
together. You do not know what has happened here. Long
ago, during the Storm Years, we had a Queen, not a very
good or brave one, but she did well enough, largely because
she had the wit to select Arktos as her consort. Ah, that was a
man to stir the blood in any woman!" she breathed.

"Unfortunately, he did. As you know, Arktos was a man of
the North, kin to the Aescir. But he had a half sister, and her
kin was with the women of Finnmark. She needed an heir for
her magic. So she cast around for the bravest, strongest man
she could find. Her brother. Under a disguise, she lay with
him. He did not know until much later that she was his sister.
And from their child came only despair. The Queen fled

south, and her land withered as she aged. That is what comes of lying with sisters."

Marric swallowed. "What happened to Arktos?"

"Certain sins cry up to heaven. Once Arktos knew his own guilt, he failed and died. As did his son—at his father's hands. But the son had a daughter who married into the Jomsborg line . . ." Luned's voice trailed off.

"Alexa is . . . like me," Marric astonished himself by trying to justify his need for her to the chieftess. "We were raised to know that we must wed one another, produce children who are doubly Imperial. There is no choice, if the Empire is to have an heir."

"You have no other heirs?" asked Luned.

Marric shrugged.

"Then I promise you, that if our nights together have made me fruitful, and if the child be a boy, when he outgrows a woman's care, I will send him to you."

Marric's hands tensed on his horse's reins, and the poor beast curveted, sending a scatter of pebbles down along the hillside.

"Idiot!" Incongruously, Luned laughed. "Did you think that the lines on my belly were all scars? I have three daughters, heir-children, and I thought, perhaps, before I grew too old, to have one more. Praise be, I will live to see them grow up, and resign power into their hands. Some rulers are not so fortunate."

"No, lady, some are not," Marric said, low-voiced.

Luned put out a hand to touch his. "Now, what I did not wish is what I have done. I have hurt you, where I meant to warn and comfort. You could be an easy man to love, but not, I think, a safe one. Yet these days and nights have been very sweet; and I wish you well."

That night was the last they spent together. The next day, Luned reached her home, and Marric the turnoff for the west. The Iceni supplied them with food, some remounts, and guides for the journey to Penllyn. Then, before Marric mounted, Luned reached up and kissed him. Her lips were dry, the kiss but a formality, but her eyes were very warm.

"Remember what I said. *All* of what I said, Marric."

He reached for her, to take her wholly in his arms despite

the assembled warriors. When she eluded him, he lifted a chain bearing a large medallion from about his neck.

"It is not a trinket," he spoke quickly as her eyes flashed, "but a token of rank in my home. My remembrance to you, or a gift to a child."

He clasped her hand about the medallion. "See, it bears my likeness."

Luned shook back her hair. "I shall remember you without such baubles. Please the Goddess, I shall return it to you, round the neck of my son."

Go now, her eyes pleaded with him. An easy man to love, she had called him. But one who was dangerous, one under a curse—and, since she had a land to guard, a man she dared not want more of than a few nights of pleasure along the road.

Marric swung up into his saddle and signaled the formation for riding through hostile territory. Moments later, he and his two *moirae* were headed west.

As they neared Penllyn, Marric felt himself to be riding back in time and into a legend. The land was filled with noises, not just the cries of birds overhead, or the thousand sounds of any army on the march, but sudden scatterings of rock, or leaf rustles that assured Marric that he and his men were being watched. Though he sent out as many scouts as he might use for a Persian campaign, they found no spies, nor could they buy any. And the only sense they had of threat was when they strayed too close to certain dense stands of trees.

At night, occasionally, they heard hoofs drumming, though they saw never a trace of the warriors or hunters who passed their way. Just carts, and ponies, and the occasional ruts of a cart or chariot: messengers and tradespeople seemed to pass freely among the tribes.

Soon they rode through mountains, or what passed for them in this island. On a much smaller scale than the massifs of Greece or the Caucasus, these mountains did not dwarf Marric and his army: they seemed a size that a man could understand, and even love.

Why had the Empire not looked north to Prydein? He wondered that time and again as they climbed. Inevitably, he found himself studying the land as if he planned to add it to

the Empire. Good land, as rich in minerals as it was beautiful.
Perhaps, after he found Alexa, he could unite the tribes and
teach them Roman military order. Then, once they had repelled Jomsborg . . .

That night, however, the hoofbeats clattered on the rock
very close to their camp, undisturbed by the thunder that
pealed from peak to peak. A gust of wind blew into Marric's
tent. He sprang to his feet, sword in hand, but found himself
slashing only at the wind that overturned his brazier. He
smothered the fire with his robe, but not before the smoke
formed into something that remotely resembled a warrior,
sword in hand, and wearing what looked like a helm with
projecting antlers. The next morning, though the ground was
muddy from the storm, they found no hoofprints. Marric had
not expected to. Now amulets hung in plain sight over his
men's armor.

I have been warned, Marric thought. There had been no
evil in the warning, simply fact: Prydein was guarded. The
very soil itself ws a ruddy color, a sign of copper in the earth,
the Goddess's own metal. So, Prydein and its chiefs had the
same relationship that he and his line did with the Empire. *I
do not want your realm,* Marric told the noises he heard. *I
have my own. I seek to ride in peace.*

As if he had made his peace with the land, the nightly
visitations ceased. Better yet, his dreams barely grumbled
through his sleep, and he had none of the waking dreams that
had made the journey north an ordeal.

Gradually, people appeared once again on the narrow
tracks: a few men in warriors' plaids; villagers who watched
him and his men pass, silently, save for the occasional child
who cried after the bright armor and weapons, or the music-
mad youths who called to one another to come see the Emperor.

It was Macsen's dream come to life, Marric realized. The
omen disturbed him. Macsen had had to regain his crown.
Marric had already fought once for it; he thought he could not
bear to do it again—yet he knew he would.

"We reach Sarn Elen at dusk," his guides told him finally,
and Marric started. It was one thing to have people think that
he was the Emperor from the old songs, but another thing

entirely to find the places that the songs taught of still in existence: like visiting Troy to seek Achilles, or Siwah, Zeus-Ammon's oracle, for some word of Alexander (both of which Marric had done). He found himself shivering, either with eagerness or dread.

Sarn Elen, the road of the wise queen, looked much like any Roman road. Then hoofbeats rang out as they neared the road itself, and a troop rode toward them, blocking their path.

Well-trained, his men reached for their weapons, not for their amulets. Marric cursed, hurried and heartfelt, in Hunnic. Then he settled his helmet and reached for his lance. A pennon bearer rode up beside him, nastily shaking out his banner's purple folds. He held up his hand.

Then two men rode forward toward the Byzantine ranks. One man was tall, with a long mane of chestnut hair, and features that Marric might have trusted had he come unarmed. The other . . .

"Kynan the bard," Marric acknowledged him. "Some day you must tell me why you always leave me. And how you manage to travel so much more rapidly than I."

The bard flushed but disdained to look away.

"Do not blame the bard, Emperor," said the warrior. To Marric's shock, he said it in passable Greek. "He but serves his first loyalty."

Marric shrugged. "Yourself, perhaps?" He could not blame the bard for serving his primary loyalty. But the armlet Marric had given him sparkled on his wrist, and made Marric wish to strangle him.

"Not I, but the order of Druids, and my sister, Queen Olwen. We were told to expect you. She bade me assemble an escort worthy of your rank. If you have no objections to riding after sundown, we should reach the Queen's maenol tonight."

Tonight! Olwen had known of his coming. Tonight, he would see Alexa, would be able to hold her and comfort her for the hardships she had suffered—and promise that never again would any harm come to her. His heart leapt.

"You know the road," he told the warrior. "And if you knew to expect me, then you know my names, Prince. But I do not know yours."

The prince stared at Marric, a measuring look that might

have offended him from another warrior. "I have known your names for many years, Emperor. I am Gereint, son of Queen Blodeuedd and of Aillel of Eire."

"I knew an Aillel," Marric began. "Horus hover over him with his wings, the Aillel I knew practically raised me." He felt his face cracking into a wide grin.

"He raised me too." The prince removed his helmet. He was taller and slighter than the guardsman Marric remembered from his youth, but the features, yes, that was Aillel's jaw, and browline.

"You have a look of him," Marric admitted. "And the same accent. Did he teach you Greek?"

"He and others. Did he teach you our tongue? You speak it with an accent too."

Marric laughed with pleasure and relief, then thrust out his sword arm in greeting. Prince Gereint stared at it a long moment before clasping his wrist in return. If Aillel were in Prydein, then Alexa was safe, and more than safe. He could hear mutterings of "Aillel . . . guard . . . remember . . ." pass down the ranks, and sensed his Guardsmen's rising enthusiasm.

But Gereint was still distant. No answering grin lit the features that were so like his father's. There had to be some reason for his reserve. Aillel was probably old by now, and he had fought hard.

"Your father," Marric asked. "Is he . . ."

"Gone," Gereint said. "He was sailing west from Eire and his ship was lost with all hands, and never a word."

Marric laid a hand on the other man's shoulder. He guessed that Aillel's son was about ten years younger than he. "Perhaps he reached the Horizon," Marric offered what comfort he could. "Perhaps he and my father guard it together."

Gereint laid a hand on Marric's, then shrugged it off a little too quickly. "I am sent to bring you to the Queen," he said with a formality that chilled Marric after the closeness he had felt only a moment before. "Emperor, will you ride with us?"

"Gladly!" Marric told him. he signaled for the horns to sound. They were swiftly answered by a blast from the curved horns, wrought in the shapes of beasts, borne by Gereint's escort. Then the Byzantine force clattered onto the ancient stone of Sarn Elen, through the assembled Celtoi, and toward Penllyn.

Hours later, they swept up a hill to the maenol that crowned it. Gereint cried out, and the gates opened wide to admit them.

"My men can camp outside," Marric mused, not wanting to strain the resources of the place, or anyone's tempers.

If he expected protestations to the contrary, he was disappointed. "That might be best," Gereint said.

There was no point asking where Gereint had learned his reserve; Marric knew where. Aillel had trained him as he had trained Marric himself. But why was the reserve aimed against Marric? Perhaps the prince resented the many years his father had served Marric's. There was no accounting for the man. One moment, he spoke with the frank warmth that Marric had learned to prize in the Celtoi. "Is Byzantium really hot and sunny all the time?" he asked during a brief stop as Marric shivered and cursed the necessity (as he saw it) to change into parade armor and purple. If he were the guest of a queen, he must look the part. And barbarians were easily impressed with splendor. Besides which (he admitted to himself), he wanted Alexa to be proud of him.

"Only in the summer. In the winter, the wind swept across all Scythia, and we all freeze. We warm ourselves by swearing," Marric quipped. He was pleased to see the man unbend. It would be good to be friends with Aillel's son. Perhaps he could persuade Gereint to accompany him and Alexa back to Byzantium.

"Have you ever wanted to see the City where your father was a Guardsman?" he asked, opening the subject cautiously.

"When I was a boy, I longed to. But I am my sister's war leader, and cannot indulge myself as my father did."

Not even the haughtiest patrician of the Empire could have phrased the reply to be more chilling. *Sneer at your father, will you, lad?* Marric thought. Enough of this hot and cold behavior. He summoned his own dignity.

"Bring me to your Queen, then."

* * *

Gereint swung down from his horse and led the way toward a hall larger than Corio's or Luned's. Torches shone outside it, and Marric sensed that it was crowded. Many people waited outside. Their greetings to Gereint were subdued, and their eyes on Marric speculative. When they had landed, he had at least been an intriguing exotic. Here, though he had been welcomed by a prince, the people seemed hostile.

Behind a stiff-backed Gereint, Marric entered the hall and stood blinking in bright light that he had not expected. Chin up, he stood motionless for the moment it took·for his vision to clear. He knew what they would see: a man tall for a Greek, broad-shouldered, dark-haired, wearing the gold and purple of Empire with casual splendor. It was a role he had been bred for, and he played it well.

The hall filled with mutterings. Marric might have spared it a glance, but his eyes were all for the people at the head table. At the center sat the Queen, a tall, beautiful woman with long golden braids that flashed magnificently against a green gown. Behind her stood a bevy of other women: noblewomen, chieftain's wives, perhaps. Beside her was an old, bearded man in a white robe, with a priest's subtlety in his face, and a strange look—compassion? and for whom?—in his eyes.

Then, out from the group of ladies surrounding Olwen the Queen, ran a woman so tiny that she had been hidden in their midst. She was slight, and her hair, unlike the red and flaxen braids of the Celtoi, hung straight and jet black over her delicate shoulders. And her eyes, set aslant in her fine-boned face, gleamed like a cat's, then spilled over into tears, as the woman ran toward him in a flurry of winking gold, white skirts, and that long, long dark hair.

"Marric!" she cried. "Brother!"

Her voice released him from the trance in which he had stood watching her and he strode foreward, holding out his arms to catch her as she flung herself at him. She twisted her fists in his cloak and burrowed against his shoulder, heedless of his armor, laughing and sobbing at once.

Even for this, his curse would permit him no tears. He

wanted to sigh with contentment, but his breath caught in his throat, and his voice was wholly choked. All he could do to greet Alexa was to stroke her hair mutely. Then, as she stopped sobbing, he lifted her chin with two fingers, and kissed her, forehead and eyes and cheeks.

There was no need, ever, for either of them to forgive the other, he exulted. Anything that needed to be said came in that first frantic embrace. He wanted to turn on his heel and, treasure in his arms, walk outside, mount, and gallop away, never stopping until he had his sister safe at home. But the people who had taken Alexa in and protected her until he could reclaim her deserved the heartiest thanks he could offer.

Still holding Alexa, Marric strode toward the Queen. Gereint stood beside her now. He was staring at them with an expression that was strange even for Gereint: grief, and horror, and pity mingled.

"With all my heart, lady," Marric wrestled the words out past the ache in his chest, "with all my heart, I thank you."

Olwen sprang to her feet, and swayed before the Druid steadied her. She would have been beautiful if she were not so wan. She looked as if she had been ill for many months. What was the matter with her?

The hall was abruptly silent, except for a child's gurgle that women tried to hush, but rose stubbornly into a wail. Alexa stirred in Marric's arms.

He bent down to smile at his sister and hug her close. "Little heart, wild bird," he crooned to her. "Glad to see me? Run through a queen's hall like a hoyden, did you, 'Lexa? Sweet one, thank the Goddess I've got you back. You know why I'm here, don't you? I've come to take you home, 'Lexa. And I promise to take care of you for the rest of your life."

The baby's cry intensified. His sister's face crumpled too, as if she wanted to weep again. Alexa pushed against Marric's chest in the signal that had meant "down!" since she was a child. Something was very wrong here, Marric thought. In a moment, he would know what it was.

"No," his sister whispered. "Sweet Goddess, help me know what to do."

The child wailed again. Just as Marric stretched out a hand to draw Alexa back into his arms, she ran forward and took the baby from one of the waiting women. Clasping it against herself protectively, she started back toward Marric.

"Brother," Alexa said. "Oh, my dearest, I am so glad to see you. But I cannot return. Not now."

Marric took an eager step toward her. "Audun said you thought you were not fit to be Empress . . ."

"It is not that, Marric," Alexa cut in. Her mouth quivered as it always did when she refused to weep. Almost fearfully, she approached him and held out the child. The baby looked up, and Marric's heart froze. The child had dark hair, damp tendrils of which clung to its face, with its blue eyes and its pointed chin, so like its mother's. The baby raised its fists and gurgled. Marric felt himself smiling helplessly.

"This is Elen," Alexa whispered. "Olwen's heir. She is my daughter, Marric; mine and Gereint's."

Chapter 20

☆

Veterans always said that the worst wounds, the ones that killed you, were the ones that didn't hurt first. Even as Marric's first joy soured into chagrin and then to a numbness that he hoped would last until he could retreat from this hall, Alexa drew closer to him.

"Your niece, Marric," she said, her great eyes begging him to accept the fact that such a child existed at all.

Gereint started to go to her, but a minute headshake, imperceptible to anyone who didn't know Alexa as well as Marric, stopped him in his tracks. Damn the man! How dared he touch a princess of Byzantium? Hastily, Alexa put herself between her brother and (Marric found the thought difficult) her husband, still holding out the child for Marric to notice, approve, cherish as she did.

"Sister mine, I am hardly a Spartan father," he got the words out in a voice that sounded like he was being strangled. To please her, he held out his arms for the baby. But Alexa recoiled, fearful. That hurt him worse than anything he could imagine.

"I used to hold you when you were that small," he said, smiling to encourage her. "You just wouldn't remember."

She smiled and flashed a brave glance at Gereint, then placed the baby in Marric's hands. It waved reddish fists at him, and he feared it might squirm. Instead, it—she—Elen, Alexa had called the child—opened heavy eyelids and regarded Marric with a steady gaze that whirled him back in time. He had been less than ten when Alexa was born; it had been a great day when their mother Antonia, still white and drawn (like Olwen! Marric realized) from the difficult birthing, permitted him to hold his sister for the first time. Never had there been such a quick and total conquest, his father had liked to say.

Marric found himself smiling at this niece, this destruction of hopes that had kept him alive when dying would have been easier. It was impossible not to smile; she looked like her mother. Then the baby laughed, and fastened a fist on one of Marric's chains, attracted by the shimmer of the gold and pearls. Marric clasped her closer and closed his eyes. Though the pain was starting now, pain that no weeping could ease, the child's weight was welcome in his arms.

Carefully, he bent and kissed the brow of a child whom his Empire's safety would force him to think of as his sister's bastard. "He looks like you, Alexa." She came forward to claim the baby, who clung still to the necklace.

"Let her have it," Marric said. "A small enough gift."

Alexa bent and kissed his hand as it touched her daughter's feathery hair. Her tears fell onto hand and child alike, and she was shivering. Marric handed her back the child, and she clung to its warmth and softness.

"Praise the Goddess." Though Queen Olwen whispered that to the Druid at her side, Marric heard, and tensed.

Sweet Isis, did the woman truly think he would turn on his

sister in front of outsiders? Or that he would simply accept that he had come all this way just to learn that his sister, heir to the role of Isis on Earth, was doing very nicely, thank you very much, with a fine barbarian husband and a half-blood child, so he could turn about and head back to Byzantium?

The woman came closer to him and welcomed him to her hall and realm in passable Greek. He replied as courteously as he might in her own tongue, then held out a hand to escort her back to her own high seat. She was very tall, even for a race that produced tall women. A scent, like flowers withering, clung to her, and he wondered why she chose it. Her skin was very pale, the veins running beneath her brow the blue of fine lapis. She wore a gown of leaf-green wool, clasped by a silver belt from which hung a dagger that seemed too black and rough for such a queen.

She gestured, and conversation rose again in the hall, a little hectic from relief. *They cannot all be such fools as to think I will not fight*, Marric thought. Judging from Gereint's intense and whispered conversation with Kynan the bard, two men were not such fools. Alexa still watched him with that mixture of hope, love, and sorrow, while the Queen, whose thin fingers gestured him to a chair, tried to preserve a semblance of gracious civilization.

The wine came watered in deference to Byzantine ways, though, Gods knew, Marric could have gulped it unwatered and been thankful.

"My soldiers, lady?"

"Food is being brought them," Olwen said. Her voice was low and pleasant. "My brother tells me you want them to make camp outside."

Marric permitted himself to nod. He was being rushed, he knew, rushed into accepting hospitality that would bind him by every code of behavior he knew. He felt himself sinking into a deep, black silence. He feared such silences, since out of them exploded rage such as he could not control, rage that came from not being able to mourn, that had been building ever since his father died. Penetrating his silence came the hag's laughter.

"Jomsborg," he broke into Olwen's measured remarks about how many stories he and Alexa must have to share, and how she was looking forward to hearing them. "They have landed in Prydein."

"I will double my guards," Olwen said. "Gereint?"

"Immediately, sister. We should send out messengers, too." He rose, cast a suspicious glance at Marric, and left. Kynan moved to take Gereint's seat.

"I have had no word yet. How could you know?" That was the ArchDruid Amergin to whom Olwen had presented him. The old man's gaze burned as deeply as that of the high priest of Osiris in Byzantium. For a moment, the laughter faded, then faded further as Alexa knelt by his chair and laid a hand on his brow.

"They've hurt you," she whispered. What else she said was rarely heard at any court. Surprised that she knew some of the words she used, Marric laughed, a brief, painful bark. Alexa flushed and took a deep breath, as if consciously controlling a rage of her own.

Marric looked down at the flowerlike face so close to his. It was a woman's face, not a girl's, he saw that now; saw how the girl he remembered had ripened into a woman as lovely as she was delicate. Only Alexa had never been delicate, he remembered; her will was as strong as his. He saw knowledge and confidence in her eyes, and power, too. Her gown, he saw now, was some version of a Druid's robe.

So Alexa had passed beyond him into realms from which he was exiled: she had a child, and now it seemed, she had some magic, too.

"I have had enough magic for a lifetime," Marric told her.

The beef and bread he choked down had no savor, and he forced himself not to drink too deeply. Finally, the pretense at a meal was cleared away, and Marric leaned forward.

Alexa tensed, waiting for the real battle to begin.

Instead, Marric thanked Olwen for her hospitality. For himself, he told her, much as he welcomed her invitation to stay within the fortress, it was not his practice to be separated from his men. In addition, he had gifts he wished to give his sister, his niece (he even managed to smile), and Olwen herself, for taking Alexa in.

Olwen, holding Elen on her lap, smiled back. "Alexa has

become a sister to me," she said. "And Elen is like my own daughter."

"A fine child," Marric remarked. "But why is she the heir?"

The woman drew in a sharp, wounded breath, before she replied. "In default of heirs of my body, Elen is heir to Penllyn. I . . . have not been well."

Marric steepled his fingers. "You of the Celtoi foster children out, do you not?" Easy enough: Olwen needed an heir; he needed a future for his sister's child that would not make Alexa hate him.

Olwen nodded, suspicious.

"So I thought," Marric said quietly. Let the idea sink in. Before Alexa could reply angrily, he had changed the subject to trade. Alexa would discover that her brother had learned to bide his time.

The days that followed were halcyons, too calm, presaging winter storms. Since there was no peaceful way to refuse, Marric had to permit his troops to mingle with the warriors. So far, no one had broken his neck on the chariots that fascinated his men about as much as their larger horses intrigued the Celtoi. When she could, Alexa stayed close at his side. At first, she came accompanied, once by Olwen herself, and they sat on the grass, talking, always talking, trading tales of the magics that hurt and healed them. Marric, who had placed himself where his body might keep the wind off both women, amused himself by teaching them to drink army-style from a wineskin.

You would hardly think I'd steal her! Marric wanted to tell the Queen. *She'd come after me with my own sword.* But there was no saying that, ever: just show Olwen that Alexa was safe. He had not meant to walk until the woman's strength was outworn; but she was pleased to take Elen back to the maenol, leaving brother and sister alone.

Marric cocked an eyebrow at Alexa. "Is it the wasting sickness? She does not cough."

"A miscarriage. From before Elen was born."

"She recovers slowly."

Alexa sighed and fingered some coarse grass stalks.

Though it was high summer, their green was pallid, and many were withered.

Thereafter, since it seemed harmless enough, Alexa walked with him alone about the maenol and surrounding villages, past what Alexa referred to as a *gorsedd* and Marric decided was some sort of shrine.

"How many men did you bring?" she asked brightly. Marric sat with his back to her while she nursed Elen. She had always had a passing interest in strategy, an interest that he had indulged.

Hearing the baby gurgle, Marric turned to face her.

"Two moira. A third is coming by water," he told her. Did she want to know the size of her honor guard, or recruit it to defend this land?

"We could use two moira," she nodded. "Two thousand men with Imperial training . . ."

In a moment, she would try to wheedle Marric's entire troop strength from him. And she would probably succeed too, unless he hardened his heart. "You *could* use them, yes," he said, and raised an eyebrow in the way he used to tell her when he would not permit her to beat him at chess.

She glared at him.

The next day she led him on a tour along defenses that clearly showed Roman influence, mentioned (but did not reveal) ample supplies of food and a water source inside the fortress.

"These defenses were your idea?" he asked her, approvingly.

"Audun had books from our grandfather's day, and I read them. But Gereint—I couldn't have done anything without his help."

"Indeed?" It would be good to have an Empress who could consult with generals while he was away on campaigns.

"Brother, let it be!" Alexa cried. "I can't plan battles. I did it once, and it cost me . . . sweet Isis, I lost . . ." She was gasping for breath.

"Hush, 'Lexa, be still." He took her shoulders in his hands. "Easy, child. Now," he unfastened his cloak and spread it on the ground for her to sit on, "you have a good mind for strategy. What has frightened you about using it?"

He leaned back on his elbows while she composed herself and gazed out over the valley. Forests and small fields were patchworked in a thousand shades of green, darker where clouds as fleecy as the sheep that grazed on the slopes scudded overhead. From here, one could see any rider or body of men who approached. Alexa had chosen her vantage point well.

Gradually, Alexa's story came out, the story of years of grief and fear, and then, gradually, her rebirth into strength, love, and power. What a woman his little sister had grown into! But she would be as formidable an antagonist as she would be an Empress: best proceed delicately.

She rubbed her hand across her face, a gesture Marric remembered her making since she was an infant, swallowed, then went on. "So you see, I am not fit, Marric. I turned on you. When Audun was in danger, I used my anger and summoned fire. And I would have done it again and again. I used Greek fire, so that the Aescir were glad to be free of me. And even in my initiation, I learned that I had...had contaminated myself and there was a price to pay.

"I dare not fight. Whenever I go near a battlefield, terrible things happen."

"Battle *is* terrible. You came to it late; you are not hardened to it. Isis forbid you ever should be," Marric soothed her.

"That is just fighting. I am telling you, I do not trust myself. I turned to darkness once. What would stop me..."

"Your own will, sister." Marric took up her hands and kissed them. "Or I could keep you safe."

"My will, Marric? It is the deepest wish of my heart to stay here with Gereint for the rest of my life."

His face must have betrayed anguish, for she was hugging him, coaxing him from his sorrow, as she had done all their lives.

He drew a long, shuddering sigh. "Alexa, forgive me. But I have to try to bring you home."

"I am home," she told him.

"Are you? When I need you, and the Empire needs you? You were born for that need, sister."

"Don't," she whispered, hands to her mouth. "Marric, this will tear me apart."

"Do you think I like seeing you torn?" Marric asked. "'Lexa, you are the dearest person in the world to me!" Stephana was gone, he thought dully; Alexa was all he had of family.

In the next moment, he would have held her and let her cry herself out, but shadows dashed across their faces. Alexa cried out, and flung herself over her child. The rasp of Marric's sword from the scabbard cut across the quiet afternoon.

"Eagles?" he asked her.

"No. Ravens." Elen began to cry, and she hid her face against the child's hair.

Those were huge ravens, then, and they circled as Marric had often seen them once they scented the dead or dying. He tensed, looking for a way to get his sister to safety.

"Warriors—down there," he pointed. Alexa ran to the hillcrest.

"That's Gereint!" she cried. "And one . . . two empty saddles. He has strangers with him."

"Sharp eyes," Marric praised her. He swept up his cloak and followed her down the hill, catching her just as she overbalanced. "Strangers," he pointed out. "And you're unarmed, carrying a child, and wearing skirts. Go home."

She pushed against his chest. "They're bringing in wounded!" she cried. "They'll need me."

Marric narrowed his eyes. Then the wind shifted and a blood-scent rose to where he stood. He coughed.

"What is the matter?" Alexa asked, her hands on his arm.

"Can't you smell it? That's the stink of shapeshifter on them. The Jomsborgers must be moving fast. You're right, they'll need you. But in the hall, where you can work safely. Now, run for it!"

She had never disobeyed that order, and he reinforced it, as he had done ever since she could walk, with a cuff aimed at her rear.

As four guardsmen, their axes out, fell in about Marric, he heard women shrieking outside the hall. Despite himself, he stopped short.

"Death wails, Majesty," one of the guards reminded him.

Gods, that sound was almost worse than battles. It reminded him of the hideous din on the shore when he had landed. Now he could smell the familiar stinks of a battle's aftermath, blood, sweat, and excrement, lathered horses, and, underlying the misery, the charnel taint of unnatural beasts.

Two horses stood trembling, barely under control, as warriors unloaded cloak-wrapped bundles.

"Sweet Mother," came a voice he identified as Gereint's, "Do you know what they did to Owain? When we found him, he looked like he had been gutted by a boar. Only boars—" Gereint's voice thickened and he almost gagged— "don't wrap men's guts about the underbrush."

The loom, Marric thought. The loom! Alexa too had spoken of that loom. It took all his discipline to keep running forward, to signal one man to fetch army surgeons, the others to lend a hand.

Gereint was unwounded, unstained, even. Grime, not battle-paint, smeared his face, accenting hollowed cheeks, and made him look older than his years. Alexa, kneeling over a man with a gash in his arm, glanced up at him. She forced a smile, and immediately, his face brightened and his eyes took on a tenderness that made Marric flush, embarrassed to have seen. Very well then, admit it: he was glad Gereint had survived.

As Alexa tried to cut away her patient's sleeve, her long hair fell free, almost into the wound. In an instant, Gereint was by her side to tie it back with a leather thong. She rested her cheek against his fingers for an instant, then bent to her work. The man had waked, and was starting to scream, his deeper voice clashing with the women's high-pitched wails.

The only women silent were Alexa and the Queen, who paced even as Marric himself did, snapping questions at her brother (and they were the right questions) as fast as he could answer them. She kept one hand on her belt near the strange black dagger. Her knuckles were very white. The fragrance of dying flowers rose about her, then faded as if subdued by the blood and sickness.

"Those wounds should all be burned," Marric got the words

out past his impulse to retreat from this place. "We had some experience with them in Gallia Belgica."

One of the Druids nodded. "They rot, or worse still, they rot the soul of the man who endures them." His hands were gentle on the man he tended, whose eyes went fearful at the thought of the burning.

"Watch for the bloodstained men too." Odd how Amergin the ArchDruid did not need to raise his voice, even in this clamor, to make himself heard and attended to. "The bears' blood forms a bond that could leave anyone whom it touches open to attack. I myself will speak with each man who . . ."

At that, Alexa looked up at Marric himself. The fear on her face—*sweetheart, don't be afraid for me!*—made him start forward, prepared to add himself to the men Amergin would chant or mumble over. Then a mad scream made him whirl around.

A warrior whose garments were soaked with reddish-brown screamed again and rushed toward the women as if he were a maddened beast, to bite or to rend. Wishing for a lance, Marric ran forward before his guard could get between him and the madman, who bellowed again, the sound of a wounded bear. If the blood had overcome him, best give him the merciful death Marric himself would want.

"No!" Olwen darted out in front of the lunatic. Her higher-pitched voice drew his attention, and his head wavered from side to side. "Gwair is mine to save, not yours to kill!"

Lady be careful . . . the words died in his throat. Gwair had stopped his mindless rush forward. Olwen advanced on him, her hands outstretched. The odor of flowers intensified. She laid one hand on Gwair's brow, then the other. The man's eyes closed, and the rictus of fury in his face began to fade. Tension hardened the back of Marric's neck. He began to sense the sweet thrum of magic, wielded to heal. A moment more, and it might sever the bond that he knew bound him to the hag of Jomsborg. Involuntarily, he started forward, wanting that healing for himself too . . .

Olwen groaned and staggered, flinging out her hands, which suddenly looked frail and useless. Before she could fall, Alexa was at her side, supporting her, while the Arch-Druid led Gwair off.

"I tried, Alexa," Marric heard the Queen moan. "This will be the last year . . ."

"No!" Alexa cried. "You did not try and fail. You tried and almost healed. Almost! Just a few more months, sister. You are getting stronger, you must feel it. Surely the risk is worth it . . ."

"Not if there's a war," Olwen bent her head to rest on the shorter woman's shoulder. Alexa's eyes met Marric's.

"You're needed there," he told her, and laid his hands on Olwen's arms, turning her. The Queen shivered at his touch, then acquiesced as he led her toward a stone. He gestured at one of the bevy of women nearby (for a mercy, they were all working too hard to shriek now), for a cup of wine, or water —anything. Though she sipped once, then gestured the cup away, Marric held it to her lips until she finished it.

"I tried," she whispered hoarsely. "I could not heal even one man. How can I keep the land whole if I cannot heal even one man?"

The grief in her amber eyes struck at Marric's own unworthiness—no magic, no power, unfit to rule—and he nodded, mute. "How, lady? As best you can."

"It is not enough. Never, never enough."

No, it never was. If only they were not one step removed from enemies, he might comfort her. But he could not afford friendship with this foreign Queen, who withheld the sister he had come all this way to claim. He began to unclasp his cloak, to wrap it about her.

"No," she whispered, recoiling, "Blood, it all smells of blood."

Marric snapped his fingers at the women who hovered nearby. "Your Queen is cold," he told them. "Bring her inside."

He too was cold, cold with knowledge. Inside his head, the hag's cackling began again. He forced his attention back to Gereint, whose call for warriors to ride against Jomsborg had turned Alexa's face chalky. The laughter rose again as he heard himself offer himself and some of his men to ride with

them, rose louder even as Alexa's glow of thanks warmed
him. He found himself offering to help with the wounded,
anything to drown out that damnable noise, that, and his
growing horror that he had only to look within himself to find
his enemies.

Chapter 21

☆

"They hide from us!" Anger warred with uncertainty in the
younger man's voice.

Marric, reining in beside him, grinned. "Patience, my
friend. They seek to draw us away from safety. You'll find it
in Caesar: an army is but as good as its line of supply."

"We drove Caesar back," Gereint told him pointedly, then
grinned back.

"Then think of it as one of those interminable cattle raids
your father used to sing about, the ones with the names no one
not of Eire could ever pronounce. Would you leave your cows
in plain sight, or hide them?" The Celtoi liked examples from
their songs about as much as Hellenes liked quoting Homer.

"You were going to say 'no civilized man?'" Gereint asked.
"I can pronounce them easily."

Marric laughed shortly. "Too easy a mark by far! If you can
do no better, let's ride on."

After a time Gereint laughed too. It had been like that between Marric and the brother he could not accept for three
days: sparring, banter that kindled into hostility, then died
away. But they needed one another now. Marric needed Gereint's knowledge of the land; Gereint wanted the massive
strength of the empire's cataphracts. In addition, he had first

whistled admiringly at the older man's skill in picking up the Jomsborgers' trail, then made a sign against evil, and now watched Marric.

He suspects, but does not know for sure that the blood has touched me. Alexa plays a double game, hoping to preserve brother and husband both, and trusting them to defend one another. Clever girl: she has us both trapped. He could almost hear her asking hotly, "And would it be so bad?"

Not at all, sweetheart, he answered silently. *I could like this Gereint of yours.* Perhaps . . . a new idea struck him until he shook free of it. *What are you thinking of, madman? You would actually consider sharing a princess of the Empire with a barbarian?* He spurred his horse, Scythian-style, and rode ahead of Gereint. But he heard the man mutter something else out of another one of those interminable songs, the one about a king's wife who fled with her lover and caused their deaths.

Best not think of Alexa for now. Best think only of battle, the sooner the better. Battle would let him forget his fears, battle might weaken the hold that daily grew upon him, and drew him toward the hag and her loom.

For fear of the trail, he did not shut his eyes, but he opened himself gingerly to that inner awareness of the bond and felt it pull taut. He reined in so quickly that his horse reared, and the men behind him fell back, swearing at the shower of pebbles and clods that it cast behind it.

"Form up," he ordered, his voice so hoarse that his officers had to repeat his order. He saw two guards and three Armenians make warding signs or reach for amulets. The Celtoi simply reached for weapons. Most had decided that the Emperor was Sighted, a reasonable enough assumption since he was their kin, a little matter of four or five generations past. But not Gereint, who had commented just that dawn that the Emperor seemed to share his sister's talent for sensing the dark.

Gereint rode to Marric's side. Under the paint, his face was strained; he probably feared his temporary ally almost as much as Jomsborg.

"Up ahead," Marric pointed at as likely a place for an ambush as he had ever seen. Ten or so men, riding there, could draw out their enemies if they were willing to fight as if possessed by Set himself until reinforcements could join them. But they would face enemies who could fight as bears or as men.

Gereint nodded slowly. "I'd wager that if we sent scouts, not a one would come back. But ten men, maybe," he echoed Marric's thoughts. Then, as if daring him to contradict, "I'll lead them."

That was a Celt for you! Though it was no business of an Emperor to turn himself into bait, as Gereint and his chosen riders trotted off trying to look like easy targets, Marric knew he wanted to ride with them. *Then Jomsborg would know it was a trap,* he told himself. But he knew that was a feeble excuse.

The Emperor, his guard, and his cataphracts rode toward the ambush. Men bearing round shields crudely daubed with bears faced them. Those spears could reach the horses before his men could ride them down, Marric thought, and cursed. He raised his arm, and a wing of his force broke away from the main body and flanked them. It would be narrow going, since the trail cut in sharply behind them, where Marric knew Gereint and his nine were fighting desperately. He thought he could hear the screams of men, horses, and bears.

The barbarians jeered, shouting insults that clearly set his Guardsmen frothing. "Give them axes, lads, not words!" Marric shouted. Rising in his stirrups, he screamed a war cry, silently damned the customs that frowned on Emperors riding in the first rank, and charged. For a few moments, the clamor and confusion engulfed his consciousness. Then he was riding free again, his lance broken, his sword and his horse's hooves dripping blood.

It was too easy to break through.

Such a clever thrall as you are. The hag's laughter slashed into his thoughts so clearly that Marric looked up. Was she here? Excellent: he would relieve Gereint and kill her. Then perhaps he would have peace.

Up ahead, he could see where ten Celtoi, no, eight, fought on. Several had learned the trick of fending off the much taller bears with spears. Two horses, though, lay dead, as much an impediment to defense as they were a temporary rampart. Marric screamed wordlessly, and spurred forward.

A giant bear loomed up in his path, its forepaws slashing down at him. His horse screamed, reared, and swerved so quickly that Marric fell against its neck. A hot wind whined past his head, and he jerked around. If he had not fallen, the bear's claws would probably have beheaded him. It was folly to leap clear and face the creature on foot, armed with a ten-foot lance. Marric could only trust his horse to slash with his hooves and come down safely. The poor beast was trained to go against armies, not creatures that stank of shape-changing magic. His heart would have ached for it if he had had time.

The bear batted at his lance and snapped it in dripping jaws. Marric snatched out his sword and slashed repeatedly at head and shoulders. The bear weaved, and he moved with it, hoping that it might expose its throat. The creature was cunning, though, and it did not.

Up ahead, the noise grew hideous, and Marric grew desperate. Leaping from his horse's back, he brought his blade up two-handed into the bear's belly, as the thing toppled. The blood was almost as deadly as its claws or teeth, he reminded himself, and dived to the side. If Isis were with him, his horse would stay nearby and he would not be trampled.

He hit hard, and rolled, coming up practically under his mount's hooves. Quickly, he mounted again. His horse trembled and danced beneath him, and he spared an instant to soothe the panicking beast with hand, voice, and knees.

Gereint feinted with a spear, then jabbed it home in a bear's throat. Marric started forward. The bear should have fallen. It was dead, he could have sworn that, and it should have fallen. Instead, impossibly, it took two steps forward. In horror, the prince slashed at the thing with his sword—

"Get back!" Marric screamed, as the bear toppled, crushing down on Gereint so that he shrieked in pain, and his bright hair vanished.

At that moment, fury slashed into Marric's brain and he reeled. His hands went limp on the reins, and his horse bolted, lacking his master's control, bolted for air clean of the stinks of battle and unnatural beasts.

Gereint would die, and Alexa would blame him, was his

thought. He struggled to rein the screaming horse in, to force it into a circle, slowing it, controlling it.

What is it to you if he dies? Then you can take the woman you want. The temptation rose in him like as lust, hot in his belly, rising, rising . . . until he spat bile and bared his teeth at his invisible foe.

That was your idea, the hag's voice told him. For once, the voice did not cackle. Its calmness was more hideous than any accusation.

Was that truly the wish of his heart? To break his sister's heart, then lie, and lying, win her back? "No," he gasped. "Not that . . . not that way."

"Not that way-*yyyyyy!*" he made a war cry of it, and galloped toward the site of the ambush. As his guardsmen finished off the remaining Jomsborgers, Marric leaped down, grasped a fallen spear, and levered frantically at the bear's carcass. The blood pounded in his temples, and the sinews in his back and legs ached, but slowly the bear toppled aside from the young man.

He lay very still on the blood-soaked ground. "Goddess, no," Marric breathed, until he realized that some of the blood came from a wound in Gereint's arm. At least it was not his sword arm, Marric thought as he bent to staunch the bleeding.

Gereint's eyelids quivered, then opened fast. "No!" Marric told him. "It's over. Lie still."

"How many?" rasped the other man.

"You lost two. I'm sorry. We wanted to save you all." Gereint turned his face away, and Marric barely heard his next words.

"Why not make it three?" he asked.

Against his will, Marric's hand tightened on Gereint's shoulder.

"Your words shame your father," Marric told him, and saw him flinch from hand and voice. "I want my sister back," he said as the wounded man flinched. "But I won't murder to get her.

"Now, keep quiet and brace yourself. I have to lift you, and it's going to hurt."

Luck was with them both. As Marric braced himself to pick

Gereint up, he fainted and did not wake until they wrapped him in a cloak by the fire of a hastily tossed-up camp.

Marric stood watching the ravens circle, black against an orange sunset.

"Emperor." The accent was Celtic, and Marric turned slowly.

"He's waked, then." It was not a question. Marric had left orders to call him when Gereint revived. He stared down at the wounded man, waiting for him to speak.

"What now?" Gereint asked. "I angered you. Will you call challenge on me?"

All Marric's anger and guilt boiled up in a yell of outrage. "Call challenge on a wounded man? I'd beat you senseless for what you said, but Alexa would kill me." He drew a deep breath and only then realized how badly Gereint's words had scored him. "I'll call challenge on you in one way. I'll challenge you to ask pardon for the insult."

Gereint shut his eyes and nodded. "I'll ask it," he whispered. "Now, and when I'm . . . home."

"So that's done," Marric sighed, and sank to his heels beside the fire. "Now, how do I get us home? We can rig a horse litter if you can't ride. Can you hold out for three days?"

"Another route . . . overhill," Gereint said, waving away the steaming potion that one of the army surgeons tried to make him drink. "It's rough. But it cuts two days off the journey."

"Can you?" Marric was frankly skeptical.

"I must. There's another thing," said Gereint. "My arm."

"You won't lose it."

"No. But you have to sear the wound tonight. Now. That will drive out the poisons, all of them."

"Gereint, man," Marric dropped his hand gently on the man's sound shoulder. "The bleeding is not that bad. You can ride with it, wait until your Druids see you—"

"No! That's it, Marric. I don't want Alexa to see it done."

Damn it all, whatever else Gereint was, he was his father's son. Who would have thought his high-strung little sister could arouse such devotion in anyone? *I wish you were my cousin, my ally, anything but a man Alexa wants me to call brother-in-law,* Marric thought, and caught Gereint's wry, weak grin.

"By the horned god, here's a tangle," he said, and held out his right arm to clasp Marric's. Despite the pain, his grip was firm.

"They're heating the iron," Marric said bluntly. "You have time to get drunk first."

Gereint shook his head and met Marric's eyes.

"Right," he said. "I wouldn't either."

As the iron struck, Gereint screamed and his fingers twisted in Marric's grasp until the pain passed into his hand too. "Steady," he whispered. "You've done well. Rest now. I won't leave you."

Gereint's head lolled from side to side. His lips moved. *Alexa* was the word they formed.

"We'll get you to her," Marric promised. "Now sleep."

Gradually, the clutch on Marric's fingers eased, and he could free them. He sat rubbing life back into his hand, staring at the fire, and knowing past a hope of doubt just where the Jomsborgers were, and where they might strike next. The maenol should be informed, but best the message not come from him, however. When Gereint woke, Marric would lead him to think it was his idea.

They reached the maenol a day later, despite their wounded. Gereint had scorned a horse litter after the first hour in it, claiming that lying still while being dragged over rough ground was worse than riding. "If you pass out, man, Goddess strike me but I'll carry you into camp myself!" Marric warned him. He had ridden strongly enough for half that day, but wavered in the saddle, shaking with the fever inevitable after such a wound, until Marric edged his horse alongside and supported him.

Ravens circled over Olwen's maenol—no good omen, that. The guards about the Byzantine camp outside the walls had been doubled. Seeing Marric, officers ran out to report. Deva, they told him, had repelled an attack, Gods knew how, seeing that the place was peopled by priests. Following them at a more leisurely pace, one of the priests who served Ares-Montu looked ironic.

Marric rode hastily by, claiming Gereint's fever as an excuse. He did not wish to speak with any of them, priest or Druid. What kind of Emperor would he be if he could not win his own battle with the hag?

The guards at Olwen's fortress looked grimly at him. When his guard tried to ride in, they turned sullen. Marric dismissed the men and rode, alone with the Celtoi, to Olwen's hall. Gereint pulled away from him, boasting that he could ride without support. Fair enough, especially when Alexa came running toward him, her lips working, and her long hair flying.

She grasped Gereint's leg and did not even notice her brother until he dismounted and went to her side. "He is too heavy for you, 'Lexa. Let me help." He eased the younger man from his horse to the ground, where Alexa knelt and held him silently, assuring herself that she had him back, and that he was not too badly hurt. Then she had time to look at Marric, and her eyes went fearful again.

"I'm walking, aren't I, sister?" He smiled at her and touched her hair.

"It's still on you," she whispered.

"Let it be. This is my fight, and no business of a priest." Or priestess. Alexa pressed her lover's face against her shoulder and hid her eyes against his hair. The Druids moved among the returning warriors, silent and worn. There seemed fewer than usual. What price had they paid for Deva?

Marric smelled dried flowers, felt a hand on his shoulder, and whirled. "I owe you my thanks for my brother's life." Against the shouts and cries of the others, Olwen's voice was low and pleasant. He supposed that the Queen of such a tribe needed all the serenity she could get. She stood beside him, watching her brother and his sister, a sad smile on her face.

"You should have seen Alexa when Audun first brought her. Even now, when we are all tired and afraid, she is happy. She is like a sister to me. She *is* my sister. *Why* can you not let her stay?"

"Lady, if there is a thing you could do for your people,

would you let it go undone? Even if you knew the hurt it would cause?"

Olwen flinched and turned away. "The Druids tell us that the Jomsborg army—can you call it an army?—roves over the countryside. At Deva, they repelled one attack. But those savages . . . they forced the Eldest Folk to show them pathways even we never knew of, and they advanced fast. Too fast. They are massing not far from here. It will be a war."

"This is a safe fortress, but too exposed," Marric said. "I would keep it garrisoned, but evacuate . . ." he stumbled over the Celtic word. . . . "Move your children and women, those who do not bear arms, to Deva, perhaps, where you need not fear for them."

She shook herself back to the present. "I must think of this. Still, before we fight or flee, we can spare time for one last feast this evening."

"And my men? Your warriors barred them from the gates."

"We are at war, Emperor. You know about war; Alexa says you are expert in it." She drew herself up and her eyes flashed golden fire. She mush have been magnificent before she fell ill. "They understand friends, and they understand enemies. But they do not understand you—and I find I agree with them. I owe you my brother's life, and that means something to me. So, appear as a friend, for now."

She left him then, in an angry swirl of cloak and skirts. Marric turned back to ask Alexa if she could move Gereint but found them both gone. He rode back to his camp, hoping to fit a bath and a few hours of sleep in among the reports he must hear, and the orders he must give. Penllyn was growing desperate: no place for a princess.

The screech of ravens was loud over the maenol at sunset when Marric and three guardsmen (he gave elaborate and ironic thanks to the warrior who had brought him that concession to his rank) rode in through the gates and to the feast.

The man nearest him, a Saxon almost as fair as Audun himself, muttered something and touched an amulet.

"What was that?" Marric asked.

"The ravens," he said hoarsely. "In my home, we call that sound 'cirm.' You would say 'charm.'"

As in spells. Wonderful. Carrion birds and carrion magic. He tried to force the dark mood from his mind and was succeeding when he entered the hall. A huge fire burned in the great central firepit, and light glistened on the sweaty finery and sweatier faces of the men and women feasting. The fire, the colors, the noise and the smell of the feast made him recoil a step. But his guardsmen were rubbing their hands, anticipating a fine evening.

A slender figure in white glided up to him and took his hand. "Stay with Gereint and me, please," Alexa said.

"He's here?"

She shrugged. "I lost an argument. I don't often lose. He said that you would not let such a small wound stop you either."

Against his will, Marric laughed. "I could like this Gereint of yours, sister. He is his father's son."

Then why don't you? Appeal gleamed in her huge eyes, but he shook his head. Alexa must lose this argument too.

Gereint sat propped by hide cushions, near Olwen herself. Marric sank down beside him. The war leader, who had been speaking earnestly with his sister, turned and smiled at him. He seemed little worse for wear. He would have to drink lightly tonight and compensate for a weak shield arm for the next few weeks, but he would be all right.

Alexa offered to mix wine for him, but he waved away the water. Gereint laughed. "Turning back to the old ways, are you, Marric? Ah, it will be good to fight at your side. Alexa has told me stories of Imperial troops. I will be glad of their aid."

Marric sipped, then set the cup down. "That must be discussed. I hire my troops and pay them well. I will not loose them without purpose or reward."

Now that was disgraceful of him. He could hear Aillel saying so. He could hear his father saying so. What was worse, he agreed with them. Though if it meant shame for him here, so far from the heart of the Empire, if his troops were a weapon to let him regain Alexa, he would use them. He drank more deeply. To risk disgrace . . . he must be desperate. He remembered Stephana's words, "I fear desperate actions." And well she might. She had died in one.

All around him, Celtoi feasted with the gusto Marric had seen in the camp of Audun Bearmaster, or the tents of the Huns. Years ago, he would have joined in—and fought the next day. Now he himself preferred to spend the night planning, or walking about his camp, or—best of all—sleeping. The din was as awesome as their energy. Even Alexa's eyes shone, and she rested her head against Gereint's shoulder. He brushed a kiss on her hair, then turned again to his meat.

"Music! A bard!"

Isolated demands for a song grew into clamor, then a steady rapping of cups on wood, and finally a loud, long cheer as Kynan approached Queen Olwen and sat at her feet. He made an elaborate business of tuning his harp and waiting until the shouting quieted down barks of laughter, occasional remarks, and loud hisses for quiet.

Alexa leaned behind Gereint, translating the old songs when Marric's knowledge of the language failed him. The noise of the feast had not quite deafened him, though; he could still distinguish between a love song and a song of arms. Several times Kynan's eyes met his ironically and he braced himself for a sharp comment, a pointed allusion, or a satire.

Finally, Kynan swung into a martial music.

> Men went to Catraeth
> Shouting for battle,
> A squadron of horse.
>
> Blue their armor and their shields,
> Lances uplifted and sharp,
> Mail and sword glinting . . .

"No," Alexa whispered. "I don't want to hear that one."

The doors blew open, and ravens screeched, then flew into the hall.

Bard that he was, Kynan's hand clashed against his harp strings, and the discord silenced him.

In the quiet, Alexa's urgent words sounded with the force of a shout.

"It turns sad," she said, and half-sang the words.

> After the wine and after the mead
> They left us, armored in mail.
> I know the sorrow of their death.

Marric tried to draw her to him, to soothe her. "Little sister, you used to weep when we read about Hector's funeral. This is just a song too."

But Alexa pulled free, trembling, and Gereint shook his head. "This is not Alexa's whim, Marric. She is like this when the power takes her."

"It isn't just a song," Olwen said. She looked up at the ravens, who darted through the hall and perched on the eaves opposite her. "Ravens. Alexa knows what that means as well as I do."

"I would be grateful if someone explained it to me!" Marric snapped. Olwen raised an eyebrow as if to note how his silken courtesy had worn shabby.

"It means," Alexa said, "that the Goddess Herself must go to war. And that she needs a human focus."

Isis, Lady of Love, of Fruitfulness . . . Marric usually managed to forget that the Goddess had a fierce side as well. Though it could be perverted into Irene's madness, or inspire men to battle, Marric preferred to ignore it. Battle was men's work, gods' work; and if that meant protecting women like Luned—or Olwen, or Alexa—whether they wished protection or not, so be it.

"Then I shall provide it," Olwen declared and rose, a shimmer of green and sweeping gold. She held out her hand toward the ravens.

"No!" Alexa darted before her and held out her arms. "You've just begun to regain your strength. That was Bodb's power. Olwen, if you draw it into yourself, do you think you will ever . . ."

"Ever regain what I lost when I lost first Rhodri, then Bodb, then—" Olwen's voice broke, and she flung up a hand. "No. But I do not believe I can regain it in any case. Penllyn withers, sister."

Alexa shook her head vehemently.

"Alexa. Can you tell me that the fields are what they were two years ago?"

Marric had seen that stubborn set to his sister's features many times. Still, she shook her head.

"On your oath, sister, now tell me. Say it!" Olwen's command rang out with sudden violence. Her voice took on resonance. My Goddess, she is magnificent, Marric thought.

Alexa sighed and, before Olwen's regal presence, seemed to diminish.

"It is either that, or wait until Beltane—if Penllyn can spare that long," Olwen said. "I even have an heir."

"Elen is a child!"

"Then it must be you. Alexa, are you ready to be Queen?"

Alexa dropped to her knees and her head drooped. "You know I cannot do that. You know that! No, Olwen. The Goddess of Battles will have her focus. But it will not be you. I will serve. When you fight against our enemies, I will take myself to the grove. I will not—cannot!—go to the battlefield. But I will look in the Water of Vision, and open myself to the Goddess; and you will live."

"You hate battles," Olwen argued.

"Better one battle than to be Queen, sister."

Alexa turned away. With immense, pathetic dignity, she rose and held out her hand to the nearest raven. It flew down toward her and hovered, staring into her eyes. At any moment, its beak could have gouged them out, or its talons could have bit cruelly into her pale flesh.

"Don't move!" Gereint hissed at Marric, who unfastened his cloak to snap it at the bird.

"A bargain, then," Alexa breathed.

The bird shrieked again, and flew in circles.

"Open the doors!" Now it was Alexa's turn to shout, to grow in majesty. The fire roared, turning the walls a brilliant red and flinging Alexa's shadow, immense and black, against them. Her outstretched arms looked like wings. The ravens flew from the hall.

Olwen sank back into her place and buried her head in her hands. Alexa turned to Kynan the bard.

"You knew," she accused.

Kynan nodded. "Did you think the Goddess meant your life or, for that matter, my own, to be easy? Think again, Princess." He gathered up his harp. "I find I am weary, and no longer in the mood to sing. I shall see you once more before I go hence."

Ironically, he bowed and left the hall. Alexa's moment of exaltation passed, and she wrapped her arms about herself, hugging herself like a freezing child. Gereint approached her carefully. When he held out his arms, she ran into them, sobbing.

Olwen clapped her hands at servants, who ran forward with wine, or mead, or ale. Some of the warriors made a noble effort at singing. Men and women rose from their places to sit with others as it pleased them; several couples slipped outside. The noise of the hall rose higher than before, and more feverish.

Shielding herself beneath the uproar, Olwen gestured at Marric. Reluctant to obey her, he rose and followed her to a corner far from the firepit.

"Alexa told me," she began, "that you have three thousand men."

"Two thousand. I expect a thousand to arrive by sea." *Liar*, his inner voice said.

Olwen shrugged. "It is still two thousand trained warriors we could use beside us."

Now that the moment was here, the words were hard to force out. "Did my sister also tell you that the Empire's army is a mercenary army? Lady, my men fight for reward. And you withhold the one prize I seek."

"You ask me to sell your sister to you?" Indignation thrilled in Olwen's voice. When she was angry, one could forget that she had been sick almost unto death.

"Queen Olwen," Marric said bluntly. "That is a crude attempt to shame me. Try to understand this: warriors have pride. I am Emperor. My pride, my honor, stand so long as

my Empire stands I have chosen to live when any warrior,
man or woman, might have chosen death, to give my Empire
a chance of life. *I* was a slave. Torque, diadem, or slave-ring
—truly, whatever metal we wear amounts to the same thing."

"Then you will not lend us your fighters."

Not as long as I have a chance of striking a bargain. Marric glowered at her and realized, with a catch of breath, that
her eyes were almost level with his.

"In that case, Emperor, I want you gone. I will not permit
an army I do not trust to idle in my land while I prepare for
war."

"Then you risk having two enemies in your land," Marric
said bluntly.

Olwen shook her head and smiled at him. The flower scent
about her suddenly seemed less sickly. "I do not think so. If
we fought, Alexa's heart would break. Since you love her,
you will protect her, whether she wants it or not. Why else do
you think I have tolerated you this long?"

The rage was boiling up in Marric, a dark, thunderous thing
that made him clench his fists to restrain himself. But the
words poured out despite his control.

"My ancestor Alexander was right about Celtoi. They ask
for help, they want advice, but do they take it? No! They're
too busy arguing. Lady, I will bid you good night and farewell."

He nodded curtly and turned. He swept up the first cloak at
hand, noticing that its plaid was subdued, and wrapped himself in it. A gesture, and his guards edged free too. Once
outside, he waved them to precede him.

Right now he wanted clear air and quiet, a chance to sort
out the pieces in this mosaic of fear and uncertainties. He
lacked some of the pieces. But one things was central.
Alexa's loyalty to this land and its queen compelled her to a
perilous choice.

Just how perilous her choice was brought Marric up short,
made Marric stop short. Years ago, Alexa had been exposed
to magic used as a weapon. She had invoked it herself, and it
had nearly killed her.

Alexa had turned to the dark briefly, and had spent years

repaying her debts. If she invoked the battle-magic and was corrupted again, her punishment would not be mere bodily death and atonement in her lives to come. She would have no chance to redeem herself, for she would be annihilated. And the idea of life after life, spent without his sister's brilliant, plotting little soul nearby made him sweat with horror.

As Marric flung a fold of the borrowed cloak over his head to conceal the anguish on his face, a man and woman ran from the shadows and collided with him. Marric steadied the woman on her feet, and she laughed before she darted off again, a hasty apology trailing after her.

They had not known him for a foreigner! If he dressed as a tribesman, he could pass for one. Oh, he was darker than some, taller than many—but if he hid his face and shorter hair, he could move among them unnoticed.

There lay the key to his puzzle!

It needed further testing, which the guards at Olwen's gates might supply.

"Best not to befriend the strangers, friend," the guards warned him. "I hear that the Queen is angry with their Emperor."

"I do not seek friends among the strangers," he replied, "but among their horses."

"Then good hunting!" laughed the guard, and let him pass. Marric hastened out, then downslope toward his camp. Gesturing at the guard, he stepped off the track, as he might if he actually planned to steal a horse. Instead, he scrutinized the ramparts for guards and torches. Ahhh, there it was, a patch of shadow where one man, if he were quiet and swift, could hurl a grapple and scale the walls, then pass unnoticed in the maenol.

He was glad now that he had never vowed not to steal Alexa. If he succeeded, he would have to resign himself to her fury. But perhaps she would be relieved to be spared a choice she obviously feared.

I cannot bear to let you risk annihilation, he told the dream-Alexa he had carried in his heart for years. *I only seek to protect you.*

Dark against the dark sky, the ravens screamed in derision.

Chapter 22

☆

Hiding the plaids of tunic, cloak, and trousers under a common soldier's cloak, Marric watched with his camp's perimeter guards as Olwen's people streamed from the maenol. Behind him, though the sky paled past sunset into twilight, his soldiers ceased their work of breaking camp, a task they had been about for the past three days. Very little remained of it now save a few tents and some cook fires.

Ordinarily, no Byzantine army would have dared to move with such lamentable slowness. It was by Marric's orders that they delayed, long enough for his spies to report where the Jomsborgers massed, preparing to meet the tribes, and to assume that none of the messengers he had sent to the eastern shore in search of his transports had survived. And—the thing that he was waiting for—long enough for Olwen to evacuate all but a few warriors from the maenol.

His only fear was that Alexa probably knew just how quickly the Empire's soldiers could work. He could only hope that preparations for the coming battle occupied her so that she had no time to cast an eye on his camp and observe that it was not shrinking. She had read her Homer and would recognize the ruse.

For the past three days, he and his guards had watched the children, the men and women too old to fight, and those women who were not warriors streaming from the maenol into some hidden fastness in the hills. Alexa had not been one of them. Today, Olwen's warriors had begun to move out, Gereint leading them. Probably, Olwen would join them once the maenol was emptied.

Alexa? With luck, she would be in the maenol. Without it, Marric would have to add sacrilege to theft, and venture into the Druid's grove to seek her out. The longer he waited, though, the greater the chance was that she finished her work and had gone to summon the battle magic. He shrugged off the cloak, picked up a rough crutch, and leaned heavily upon it.

As he limped toward the maenol, he warmed himself by remembering how his guards had grinned at his plans to steal his sister. Apparently, bride-stealing ranked with horse theft among barbarians. They had even suggested that he pose as a man too lame to fight rather than risk discovery as he scaled the wall.

The rest of his staff, however, had not been as encouraging. To lay violent hands upon the heir to Isis on Earth alarmed the senior officers; the priests frankly warned him of hubris. But what else could he do?

As he limped up the hill toward the maenol, he hoped that his limp and his scowl of frustration at being left behind were convincing. He always had been a good actor: pray the gods who governed trickery—and the stage—that he was good enough.

He had spent enough time in the camp that the guards recognized his face without being quite able to place it: he was there, he was familiar, it was enough. He drew a deep breath, growled agreement to hopes that Prince Gereint and the Queen would make fur rugs out of those damnable shapechangers, and limped past the fortifications toward the Queen's hall.

Once away from the gate, he discarded his crutch and twitched his sword hilt within easier reach. His weapon was the one piece of his gear that was stubbornly Byzantine: superbly balanced, familiar in his hand, he would not be parted with it.

He wet his lips and told himself that this did not at all resemble the time he had had to sneak into Byzantium after his father died and Alexa had sent for him. He had been younger then, rasher and less wary. This time, he would not make the same mistakes. This time too, Alexa would not turn corrupt battle-magics upon him. This time, he would not fail to spirit Alexa away from danger.

The usual blaze of torches about the hall was quenched, and the place looked forlorn. It was even bereft of the clamor that Celtoi made when they did even the smallest thing. He found himself missing the noise and light. But the dark plaids he wore let him slip into the shadows, past the hall, toward the nobles' living quarters.

Quiet as a stalking leopard, Marric padded inside, listening for voices or footsteps. The rooms were empty. He prowled from room to room, noting as he went that the fittings grew increasingly rich. In leaving their home, the Celtoi traveled light. He nodded brief respect at the spirit that let them abandon their homes and goods.

There! Marric flattened himself against a wall. He heard footsteps and voices, women's voices. Alexa! If he were in hell itself, he would recognize her voice.

"Go on, Olwen. The people who were to leave are long gone. You don't want to waste your strength—or your horses'—by having to hurry. Gereint's got the warriors in hand; the Druids who do not fight or make for Deva will help me manage here.

"Once you leave, I will go straight to the *gorsedd*. I can watch the battle there and call upon the Goddess to aid us." A long pause, and a gentle ripple of sound.

"If it comes to that pass, sister," Alexa's voice was tender but quite firm, "better that I invoke the battle magics than you. Perhaps the Goddess will smile upon us all, and I will be spared the need." Alexa sighed. "I wish that my brother . . ."

The women's footsteps drew nearer and nearer. Marric had counted on finding Alexa alone. Olwen might be a warrior, but she had been ill. He would have to surprise them and move very fast to avoid using force against them.

Now his sister and the Queen walked past the room in which he hid, Olwen slightly in the lead. Marric stepped between the two, barring Alexa's way.

"Marric! How—" Alexa went quiet, her eyes taking in his disguise. She shook her head, her eyes going narrow. "Brother, this is folly. I don't want to go. I can't!"

"Leave here!" Olwen hissed. "Before I call guards."

"You have no guards here," Marric said. "None I cannot take. Lady, I wish you well in your battle and I mean you no harm. But I must and I will take my sister home with me."

He turned to Alexa and let her see the longing in his face.

"I know," she whispered. "When I thought you were dead, I wanted to die too. I tried, but Audun pulled me back. The night of my initiation, I saw you in a vision. Marric, that moment was the happiest of my life. Even though I had done things for which my soul should have been forfeit, the gods were kind. They spared me, and let me see you.

"But they let me see other things too. I had to pay a price for what I've done. I cannot attain a priestess's full power, and I cannot rule."

"You do quite well here," Marric observed. Abruptly certain that Olwen had gestured "keep him talking" and would edge past to call help, he whirled, seized her by the wrist, and pushed her toward his sister. A faint odor of flowers prickled in his nose, then faded.

"I manage here because Olwen loves me. And Gereint." Alexa's voice went tender as she spoke of the man who had taken her. "He is my husband, Marric. It would rip out my heart to leave him and Elen. And even if I survived that, I still could not be your Empress and your wife. You heard the story of Arktos. That marriage would be just such a sin that—"

"Isis and Osiris Themselves were brother and sister! We are their heirs. How can it be wrong for us?"

Alexa sighed. "Marric, I am no longer heir to Isis."

Cunning though she could be, her face held only grief. It was Olwen's quick gasp that warned Marric, that and the glint of light that had to be a spear or blade aimed at his back. Instinctively, he whirled, his sword hissing from its battered scabbard to strike the Druid Kynan in the chest.

The bard reeled back and crumpled, and his blood pooled, impossibly red against the scrubbed floors. His harp, copper and silver inlays glowing in the scant light, smashed with a wail of snapping strings that glinted briefly before they trailed in the blood.

"Kynan, no!" Marric's cry echoed the women's.

He had expected a guard, a warrior, not a bard unarmed,

save for his harp. Seeing metal behind him, he had struck by reflex. And slain not just a priest, but a bard.

"Ah *gods!*" he gasped, and toppled to his knees. His hands reached out toward Kynan, then fell limp.

Though life and sense were fading from Kynan's eyes with every heartbeat that sent blood spurting from his wound, for a moment, the bard's lit with their old sarcasm. "Now I wish you had been a bard, not a warrior," he gasped.

Marric moaned, shaking his head in rejection. He reached for Kynan to staunch his wound. The bard's blood spattered his hands and face.

"Get back!" snapped the bard. "Are you Emperor or an idiot?"

Marric let his hands fall, waiting for the bard's death curse. He had struck a man whose dual callings made him doubly hallowed, doubly owed any man's respect and protection. How much more should he have been able to expect from an emperor? Head bent, Marric knelt, chin against his chest, waiting for the lightnings.

Kynan leaned on his elbow, gasping with the effort of movement. Now his blood pulsed from his wound more weakly and pinkish spume trickled from his mouth. He coughed and gasped for breath, and it turned into a darker flow. Olwen knelt behind him to support his back.

"Even if you could heal," Alexa said, "Queen's touch was never proof against death wounds."

The bard dabbled shaking fingers in his own blood and dashed it in Marric's face. "Not a curse," he gasped. "But knowledge. See what I see. See the consequences—your future, Emperor!" He fell back, and gasped once or twice. Then his breathing ceased.

Marric buried his face in bloodstained hands. For the first time in his life, his courage failed him and he flinched from the atrocity of his deed. A bard, a priest, an unarmed man: he had not meant to kill him, but the gods saw only guilt, not ignorance. Had he thought to preserve Alexa's soul? He had lost his own.

There would never be an heir now. He was accursed.

He forced himself to look at the dead man, to shake free his cloak to spread it over the body and the spreading, darkening pool of blood—sweet gods at the Horizon, what was that?

Like oil floating in a bowl as it shimmered and re-formed into patterns that only a seer could read, the torchlight touched the pool of Kynan's blood, and it appeared to shiver.

As a hot tide of power swept up his spine and into his temples, Marric whimpered. For the first time in his life, he scryed, saw patterns in the blood below him. It faded to the purity of a mountain stream, then darkened into blackness against which a pale face and form glowed out from a soft lunar nimbus. Or was that simply the effect of the silvery hair that turned the spirit's braided hair into a crown, or the sheen of the huge blue eyes that looked at Marric and wept?

"Stephana!" he gasped. "Oh, my heart, my dear one—"

"My guide!" Alexa cried behind him. "How do you know my spirit guide?"

"In Egypt I met a seeress who showed me you, standing between Olwen and Gereint. I thought—I was wrong in what I thought. But Stephana was that seeress, and I loved her."

"My Marric," the figure whispered. "Oh Marric, another folly. How could you?"

Marric's head bent. He prayed that the pounding in his heart meant that it would burst and spare him the rest of this agony. Like a wounded beast, he shook his head in denial of his pain. "I never meant to . . ."

"No, you never did, beloved. No more than your sister, to whom I was sealed as a guide when she received initiation. You should be proud of her, my love. She is much like you. And she loves you dearly. As do I. But," Stephana's soft voice went chill with the anger that Marric remembered, "you must see the consequences of stealing Alexa."

She pointed at him, and white light shot from her finger to brush his forehead. He recoiled, then leaned forward. The figure of his slain lover vanished from the pool. Instead he saw himself bringing Alexa back to Byzantium. The triumph was no triumph, as guards attended her day and night to prevent her escape or suicide. And the wedding was no wedding, but—Marric gagged and swallowed bile—a rape as a grim-faced Emperor forced himself upon the struggling body of the one person whom he had most reason to love and revere.

Again the vision shifted: Alexa, wrapped in a fraying gown, her belly swollen, her expression blank and hopeless; Alexa writhing upon a bloodstained bed, women and priests helpless as she gave birth, then gasped in relief, and died. Her face relaxed into a smile of peace.

"Do not expect that the child whose mother's life you cost will love you, Marric. Or that, as his father aged, he would respect and spare him. Without doubt, you have heard the story of Arktos that they sing here?"

Kynan himself had sung it. The patterns swirled and re-formed: a young man, as dark and slight as Alexa, with her cleverness in his face, striding through Byzantium's streets, drunk . . . drunk again, and surrounded by drunken young nobles, all wearing the garb of barbarians fashionable among them; a young man who quarreled with his father, who struck at him, then fled . . . only to return with assassins and watch laughing as Marric seized a dagger, then met his son's eyes, flung it aside, and, despairing, let himself be butchered.

"A parricide and a waster," Stephana's voice was gentle, but ruthless. "What a fine Emperor he will make, my Marric. After all your pains. And mine. I beg you, turn aside from this course while you can."

Stephana in tears, Stephana angry, Stephana begging him for anything? "My love does not beg!" Marric rasped. "Least of all for this. Alexa," he turned to his weeping sister, "forgive me. Go free. Be happy with your Gereint. But Stephana, what shall I do?"

"What you must," she whispered. "Just as you always have." Her image flickered, and faded.

"Alexa, little sister," he heard her gentle voice. Then it, like her face, faded from his consciousness. Then it was Alexa's turn to pale and stiffen as the power touched and took her.

Marric looked about. Though he felt a lifetime older, the torches had not burned down. He rose and draped his cape over the dead bard.

Alexa moaned, and her hands came up.

"When she is like this, she prophesies," Olwen said.

"I wish she would prophesy what I should do," Marric mumbled.

The Queen rushed forward, her golden braids flashing against the dark green of her robes. "I can tell you that."

Numbly, Marric looked at her. All his actions and schemes had come down to this: abomination, utter and total sacrilege. If she commanded him to fall on his sword, he might even obey her.

"I have done that which is past all redemption. What can I do now, lady?"

She grasped at his arm. Quickly he stepped back, to spare her the contamination of touching him. "Don't be foolish!" she ordered. "Help us!"

Olwen went to fight a battle against evil men, shape-shifters, and a hag, a battle she feared she could not win. He had two thousand men more highly trained than anything seen in Prydein for a thousand years. Though they might have meant life for the people who had taken in his sister, he had denied Prydein their help. Now he had a chance to redeem one of his misdeeds, in any case.

"Yes," he said hoarsely. "Yes." He would lead his men against the Jomsborgers. Perhaps he would die in battle, though he prayed that before he fell, he be permitted to strike down the hag whose demon laughter had tormented him, waking and sleeping. He drew a shaky breath. That presence in his consciousness . . . "It's gone," he said.

"What is?" Olwen said.

"The laugher . . . the blood," he muttered. "In Gallia, I fought a shapeshifter. Though its blood splashed me, I wouldn't see a priest or a Druid. I thought I could fight its effect—nightmares, temptations to murder—by myself. Gods help me, I even refused to let Alexa help me! Lady, you shall have your help. My men shall march with yours. I myself will lead them. But I beg you, the hag who rides with her grandson the Jarl: her life is mine to take! She has turned my life into a waking hell."

"She is yours." Emperor and Queen alike recoiled from the new, resonant voice that filled the tiny room. Alexa rose to her feet and stood beside Kynan's shrouded form. Tiny though she was, in that moment, she seemed to tower over the other two.

The power of prophecy had touched Stephana gently, Mar-

ric remembered, like water being poured from a vase into a
clear pool. It raged through Alexa; her green eyes shone and
her entire body quivered with a vitality that was supernal, not
human.

"You are brother and sister to me," she declared. "Heirs
you need, and heirs you shall give to one another."

"What—!" Marric and Olwen both cried, broke off, then
glanced at one another.

"It is true that we are kin, but our kinship is far distant. Too
far distant," Marric said.

"Sister, there is but one father for your heir, and there he
stands. Brother, my sister shall be your bride: none other. And
lest you fear the blood runs thin, Olwen, give me your blade."

Before Olwen could protest, Alexa leapt forward and drew
the rough-hilted blade that the Queen always wore. Un-
sheathed, it looked no fairer than it ever had to Marric, though
the blade looked well-kept.

Alexa nodded gravely in satisfaction, and tested the blade,
not on the ball of her thumb but against the inside of her wrist.
In her exaltation, she did not flinch as the blood welled out
against the fragile whiteness of her skin, but turned to Olwen
and held out her hand for the Queen's. She made the cut, then
pressed her wrist against the Queen's, raising them so that the
blood trickled down their arms for perhaps the space of thirty
heartbeats.

"There!" she said, her voice softer and a little breathless as
the power abandoned her. "Can you say, brother, that Queen
Olwen is not of my blood?"

Marric shook his head.

"Now, as for your own . . ." she held out her hand for his.
The blade's edge was thin and lovingly honed, but Marric
trembled with more than pain as Alexa drew it across his
wrist. "Olwen, give him your hand."

Fiercely, Alexa pressed the Queen's hand against her
brother's as if she were a priest solemnizing a marriage. "You
need an heir. Take one another, take one another now, and I
promise you that you will conceive such an heir that Penllyn
and the Empire both shall rejoice. You are blood of another's
blood: Isis and Osiris on Earth. Go now, and go quickly. I
shall come for you before dawn."

Still handfasted, dumbfounded by Alexa's revelations, Marric and Olwen said nothing as Alexa tugged at their linked, bloody hands and drew them down a corridor to a room in which the sleeping furs were so rich that they could only belong to a queen.

Deftly, Alexa kindled fire in an ancient brazier, then rose on tip-toe to kiss first Olwen, then Marric. "I shall bring you linen and hot water," she said. "Brother, you look as though you could use them. And," she surveyed him critically, "fresh clothes. I take it you have no objections to trousers? Good. That makes my task easier."

Alexa hastened, all magic and practicality mingled, from the room. If she had continued on like that for a moment longer, he knew he would have laughed like a madman. He looked down at his fingers, entwined with Olwen's, blood-stained.

Alexa slipped into the room, her arms heaped with a wool and linen, then darted out, to return almost immediately with a steaming pot. She regarded the two of them with an enigmatic smile that reminded Marric of Stephana. "The Goddess bless you," she said, then left them.

Marric loosened his grip to let Olwen free herself. When she did not move, he raised her hand and kissed it, silent tribute to the strength that enabled her to tolerate him and his sister. At that, she withdrew and walked over to sort through the clothing Alexa had brought. She steeped white linen in the steaming water—it smelled of herbs, of spring flowers, fresh, strong, and sweet—and looked at Marric, who sank down on the nearest bench.

"You look like you fought a war," she commented. "It is a custom of my land to bathe our guests. Let me help you get clean."

"Clean?" he whispered. "I shall never be clean again." Nevertheless, he pulled the blood-sodden tunic over his head, wadded it, and tossed it with loathing into the corner.

Olwen gasped as he turned. Marric glanced down at himself sardonically. Scarred and smeared with blood, he looked like something that any sensible woman would flee.

The Queen, however, drew closer. "Sit down . . . Marric. No, not on the bench. Be as comfortable as you can." She stood over him and began to wipe his face with the wet linen. Marric turned his face up and shut his eyes, savoring the warmth and the welcome cleanliness. Something warm fell upon his cheek, and he opened his eyes. Olwen's wrist still bled from the cut Alexa made.

He touched her hand with a fingertip. Olwen followed his glance. "Oh," she breathed. "If that is all . . ." she touched the cut with a fingertip and closed her eyes. An instant later, it healed to a faint pink scar. An instant more, and even that faint line thinned out and disappeared.

Olwen gasped. "Give me your wrist!" she demanded. She laid fingertip beside the cut, concentrated for a moment, and the tiny wound closed. The fragrance of flowers that rose from the hot water intensified, reminding Marric of the palace gardens in high summer, or of roses, the deep red blooms that Stephana had loved.

The Queen drew back, her eyes wide and wild with a gladness he did not understand. She seemed to glow with joy. After a moment, Marric realized that a golden haze actually did surround her. And the scent of flowers in the room rose not from the water but from Olwen herself.

"I can heal again!" she cried. "I am whole!" Then she paled. "And if I am whole again, I am no longer barren. Oh Goddess, I thank you!"

She drew a deep breath, then bent to wash the blood from Marric's shoulders and chest. Though her touch was delicate, his entire body quivered with awareness of her fingers moving on him, tracing the slick weals that marred back and sides. His skin tingled as the warm water dried. He caught her hand and held it against his heart. His nipples hardened at the touch, a womanish trick that women who shared his bed had sometimes remarked upon.

"Olwen," he breathed. "Will you really do this?"

"I like how you say my name," she told him.

He waited for her to answer his question.

"I think, Marric, that we must. The Goddess has spoken through Alexa and given you to me, and me to you. Granted, I know I am not the woman you would have chosen. Well enough: Once I chose another man to father my heir."

Marric looked up wordlessly.

"His name was Rhodri," Olwen said, her voice leached dry of emotion. "He was a Druid, a speaker of laws. Jomsborgers killed him."

The compassion, the sense of understanding that had flickered between them from time to time, rose in a warm tide.

"The night I won my throne, my enemy murdered the woman I loved."

"The seeress Stephana who appeared to you and Alexa tonight?"

Marric nodded.

"Then we have both been ill-treated, no less by one another than by anyone else. Perhaps we can be gentle with one another, even just for a little time. There is—a fate laid on the queens of my line, Marric. They may rule only as long as they may bear. And when they cease to be fruitful, why then, it is time to pass within the groves, and give back the gift of life."

He didn't think he understood what she was saying, that Olwen, golden, vital Olwen feared she was barren and would have to—what? abdicate? sacrifice her life? Luned had told him something of the sort . . . he shook his head in rejection.

"I want to live, Marric. I want to, very much."

So do I, but I have doomed myself now. Marric groaned and slipped to his knees. Olwen took his head in her hands and guided it to rest in her lap. He rested his cheek against her and shut his eyes. Her hands slipped from his head to ease taut muscles in his shoulders and back.

"Why would anyone do this to you?" she whispered. "And such scars . . . do they give you pain?"

Marric's bleak laughter surprised even himself. "You have seen, lady. I am skilled at angering people."

"Perhaps I could heal you," Olwen mused. Her fingers warmed as she stroked his shoulders. It was almost unbearably pleasurable, and Marric shivered. He locked his arms about her waist. "Olwen, Olwen, no," he whispered. "My back is healed as well as Stephana could contrive. We had very little, both being slaves at the time."

He shivered again and looked up at her, letting her see the frank desire in his eyes.

"Perhaps this too is a kind of healing. For you, as well as for me," she breathed.

He buried his head in her lap again. His hands stroked along her back, then down along her sides to clasp her hips. Her fingers tangled in his cropped, curling hair and pulled his head up, then caressed his cheek and brow.

"Yes," he whispered, and flung his arms about her. This time, she pressed his face against her breasts. The fragrance of her skin made him tremble. He cupped her breasts and kissed them through her gown, then moved upward to let his mouth linger on the hollow of her throat, just beneath the gold of her torque. The metal distracted him, and he removed it, then kissed up the long, smooth line of her neck to her ear.

"Let me undress you," he whispered, as his mouth sought hers and she turned her head.

She nodded. As his eager hands dropped to the girdle she wore with the black dagger in its sheath, she forestalled them and removed it herself. Then, while he puzzled out unfamiliar ties and pins, releasing each in its turn, she sat as if this were a new form of worship. He pulled wool and linen over her head, then leaned down to smooth the wisps of rich, red-gold hair from her forehead and temples. "Your hair is beautiful," he whispered. "I would like to take it down."

He kissed her eyes. "Let me unbraid it?"

Olwen laughed. "We have very little time. Afterward..."

If we both live, Marric thought. Olwen would live. Alexa had prophesied that she would emerge from his embrace bearing his heir. But he himself? That did not matter. He had no doubts that an heir would be born, and it would thrive. Olwen, Gereint, and Alexa among them would see that it did. So this would be the last time he would enjoy any woman, let alone one like this.

"Marric?" He made himself smile for Olwen. She watched him, evidently expecting that he would press her beneath him onto the sables and wolfskins of her bed. But she was not just a woman he desired, she was a queen.

He knelt away from her, his glance caressing the long, supple curves of her body. "You are magnificent," he told her hoarsely. He stroked one hand up her thighs, to part them and seek out her warmth. "Invite me. Please."

Never taking her eyes from him, Olwen reclined on her side and held out a hand. Marric stripped off the rest of his cloth ing and lay beside her. She looked down his body as he had examined her. He had pleased many women in his life, and now in Olwen's glance, he saw and savored what they had enjoyed in him. He reached out and took her in his arms carefully, holding back to let her refuse if she chose. She put her arms about him too.

"Your skin is warm," she murmured.

"The songs didn't lie. You smell of flowers."

Time seemed to slow for them as they held one another for a long time, time enough for their bodies to learn one another, to reach a kind of ease and peace with one another. They were both tall and long of leg: they fit together well. Experimentally, Marric moved his hips against hers, and felt her respond almost as if they danced, body to body. He leaned against her, easing her onto her back, and the dance continued.

The flower scent grew strong and sultry. Marric breathed in gasps as he explored her with hands, lips, and tongue and felt her answering caresses. He was thirsty, he was parched with thirst, and he raised himself to her lips, but she eluded him.

"Later," she whispered.

The prohibition inflamed him. He drew his hands down her breasts, over her belly, and between her thighs, probing until she gasped and he knew she was ready.

When they united, she raised her legs to clasp him close. Abruptly, her refusal to yield him her lips become unbearable.

"Olwen," he mouthed against her neck, kissing up toward her mouth, and finding it as the long tidal surge of pleasure caught them up in a great cycle of sun and moon, earth and water and standing-stone. He heard her breath pant against his mouth, and opened it to probe hers deeply. They were soaring, they could lose themselves in the sky; and they held one another close to protect themselves and the pleasure, the ecstatic oneness they found. She arched her back and took him deeply into her, and he cried out in pleasure.

He had a brief vision of golden wheatfields, rain falling on green leaves, or animals mating in a leafy wood, and then pleasure blazed up along his spine and exploded into light past his power to bear or remember.

After what felt like hours in which they lay joined, at the center of the great dance of the earth and stars, the cycles of cold and heat, rain and drought, life and death, Marric lifted his head from Olwen's breasts. Kissing her lightly, he turned on his side and bore her with him, easing his weight from her body. He laughed and laid her head on his shoulder.

"There will be a child," he said confidently. "A son."

"And how do you know that it will be a son and no daughter to inherit my lands?"

Marric smiled and shook his head at her. "It will be a son."

"Then we must try again," Olwen laughed. "And again and again." Her eyes were warm, and she did not move for him to withdraw from her.

He kissed her eyes closed. "Rest as long as you may," he said. "Alexa will be here soon."

Olwen smiled. "So you already think I need to rest, is that it?"

It was hard to leave her, to wash the scent of flowers from himself, and to dress in the plaids—Gereint's clothing, judging from the colors—Alexa had left. He left the blood-soaked clothes lie as they had fallen.

He turned to see her smile at him. "I am not through with you," she told him forthrightly. "Keep yourself from harm."

Marric made himself laugh, and then he left her.

He strode from the near-empty maenol to his camp and found a knot of soldiers and officers armed and jittery. Gods, they had been within a hair of charging up the hill, into the maenol—he had a moment's mad vision of mercenaries crashing in on him as he lay in Olwen's arms, and stifled a laugh.

"The Princess?" one officer asked.

"She does not return with us."

"So, Emperor, now what?" asked one of the guard. Marric's Greek officers always condemned his frankness, but nonetheless, they valued what news it brought. "Do we leave?"

"No," Marric said. "We fight alongside Prince Gereint and his men."

That, he saw instantly, was a popular decision. It was a matter of a few moments to issue the orders that would form up his soldiers and send them riding out to fight Jomsborg. Marric hastened to his tent, the last one left standing.

Even as he changed tribesman's clothing for cavalry officer's gear, he stretched, savoring the afterglow of loving Olwen until his well-being faded into melancholy. He remembered his Aristotle: after they couple, all creatures are sad. His troops said it more coarsely.

After all, why should he mourn? With the gods' grace, it would all be over soon. He reached deep within himself, testing as a man tests a half-healed wound, for the familiar torment inflicted upon him by the hag. To his astonishment, it was gone, washed away, perhaps, by Kynan's blood or healed by Olwen's caress.

He stood motionless as his men aided him into mail so heavy that it weighted him the way Osiris's gravebands must surely constrain the god. Leaving his tent, he mounted to ride out toward what he knew would be his last battle.

Chapter 23

☆

Just before dawn, the wind rose as Alexa slipped down the path to the *gorsedd*. Long grass shivered on the ancient mound. Overhead, the leaves rustled. Leaves and grass did not seem as parched as they had been. The Water of Vision lay unmoved by the cool wind.

Alexa knelt before it and sighed as she unbound her long hair and shook it free. She dipped a hand into the water and poured the water back into the pool and knew the gesture for one of Stephana's memories as well as her own. The ripples seemed to chime within her consciousness as they spread out, then subsided. Overhead, the sky paled. By now, she expected that the remaining Druids would have left for Deva, taking Kynan's body with them for burial.

Grief for the bard stabbed at her then, and she forced it back. Kynan had known what he did. Alexa would have wagered the soul she had reclaimed that the bard had sacrificed his life to force her brother's hand and conscience. How quickly he had changed, too. One moment, she expected Marric to sling her over his shoulder and bear her off; the next, he was all repentance and submission to fate.

Well, she hoped with a wicked little smile, not all submission, or Olwen would have found her hours alone with him a waste of time. Amusement rippled in her thoughts, as Stephana's thought entered her consciousness. *No chance of that, is there?*

It had been dry all summer, but now the air was moist and sweet. A deer emerged briefly from the trees and regarded her with grave wide eyes, then turned toward a shadow that had to be her mate. She flicked a smile up at the *gorsedd* where she had lain with Gereint, Goddess to his Horned God. Fire had smoldered between Marric and Olwen before; it had taken shrewdness, not magic, to bring it to a blaze. But her prophecy was true. There would be an heir. That left Alexa free.

She gazed down into the water. Not even the Jomsborgers would fight in the dark, but the sky was lighting now, and the water reflected it. Centering on that waxing light, she cast her thoughts toward the people she most needed to see: Gereint, Goddess smile on him, donning his favorite ornaments before battle, standing with his friends; Olwen, driving in her chariot, her mind occupied with a healthy fear of the upcoming fight, yet already triumphant. *I can heal, I can conceive, I can live!*

And then there was her brother, his face shuttered, then hidden beneath his helm, as he rode toward the people whom, finally, the Goddess commanded him to accept as allies. His body, eased by Olwen's embrace, sat confidently. His mind seemed curiously detached, but, for the first time in months, it was free of the taint laid on it by the hag. Kynan's blood or Olwen's hand had released him. Her heart beat in sympathy with her brother's as she remembered how she had freed herself from the hag's thrall. Never again could she reach them, threatening to hang them on her loom and weave them into her spells.

A sudden vile gust struck at him—it was the hag, cursing at the prey that had escaped her. Marric thought death and vengeance at her, and the purification of fire before the hag withdrew. How fierce he was! Alexa thought proudly. The hag had to fear the man who was free of her power. Marric's eyes blazed. He tried to regain his earlier peace, but his concentration had been broken. Now all the tiny hopes and doubts could creep in.

He was a fine general and a better warrior; there was no reason he should not survive this battle, and even slay—as he had vowed—the hag who had haunted his life and her damnable son. No reason, except that he had committed a deed for which there was no forgiveness. From nowhere, lines from a play he had read as a boy floated into his consciousness, sounding with each beat of his horse's hooves:

And yet one word makes all these difficulties disappear.
That word is love.
You never shall have more from any man
Than you have had from me.

Disquieted by the poetry, Alexa reached to Stephana-within for the comfort that her guide never failed to give her. Despondent Marric might be; fated to die—no.

Marric believed that he and Olwen would have a child. So he had his heir, he had his guilt—he had no reason, now to live. The last line of the verses Marric remembered thrust into Alexa's thoughts. *And now you must spend the rest of life without me.* He wants to die and be at peace.

Alexa bent her head over the water. It had begun to ripple and to steam gently. Now she could see the Jomsborgers. Some had chosen to fight as men. They stood drawn up behind a shield wall, with a troop of rough horsemen to either flank. She had little heart to study the others, who ramped and shambled in the shadows, sometimes on two feet and sometimes on four.

Her brother's troops tensed as they saw Celtoi and Jomsborgers facing one another, testing with arrows and shouting

insults before they fought in deadly earnest. As Marric flung
up a hand, they rode faster. Gereint, on the other side of the
field, saw the Byzantines riding toward him, sun flickering
off their weapons and harness. The sight made him grin as he
screamed a battle cry and led the Celtoi against their enemy.

If anger and sheer brilliant courage could win battles, Gereint would win his. He led his warriors with ax and sword
against the Jomsborg center while Olwen and the other chario-
teers dismounted to the side of the field and used their long
spears to keep the shape-changers from circling and attacking
the striking force from behind.

Marric grimaced and signaled for greater speed. Alexa felt
his disapproval as if it were her own. This was no way to plan
a battle. One surveyed the field, set out archers on the wings
to fire into the enemy's lines, and tried to draw them into
charging you. If possible, one used engines to hurl missiles at
them.

Not the burning! Alexa recoiled. *Never that again.*

Gereint is brave, Marric thought. *There is nothing like
courage for getting yourself killed fast.*

Not like you, manling. You fear death, so you study killing.

I will not fear your death. I will rejoice at it. Marric
screamed pure fury at the hag and, disregarding his own
counsel, which was to stay with the second line and order his
men, he galloped toward where the press of Jomsborg seemed
thickest. A reiver who had lain facedown suddenly leapt up at
him, his hands dropping weapons and sprouting long claws.
Marric sheared down on his shoulder and dropped him.

Alexa, kneeling in the grove beside the pool, gasped. Gereint's ardor had misled him. He and a small force were surrounded. Two men had spears and used them to good effect
against the shapeshifters; but they faced more than bears; they
faced a much larger force with axes and swords that could
beat down resistance as they hacked through shields. One man
fell, then another. Alexa knew their faces, even twisted with
pain and astonishment. The survivors screamed with rage and
grief, then turned at a new sound . . . six mounted Jomsborgers
armed with ax and club. One of them was Jarl Grettir himself.
Gereint drew himself up, determined to give a good account
of himself.

And half a battlefield away, Marric saw Gereint about to be cut down. He turned his horse's head so quickly that the beast pivoted on its hind legs, sharp hooves battering at two men who dashed in, and rode back across the reddened field toward Gereint. His sister's husband should not die, not if he had anything to say about it. Alexa loved him, and that meant that he had to live.

"Grett-iiiir! To ME!" Marric screamed as he had heard the Huns do. The sound was barbaric, horrible, and Grettir turned toward it an instant before Marric's horse steadied from a wild run into the charge that made the Empire's heavy cavalry so deadly. After so many weeks of inaction and frustration, Marric was almost relieved to strike out at an enemy he hated as much as Grettir. He had pacted with Irene, he had destroyed Marric's towns, he had haunted Marric's dreams—and now he was going to die for it. The impact of his blows traveled up his arm and resonated throughout his body.

Grettir fought like a Fury rode his back, but he was no match, Marric exulted, for a man who could think and fight. He saw the man's snarl change to uncertainty, then fear. Behind him, he heard a harsh shriek, "It is the Emperor himself! Run!"

Grettir turned to scream back at the coward. And in that moment, Marric struck. The Reiver Jarl's torso spouted blood, then toppled as Grettir's horse panicked, turned to run, and toppled.

The Jomsborgers' shield wall dissolved. Their horsemen turned, and the wolves slinking on the edges of the field seemed fewer now. But one small blot formed there, and darted in toward Jarl Grettir's corpse.

Cowards! Oathbreakers! Is this how you repay my grandson for blood and meat, swords and power? Devour them all—or face me!

Marric's horse reared, screaming. Nimble despite her age, the hag dodged its hooves, rolled, then rose to face the Emperor.

Deliberately, Marric sheathed his sword and reached for the ten-foot kontos he had kept in reserve.

You cannot kill me, manling. You dare not. I will weave

your entrails on my loom, the hag threatened. Her threat made every warrior on the battlefield turn. *I will eat your soul.*

"No," Marric whispered. "I swore to end your life. And I will end it."

Abruptly a reddish haze surrounded the woman. Fire lashed out and sent Gereint tumbling to the ground. He rolled and came up, unhurt. Marric's horse tried to bolt.

Alexa tensed as she perceived the hag's intent. "Why?" asked the hag. "See how I can help you. Shall I slay the man who took your sister? With him dead, she will turn to you once more. But you are a lusty one: why should you not have them both, your sister and the Queen? Just say the word, and I shall strike. Or would you rather trample him beneath your horse's hooves?"

Marric spat. "What manner of beast are you to suggest that? And what monster am I, that I listen?" His voice choked with loathing. "Doomed, perhaps, criminal, but I will not let you damn me!"

He wrenched his horse's head around (Alexa sensed his hurt at the cruelty), and spurred it toward the hag. Weaving, bloody apparitions reared up between Marric and his prey, but the horse, spraying froth and lather, trampled them as Marric, his mouth squared as he screamed in rage, lowered his lance and struck.

The lance transfixed the hag, stabbing her to the ground. Even as the lance snapped from the force of the impact, its butt recoiling against Marric's chest, red light crackled up the wood and it burst into flame. The fire leapt from the charred wood and wound around Marric as wire winds about a sword hilt, pulsed and pulled tight, then faded with the last of the hag's life.

Even through the Water of Vision, Alexa could smell the stinks of battle, blood and sweat and beasts, now augmented by metal and singed leather of Marric's armor. For a moment, her brother sat motionless in the saddle, horse trembling beneath him.

And then, very slowly, he toppled to the fouled ground and lay in a welter of broken bodies and weapons.

His horse sidled forward a step or two and stood over him. The battle split on either side of them and raced by. Seeing him fall, the Byzantines shouted in horror. The Jomsborgers roared, a throaty, feral sound that was almost enough to make her brother's men begin to pull back. Gereint—safe for the moment, at least—began to slash his way toward the fallen Emperor.

Alexa hurled herself forward, staring frantically into the pool. Her knees ached from the long stillness and her hands clutched at the grass. She drew a sharp, aching breath, the first for quite a long time. Only then did she realize that beneath his armor, her brother was not struggling to regain his feet. Even the rise and fall of his chest had stopped.

"He cannot die yet! It is not his time! Alexa, help him!" The terror that echoed in her skull, feeding on her own panic, was Stephana's. That her guide's visions should fail them both, that she would have to kneel alone as she watched her brother die—they would all die now, and she would be alone.

"No!" Alexa wailed.

Despairing, she fled into her own awareness, back along mental byways scarred from the way she had misued her powers, until she found the core of her fears, her hatreds, and the source of the battle-magic deep within herself, coals awaiting only a breath to stir them into brilliant flame. It was not evil, not of itself. And it was not the thing she feared most. What she feared most lay before her, mirrored in the Water of Vision—the death of those she loved.

In her mind's eye, she saw herself thrusting hands into that flame. It hurt, and she screamed again. Frantic for water, she hurled herself into the pool . . .

. . . and through a darkness that hurt like dissolution itself. She was falling into a waste like the wilderness of Tuat, where the sun fled at night. Monsters clawed and scaled, with curved teeth, or a jackal's fur, snatched at her. But she was not damned, and she eluded them . . .

. . . to slam against something hard, and roll and land sprawling on the battlefield. Cold wind lashed against her naked body. Her robe had not survived the journey.

Stephana-within wept, a dirge within Alexa's head as she hurled herself at her brother. She pulled his helmet off, then tugged at the throat of his gear. Some detached awareness observed that light shone from her hands, but the thought vanished, forgotten, as Marric's body rolled toward her, then lay quite, quite still.

Gone? She could not believe that that vitality of his could be snuffed out. But his eyes were shut, and his head lolled back. The pain and shock were fading from his face that assumed the severe, distant beauty of a funerary carving. She touched his dark, matted hair, and sat back on her heels, her eyes and mind vacant save for a stray line or so of verse. *But with my parents hid away in death, no brother, ever would spring up with me.* The tears began to come then, and she yielded to them until Stephana's thoughts shocked her back to awareness.

Pain had yielded to the languor of death. She drifted amid the odors of ash, incense, and roses . . . Marric leaned over her, anguished, and bent down to catch a last breath in his own mouth . . . Breathe for him, Alexa, little sister. Since I cannot, give him back my breath.

With a moan of loss, Alexa hurled herself forward. "Wake up!" she wailed. "Marric, we need you!" Her small fists beat against his chest, and she flung herself over his body. As she would never do in life, she covered his lips with her own. They were cold, rigid, and she breathed against them, hoping to warm them, hoping to restore breath, or failing that, lose her own.

A reddish tinge hid Marric's face from her. Now his body was the only anchor she had as the battlefield rocked about them. She had a brief glimpse of light, beckoning at the horizon, but falling beyond her reach. Gasping, Alexa collapsed and fell beside her brother. Soon their enemies would come and find her, she thought idly. Somewhere about her brother's body she could find a weapon to ensure that they would not take her alive.

She shook her head to clear it, and fumbled for the dagger at Marric's belt. As she reeled and pitched against him, she felt his body stir.

"Marric?" she whispered. "Brother?"

She heard a shallow, rasping breath, then another. His eyelids quivered open. One tear rolled down his cheek, then dried as Irene's curse took hold once more.

"I was at peace," he murmured. "Cruel sister, why did you force me back?"

"No peace for you," she sobbed. "Not yet."

His arms came up to hold her, and she wept against his hair. Within her mind, Stephana was weeping, as Alexa had not known that spirits could—or should—weep. Finally, Alexa pressed her hands against Marric's chest and pushed free.

"Your battle," she gasped.

Marric snapped alert. Instinctively, he reached for helm and sword, then whistled for his horse.

Only then did both of them become aware that Alexa stood clothed only in the nimbus Stephana had cast about her for protection—and that it was fading fast. She shivered as the air touched her skin. A hundred feet ahead, two men saw her and shouted with glee.

Marric shook his head. Despite the shadow of his helmet, she could see his mouth quirk. He shook loose from his cloak and tossed it at her.

"Quick!" he snapped, then lifted her to his saddle and swung up behind her and raised the shield to cover them both. "Make yourself even smaller!" he ordered, and drew his sword.

Alexa crouched beneath her brother's shield, her arms about his waist, wishing to the Goddess that Marric would finish off these two, then retreat long enough to set her down somewhere while he showed himself to his men. She was worse than useless on a battlefield.

Then she remembered. She had drawn upon the battle-magic and not been struck down. She lifted her head (despite curses to the effect that she should keep it down!) and looked out. Ravens circled, and the Jomsborgers—those who fought on two feet, and those who ran on four—closed in, maddened by the deaths of their lord and his foul grandam. She reached back into her mind where the fire burned merrily now, and plunged hands into it once again.

The fireglow leapt up to surround them. This light was the red of a flame under control, not the wildness that had almost destroyed her. Marric swore in astonishment, and Alexa laughed. She would not need to be set aside, out of harm's

way. Not now: and not ever while she could fight to defend
her home and family. This was not the darkness of Irene's
power or the hag's, nor the rage, barely held in check, that
she had feared in Bodb. Sure of her control now, she drew on
her power. Exultantly, Marric wielded his sword against their
enemies; she unleashed her flame.

"What's that shouting?" his voice muttered against her hair.

She had to shake herself to remember that the world con-
sisted of more than her, her brother, her power, and her war.

"Oh, sweet Isis!" Marric breathed. "My lost thousand! My
men!" His voice broke.

Though their standards were furled, and no horns sounded,
the lost moira rode toward their Emperor as if accompanied by
banners and trumpets. The other Byzantines cheered. They
rallied and advanced, catching their enemies in a pincer, while
the faster-moving Celtoi darted back and forth in their chariots
to harry Jomsborg where the need was greatest.

"There's Gereint!" Alexa pointed.

"I see him," Marric said. His voice was remote as he focused on the battle. "I can set you down now, 'Lexa, or take
you with me. Will you fight?"

"Yes!" she cried, and cast the fire around them more widely
to sear the fur of the shape-changer who launched himself
toward them. Soon no one would approach the Emperor on
his tall horse, a nimbus of power blazing about him; and Marric rode back and forth as he would on the trampled battlefield
that was now his—his and Olwen's.

A shout hailing Marric as Emperor and Pharaoh rang out as
officers from all three moira approached. But Gereint called
out too, and from the corner of Alexa's eye, she saw Olwen
jump onto her chariot and hasten toward them.

Marric turned to face Gereint. He swept off his helmet, fear
plain on his face for Marric to read. Here rode an Emperor,
surrounded by his officers in the midst of a victory that Gereint's warriors could not have won alone. Clinging to him was
his sister—Gereint's wife. If Marric chose to ride off now
with Alexa across his saddle, there was nothing Gereint could
do to stop him; and they both knew it.

Slowly, Marric removed his helmet and sheathed his sword.
Then he grinned. "Brother, can't you keep your wife decently

clad? I found her stalking the battlefield wearing only her skin!"

Alexa gasped in indignation, but Gereint laughed. "I never had this problem with her before, brother. Give her back, and I'll promise to do better."

"Just hand me over like a trophy, is that it?" she hissed. She tried to poke her brother's ribs, but bruised her forefinger against his armor.

"Don't you want to go?"

She glared at him. "Of course!"

"Then hush," he told her. Then, pitching his voice louder, "See that you do so, Gereint. Alexa is my only sister."

His horse sidled toward Gereint's. Carefully, Marric lifted Alexa from the saddle and into Gereint's arms where she could nestle against him. Then Marric held out his hand to Gereint. Impulsively, the Prince disregarded it, and caught him in a rough hug. Muffled between the two men, Alexa laughed, protested, and wept.

When she emerged somewhat later and more tousled than she had been even before that, Olwen was smiling.

Truly, they had won more than one battle today.

Chapter 24

☆

"If I had lost today," Marric remarked to Gereint much later, "I would not be this tired." He laid a hand on his chest. The place where the broken lance had struck him felt as if he wore a burning coal as an amulet.

Gereint chuckled as he rubbed a cut on his arm. "We would all be dead," he observed. Then he turned back to the more important business of praising those Celtoi who had taken heads. Marric, unused to the custom, looked away. He was relieved to see that Alexa, who had had years to become hardened to the practice, looked away too. Not that there were that many heads—or bearskins—for the taking. Many of the dead Jomsborgers seemed to have dissolved like the ones he had killed in Gallia. The places where they fell were marked by little withered patches in the grass, scorches on bare earth.

Half the battlefield away, Olwen was seeking out those places to heal them. Wherever she walked, a scent like that of apple trees lingered.

That left the bodies of Marric's own men and the dead Celtoi to bury. Since the men of the third moira were relatively fresh, he ordered them—from substrategos on down to servants—to aid in the digging of burial pits. Generals should share in their men's labors. If his chest hadn't hurt so fiercely, he'd have stripped down and taken pick and shovel too. The sounds of digging grated over the field, mingling with the chants, the horns, the sistrums of Druids and priests alike.

The sunlight had deepened to mellow gold: hard to believe that this was the afternoon of the same day of a battle in which Marric, apparently, had died and been compelled from escape into the Horizon's peace back to life. Irene's curse had said that he would know no peace as long as he wore the crown. He wondered if that would make him immortal. Surely the gods would not permit such cruelty to a kinsman and servant —would they? He was very tired. But now that Alexa had drawn him back, he rejoiced in the sight of each man or woman who had not died in battle, in the awareness that he would live to see an heir. Once again, he wanted to live.

Long shadows stalked Marric's officers across the field when they finally informed him that their comrades' graves were ready. Greeks by birth or loyalty, in death they would belong to Prydein. He cast an eye over his surviving men, some standing among the Celtoi, and thought that he might lose a few more to marriages with local women.

That was well enough; he supposed he himself would set the example. Not that he had any idea of quartering an army in Prydein and conquering it by colonization if no other way: Olwen would murder him for even the thought. But they were akin, Prydein and the Empire; their bloodlines should meet and mingle. If some men from Byzantium chose to stay here, their sons and daughters might journey east or remain here, to serve Olwen and her heirs—hers and Marric's.

All along the field, the priests of Horus and Ares-Montu aligned themselves with the Druids. Alexa stood among them, decorously robed in white, Gereint at her side. Sunlight crowned him, and Marric remembered how a Druid had called him "Lugh come again." Naturally he had inquired, and learned that this Lugh was a god of sunlight, of virile youth, and of war, a hero who fought his dark brother and won.

A god, he concluded, as much like his own patron Horus as made no difference. That would explain the kinship he had felt with Gereint from the first. It was logical; and Hellenes were justly famed for their logic.

But it was neither logical nor reasonable of Marric to escape into his thoughts while his men stood by, their wounds stiffening as the air cooled, and the priests waited for him to give an invocation. Though he was not a priest himself, he could act as one in so small a thing, for his men's comfort, if not for his own.

A shrill cry belled overhead. Flinging up a forearm to shield his eyes against the molten disk of the sun, Marric blinked tearlessly at the sunlight glittering on the back of the Hawk that circled slowly overhead. He flung out his arms in welcome.

"Homage to thee, who at thy birth dost make the world bright with Light," he greeted his sigil, which circled lower and lower.

"Hail my lord, thou who passest through eternity, and whose being is everlasting. Hail thou disk, lord of beams of light. Thou risest, and thou makest all mankind to live."

His own warriors were dead, and their bodies lay before him. But, like the sun's night, this death of theirs was a fleeting thing. Marric knelt beside a grave and buried his hands in the dirt.

"Grant that I may behold thee at dawn each day. When thou risest in the horizon of heaven, a cry of joy cometh out of the mouth of all people.

"Thou stridest over the heavens in peace, and thy foes are

cast down; the never-resting stars sing hymns of praise unto thee."

In each hand, he brought up a handful of cool, moist dirt and displayed it to his army. Then he opened his hands and let it fall onto the bodies beneath him. The burn on his chest ached fiercely and dizziness shook him as the Hawk descended still farther. The sunlight on its feathers seemed to transform it into a disk, a tiny sun itself. He met the Hawk's dark eyes until his men muttered in awe. But he was Horus on Earth; why should he cast his eyes down? Light flashed from the Hawk to Marric himself, and poured down his spine and out along his nerves to sink into the earth, gilding it and hallowing the dead warriors.

As the glow faded, Marric swayed, as drained and humbled as his youngest soldier. He bowed his brow to the tumbled earth, then looked up. As the Hawk rose on an updraft, he held up his hands in supplication.

"May there be prepared for me a seat in the boat of the sun; and may I be received into the presence of Osiris in the Land of Triumph."

A last beam of sunlight flashed down and filled his outstretched palms with gold. Then the light darkened toward twilight, a sistrum rattled out, the priests paced forward with burning incense, and the burial party heaped earth over the graves.

After a time, gentle hands and a warm weight dropping suddenly on his shoulders restored Marric to full awareness. He looked up to see Alexa, Olwen with her, then raised one hand to touch the cloak Alexa had laid over him.

"You looked as if you could use it," she told him.

"Now that you no longer need it." Marric gestured at her coarse Druid's robe. It suited her, though he preferred to see her in silks and jewels. That reminded him: he had brought a small pack train full of gifts for Alexa all the way from Byzantium, and not found the moment yet to give them to her. Silks and jewels, cosmetics in fine alabaster jars, sweet oil— there were enough treasures to dazzle two princesses, even two as unlike as Alexa and Olwen.

He signaled for an officer and gave swift instructions for a feast in his camp that night, no matter how late they arrived there; and funeral games on the morrow. Then he followed his sister over to the graves dug for the Celtoi, and stood, shoulder to shoulder with Gereint, shadow to his sunlight, as the Druids sang farewell.

Braziers smoked in his tent, and Marric reclined, sipping red wine. The salves and bandages of his surgeon had eased the burn on his chest, and the crimson silk of his robes lay sleek against his shoulders. Gereint stood at the opened flap of the tent, enticed by the smells of roasting beef and lamb, spiced—Marric sniffed appreciatively—with pepper and cardamom brought by caravan from the farthest East.

From behind a partition of rich brocade, women's voices exclaimed and laughed as Alexa and Olwen divided the gifts he had brought for his bride.

"They have been in there for hours," Gereint complained. "My sister barely has time for merchants when they come each spring. As for my wife—!"

Marric raised an eyebrow slowly, skeptically.

"What sort of treasure did you bring?" Gereint asked.

"Do you really want to meddle in women's mysteries? Evidently I chose right. Why not sit down and wait until they finish dividing the spoil?"

Gereint turned back and seated himself with some caution in an unfamiliar chair. Marric gestured toward a silver goblet, the match of his own. "My surgeon will probably give me a second burn if I move about. The unwatered wine is in the black and red amphora."

"Which are you drinking?" asked Gereint.

"It is bad enough that I cannot serve my own guests properly. I will not insult them a second time by not drinking with them." He held out his cup for more of the thick, neat wine.

Behind the curtains, Alexa's voice rose in delight. "That one!" she decreed. "It is perfect!" Marric heard Olwen laughing and smiled into his wine.

Gereint drained his cup and refilled it. "If that's the one," he shouted, "perhaps you can finish gloating over your prizes and come out here!"

Both women laughed. Olwen shouted back something too rapid for Marric to follow.

He laughed anyway, then bent over, one hand pressed to his bandages. The laughter strained his burn. He gestured to various servants to bring in dinner and fetch the rest of his guests.

The hangings slid aside as Alexa and Olwen came into the outer room. Alexa wore the violet of a princess of the Empire; amethysts and aquamarines glittered on her fingers, dangled from her tiny ears, and shone on the gemmed circlet, wrought in the form of flowers, that held her long black hair. Those jewels had belonged to their mother; Marric had heard her weep when she discovered them.

Olwen . . . Marric gasped and rose to his feet in unbidden homage. He had longed to see her hair loose, and golden, shimmering over her back and shoulders like wheat playing in the wind before harvest. He went over to her and boldly filled his hand with it, lifting it from her shoulders to smooth it down her back and reveal the robe that Alexa had admired.

Marric remembered that one: green silk brought over desert and mountains all the way from Ch'in, and embroidered with a garden of blossoms. Kingfisher feathers trimmed it, more brilliant and changeable than any jewel as they rose and fell with Olwen's breathing or as the firelight struck them. Even though he had known it was far too large and too heavy for Alexa, and the merchant's asking price was enough to appall even an emperor, he had refused to bargain and tossed the man a purse of gold simply because Alexa might enjoy possessing such a wonder.

"Magnificent," he breathed, and kissed her forehead.

As Olwen smiled and freed herself, he looked over at Alexa, smiling his pleasure.

Olwen's fragrance drifted in the cooling air. Marric knew he was staring like a boy falling in love for the first time. When he was a child, nurses had told him that if a man sought Isis-Hathor, she could be found in a grove of flowers at the farthest land west before the Horizon.

I must bring her home, he thought, *though I cannot hold her there.* The Empire would acclaim her as Isis on Earth, and be healed, just as this land—and Olwen herself—had been healed by his intervention. And he—they—would have an heir.

He spent the feast staring at Olwen and Alexa, occasionally looking at Gereint. How long it had been since he had a family! When he remembered, he ate, or forced himself to return his guests' courtesies. Alexa, who knew the ways of Byzantium and Penllyn both, would see that they lacked for nothing. The sheen of light on Olwen's hair fascinated him. He watched it until Alexa caught his eyes and grinned like the mischievous little wretch she had always been.

As the feast wore on, Marric suppressed a yawn. The drugs in the salve on his burn had worn off long since, and the pain was growing. He hunched forward to ease it and reached for more wine.

Olwen laid long fingers on his wrist to stop him.

"I did not know you were wounded," she whispered.

"It is only a burn."

Olwen regarded him skeptically, then took his cup from him, her fingers brushing his.

"You need not serve me," he managed.

"I am not serving you. I am preventing you from moving," she told him. He noticed that she refilled the cup from the jar of watered wine and smiled ironically when she handed it back.

He watched her sink down by Alexa and whisper to her. Alexa sat up straight, her eyes flashing indignantly. Marric sighed. That afternoon, he had thought, he could not possibly be more exhausted. He had been wrong. Isis grant he did not have to deal with his sister's indignation too.

Olwen shook her head emphatically at Alexa, her hair swaying down her back almost to her knees. Though Alexa stayed where she was, she gestured imperiously at Marric's staff, and the tempo of the feast picked up.

At some point, Marric thought he heard Gereint lament that they were running short of wine (if that were Alexa's doing, it was poor hospitality, Marric thought). His idea that Celtoi and Byzantines alike stagger happily up to the maenol to see if any had been left behind produced drunken cheers. Marric started to rise, to accompany his guests at least to the flap of his tent, and—given the strength—to the outskirts of his camp, but a hand pressed him back.

People jostled one another, laughing, as they left. After a

time, only the remnants of the feast—bones, plates, and the dregs of the wine—were left. The servants had vanished; all but one of the braziers had burned out. Marric thanked the gods for the sudden, welcome silence and solitude. A moment more, and his guards would take up their usual positions circling his tent. No one would disturb him until dawn. If Alexa had been her usual busy self, they might let him rest even longer.

The tent flap lifted as Olwen entered, pulling it closed behind her. The firelight shone through the fine silk she wore, outlining her body.

"I told Alexa that I would stay."

"You are most welcome," Marric levered himself to his feet and caught his breath as the bandages stuck to his burn. Seeing that, Olwen pursed her full lips and moved in to support him.

"I can walk, lady," he said, feeling some offense. Her body was silk and steel against his, "but I regret . . . I am in no state tonight to afford you any pleasure."

"I understand that," she told him. "I watched you. All this evening, you were in pain, and you said nothing. Perhaps I can bring you peace."

Marric caught up her hand and kissed it. "No one can do that. I am under a curse."

Olwen scowled in displeasure at his literal-mindedness. "Does your precious curse forbid me to ease your pain, or even—Goddess forbid—heal you?"

Marric chuckled weakly. In Alexandria, Stephana had been even sharper-tongued to coax him back to life and health. In that one way they were alike, the lovely, doomed Stephana and this vital, glowing Queen. "Can you heal me?" he asked.

"Why don't we see?" She urged him toward his bed, and began to ease him out of his robe and tunic. As she bent forward to inspect the bandages that strapped his chest and shoulder, her breath fanned his cheek.

"I do not think we will have to soak these off," she said. "If I hurt you, let me know."

It would be a wet day in the desert before Marric did that.

"I mean it!"

Marric sighed. Her hands were gentle as she unwrapped the

bandages. But as the air touched the angry red burn, centered between his breasts, he drew in his breath sharply.

"Lie back," Olwen ordered. Her brow furrowed as she thought. She began to stroke his shoulders with cool, deft fingers, then slide them down his chest. Marric breathed quickly, braced for a stab of pain.

"Trust me to touch you gently," Olwen breathed. Her hands were soothing as they glided over him. Marric wished he had the strength to desire her as she deserved.

Finally, she centered her hands on his chest, cupping lightly right above the burn.

"I am going to try and heal you now," she said. "Yes, if you will be easier for it, you may place your hands over mine."

Her fingers, so cool a moment before, began to warm. The warmth pulsed from her hands down into his chest, pouring into the burned flesh until it tingled with renewed health and life. His pain faded, to be replaced with a relief almost as exquisite as the way Olwen's hair felt as it trailed across his face and neck. Warmth passed out of her hands into him, and she sighed, then toppled against him.

Marric flinched, yet raised his arms to catch her against his shoulder. To his surprise, he felt no pain. When he glanced down, he could see only the healthy pink of new skin where moments before an angry burn had ached and oozed.

Olwen was trembling. He had to warm her. She shook her head at an offer of wine. He fumbled at the fastenings of the Ch'in silk she wore. A little later, he had pulled the beautiful, extravagant thing from her, and had started to strew it—and his own remaining garments—on the floor when Olwen shook her head and whispered something. Her voice was so soft that he had to ask her to repeat herself.

"Neatly," she repeated. "Don't catch the embroidery. You will ruin it."

"Olwen, what do I care about one robe?" he started to ask.

"Well, I do. We see less of such treasure than you in the Empire. But when we do see it, we treat it with respect. Neatly."

Marric chuckled and obediently draped the robe over a nearby chair before stretching out beside Olwen and embracing her. He ran his hands down her back, then over her arms, seeking to warm her. The ease and pleasure that had allied their bodies the night before kindled between them again, and she clung to him, savoring his warmth.

One hand under her chin, Marric raised her face and kissed her, parting her lips with his own.

Olwen felt him against her and laughed, deep in her throat. "What did you say? that you were in no condition to afford a woman any pleasure?"

"I lied," said Marric. "But let us lie together now, just lie here. I will keep you warm."

Olwen pressed against him, shivering. Perhaps it was just imagination, but Marric fancied that her body was fuller than it had been the night before. Had healing him drained her so? What of—

She shook her head once. "Always . . . like this after I heal . . ." she whispered. "Don't worry. It will not hurt the child."

"You tell me not to worry? When I have never been a father, at least not that I know of?"

Male pride and duty made him long for a son. He would be proud of a boy who combined his strength and Olwen's. Such a son would likely be as tempestuous as his parents. They would know how to raise such a boy, to train him without breaking his spirit. But a daughter, such a child as Elen was, and Alexa had been: he would treasure such a daughter with his whole heart.

Olwen laughed through chattering teeth and flung her arms around him, much to his surprise and pleasure. Her body was warming now, and the added warmth made him drowsy. It would be good to sleep in her arms. Perhaps they could sleep now, wake before dawn and make love, then sleep again. Marric stroked her back suggestively.

"I promise," she murmured, "that I will share them with you."

"Them?" Marric asked.

"Our children," she said, and embraced him again, drawing him down against her with a little laugh.

"Children?"

Olwen arched her back, stretching, inviting him to kiss and stroke her breasts. "Certainly, children," she said with mock sharpness. "Alexa told me much about you, but she never said you were a fool. One child is not enough to ensure one succession, much less two—ah!"

"Now?" Marric asked, his lips grazing her skin, savoring the odor of apples and blossoms that rose from it. "Or after we sleep?"

"You give . . . hard choices." She broke off to shiver, not with chill but with desire, and locked her legs around him. "I choose . . . both."

After their sudden, drowsy passion ebbed, Olwen slept, her hair trailing over Marric's shoulders and arms. He lay watching her. She had not Stephana's fragile, lunar beauty, which had broken his heart. She was not kin to him in the sense that Alexa was, their minds alike as twins. Nor did she possess Luned's gift for easy acceptance. But their bodies had known long despite their haughty tempers and anxious, questing minds: they were fit mates for one another.

It would not be easy. Olwen could not live in Byzantium any more than he could live in Penllyn. There would be much traveling to and fro within the Empire and across the Sea. There would be a child . . . no, children . . . to raise, heirs for them both. They would have to learn to deal together. Mated in the flesh they were; they had yet to learn to be friends and companions.

Probably the God and Goddess fought together too.

They *could* achieve harmony and love, he thought as he brushed a strand of amber hair away from Olwen's eyes, then bent to kiss them. How beautiful she was now, and how serene.

He let himself sink toward sleep. He was not at peace, no; never that. But for the moment, he hoped he might be allowed to call himself happy.

The instant she heard the shouting start, Alexa ran from the maenol to the field where Marric and Gereint had gone to inspect horses, so quickly that she did not even have time to put Elen down. The child wailed, but Alexa pressed her head against her breast and pushed her way through the knot of Celtoi and Byzantines. As far as she was concerned, they were equally curious, equally noisy, and equally infuriating. What if Marric had fallen—or Gereint? She could not imagine her world without either of them.

"Let me take her, my heart," came Gereint's voice, laugher rumbling in its depths. Her knees failed her and she passed the child over. She had feared him dead, his neck snapped, and here he was laughing! It made her palm itch to slap him.

The shouting grew louder, until Alexa felt like joining in on the choruses. Chuckling indulgently at her, Gereint helped her wriggle through the crowd to where Marric and Olwen glared at one another, clearly in the middle of a fine quarrel.

Alexa recognized the horse Olwen rode as one of her brother's finest and most spirited. Even as she watched, it bucked and sidled. Marric stepped in, his fingers tightening on the reins he had snatched.

"I don't need you to hold my reins!" Olwen shouted at him. She tried to pry his hand from the reins but Marric kept his grip.

"You need me to talk sense into your head!" he retorted, his face dark with anger and fear. "That is a war-horse, a stallion, not a horse for a madwoman!"

"So you think a woman cannot ride your horses, is that it? What do you think I am, some soft kitten of Byzantium, sheltered in the innermost courts?"

"Like my sister?" Marric's voice went up in amazement, and he broke into a laugh.

Olwen looked as astonished as he to find herself laughing too. "Alexa clings to a horse's back like a cockleburr," she said.

"I wouldn't ride that one," Alexa declared. "Look, you made Elen cry." She glared at the knots of spectators, jerking her chin at them to suggest that they take themselves elsewhere—fast.

"Olwen," her brother said urgently, his voice as persuasive as he could make it (which was saying a good deal), "if you want to ride my horses, go ahead and ride them. But must you ride them now?"

"You do," Olwen said.

"Set take you, woman, I'm not bearing a child!" Marric

shouted. "Break your neck, go ahead and break it. But *after* you give birth!"

Alexa turned around in time to see the consternation on Marric's face and the delight on Olwen's at shattering Marric's composure. It had been a challenge to her since the moment they had laid eyes on one another. The horse decided to buck again, but Marric had him under control now, and soon he stood quietly.

"Olwen, please," Marric said. "I will never stop you from taking any risks you need to take, but this one is folly. Soon we will go to Byzantium. The sea voyage should give you all the adventure you can use for now."

"And if it doesn't?" Olwen was challenging him, testing him, still unsure of whether he would try to master her as now he mastered the sweating horse.

"They have a lively idea of entertainment," Gereint remarked. Alexa leaned against him comfortably to enjoy the show. She expected that Olwen and her brother would enjoy some lively fights. How those two fine, carrying voices would echo in the Palace's marble corridors!

Marric laughed. "Then we will ride, you and I, out to see the Huns. I understand that their women dismount only to give birth!"

"That can't be true!" Olwen laughed.

"Of course it isn't. But Olwen, dear one, let me lift you down now."

"I am not a Hun and about to give birth. I can dismount myself." Nevertheless, Olwen let herself be eased from the saddle into Marric's arms. Behind her back, he snapped his fingers for a groom to lead the horse away.

"Of course you can," he said and drew her close. "But this way, I have you in my arms, and I can kiss you."

Their kiss was long and deep enough that both of them ignored the cheers and friendly hoots that rose about them.

Gereint eased their child back into Alexa's arms, then put his own about them both.

"Which do you think will tame the other?" he asked.

"Neither," she replied promptly. "And I think that may be how they want it." She sighed, thinking of the trip east, of a triumphal return to Byzantium through the Golden Gate re-

served only for victorious emperors, of Olwen, shining in the
Moon Crown of Isis Incarnate as she was acclaimed Empress.
The thought of Olwen's gold and white beauty set against her
brother's darkness like diamond and ruby paired in the same
clasp took her breath away. She wished she could see it, and
yet—

"A deep sigh, my heart. Do you regret your home?"

Alexa turned on her husband so quickly that Elen began to
cry. Better than anyone else, she knew Marric and Olwen,
knew the life they would make for themselves. It was impossible that they would not come to love one another—in their
own, turbulent fashion. Best not to think, right now, of what
would happen, as they aged, to an Emperor under a curse and
a Queen who wore a dagger wrought from a fallen star, a
dagger that would one day seek her heart. That lay, as it had
always lain, in the hands of the Goddess.

But she had Gereint to answer and to comfort. For once and
for all, she vowed, she would wipe from his face that wistful
look he got when he feared she dreamed of the Empire. "Let
my brother and Olwen have what love and splendor they may,
for as long as they may. This is my home," she told him. "I
have everything I want."

Author's Note

☆

Though Julius Caesar first led legions into Britain in 55 B.C., most of what we think of as "Roman Britain" dates from the reigns of emperors such as Claudius. But if the Roman presence in Britain had ceased after the assassination of Julius Caesar, the history of the British Isles would have been much different—no Roman roads, no revolt against Rome by Boudicca, no Hadrian's Wall . . . and no Arthur.

The Woman of Flowers is a fantasy, second in a series of books set in an alternative empire created when Antony and Cleopatra defeated Caesar's adopted heir, Octavian, in a bid for power, and won dominion over Rome and Egypt alike. From the strategically located capital they established at Byzantium, their heirs rule as emperors and pharaohs, extending the empire to the east and south . . . but not to Britain. It is primarily a pagan empire; emperor and empress are the earthly incarnations of the ancient Egyptian gods.

It intrigued me to speculate on what a Britain devoid of Roman rule (but still subject to the Germanic tribal migrations and invasions) might look like. Readers will note that my speculations could not have begun without the Four Branches of the Mabinogion, which I have chopped and rearranged quite deliberately to suit my own purposes. I hope I may be forgiven both this and my scrambling of Arthurian romance; I suspect that the ancient bards might have understood.

For anyone interested in retracing the trails I've followed, I've listed some of the books that I drew on most heavily.

British, Celtic, and Roman History:

Nora Chadwick, *The Celts*. London: Pelican Books, 1985.

John Morris, *The Age of Arthur: A History of the British Isles from 350 to 650*. London: Phillimore and Company, 1977. Note: Volume II provided me with Aneirin's song about the Battle at Catraeth.

Alwyn Rees and Brinley Rees, *Celtic Heritage: Ancient Tradition in Ireland and Wales*. London: Thames and Hudson, 1961.

Northern Byzantine Empire and Viking History:

H.R. Ellis Davidson, *The Viking Road to Byzantium*. London: Allen and Unwin, 1976.

James Graham-Campbell and Dafydd Kidd, *The Vikings*. Metropolitan Museum of Art and British Museum special exhibition catalogue, 1980.

Gwyn Jones, *A History of the Vikings*. Oxford: Oxford University Press, 1985.

Tre Tryckare, *The Vikings*. New York: Crescent Books, 1966.

Folklore and Mythology:

E.A. Wallis Budge (translator), *The Egyptian Book of the Dead*. New York: Dover Press, 1967. Note: I adapted various invocations to the sun from pages 250–52.

Robert Graves, *The White Goddess*. New York: Farrar, Straus, and Giroux, 1982.

Stuart Pigott, *The Druids*. London: Thames and Hudson, 1986.

Ward Rutherford, *The Druids*. Wellingburgh, Northamptonshire: Aquarian Press, 1978.

Nikolai Tolstoy, *The Quest for Merlin*. Boston: Little, Brown, 1985.

In general, Osprey's Men at Arms series and *The Golden Bough* provided valuable pictures—whether pragmatic or mythic.

Good reading to you—and happy hunting!